Greedy Heart

Greedy Heart

A.P. Murray

TULE
PUBLISHING

For where your treasure is,
there your heart will be also.

Matthew 6:21

Dedication

To my husband, Christos J. P. Moschovitis,
the love of my life and the light of my soul.

Thank you, *o syzygos mou*, my yokemate,
for pulling along with me in work, life, and love.

Acknowledgments

At Tule—Thank you to Jane Porter, Meghan Farrell, Jenny Silver, Cyndi Parent, Helena Newton, and my brilliant editor Kelly Hunter. Thank you for "getting" my book and giving it a home.

At David Black Agency: Immeasurable gratitude to Gary Morris for your enduring support.

To Sheila Levine for your patient, practical and wise advice.

For all in the writer world who put a hand out to help me up, pull me along, or sometimes just offer a hug: Lynne Barrett, Kristan Higgins, Lisa Halliday, Colette Sartor, Janet Reid, Katie Wech, the IWWG, the RWA, the Golden Network, and my incredible Persister Sisters—the Golden Heart Class of 2018.

To my friends and family who encouraged, beta-read, suggested and championed. Mara Fisher, Stephanie Long, Marci Weisler, Johanna Prinz, Andrea Bradbury, Colleen Burke, Sister Marlene Brownett, Sheryl Jones, Chantal Parker, Isabelle McDonnell Catino, Charlene Weisler, Anjali Kiggal, Lynn Marie Hulsman, Katie Kenney, Ellen Gandt, Sarah Hall, Kathy Buccellato, Mari Andreou, Koralia Tsagaratou, Dimitris Koutsorrizos, Jessica Mitchell, Stephen and Barbara Pearlman, Kristin Rath, Susan Monshaw, Kirsten Bischoff, Miller Murray Susen, Zoe Bouloutas, Toni Tugenberg, Hilary Poole, the monthly Women's Discussion Group, my sister, Mom, and Dad. And for two who will be deeply missed at the launch party, Connie Murray and Jeanne Frank.

And, most importantly, to every reader who spends time with this book.

Part I
GREED

Chapter One

I'm a little leprechaun dressed in green.
The tiniest man you've ever seen.
If you ever catch me, so it's told,
I'll give you my pot of gold.
—Irish verse

M ORNING SUNBEAMS POKED through my blind slats. The rays were long and warm like yellow fingers, touching my shoulder as I straddled my "boyfriend," Eric (quotes stet).

"God," Eric said, thrusting slowly. "It only gets better with you."

For me, not so much. Sex with him had lost what made it so special: that impersonal, transactional quality.

Our first encounter, Eric hinged me forward over a desk, pulled up the back of my dress and spread my legs with his knee. Next, we did it against a campus palm on a moonlit night. Then on the couch in his office. Our relationship started to develop a great rhythm: rendezvous, screw, carry on.

Now he was spending the night. He was leaving a change of clothes. He was *resting his hand at the small of my back*. The implication was clear. I was transforming into a girlfriend, someone he might even want to marry. Have kids for him.

Make sacrifices for him. Move for his career. He was planning to fuck me all right, just in a different way.

But I wasn't after love or a relationship. My goal was money.

"Oh, baby," he groaned, as the dawn stretched into the corners of the cave-dark Florida apartment. His hands tightened on my waist. My cell phone's screen animated, flashing and glowing. I glanced to see the caller.

No. It couldn't be.

I looked again.

It was true.

In a single sweep of my leg, courtesy of equitation lessons from back in my finishing school days, I dismounted Eric's cock and grabbed the phone.

"Hello?"

The recruiter got right to his purpose. I was being considered for a position as a "quant." He schpeeled off phrases: *absolute return, trading techniques, assets under management* and *shorting.*

"You said you were from...?" It was too much to believe. I sat up on the edge of the bed while Eric stroked his dick to finish himself off.

"Odyssey Capital," he said. "We're rated number-one in *Barron's* based on performance." As if I didn't know. As if Odyssey wasn't legendary.

Somehow *they* were calling *me*? I was not a Stanford-minted PhD. I was scratching out my dissertation at a third-tier school in central Florida, making $25,000 a year as an adjunct with a hundred grand in student loan debt, living in a crappy apartment with powdery sheetrock and moldy bathroom tiles. So far, my best job offer was from an automated calling center in

Minneapolis.

Odyssey was, to use my mother's term, *crème de la crème*. Its founder, the inscrutable, young Peter Priest, sat in the pantheon of new hedge-fund gods. Today, in 2006, the people at these hedge funds raked in millions, tens of millions, even hundreds of millions. It was a level of wealth few people could imagine. *I* could imagine it—I who was born in a modern-day castle. Of course, that was before The Great Family Financial Disaster of 1986. That was when wealth, family, love, future hopes—all of it went out the window. In one case, pretty much literally. I spent twenty years in exile. Now Odyssey was materializing like a rainbow out of the clouds—the kind of rainbow attached to a pot of gold.

"How'd you guys find *me?*"

"We have a very good research department, Ms. Mulcahy."

"Researching *what?*" I was a nobody with nothing to my name. These days, anyway.

"Can you be here on Tuesday? You'll need to block the whole day to accommodate Mr. Priest's schedule. His assistant will send an email the night before with your appointment time. However, we request you clear the entire day."

Oh, my God. *Tuesday.*

Tuesday was the day after tomorrow and my last interview with Telefony, the call-center company offering me a six-figure salary. It was a lot of money to me, though nothing in comparison to what I once lost. The Telefony technology replaced humans with automated systems that said, "If you are calling about an existing reservation, say 'existing reservation.'" They were hiring comp-sci PhDs to trick out their artificial intelligence algorithms, bringing the firm to the next level. They had a plan to replace the 911 operator.

If you are calling about a heart attack, say 'heart attack.'

The $150,000 offer was practically in the bag. My almost-employer was talking to me about options and an eventual IPO. If they went public in a few years, I could cash out for half a million. These numbers represented a fortune just yesterday. There was only this last interview, with the twenty-nine-year-old founder, a guy six years younger than I was. The Telefony HR woman told me my offer would come at the end of the Skype.

The Odyssey recruiter continued to give me instructions over the tinny cell phone connection. "You'll need to stay through Thursday in case there's follow-up or negotiations," he said. "Though you may be finished on Tuesday," he concluded ominously.

A bird in the hand, whispered Aunt Kathleen. But your aphorisms don't get listened to when you jump off a roof and land in a fountain in the garden.

"You'll pay my way?" I asked.

"Of course. Simply submit the Odyssey expense report when you return."

Great!—except my credit cards were maxed out. I told him I was a libertarian who didn't believe in credit cards, so I needed him to wire the anticipated expense funds to my checking account. He agreed. No doubt because three grand was a rounding error for him. Then I phoned my mother whom I hadn't called, much less seen, in five years. I needed to stay at her house, so I could pocket the cash from Odyssey. I would fake all my receipts.

"You won't get another opportunity like this." Eric slouched to my bathroom with its poorly laid floor tiles that petered out at the corners into exhausted rhombuses and trapezoids. Eric was right. By now, 2006, hordes of programmers were specializing in exactly the kind of math Wall Street wanted. I'd started on the path too late. My credentials didn't attract even one Wall Street interview. Yet, suddenly and inexplicably, here was Odyssey, appearing out of nowhere like a fairy godmother with an invitation to the high-finance ball. This was real money, not some lousy hundred-fifty kay. It was the kind of money that might even reconstitute a lost fortune. I would need to go back to the scene of a crime that destroyed my life before it had a chance to begin. It meant jeopardizing a certain future and certain money. Could I possibly land the Odyssey job?

I booked my plane tickets and told Eric to drive me to the airport the next day. I lied to the Telefony HR woman that my mother, to whom I was devoted, was scheduled for emergency surgery on Tuesday. I was flying to New York and would not make the Skype. She seemed to have heard this story before and said while my situation was regrettable, the job market was competitive, and if I missed the interview, they would make an offer to another candidate.

Two in the bush.

Chapter Two

Audentis fortuna juvat.

(Fortune favors the bold.)

—Latin proverb

M OM WASN'T ALWAYS a basket case. Once, she was a glittering socialite, a former model who'd married a fortune and given birth to an adorable daughter. But when Mom's world collapsed, she did too. Mom withdrew and her universe contracted. She transformed from outgoing and vivacious to miserly and suspicious. For all practical purposes, she quit being my mother too.

Mom's one enduring contribution to my life, bequeathed through her DNA, was her beauty. On our way to the airport, Eric stole glances at me in the car, still entranced after all these months. It was a fact. I was gorgeous. My looks didn't help much in the money department, as happened with Mom. These days, rich men wanted ironclad prenups. My appearance did pave the way for good, easy fucking. Which was handy. Because even if love was for suckers, screwing was for everyone. What made me even hotter to men was my profession. I was a female programmer, fast and good and smart. I talked about compiling, integrations, data ingestion, AI, and performance under load. I was Xena, Warrior Princess, but better. I knew instinctively when one of my colleagues, other adjuncts in my all-male PhD program, or administrators, or professors, or college presidents went hard with desire. Eric was the Provost.

"What are you thinking?" Eric asked on the off-ramp to the Orlando airport.

"Nothing."

He sighed. "We never talk, Delia. Not really."

"Isn't that something the girl is supposed to say?" I asked. He looked at me confused, but we were at the curb.

I proceeded through check-in and security. When I settled in at the gate, I texted Eric to say maybe we should see other people.

❧

MY PLANE LANDED at LaGuardia, that battered old washer-woman of an airport. Grungy, careworn, poorly lit, and host to millions, she seemed to be saying, "I don't have time to fix myself up. Can't you see how much work I have to do?" I adjusted my backpack and marched through the doors marked, "No re-entry."

I passed guys whispering "need a cab" under their breaths like drug dealers. Bert waved from amidst a gang of limo drivers carrying scrawl-lettered signs. Bert fit in well with the group because of his overhanging belly, mid-priced suit, and thick-soled brown tie shoes. Funny how limo drivers and retired New York City cops all look alike.

"Hey, stranger!" Bert was my mother's…well, my mother's nothing actually. He was her neighbor and—for reasons passing understanding—amanuensis. Thank goodness someone was there to look out for her. Bert let Mom "rent" (quotes stet) a house he owned, and took care of her, doing anything she needed, from cleaning her gutters, to raking her leaves, to resetting her circuit breaker, to driving to the airport to pick up the daughter she hadn't seen in years.

"You look the same, Bert." He swung my duffel into the back of his Jeep Grand Cherokee. Bert retired from the force after a long and varied career as a beat cop, a mounted police officer ("to get off my feet"), and finally a detective.

"How's Mom?"

"More gorgeous every year."

"I'm sure." Bert wasn't being sentimental. Age only enhanced my mother's exquisite face. Mom's beauty was her ticket to ride away from her Queens' roots, transporting her onto magazine covers and into a marriage with my lace-curtain Irish father and his Old New York money.

"She still won't let you make her an honest woman?" I asked.

"Your mother *is* an honest woman!" Bert's voice rose in outrage.

I put my hand on his arm. "Just kidding." He proceeded with the story I'd heard a thousand times as if he were telling it for the first time.

"Senior year in high school, she was at Cathedral and I was at Cardinal Hayes. I asked her to marry me on Valentine's Day. Right then and there she said she'd never marry a cop." Bert laughed as if my mother's rejection was one of his fondest memories. Bert forgave her for dreaming bigger than himself. Not marrying a cop was my working-class mother's *raison d'être*. And the one goal of her life at which she had colossally (if temporarily) succeeded.

Instead of Bert, Mom landed my dad, the heir of an industrialist family. He was fifteen years older than she, softhearted, shy, and intellectual. Dad used to come into my room while Aunt Kathleen read me stories. Which made me wonder if any of his strict nannies ever bothered to read stories to *him*.

Mom pestered Dad to be more ambitious. He was from a family of inventors, she reminded him. He should look at what was next. Like computers! She really should have nagged him about his smoking because Dad died of a heart attack at the end of my sixth-grade year. The first blow in what was to be a long boxing match with fate.

Bert continued with his story, "I ask your mother again every year! She still won't marry a cop, though. She's better than that."

The drive to Centerville was long and flat and depressing, as the hills of Long Island flattened into the scrubby pines and sandy berms of the east. A few miles south, the Hamptons towns dotted the shore like a necklace of jewels. The Hamptons were the South of France, Amalfi Coast, and the Greek islands all rolled into one. Where we were headed, fifteen miles inland, it was all the same tacky stuff—four lanes of traffic and strip malls, garden centers, Jenny Craig franchises, and purveyors of cemetery monuments. The center-of-Long-Island-ness of Centerville was one reason I never came back. Mom was the other. Mom and I both became different people after the family disaster, and neither of us was particularly nice.

"Seems like a lot of new construction."

"Yeah. Boom times. You haven't been around in a while." This was as close as Bert would come to chastising me for staying in Florida, even during holidays. Neither Mom nor I cared, but Bert did. After a short silence he said, "Hedge fund, huh?"

"Yep."

"Big time."

"Yeah."

"Delia . . ." Bert's accent, rich and dense as a slice of New York cheesecake, transformed *Delia* into *Deel-yer*. The sound reminded me of Aunt Kathleen, who was both my aunt and my nanny. When I was born, Aunt Kathleen had just left the convent. Mom was struggling to adapt to her role as a wealthy socialite and new mother. She was overwhelmed by the troops of British nannies on offer. With her sister conveniently available, Mom pounced on the opportunity. Aunt Kathleen arrived, quickly becoming not only my nanny, but an indispensable support for Mom, Dad and even Grandmother.

"Those finance guys are real dicks," Bert continued. "Excuse my French. Better watch yourself."

"I can deal with them, Bert."

"Strong like your mother." He smiled at me. "Almost as pretty too."

"Thanks." I didn't remind Bert that Mom wasn't very strong. Nor did I take offense at his *almost as pretty*. Any woman would have given her eye teeth to be almost as pretty as Mom on her worst day.

"Some guy'll be lucky," Bert said fondly. Bert saw qualities in me I left behind years ago.

Sure, I could have grown up differently, if my world hadn't been blown to bits; if there were still money; if Aunt Kathleen and Dad were alive; if, after losing it all, Mom hadn't had a nervous breakdown. But that whole fleet of ships sailed a long time ago.

"I heard fromma buddy whose son says these Wall Street guys are nuts in interviews." Bert cornered his Jeep down a cul-de-sac with the skill of a guy trained for high-speed chases. "They say some'm like, 'spell diverticulitis.' If you can't, it's out on your keester."

I knew the stories. One guy wrote on his blog he stepped into an office and had a crystal paperweight hurled at his head. He ended up in the trauma ward at Bellevue.

Bert parked the truck in front of Mom's residence—a 1970s' split-level with a roof low and overhanging as a Neanderthal's brow. Mom acidly described her domicile as "a ranch on a slab," even in front of Bert, even though the house belonged to him.

"Here we are." Bert heaved a contented sigh. Bert gave Mom the house in her hour of need and bought another place a block down. I didn't know what she paid to live in Bert's house, if anything. Bert's pension didn't seem as if it would stretch to cover two houses and Mom's expensive tastes. Worrying about Mom and Bert, however, was not my job.

"Thanks, Bert." I approached the house. Mom didn't look out the window.

"Your mom can't hardly wait to see you."

MOM'S FRONT DOOR opened to a small plateau. My mother compared this foyer to the state of limbo where unbaptized babies go—neither here nor there, but hellish nonetheless. A fussy white iron railing proceeded up to the bedrooms and down to the sunken living room.

In the living room, surrounded by cheap aluminum windows, my mother sat amidst my grandmother's furniture and art. All the pieces that did not go to Christie's for auction after

The Great Family Financial Disaster of 1986 because they "fell off the moving truck." In those final days, Mom stole furniture, jewelry, clothes—anything she could fit in a suitcase or on a U-Haul. It was a sign of Mom's unraveling. Over about a year, Mom morphed from an effervescent socialite into a mash-up of Gollum and Miss Havisham.

An escritoire with legs fragile as an Italian Greyhound's, Queen Anne chairs, Chippendale sideboards, a French mahogany dining table—it was all here in Centerville. The tables stood ankles deep in the shag carpeting and supported Ming vases, Staffordshire figurines, and Waterford candy dishes, while Hudson River Valley paintings graced the cheesy 1970s-style wood paneling.

My face hung over the faux-stone fireplace. It was a copy of a portrait painted of me when I was eight. According to my grandmother's wishes, all family portraits remained behind, in the gallery of the Fifth Avenue mansion after the house was sold to become the Greek embassy. I think Grandmother was trying to console Mom by giving her the facsimile, unaware Mom had absconded with so much else.

The quality of the duplicate was pretty good. It captured the expression of the original. I was impish and sparkly-eyed, beaming down with hope and purpose. For Mom, though, it was the ultimate booby prize. To a woman obsessed with appraisal values, what could be worse than having a picture of a daughter from whom she was estranged that was worthless to boot?

My mother, still the same 123 pounds she'd been at twenty-five sat straight-backed and perfectly coiffed on a velvet settee, needlepointing. The custom pattern ($450), executed with hand-dyed yarns ($175) was of sandpipers with tiny cross-hatched feet.

"Thank you, Bert," Mom said, finishing the stitch she'd begun.

I watched my mother's inclined head. Her beauty was startling. Even at sixty-eight. Even to me. She was Audrey Hepburn, Grace Kelly, and Ingrid Bergman all rolled into one. Add to that the charisma of Zsa Zsa Gabor, which she preserved, despite her eccentric state. It affected not only Bert, obedient after fifty years to her smallest whim, but also all tradesmen, meter readers and bill collectors. Years ago, as her world was collapsing, she even attracted the attention of a Greek shipping magnate. The end of that relationship was the last straw in a haystack of last straws.

Her stitch safely accomplished, Mom rose, took off her glasses and looked me up and down. "I hope you'll do something with your hair before tomorrow."

That was another thing. After her world disintegrated, Mom gave up on tact, especially toward me. We shared a painful past; I was the only one left to remind her of it; and she took it out on me. I didn't mind Mom's sharp tongue. In a way, I admired her authenticity. Because bottom line, I despise a hypocrite—someone who is secretly not what you think they are. That's the thing that rips you up.

Like Aunt Kathleen, who began as a mannish Mary Poppins from Queens, holding a Schlitz in place of an umbrella, carrying a carpet bag full of love for me. She was the center of our family, the gravitational force that grounded everyone. Even when things were at their worst, I always had stalwart Aunt Kathleen. As my world was dissolving in front of my eyes, and my mother seemed as if she might crack at any moment, Aunt Kathleen assured me, "We'll get through this together.

Somehow, pal, we will. You *will* have a future." And then—she was gone. As is the wont of magical nannies, she sailed into the sky one day without warning.

"Your only hope is to tie it back," Mom said. My hair was red and Celticly wild, just like hers. The frizz offended her sensibilities. Too working-class.

To this day, Mom went to a Madison-Avenue stylist at $475 a visit to master her own tresses, now a regal, silvery white. It was hard to tell if Mom was delusional, determined to live as she once had despite financial realities. Or if she was simply too stubborn to change her ways. I suspected it was probably both and wondered what financial alchemy, including Bert and the furniture sales, paid for it all.

My wild curls were like catnip to men, so I kept them that way. Tomorrow, on the other hand, was a Wall Street interview. "I probably should do something about it," I mused.

"You'll notice the River Valley oil is gone," Mom said on her way to her avocado-colored kitchen. Bit by bit Mom was selling my grandmother's things to make ends meet.

"Did you get what you wanted for it?" I called into the kitchen, trying to sound nonchalant. Mom emerged carrying a Spode teapot surrounded by chip-less sixty-year-old cups. The china had tracery crackling on its surface and was covered with birds. Birds were my family's coat of arms, as it were, and all our china had been made by Tiffany in a custom Audubon pattern.

"Mmmm," she said. It was déclassé to talk about money. I wondered if Mom would outlast the art and furniture or if it would outlast Mom. I pictured her, in her nineties, confined to one small corner of her house, sitting in a final remaining chair, drinking from a penultimate teacup.

Aside from Bert and art sales, Mom had one other ace in the hole to rescue her from penury: if she could cash in on a lease she still held to a rent-controlled apartment. She took the apartment in 1969. Later, Aunt Kathleen moved into it and her name was added to the lease. When her sister died, Mom retained the lease, and kept it all these years.

Rent-controlled leases were worth their weight in gold because they gave the leaseholder a lifetime right to their apartment. Landlords, eager to redevelop their properties, paid huge sums, six figures or more, to get tenants like Mom out. They converted their buildings to luxury apartments or, even better, ripped them down and put up huge towers if zoning laws allowed. Mom bribed the super to say she spent the required 183 days there. Mom didn't set foot in the place because Aunt Kathleen had jumped from the building's roof.

"Is your art dealer that lady you used to know?"

"Judith. Yes, she's still at the Grandhope."

What an Old New York phenomenon the Grandhope was! A hotel where people real-life lived. It conjured up Eloise at the Plaza, Elaine Stritch at the Carlyle, Sylvia Plath at the Barbizon. Nowadays, these old hotels were being turned into co-ops. "I don't know how long it'll last. Judith's nearly ninety and going blind you know."

"I didn't know."

"I hear Angela is in the neighborhood, too." Angela was my childhood "best friend" (quotes stet). "I *don't* say hello." Mom never really liked Angela, though Angela worshipped Mom. Mom called Angela *a climber.* Pot, meet kettle. Please discuss amongst yourselves. "Do you have any plans about where you'll live when you get this job?" Mom's *when* was subtle, but I heard it. No matter how estranged we became, Mom never doubted my capacity.

She didn't offer me her rent-controlled apartment, nor did I ask about it. The rule with Mom was her stuff was *hers*. Given city housing laws, a daughter could claim the right to a rent-control lease if she lived there. Mom didn't have to worry, though. Years ago, when she retreated into her pain and left me to mine, I decided I didn't want anything from her. Not that she would have given me anything if I asked. Now, I would rather die than accept a single teacup.

"I was thinking I'd buy my own place." Just saying those words gave me a thrill, as if uttering some incantation with the power to restore a lost life.

"You might want to read this." Mom passed me several ink-jet pages. "It's from the *Vanity Fair*." Bert had set her up with the internet and email. She kept the computer, which she considered aesthetically objectionable, in the laundry room. Mom was surprisingly adept on the thing, using it to track the art market.

The title on the printout said "Hedge Fund Rivals." Underneath was a photo of two men back to back, both good-looking, fortyish, in the immaculate suit-jacket-no-tie-gold-cuff link uniform that screeched, "high finance." The caption read: "Arch competitors Peter Priest of Odyssey Capital and Robert Goodman of Hermes Fund." Mom pointed to the second man, the one called Goodman.

"You think it's the same guy?" I asked. "There could be a hundred Robert Goodmans."

"It's the same," Mom said.

"How can you be sure?"

"I read the internet, darling." She looked over her glasses at me.

"He's your landlord these days, right?" The Goodman family owned Mom's rent-controlled building. If it was the same Robert Goodman, he inherited the building from his father.

"Yes." Boy, New York was a small world, everyone cramming together with the density of iridium. "Good-looking fellow." Mom examined the two men on the printout. "The other one is kind of dark." Mom's taste for Mediterraneans soured after the incident with the Greek shipping baron. "Delia, if you should ever run into Robert Goodman, you won't mention your connection with me?"

There was a plaintive quality under the steeliness of Mom's tone. Perhaps a note only a daughter could pick up. It was Mom's paranoia about her lease—the possibility, however remote, I might try to claim to it, or spill the beans she didn't live there. Mom thought everyone, except Bert, was out to take what little she had left.

"My interview's not with that one. He's Hermes Fund. It's with the competitor, Peter Priest of Odyssey Capital. In any case, no. I wouldn't ever mention it."

"Good," she said. "I'm just another name on a lease to Robert Goodman. It still has my maiden name." She really *was* staying off the radar.

Mom was welcome to keep everything to herself. I didn't want any of it. Besides, I was about to make a fortune of my own.

Chapter Three

The king was in the counting-house
Counting out his money.
—Mother Goose, "Sing a Song of Sixpence"

THE WINDOWS OF the LIRR train into Manhattan were scratched and foggy as a pawnbroker's. The train shrieked and heeled on its track as stands of sumac trees bent in its wake. Gradually the skyline came into view, a vista powerful as myth. New York was a fairy-tale kingdom, a glittering citadel of towers and turrets, with heroic bridges and leaping trestlework bracing the island like flying buttresses.

My lost castle was at the center of this kingdom, one of the greatest mansions on Fifth Avenue. A grand white wedding cake of a house, it presided over the corner of 80th Street and Fifth. Once upon a time, the mansion housed one of the city's First Families. Mine. I was the scion of this family, a modern-day princess, with roots extending back generations, into the literal fabric of the city. The mansion was a place of great wealth, of course; but for me it also held love and the promise of my future. This kingdom and that castle were my birthright. I was here to storm the shores.

My suit of armor was blue and from Brooks Brothers. I wore virtually no makeup and tied my hair back into a tight incognito knot. If you were a woman who wanted to be taken seriously as a quant in the extreme-bro culture on Wall Street, it was better to be homely, acne-riddled or—if you could possibly manage it—Asian. I unfolded Mom's ink-jet pages and began to read.

It was too boring and complicated to cover what hedge funds actually did, so this article focused on the testosterone-fueled rivalry between the two media-genic billionaires, Peter Priest and Robert Goodman. According to *Vanity Fair*, Priest and Goodman were opposite "to a Shakespearean degree." Goodman was handsome, tousled-haired, and towheaded with a chip-toothed smile. A hail-fellow-well-met media darling who always dressed the part—gemmed cuff links, brightly colored handmade silk ties, and Italian shoes—Goodman drove a Lotus that he self-deprecatingly joked was evidence of an early midlife crisis. He was constantly photographed with high-profile women of international pedigree. He was "a man seeking princesses to complement his kingly fortune." Goodman was famous for owning a quirky rent-controlled building—Mom's. The article portrayed him as a benevolent landlord, who left the building alone, despite the prime location. "Why touch it? It's filled with great New York characters. And I have enough money." Too bad for Mom and her longed-for payout.

Peter Priest, Odyssey's founder and the man to whom the LIRR train transported me, was mysterious and press-shy with the demeanor of an "Eastern-bloc diplomat." In contrast to the charismatic MBA and deal-maker Goodman, Peter Priest was an academic and a mathematician. Famously, he shunned the media and would not agree to pose for the article. A subtitle said the piece's cover had been Photoshopped using a file image of Priest from a recent Capitol Hill banking hearing. Priest did not own an apartment and was instead living in a high-end hotel. There, the fee for things like doormen, fresh flowers, and maid service was forty grand a month—or twelve new BMWs a year.

Neither man was ever quoted on the record about their falling-out. In 2001, Rob Goodman left Odyssey, the fund Peter Priest had started, and went on to found his own firm. The article cited all the current rumors: a disagreement over strategy; a disagreement over money; a disagreement over a woman. I put down the printout.

On the horizon, the buildings of the New York skyline shifted with the movement of the train, like chess pieces arranging themselves for the biggest game in the world.

I WENDED MY way through the greenly lit rabbit warren of Penn Station. Is there a train station on earth where the fluorescent lighting is more fluorescent, or the linoleum more linoleum-er? I descended to the subway. On the Number-1 platform, an Asian man played a wobbling version of "Ave Maria" on a zither. It was the closest I'd been to anything religious in years.

I began toying with atheism when I was seven and preparing for my first holy communion. It was my first real exposure to religious studies, and I quickly pegged Jesus as a Big Red Socialist. It was clear to me Christianity was a religion of the poor, by the poor and for the poor. Throw a dart into any of the Gospels and you'd hit something about how great it was to be poor. Blessed were the poor. They stood to inherit the Kingdom of God. Woe was coming unto the rich, not least because they were going to be squeezed through eyes of needles. Homilies attempted to soften the severe pro-poverty doctrine of Christianity. But it was obvious that adults were doing what adults *always* did when the facts didn't suit them. They lied.

I knew spin when I heard it, even at seven. I was rich and liked it. So that was the end of the Jesus nonsense. I panicked my parents by informing them I would not be going through with communion. Aunt Kathleen, former nun that she was, handled things. She shrugged off my anti-Jesus stance saying, "Religion is like language. You speak the one you're born into," and marched me to first communion. She then took charge of my religious instruction, teaching me my prayers and reading me the lives of the saints. I went along with it, because I loved her.

Turns out, I was just ahead of my time in the matter of religion. Hardly anyone believed in God anymore. His branding had been tarnished by frauds, zealots, and maniacs. The Catholic Church itself was on the skids, like a home team that hadn't won a pennant in decades. Even redoubtable Aunt Kathleen joined the apostasy with her spectacular leap off a roof. That was the moment I decisively gave up on God.

God had been replaced by things like spinning and kale. Also Reiki, Steve Jobs, airline points, Landmark seminars, iron man triathlons, colon cleansing, TED talks, veganism, helicopter parenting, social media, and discovering Reykjavik. It struck me this could be problematic for society in the long run. If you cared about such things. My current chosen deity, Money, was a concrete and reliable god. He had an exchange rate.

ODYSSEY'S HEADQUARTERS WAS in Nolita, a freakishly hip downtown neighborhood I wasn't sure existed when I was a girl. Here the streets were cobbled and ran diagonally. Standing on a corner, I noticed a small bronze plaque on the sidewalk. It said, "Property Owned by Herbert Ivers, 1923." I knew what this was. Aunt Kathleen and I used to hunt for them. The plaque marked one of the smallest pieces of property in the city. A plot so tiny, you couldn't even erect a flower stand on it.

It was all thanks to city planning. When eminent domain plundered through, commandeering land for a subway station or Lincoln-Tunnel ramp, a tiny slice of property might remain behind, maybe four feet by four feet. The owner and his descendants sometimes kept the lot and marked it. Sure, it was a little silly, because the sliver was useless. But a legacy, no matter how small, could be bigger than what it was.

I stepped over the Ivers's estate and headed toward Odyssey. The building was a former light-industry edifice—maybe a button manufactory—made over in granite and glass. The internet backbone ran under the building, and high-speed fiber-optic cables snaked down the Odyssey walls mainlining the web. I swung through a revolving door. The silhouette of a trireme, an ancient Greek sailing vessel, was etched in the glass. The door whirred me into a lobby done in a pale earthen color: neither gray, nor tan, nor white, it's a hue the Lands' End catalog calls "stone." The custom buff-toned wallpaper was embossed with more triremes. Metal lamps cast no light on a credenza made of unpolished marble. There a khaki-suited receptionist sat camouflaged like a chameleon.

She rotated her head, regarding me with detached, reptilian interest.

"Delia Mulcahy for Peter Priest," I said.

She took my ID and snapped my picture via a small webcam on the credenza. Then she printed out a pass with a speckled QR code. "You'll be met on fourteen."

I beeped my way through the turnstile and noticed there was no *up* button for the elevator. Nor a down button for that matter. Only a keypad.

"Your floor," the receptionist said wearily. "Punch in your floor."

When I did, the display came alive and said, *Proceed to Elevator D*. I stepped inside Elevator D and the doors murmured shut. I searched again for a button, any button, on the car's smooth birch-wood walls. I wondered if this were part of the hazing process Bert had referred to. I must stand in this featureless box and figure out how to escape. Unbidden my elevator began to move. I realized it was fully computerized, taking me where I needed to go.

The elevator's sleek and costly interior reminded me how out of place I was. My journey since college was so lacking in money or accomplishment, I couldn't believe I was here.

I had started out as an insurance adjuster in Columbus, Ohio, eight years ago, but an event at the insurance job changed my course. I was visiting the site of a tornado with a bunch of newly erected McMansions that were wiped out. Walking among the faux castles' remains was like a metaphor of all I had lost. I felt bitterly resentful that all the homeowners would be paid to rebuild these counterfeit castles, when my *real* castle, my family, and my future had been irrevocably lost.

Amidst the flattened great rooms, twisted wraparound decks, and hot tubs turned into kindling, it was all remarkably clear. I needed *money*. Not McMansion money. Real money. Mountains of money. True, the obliteration of my family fortune was just one of my losses. I also lost a mother, a might-as-well-be-mother, and my future as head of our family company. Along with all of it went my belief in people and the power of love. Still, the money part was the thing that could be *fixed*.

Why had it taken me so long to figure this out? My memories of high school were dim. Back then, it was as if I had survived a bomb blast and couldn't hear much over the ringing in my ears. I lived out those years in a remote Virginia boarding school. Later, at Ohio State, I continued purposeless. The life I had been raised to live, as the head of a company, was gone. I floated along alone, no parents to guide me, completely unprepared for how one managed life in the middle class. I ended up majoring in English, by the luck of college-credit roulette, and got the job in insurance so I didn't have to leave Columbus.

With my new discovery—that money was my true goal and purpose in life—I realized my literature degree was as useless as a trapdoor on a lifeboat. I read the finance news and learned about a new Wall Street trend: hiring math majors. Wall Street was the big money. I was late, but still had a chance if I could get my act together. I took night courses in math and hard science, then I enrolled at the only PhD program that would take me. Despite killer GRE scores, and a 155 IQ, I was not a great candidate. I didn't have an undergraduate math degree; I had been farting around at an Ohio insurance company; and I was a woman. I did fine in the program, but fortune-making job prospects did not pan out. And yet, today, I was inexplicably interviewing at Odyssey.

The elevator arrived with imperceptible deceleration. The doors opened to a diminutive fellow of South Asian aspect wearing fine-gauge brown wool trousers and a blue dress shirt rolled at the sleeves. He greeted me with a flat, "This way."

The extensive cubby-land trading floor was nearly silent, only the low whirr of computer fans and keyboards clicking like a forest of cicadas. Five monitors overhung each trader's desk. It was the kind of command-center setup that might launch satellites. Mom's article confirmed the startling fact: Odyssey had never lost money.

Up half a flight of stairs, Priest's office spanned the mezzanine. The South Asian fellow held open the door. The office's wall of glass overlooked Priest's trading floor. The other walls were upholstered in floor-to-ceiling suede panels the color of cappuccino foam. The surface cried out to be touched, soft, pearlescent and nubbly. Researching the wealthy was a hobby of mine, so I knew what an interior like this cost: I estimated the walls alone in here topped a quarter-million dollars.

My guide offered me a chair facing Priest's desk and left. On the shelf behind the desk were pictures of rocky beaches like those I combed one summer, on a nameless Aegean island, trying to occupy myself while my mother pursued the affections of the island's owner.

Priest entered through a side door in the suede paneling. He was well over six feet tall, looked forty-two, and reeked of intelligence, sophistication, and money. Trim, with the broad shoulders of a rower, he had olive skin, black eyes, a roman nose arched at the bridge. He wore a custom-made Italian sport coat over navy wool slacks. Along the back of his neck, small dark curls with the tiniest fleck of gray edged the collar of his jacket. Unlike as with my mother, dark men *were* my type. I reminded myself I was not here for that.

He extended his hand. "Peter Priest."

I happened to know, from the bits of Greek I gleaned that

one summer, "Peter Priest" was a simple translation of Petros Pappas, a name he had in common with six dozen New York deli owners. He anglicized his name, no doubt, to distance himself from them.

"Thank you for seeing me," I said.

"Please sit down." I also remembered that accent—of the urbane, internationally educated Greek. Priest, I suspected, would be fluent in French and German as well English. But he would still have a sibilant S, and his H would rasp from the back of his throat. Schooled in Britain, he would use the phrase *obliged to* instead of *have to*.

Priest retrieved two Pellegrinos from a refrigerator behind the numberless suede panels. He leaned forward to give me one. I declined. As he leaned back, I caught a whiff of his cologne. American men almost never use it. This expensive scent was something the Greek shipping baron might have worn. Nothing screws with your memory like the sense of smell. Suddenly, the noise of the sea filled my ears, and in my mouth, I tasted dill.

Priest's cologne and accent, the pictures, the beach-colored walls all whirled together to evoke that Aegean summer when I was also on a treasure hunt. I saw the face of the teenage boy whose name I could no longer recall, and perhaps never knew in the first place—the *palikari* who took me diving in crude scuba gear. The boy and I flippered through the cold and clear water looking into caves and sea-floor reefs where, it was said, valuable artifacts could be found. Black eyes smiling behind a snorkeling mask, the *palikari* gave me a small stone figure. It was the only moment of joy I remembered from that entire summer. It seemed as if the boy was presenting me a sacred object with the power to mend my shredded heart.

Priest twisted the cap off the mineral water, which exhaled with a sizzle. "I assume you know how lucky you are to be here."

I *was* immeasurably lucky. Still, I bristled. Priest made me sound like Lana Turner at a lunch counter, sitting around waiting to be discovered by *him*. I had spent years climbing out of depression and the wreck of my past. It had taken time, guts, and the evisceration of all softer feelings.

"Yes," I said, snuffing any irritation.

He nodded once, then leaned forward in his custom-made ergonomic chair that cost twenty-five hundred dollars if it cost a dime. He was a young man to be so immensely rich. His cool demeanor suggested he was jaded, unimpressible. He bent to a file drawer and pulled out a bound document. He set it in front of me and leaned back again.

I recognized it immediately. "Where did you get *that?*"

"I have an enviable research department."

It was my PhD thesis. A draft of my unfinished and *unpublished* PhD thesis.

Holy shit.

My thesis was in the most arcane corner of finance. Something called mortgage-backed subprime.

"I am impressed by your work, Ms. Mulcahy. It is truly remarkable."

Well, that was a new reaction. The minute my professor heard my proposed topic, he told me to pick another subject. I forged ahead. I thought my idea was original. Most importantly, I was sure it could make money. Evidently, Priest thought so, too.

"How much did you pay my thesis advisor?"

Priest's smile glinted. "That's none of your business. You

stand to be compensated plenty."

My thesis was based on a popular new kind of bond called a *mortgage-backed security*. A mortgage-backed security was created when investment houses bundled up hundreds of thousands of home mortgages belonging to hundreds of thousands of regular Joes. They then sold the bundles to other people, governments, and institutions. The nickname for this new financial phenomenon was simply *subprime*.

As hot as these investments had recently become, no one really understood them. *Understanding* was exactly what I set out to do. I dug through proprietary databases and pored over research material, most of it not even computerized. Compiling and keying in the data took months. Next, I wrote the complex and custom computer code to analyze it all. A picture emerged. To wit: the only thing standing between most US mortgage holders and default was the expense of one busted dishwasher. That meant all these subprime bonds—a market in the billions invested in by people, institutions, and world governments—were a ticking time bomb. I had discovered the inevitability of a market crash of unprecedented scale.

More importantly, I had found a way to make billions on it.

Priest continued. "I agree the market is destined to fail. I am amazed things have lasted through 2006. It seems you have found a previously unknown way to make money on the bubble bursting."

"Yes," I said, impressed. My thesis advisor hadn't been able to follow my analysis or my math or even the syntax of my title: *Shorting Mortgage-Backed Subprime Bonds via Credit Default Swaps*. His mind engaged, Priest's strong charisma expanded, surrounding him like a force field made of brain waves. With his quick intelligence, he instantly understood my discovery.

"You do it through credit default swaps," I said.

"Swaps," Priest mused. Swaps, as he well knew, were a kind of insurance. Like buying fire insurance on a house. If the house burned down, and you had an insurance policy, you got paid. The magic of swaps, though, was you could buy insurance on a house you *didn't actually own*. I researched swaps and learned all about them from an obscure academic bond expert, including the fire-insurance metaphor.

Using insurance to bet against subprime bonds was, if I do say so myself, a stroke of genius. Bonds were trickier than stocks. Betting against *stocks* was easy. You just shorted them. As for bonds—my swaps strategy was the *only* way to bet against them. No one had ever bought insurance on subprime bonds. But, right now, with a subprime bond crash looming of the size I predicted, the *one* thing you *really* wanted insurance on was subprime. What's more, it was perfectly legal. Though we all knew what Aunt Kathleen would have had to say about that.

"Fascinating." In that moment, his black eyes looked so much like the handsome scuba-boy's I caught my breath for a second. "Still, what makes you think someone would actually *sell* credit default swaps on a subprime bond? It's never been done before," he challenged.

"Because I asked them," I said.

"Of course, you did." Priest flashed a smile, leaning forward, stretching the fabric of his jacket against broad shoulders. I warmed under his approval, flattered that a man at the very top of the finance industry admired my work. I thought again about my difference with my mother regarding Mediterranean men.

"I called Deutsche and AIG as part of my research." I did not mention that I impersonated a partner at a hedge fund whose name I found on LinkedIn. "I'm not saying they understood it. But their reaction was, 'Sure. It's possible. Why not?'" Then I added, because I liked the metaphor, "It's like buying home insurance on a house that you don't own, but one that you *know* is going to burn down."

Priest rubbed his chin. "Perhaps not quite the right turn of phrase since, theoretically, house fires are isolated events. The impending crash is something that will happen on a mass scale. More like, say global warming, which will destroy the planet. That's the correct metaphor. You have found a way to take out life insurance on all the polar bears."

Polar bear life insurance. That was also pretty good. There was a definite intellectual spark between the two of us. But Priest evinced no signs of physical attraction to me, which was mildly disappointing. I had never slept with a guy who was my intellectual equal.

"Yes. Like life insurance on the polar bears."

"Now I must ask you a question."

"Sure."

"How do you feel about this strategy?" He twined his long fingers.

"I beg your pardon?"

Priest swiveled in his chair. "If I may continue the metaphor, you propose a strategy to bet against the planet's doomed polar bears. However profitable it might be, one might feel conflicted. One is not, for example, trying to solve global warming or save the bears."

"No, one is not," I said, feeling renewed irritation. "One is only trying to make money." What was he playing at?

Priest gave a half smile, acknowledging my sarcasm. "And if I understand your theory correctly," he proceeded smoothly, "the strategy is not simply to bet against the polar bears, so to speak. You will also turn up the heat."

Right again. Anyone executing my strategy would unquestionably *accelerate* market meltdown. If a crash came, a technique like mine would quadruple its impact. Not only would all of Wall Street collapse, but so would the entire insurance sector. It was something never seen before. It would create the biggest crash since the Great Depression. Bigger, even. I wouldn't care because I would be rich. Wasn't that the idea?

"Correct," I said.

"Does that cause you any qualms of conscience?"

"I'm sorry, but didn't you say you run a *hedge fund*?"

Priest chuckled, seemingly not offended by my sharp tongue. "Indeed, I do. Your point?"

"Qualms of conscience, as you put it, could be inconvenient in your line of work." My growing familiarity with finance taught me one thing for sure. The business was dirty. Wall Street classed up what they did with complex math, and they paid lobbyists to keep it all legal. Still, choirboys did not run hedge funds.

Priest's smile dissolved. "I have a father who says things like that. For centuries, my country has suffered from endemic corruption. The system keeps the wealthy wealthy, no matter the cost to society. My father has many government connections and wanted me to follow in his *line of work*, as you put it. I came to America instead, to make money on my own. Without such corruption."

Quickly, I went from thinking how brilliant Priest was to

wondering if he was right in the head. I opened my mouth, then closed it. I really wanted this job.

"What were you about to say?" he asked.

"That you're deluding yourself. And that only people with money have the luxury to debate ethics."

"You could be quoting my father." Priest's tone indicated this was not a compliment. "Of course, there are compromises, as in any business, but I try to adhere to my principles."

"Do you succeed?"

"I believe I do," he said. "I flatter myself that, at least, I am not among the worst."

"I have a question." This academic debate was not going anywhere. We needed to get to the point.

"Yes?"

"If my theory kills the polar bears—or whatever—why did you invite me here?" My strategy was not just *among* the worst, I was pretty sure it literally *was* the worst.

"My motivations are not your concern." Priest paused, sipped his Pellegrino, and walked to the windows looking over his trading floor. He stood there a moment, then turned around. He took a document from his desk, a copy of my C.V., which was stapled to something that looked like a dossier from his research department. "You somehow worked your way from an insurance company in Ohio to placement as a PhD candidate in abstract mathematics. Then, with virtually no background in computer science, data analytics, or banking, you developed one of the most brilliant theories in all of finance. Frankly speaking, I admire your work, and I admire *you*."

"Thank you," I said proudly.

"*Your* motivation for all this?"

Well, that was easy. "Money," I said. "Doesn't everyone want money?"

"Much of the time, to be sure. Yet there are dozens of easier ways to make money."

"Not *this* kind of money." I tilted my head to his suede walls.

"True." His inflection suggested a puzzle piece falling into place. "I understand." Exactly *what* did he understand? "Also, I can see you are no fool. I am guessing there is a fair amount of information you did *not* put in here." He tapped my thesis with a manicured index finger.

"That's correct."

"Exactly as I would do." Priest shrugged and walked back to his desk. "Your thesis and your mind are very valuable. I want to have you here. I would like you to join Odyssey Capital."

My heart did a triple Lutz. "Great!"

He set the document aside. "Now, there is the matter of other offers."

"I don't have other offers. Your *research department* must know that already."

"The mere fact of my interest in you will trigger other offers." Huh. Intriguing. "I find the whole offer-counter-offer process inefficient and therefore irritating. We'll sort it all out now. If you do indeed receive another verified offer, I'll beat it by 20 percent. One round. That's it. The job starts at five hundred, plus bonus. Which you will find above par for similar positions at other firms. In answer to your next question, last year my lead quant received a bonus of one point three."

Five hundred thousand. *One point three million dollars.*

"I accept."

"I haven't officially offered yet. Your background check will take another few days. You must stay in town. If you pass, you start immediately." Priest slid a heavy piece of card stock across the desk. "One more thing. I've asked for your name to be put on the list for our event Thursday night. Something to do while you wait for your background check. I thought you might be interested."

Have I mentioned New York is a small world?

The embossed lettering said, *The Embassy of Greece, 990 Fifth Avenue.*

My lost castle.

"This year, Odyssey is hosting Wall Street's Poker Night. I used my government connections to gain access to this particular historic venue."

"Thank you for the invitation," I said, determined to remain impassive.

Priest's smile was that of someone enjoying a private joke. "I think the portrait on the second floor is an incredible likeness." Some research department, indeed. "The girl's expression is—inspiring. I hear *that* version of you would be priceless these days."

I winced as he touched a nerve. "That girl no longer exists."

"Shame," he said, evidently disappointed to be meeting the one in her place.

Chapter Four

He is not a full man who does not own a piece of land.
—Hebrew proverb

MY LIFE ENTERED its Hellenic period when our family mansion was sold to the Greek government in 1986. Grandmother seemed happy about the sale. She cared about honor, and a country owning the house felt regal. Much better than another private family or foundation purchasing the place. As for the Greeks, they appreciated the mansion's neoclassical grandeur.

Throughout the negotiations, a stream of diplomats and influential Greek businessmen flowed in and out of our mansion. A gorgeous young widow like Mom was bound to attract attention. From a Greek shipping baron, for example. At that time, with her sister dead and the world coming apart around us, Mom started to behave erratically. Much of the time she wore the expression of a cornered animal. A shipping baron—now *that* was a solution. If ensnaring a wealthy Greek to save oneself from financial distress was good enough for Jackie Kennedy, it was good enough for Mom.

"You see, Delia," she said. "It's all going to be okay after all."

The house was sold, and a summer cruise decided upon.

Since Aunt Kathleen inconveniently killed herself the previous April, and my boarding school didn't start until September, along I went. That was how, the summer after I lost everything, I found myself, stunned and stricken, on a bleached white comma of an island, steeping in an expanse of the Aegean the color of Ty-D-Bol.

Things were not going to *be okay*. Mom felt less and less like a parent I could rely on. Aunt Kathleen had promised to help me through it all, and she'd checked out.

Here's what happens when you are left behind by the suicide of someone you love without so much as a note: you can't make the pieces fit. You turn into a fucked-up Don Quixote questing for a reason. So, while my mother was off ensnaring her Greek magnate, I was left in a marble villa perched like a pelican on a cliff. Most days, I wandered down to the harbor, zigzagging through the donkey-wide streets with their jaunty sherbet-colored houses.

A villager sitting on a bench, shelling pistachios, and humming along to Greek music on an old radio, greeted me as he usually did, "Where you from, little girl?"

"She from Greece!" answered a second, familiar, bushy-eyebrowed fisherman, mending his mound of orange nets. The net-mender and the pistachio-sheller laughed with volcanic rumbles, throats phlegmy from unfiltered cigarettes.

This "where-you-from-she-from-Greece" was like the new village knock-knock joke. Word had gotten out that our house in New York City was the new Greek embassy. As the Greek embassy, it was literally Greek territory. Hence the punch line that I was "from Greece."

I didn't mind the avuncular joshing that day. I was lost, bereft, my life blown to bits, and I was about to head to a remote boarding school in Virginia. The particular school was chosen because Aunt Kathleen once told Grandmother she wanted me to attend as she knew the headmistress. When Aunt Kathleen died, Grandmother classified the request under "Dying Wish." A small sum was set aside from the liquidation of family assets to cover my secondary-school education. It wasn't a very good school, so it didn't cost that much. Mom immediately approved the idea. She couldn't handle her own life anymore, much less mine.

"You get *another* home, *koukla*," encouraged the net-mender. *Koukla* meant doll. "You know," he confided to the sheller, "in American they have scheme called mortgage. The bank buy you a house, then you rent it from them!" I felt I should disagree with this but couldn't find any aspect of his statement that was wrong. Maybe I would know when I was older.

"Why they do that?" asked the sheller.

The net-mender shrugged. "Americans don't like same house all the time. They always moving. Sometimes to other side of the street. Someday, this coming to Greece."

The pistachio-sheller snorted his disbelief and handed me a nut. "We not making fun of you, *koukla*. Greek different than American. We old civilization. Family home is passing down father to son, and he is passing down to son, and he is passing down to son. And then *he*—" a wink "—is passing down to *daughter*."

I ate my pistachio, which was sweet and Statue-of-Liberty green. What the pistachio-sheller described had, in fact, been the plan for me. "I think that's important, too."

"See what I say! You Greek!" They bellowed laughter, which ended for the net-mender in a fit of coughing like my three-pack-a-day father used to have. The men regarded my sad face.

"*Palikari!*" the net-mender yelled at a boy loitering nearby, clearly fascinated by my red hair. A colorful word, *palikari* meant "brave young hero," but was applied so randomly as to signify, "Hey, you there!" The wiry teenager approached, tan above his cut-off jean shorts. The boy and the net-mender exchanged some words in Greek. The boy nodded agreement and looked at me. I looked at the net-mender. "He take you on adventure. For *secret underwater treasure.*" The net-mender's eyebrows bristled portentously. That was the day the handsome boy took me scuba diving and we found the small, stone statue. It was the happiest time in the entire summer.

Sadly, at the end of our sojourn, Mom discovered the Greek shipping baron was married. I imagined she learned this fact as she desperately pressed him for commitment. We returned to New York in disgrace. In 1986, the mores of our social set had progressed to approximately 1952. A woman who spent the summer alone on an island with a married Greek millionaire could not expect to attract a respectable husband at the country club, especially if she had no money of her own. Bert offered Mom a haven in his house. There, Mom withdrew from the world, folding into herself, becoming, and remaining, the woman I saw in Centerville.

⌒⌒⌒

NOBODIES ALWAYS PASS background checks. Still, it takes time to find out nothing about someone. I had days to kill. The last place I wanted to kill them was in Centerville with my needle-pointing mother.

Besides, I could hardly sit still. I was giddy with possibilities. The money I would have! The ever-loving piles of money!

Don't count your chickens, Aunt Kathleen whispered in my head.

I ignored her. I was going to be the Frank Perdue of poultry demographers if I felt like it.

I reminded myself of the net-mender's comments all those decades ago. What seemed ridiculous then—I was a little girl— was eminently possible now.

You get another home, koukla.

Don't mind if I do.

❦

THE REAL ESTATE agent I contacted through the Corcoran website hopped to it when I said, "hedge fund." We set a meeting that afternoon.

Early for my appointment, I paused outside the Corcoran office on East 34th Street to review the extensive selection of modern-day castles posted in the window.

795 Fifth Avenue, Pre-War Penthouse

This incomparable penthouse encompasses the entire forty-first, forty-second, and forty-third floors with awe-inspiring 360-degree views. The residence boasts sixteen grand salons, with a living room considered the most magnificent privately owned room in the world. There are four adjoining terraces, five master bedrooms, six full baths and three half baths, five working fireplaces, separate guest suites plus staff quarters. The residence will forever remain without peer in Manhattan.

$95,000,000.00

I needed a moment to count the zeros. Ninety-five million. I read that New York had yet to crack the legendary hundred-million-dollar mark for a single apartment. This one was inching close.

How to put that number in context? What else did ninety-five million buy? A fish tank filled with diamonds. A satellite orbiting the earth. No, two satellites. A new cancer drug. That apartment that might even tax Peter Priest's bank account.

Next up—a Soho triplex with six bedrooms, a chef's kitchen, media room, two dressing rooms, and two staff rooms. Designed by a celebrity architect, the building had "a façade of flamed charcoal-grey granite colour with large glass windows." As if the British spelling wasn't quite enough, the listing enthused the luxe co-op offered "a gym with a double-height lap pool under a sensually curving wood ceiling." Despite the peerlessness of the previous listing, this abode was also "without equal in New York."

$80,000,000.

A diamond-filled hamster habitat. One-and-three-quarter satellites. Two private Caribbean islands.

Next, a forty-two-million-dollar Tribeca townhouse had succeeded in transforming the "blank canvas of raw space into an airy and sophisticated family home." It also possessed "random-width plank oak flooring."

A diamond-filled Tupperware. One island. A commercial jet (Embraer version).

I worked my way down the window. There were some nice one- and two-bedrooms in good neighborhoods.

$2 million.

Just my speed.

I fully understood some might view this as crazy—paying

two million dollars for a 2,200-square-foot apartment plus another $3,500 dollars a month in "co-op maintenance fees." How could I consider such a thing when, at that moment, there was a five-bedroom, five-thousand-square-foot house with a pool, a deck and a built-in spa for sale in Kansas City at a fifth the price?

Honestly, though, if we're talking about crazy, who in their right mind wanted to live *there*?

The Corcoran agent spotted me and poked her head out the door. "You *must* be *Delia*." Shaking my hand with the firm grip of a politician working a rope line, she said, "Let's get *started*!" A sixtyish woman with a blond bob and faint Southern accent, Sarah, I learned, always spoke in italics.

⟜⟝

FOR THE NEXT three days she marched me through the city, apartment by apartment. We saw everything: big-windowed abodes in blustery Battery Park City with cheerful views of Lady Liberty on one side and the tragic gouge of Ground Zero on the other; brick-walled lofts on the Lower East Side converted from old liveries and sewing factories; lugubrious Hogwartian towers on the Upper West Side. We apartment hunted our way through SoHo, NoHo, Nolita, Meatpacking, Tribeca, Bowery, Alphabet City, Greenwich Village, Washington Heights, Kipps Bay, Clinton, Inwood, and Murray and Carnegie Hills. Nearly every apartment was not only eye-blinkingly expensive, but also likely to enter a bidding war that would drive its price even higher.

If the housing bubble was going to burst, it showed no signs of ending here. Sarah said New York prices kept rising as if sprinkled with magic beans.

Working for Priest, I would have the money to purchase one of these fantastically priced places. There was only one problem: I didn't like anything. Nothing cried out, "Buy me!" What was the matter with me? I tried to put my finger on it.

One issue was that every apartment was so strenuously renovated, it seemed like a movie set of some other place. The twin AGA stoves in a Tribeca kitchen were right out of the Cotswolds. A master bedroom on the West Side with custom stenciled cabinetry seemed to hail from a Loire Valley chateau. A Murray Hill bathroom with tumbled pebble walls and plashing mini fountain evoked a Canyon Ranch spa. An inorganic postmodern living room in the Meatpacking District with severe Mies van der Rohe chairs and command-center track lighting suggested an off-earth space colony.

When I mentioned my observations to Sarah she said, "This is 2006 in New *York*, honey. You buy an apartment and you *renovate*. Rip it all out! Make it *you*. If you sell in two months, the next person will rip it out again. No one wants to live in an *unrenovated* apartment. That's like wearing someone else's *underwear*."

Maybe exposure to nothing but generic middle-America dwellings and Pottery Barn furniture had impaired my aesthetics. Still, even considering my own renovation, none of these places felt like *me*.

"I don't know why I'm so hard to please," I said, taking off my shoe and pondering a possible bunion.

Credit where credit is due, as I became increasingly discouraged and foot-weary, Sarah remained implacably patient and unswervingly italicized.

"*I* do." Sarah blinked her eyes several times, hard, because she was wearing too much mascara. "Buying a *home* is like falling *in love*, honey. When you find the *right man*, he makes your *socks roll up and down*. It's the same with buying an apartment. You have to find *something* about the place that rolls your socks. Even if it's just *a window*."

I had never experienced sock-rolling. Certainly not of the man variety. I was pretty sure Sarah meant something different than horny.

"Why don't we go back to the office and work on finances? A little paperwork to fan our spirits."

SARAH'S STUNNED SPEECHLESSNESS was itself a form of italics. Finally, she stuttered to life.

"What do you mean *no savings*?"

"I mean no savings."

"I thought you *said* you worked for a *hedge fund*. I mean I've seen *cash burn*, honey. Boats, airplanes, fourth homes, *giraffes*. But I've never seen anyone spend *all* of it."

Giraffes?

"I haven't spent all of it. I don't even have it yet. I'm waiting for a job offer. I thought I told you that in our first conversation."

Sarah turned over my financial application with a big sigh. "Maybe you did. All I heard was 'hedge fund.' The best clients are in hedge funds. I hope you will *be* one of *mine* in a couple years."

"A couple of years!" A five-hundred-thousand-dollar salary, minus taxes and sundries, was nearly thirty grand a month. Bonus aside, that was more than enough for any of the apartments I was looking at. In point of fact, I was being conservative.

"Delia, *honey*, how *exactly* do you plan to meet the co-op board *financial requirement?*"

"The what?"

In a few brutal minutes, Sarah explained that despite the farmers'-market ring to the term "co-op," New York buildings were the strictest, most exclusive, and closed-est of clubs.

"The co-op board can reject you for any reason. They don't even have to tell you why."

They don't tell you why. No reason. No note. Just a figure, face down, wearing familiar shoes and fingers trailing in a fountain.

Sarah tapped her pencil to get my attention. Buying into a co-op, she explained, was not a traditional purchase of property. You literally bought shares in the building, like stock. Your stock entitled you to your residence. That allowed the co-op to be managed like a private corporation. The board said who got in and who didn't.

"The last legal form of housing discrimination," Sarah said. "It used to be boards were racist. Now, they're cash-ist. It's all about the financial requirement. Most co-ops want a buyer to show two times the purchase price in liquid assets *after* the sale. It's not even written down anywhere. It's just *understood.*"

Two times purchase price in savings. That was *four million dollars.*

The co-op board, she further informed me, also controlled how much of the price you could mortgage.

"The most lenient co-ops, the really *loosey-goosey* ones, will absolutely require *25 percent* down."

Six hundred thousand dollars up front.

Two years my ass. If I lived in Centerville for the next four years, maybe I could swing it. The fact that I didn't like any of the apartments was now a moot point.

"You could always just rent. On your salary, you'd get a really nice place."

"*Rent?*" Renting was like being offered a chance to look in the windows of Cinderella's ball when you wanted to be *at* the ball. When you had once *hosted* the fucking ball.

"It's not the worst thing in the world."

Yes. It was.

I left her office.

Chapter Five

If you must play,
decide upon three things at the start:
the rules of the game,
the stakes,
and the quitting time.
—Chinese proverb

I DID SOME quick calculating. The plan of living in Centerville would never work. Aside from the fact that my psyche
might crack under the strain of living with my mother, it was a
full two-hour commute to the Odyssey Nolita office. I would
be expected to put in eighty-hour weeks. It was a nonstarter.
That meant paying New York rents, which would take a big
chunk out of my paycheck. Even with my soon-to-be enormous
salary and bonuses, my best-case scenario would take me seven
years to save enough to buy my own place. Worst case, say if
bonuses were slashed, it could take fifteen. I would be fifty by
then.

For kicks, I ran the numbers on buying the ninety-five-
million-dollar pad. That would take me a hundred and forty-
seven years. With bonuses.

I AM GOOD at disappointment. Because I've had so much practice. The shrink I went to in high school called my ability to ignore my feelings "repression."

Here's what I like to call it: "coping."

I had a party to go to. Wall Street Poker Night, hosted by Odyssey Capital. The event was just a few hours away and in my old house. I longed to be there again, to coat myself in it like a salve and lose myself in the pages of that defunct fairy tale.

Cinderella got her ball gown from a whack with a magic wand. I got mine from my mother's cedar closet, which was like a rack at a high-end consignment store. She still had all her old Gucci, Bob Mackie, Balenciaga, Diane von Furstenberg, and Ungaro. It all still fit her—and me.

"This, I think." Mom pulled out a seafoam-green silk Valentino. It was the same color the Russian portrait-painter chose for me all those years ago. "I wore it when your father and I were dating." I slipped it over my head. Mom stood back. "Perfect."

Mom placed me in front of her vanity while Bert waited in the one living room chair he was allowed to occupy. Mom used exclusively Chanel makeup. She swiped primer ($65) on my face in a businesslike way, following it with foundation ($115). She learned her techniques from professional makeup artists back in the day. A dozen cunning powdered eye shadow squares ($45 each) smelled like lilies and looked like little jewels. Heating up on the glass surface of the vanity was a flat iron called the "gdh gold® styler." ($225).

An observer might have misinterpreted all this primping as

motherly. Knowing Mom and her priorities, I felt more like a Ming vase, being dusted and packed for shipping to an art sale.

Mom separated two-inch locks of my hair and let the iron sizzle fiendishly down their lengths. When she was done, a curtain of glossy red fell around my shoulders and to the middle of my back.

"There."

Mom palmed the key to her nightstand. She opened it and extracted her green leather jewelry box. Inside lay a glittering collection of jeweled bird brooches. They once belonged to my grandmother, and also fell off the moving truck.

Mom selected a diamond-emerald-and-sapphire humming-bird, his wings arched at the apex of his stroke. She pinned it to a place where the green Valentino silk caught at my waist. Emerald earrings, my father's wedding gift to her, clamped my ears hard, like a childhood pinch.

We emerged into the living room and Bert shot up from his chair with an alarming creak.

"Jesus, Mary, and Joseph. It's like stepping back in time. You'll have to beat the fellas off you with a stick."

Bert gave me a ride into town and dropped me off on Fifth Avenue.

CHATEAU, SCHLOSS, ALCAZAR, palazzo. My former home stood there as if materialized out of a storybook. The colonnaded façade took up the entire 80th Street corner, stretching half the Fifth Avenue block south to 79th Street and half the eastward block toward Madison. When we lived there, it was the last great Fifth Avenue mansion in private hands. All the rest had been transformed into schools, museums and embassies. There were dozens of privately owned *townhouses*—those narrow, five-floor former middle-class domiciles cramming side streets like the spines of books. The mayor lived in one. But those places were not castles like mine.

My castle said, "Fuck you, Mr. Ninety-Five-Million-Dollar Penthouse and your lousy sixteen rooms. I have thirty-five."

Nine ninety Fifth was a great white confection of a house, embellished along its roofs and windowsills with piping and rosettes as if decorated by some crazed hybrid of pastry chef and plaster mason. Magnificent windows arched the ground floor. On the second, third, fourth and fifth floors, the windows grew smaller, until, at the top, where the servants lived, portholes peeped out under the eaves. Slates tiled the roof, overlapping each other like feathers on the back of a giant bird. Speaking of birds, avian motifs were in every architectural detail, in the wrought iron, armatures, brackets, column capitals, moldings, and roofline parapets. This was an eccentricity of my industrialist and inventor great-grandfather, who built the house in 1915 and was an amateur ornithologist.

Back then, Great-Grandfather was in the vanguard of the Real-Lace Irish bursting into New York society. His crew included the Kennedys, Murrays, McDonnells, Skakels, Cuddihys, Buckleys, and Bradys. We were the new New York aristocracy, outshining the dusty Dutch and dreary WASPS with our bright Celtic glare. We had good looks and glamour, charisma and humor, sex appeal and JFK.

New York is a place of opposites, where rich and poor, clean and dirty, high and low cram together cheek by jowl. The corner of 80th and Fifth was no exception. Another building stood adjacent to the grand Mulcahy Mansion. Or rather, the building skulked next to it. This dingy thirteen-story toad of an apartment structure had no liveried doorman. No freshly planted flower beds. No brass accents requiring daily polishing. Nothing like the other fine, limestone buildings off Fifth Avenue. Its awning tried to announce its number—*TEN*. But since the first two letters exhausted themselves in the seventies, there was only *N* left.

It was, of course, my mother's rent-controlled building, sitting right next to the fairy castle.

The proximity of the two buildings was precisely how my father and mother met. She, an upcoming model, moved away from Queens to this reasonably priced apartment smack in the midst of the class she aspired to join. He, the shy, bookish, still-single millionaire bachelor suddenly got one of the world's most beautiful women as his neighbor. It was a story made for the society pages.

Mom's paranoid, survivalist tendencies—in full flower these days—must have always existed. Even after she was married, Mom didn't give up her rent-controlled lease. This turned out to be a lucky break for Aunt Kathleen. When she was kicked out of the convent and recruited to help raise me, Aunt Kathleen moved into Mom's apartment and her name was added to the lease. Since Aunt Kathleen was both a literal sister as well as a former nun, Grandmother agreed the apartment, rather than the servants' quarters, was most appropriate.

Tonight, in the soft, late-summer breeze, the blue-and-white flag of Greece fluttered outside my former mansion. A sign announced, "Wall Street Poker Night." It was a famous event since Wall Streeters were inveterate gamblers. They placed bets on anything. On how many sesames would be on today's bun, or which drop of rain would beat the others in sliding down the windowpane. Mom's *Vanity Fair* article said Priest got himself banned in Vegas for card counting.

A tent shrouded the mansion's swooping marble staircase, continuing along the sidewalk, a red carpet peeking out of it like a tongue. I joined the queue inside the tent. The men in the line wore tuxedoes. The women were extraordinary—clearly not wives or girlfriends, those concave-chested mates of finance professionals in Lilly Pulitzer dresses and Jack Rogers sandals. These dames were busty swans, long legs striding confidently in towering shoes with red soles. Models maybe. Or something else.

I climbed the front steps. Under the soles of my mother's Ferragamo pumps, I felt the small dip in the center of each stair where the marble was worn away, the same indentation as decades ago. I held my breath and entered.

Things had changed. In the small anteroom, the Italian marble floor was scuffed and worn. I saw no brass umbrella stand, nor massive vase atop an elegant mosaic-surfaced table. Of course not. Mom had the vase, table, and umbrella stand.

I longed to glimpse the main entrance hall, wondering if the crystal chandelier, the size of a small pony, still hung overhead. The tuxedo in front of me moved away, revealing a security checkpoint, screened top and sides by curtains. I couldn't see anything.

I presented my invitation and ID. A woman in a black suit and crisp white blouse checked me off her list. I opened the snap on Mom's Chanel clutch, which gave a satisfying pop. The guard fingered my wallet, a lace handkerchief with my grandmother's initials, and Mom's lipstick, then he directed me to his left. More curtains and arrows tunneled down a side hallway dumping me into the garden under a tent. The party was not in the house at all.

The crushed stone and shells crunched familiarly under my feet. The gracious garden with its geometric paths and beds and decorative dwarf trees huddled under the tent. Long white-clothed buffet tables spanned the length of the tent, and roaming waiters carried silver trays of fizzing champagne flutes. I looked for a way back into the house.

I noticed a line forming at the doors to the conservatory, a glass sunroom where Grandmother once drank tea with her lady friends. I joined the queue. Oddly, everyone in line was male. I got a look or two. Was this the line to the men's room?

"Credentials?" said the guard who was checking badges.

"Where do I get credentials?"

"From your checkbook," one of the tuxedoed men tossed over his shoulder. He held out the badge on a lanyard around his neck, and the guard waved him around me.

"Excuse me?"

"Players only inside," said the guard.

"I really want to see the house," I said, surprised I sounded so much like a little girl. "I used to live here."

The guard looked at me as if I had said *I used to be a platypus.*

"Players only. Buy-in ten grand." He gestured to the cashier's table.

Chapter Six

Should auld acquaintance be forgot,
And never brought to mind?
—Robert Burns, "Auld Lang Syne"

I WANDERED AMIDST the skirted tables and the gold-painted bamboo chairs. The buffet was a Noah's Ark-worth of animal ice sculptures surrounded by an ocean of seafood: caviar, raw oysters, shrimp, smoked salmon, lobster, rock crab, crab legs, crayfish, langoustines, sushi, and sashimi.

I felt the stares of men as if they were palpable taps on my shoulder, trying to get my attention. I had a transfixing, honey-pot kind of beauty, sharpened by Mom's Valentino and expert hand on my hair and makeup. The male attention had its usual effect of piquing my own desire. One fellow broke away from his friends and came my way. Hmmm. Possibly fun. On the other hand, I didn't know who he was. He could be a future competitor, or colleague, or someone I might even report to, who had made the assumption I was a high-class call girl.

Awkward.

I sighed with regret and melted through a stand of people toward the fountain near the eastern wall. Familiar ivy climbed up the wall, and nearby a Japanese maple bowed its miniature trunk, red leaves glowing. The fountain was a large stone urn with figures of birds perched on its edges to set an example for the real ones. The water burbled and purled.

Just as it had decades before.

⌒⌒

IT WAS 1986, and an April sun warmed the city. Dad had died almost two years before. I was starting to heal from my grief, with a lot of help from Aunt Kathleen. She was more grounded than Mom, who had been catapulted from the working class to modeling fame, then to Lady of the Manor. Even though Mom had gotten the life she aspired to, it was as if the steep ascent gave her the bends. I remember Mom all fluttery and breathless, trying to project a confidence she didn't feel. It got worse when she didn't have Dad as a shield.

Aunt Kathleen, former nun that she was, didn't care about social class. Practical, cheerful, reliable, she would have been as at home in a hermit's hovel as a mansion. In the years after we lost Dad, Mom coped with her own shock, and Aunt Kathleen took over mothering me almost completely.

By the spring of 1986, it seemed like things were finally getting to some kind of new normal. Then the atmosphere in the house went electric with a different kind of tension. There were some "financial problems," Mom said. I wasn't sure what that meant. "Do you think it would be fun to live somewhere else?" she asked me one day. That's how I learned Grandmother was contemplating the sale of the house.

When I asked Aunt Kathleen for some explanation, she said, "We'll get through this together. Somehow, pal, we will." I believed her.

Those were the conditions on the April morning in 1986

when, just before breakfast, I marched into the sunlit garden, notebook in hand. In the back of my mind, I was scared about "financial problems," and wondered whether it would, in fact, ever be necessary to live somewhere else. Still, I felt immune from true harm. I had Aunt Kathleen in my corner.

The eighth-grade science assignment required us to measure the bean plants we were each growing. My sprout was just forming an apostrophe, unfurling in a small terra-cotta pot on the southern wall of the garden. It was shaping up to be a bright day, but I recall feeling a knot in the pit of my stomach. Something felt off-kilter, in a foreboding way.

My feet crunched down the path. Some yards away, I saw a figure lying on the ground, one arm flung awkwardly out, pale fingers dangling in the water of the fountain. I struggled to understand why there was someone sleeping in the garden and why she was wearing oddly familiar shoes. I approached the figure, transfixed.

A white-faced gardener manhandled me back into the house.

Next, there was a gap in my memory. Like a data corruption. I believe I sat in the front hall, sketching the garden fountain scene in my science notebook, waiting for Aunt Kathleen to walk me to school. There was confusion all around. The next thing I remember were the police faces, and someone saying Aunt Kathleen had committed suicide.

That's when my world shattered into a billion shards. It was now a grand puzzle where the pieces would never fit together again. It simply *couldn't* be. Aunt Kathleen had not committed suicide. It was not her. That must be some other woman wearing her shoes. My grief had infinite elasticity. It stretched to cover many years after her death. It spanned my entire boarding school career at the aptly named Our Lady of Sorrows.

⌒

THIS EVENING, AT Wall Street Poker Night, a woman arrived in my garden spot, interrupting these memories. She wore a hot pink, black, and orange Roberto Cavalli dress with see-through lace over her enormous fake boobs. She struggled to balance her champagne flute and hors d'oeuvres plate. She looked for a place to put her dish and decided on the edge of the fountain. She set it down, the plate tipped, and a veined thumb of a shrimp tumbled into the water, streaking the surface in bloody cocktail sauce.

I decided it was time for a new assault on the house. "Bathrooms?" I asked a waiter.

He pointed to a sign with arrows and a female icon.

A flagstone path ran along the perimeter wall. I followed another bathroom-bound woman in a white dress transparent enough to show an underwear-free ass.

Through a side door, I found myself in the familiar back hallway, dark, wood-paneled, and beloved for games of hide-and-seek with my childhood "friend" Angela (quotes stet). There were closets for linens, and storage rooms for food, tools, buckets and brooms. Various thresholds gave access to four servants' staircases, the kitchen, and, finally, the butler's pantry, a former treasure trove of crystal, china, and trunks of silverware. Angela and I used to spread the silver on the floor and play.

I remembered Angela's eyes, owl-wide, marveling at all the types of spoons—soup spoons, teaspoons, and consommé spoons; and fork species—dinner forks, fish forks, and oyster forks. I taught her vocabulary like *vichyssoise, chateaubriand,* and *hollandaise.* I oversaw the setting of make-believe tables with real-life banquet-ware and divulged the trick for remembering where the bread plate and drinking glasses went: hold up your hands, palms out, thumbs to forefingers. The left makes a lower-case *d,* the right a *b.*

Today, I tried each doorknob along the hallway. All locked. The woman in white looked back to see what was rattling. At the hallway's terminus, a cross-armed guard blocked the door to the rest of the house. Past him, I saw the poker tables and players, jackets on, bow ties tight. Priest was somewhere in there, arranging cards in his hand. "Badge holder and embassy personnel only. Ladies' room that way," the guard said, gesturing to his left.

A small powder room from olden times had been extended into a four-stall bathroom for embassy workers. Two storage closets had been knocked down to create a sitting room with mirrored walls and upholstered ottomans.

I collapsed on an ottoman, defeated. This field trip wasn't working out like I planned. I wanted to get inside my former home, to relive that world if even for a few moments. Maybe I also harbored a screwball fantasy that somewhere inside my castle still hid the secret key to my future.

Yet here I was in a cramped ladies' room, hemmed in by women with bald-waxed pussies, rustling inside jeweled evening bags for cocaine.

"Is that Dee-Dee Mulcahy?"

I couldn't see the speaker because she was shorter than the surrounding population. But I could think of only one person who would use my childhood nickname. My "best friend" (quotes stet) Angela Conti forcibly parted a curtain of long-legged women.

"Oh my God!" Angela exclaimed. She stretched out her arms.

"Oh my God back!" I rose in response and embraced a pair of straight shoulders with palpable biceps. I stood back to take her all in. Or rather to take in what was left of her. Her triple-D breasts were missing. As was her former nose. She turned to show off a fabulously fit figure displayed to full effect in a Nanette Lepore lace-over-taffeta cocktail dress. Her hair, long since grown out of its eighties perm, was swinging glossily at her collarbone. A ten-thousand-dollar poker-playing badge hung from her neck.

"*Pardon* me." A woman adjusting her hair extensions was jostled by Angela's pirouette.

"Never mind." Angela waved a dismissing hand, sat down on the ottoman, and patted for me to do the same.

"Wow. Angela! Look at you!" I was surprisingly glad to see her.

"Like it?" Angela modeled her profile.

"You look like a million bucks."

"Oh, it didn't cost *that* much." Her eyes twinkled. "Almost. Nose job, breast reduction, and Pilates four times a week. It's *so* good to see you, Dee!" She reached over and squeezed my forearm. "I've googled you every now and then. But you're not on Facebook, or LinkedIn or anywhere."

She was right. If anyone asked about my lack of social networking, I would say, "I don't like people." They would think I was joking.

"You *searched* for me?" I asked.

"I tried everything. Dee-Dee Mulcahy. Delia Mulcahy.

Even Brigid." This was my name, though virtually no one knew it. Aunt Kathleen, my godmother, chose it. In the insanity of Irish nomenclature, one nickname for Brigid is Delia.

There was a pause while I didn't explain to Angela why I'd never looked for her, so Angela continued, "It's like some kind of karma we'd run into each other *here* of all places." She put her hand over mine on the ottoman. "I can't believe you're back in New York. What are you doing here?"

"Odyssey Capital. I'm interviewing for a job with them, and they gave me an invitation to this shindig."

"You were always so smart!" She nearly squealed. No one knew my academic history better than Angela. She and I were double classmates. We first became "friends" at Rosemont, the Catholic grammar school around the corner from the mansion where we now sat. Then, when Sorrows was selected as my high school, Angela followed me there. Her father insisted. "Interviewing for Odyssey! That's a really big deal."

"What are *you* doing here?"

"I'm on the board."

"Of what?"

"Everything!" Angela's laughter pealed. "Like a dozen non-profits. It keeps me busy. The best part is I can get any invitation I want. But this event isn't a party women go to, unless they're...*you know*." She raised her eyebrows at our ladies' room companions.

"So why are you here? The killer venue?" My house was once Angela's favorite place on earth.

"How could I resist?" She squeezed my forearm. It was like we were back on our side-by-side boarding-school beds. "Have you seen the *men*?"

"Uh-huh. You single?"

"Divorced. I have a little girl. She's five. You?"

"You're kidding, right?"

Angela tossed her head with another laugh. "Same old Dee. Such a loner. We'll have to fix that." Angela took a lipstick out of her bag, snapped open its mirrored case, and applied a swipe. "To be honest, I'm not interested in the men for anything romantic right now either. I'm here looking for a deal."

"What kind of deal?"

"An investment deal. Get in on the ground floor of something. I don't know what. Just *something*. I want my own money."

Sing it, sister.

"But you have a ton of money. Has anything happened?" A row of rings was stacked on Angela's hand: emerald, sapphire and diamond. Two-carat diamond earrings studded her little lobes.

"Dad still controls everything."

"You're kidding. Still? We're like thirty-f—"

"Shhh. Don't publish our age." Angela held up a hand. "That's the way it works with a trust fund these days. They don't give you access to it. So nobody blows it all." Angela paused while we both thought of my family who blew it all. "Dad appoints the trustee. They have to approve everything— the apartment, car, school for Madeline. I get zero say. Not even when Dad dies."

I remembered Papa Conti from childhood. He gave Angela everything—except her independence. The girls in school gossiped he was in the mob, and Angela never corrected them. When she was in first grade, the short, wealthy Sicilian decided Angela would achieve a social class he never had. He took her out of her parochial school in East Orange, New Jersey, and had her chauffeured daily to Rosemont on 81st Street. There, all the girls instantly hated her. Angela learned to be ashamed of her roots and longed to escape from her father.

"Dad doesn't take me seriously. He says if I want to make my own decisions, I should make money of my own. But how am I going to do that? Get a *job?*" Angela paused to let the ridiculousness of that sink in. "He says maybe if I find some good investment, he'll approve using money from my trust."

"Where are you living?"

"You'll never believe it. I'm across the street!"

Coulda predicted that one.

Angela always coveted my life. I had what she wanted: wealth and class and a society family in a Fifth Avenue mansion. Even as a little girl, Angela maneuvered for playdates and tried to ingratiate herself with my mother. She loved playing silverware games in the butler's pantry. She said when we were both grown up, she'd live next door and we'd give soirees. Evidently, she'd achieved the part about living next door.

"I have an apartment at the Grandhope," Angela continued. "It went co-op ten years ago."

"I remember reading about that in the *Times*. They auctioned off all the hotel paraphernalia like teapots and towels. The sale was mobbed."

"We don't like to remind people it was a hotel," she said.

"I'll watch my mouth, Sister Scholastica." For a moment, it didn't look like Angela would laugh. Then she guffawed at the mention of our long-ago nun nemesis from Sorrows.

Sorrows, our alma mater, was a rural Virginia anachronism, caught in the bend of the Rappahannock River, where the nuns wore full habits, and we girls studied elocution, archery, and horseback riding. Scholastica was the thin, humorless, former-friend-of-Aunt-Kathleen headmistress who watched the two of us as if we were her special project.

"Oh, Dee. It's like old times. What about you? With this fancy new job, you must be looking for a place to live."

Maybe it was because Angela was one of the few people who'd ever seen me cry. I found myself telling her all about my shabby life in Florida, the job hunt, the incredible Odyssey offer out of the blue, Priest's interest in my thesis, my dream of having a home again in New York, and finally the impossibility of that dream coming true, at least for a very long time.

Angela listened, nodding sympathetically, as she used to do. "I wasn't the best friend to you." She looked down at her ringed hands.

"You were great, Angela," I corrected, feeling slightly guilty. After all, I was the one using the quotation marks on *her*. This was because of the way our friendship started—with Aunt Kathleen insisting I invite the unpopular new girl over. *Just one playdate*—that was the deal. But Angela stuck like glue, wheedling more invitations, saying I was the only one who was nice to her. Papa Conti was so thankful to Mom and Aunt Kathleen there was no way to stop. With all the playdates, everyone assumed we were friends. In my head, I always inserted quotes around the word. A forced-to-be-friend wasn't a real friend.

"I *wasn't* great," Angela continued. "That time in Ohio. I upset you, and you never called after that."

"Never mind," I said.

"Now I have the chance to make it up to you." I thought for a moment she might approach her father on my behalf. Then I realized how nutty it was to think Mr. Conti might lend four million dollars to a person he hadn't seen in over a decade. Besides, it would be an impossible situation, since he wouldn't give Angela a dime. "There's an apartment about to come available in *my* building," Angela said.

"Angela, I just finished telling you, I don't have the financial qualifications or the down payment." Sometimes Angela wasn't such a great listener.

"Remember I said I'm on a lot of boards? That includes my co-op board."

"I can't believe you could get them to waive their requirements completely. I have zero."

"Just come see the apartment tomorrow."

"Fine." For all the good it would do me. But as long as Angela was in the mood to dole out favors... "Listen, do you remember that trick of yours with the dormitory doors?"

Chapter Seven

Τὸ μέλλον ἄδηλον πᾶσιν ἀνθρώποις, καὶ μικροὶ καιροὶ μεγάλων πραγμάτων αἴτιοι γίγνονται.

(No man can tell what the future may bring forth, and small opportunities are often the beginning of great enterprises.)

—Demosthenes

"IT MUST BE killing you not being able to see the place," Angela said, an unbent paperclip in her hand, jiggling a lock. At Sorrows, she could get into her enemies' dorm rooms at will.

I kept my eyes down the hall, feeling like I was fifteen and Sister Scholastica was just around the corner. The door sprung open, Angela waved me inside and hightailed it the other way.

I stopped to let my eyes adjust to the dim light of the servants' stairwell and took off my shoes, anticipating the squeaky boards. I switchbacked up the steps and popped out a side door onto the spacious second-floor landing. To my right, the main staircase spiraled upward like the inside of a giant seashell, winding through the center of the house, growing ever more tightly coiled.

I caught myself in a gilt mirror. God, I was the image of Mom, standing here, in a dress she'd worn at soirees like this

66

one. Well—I considered the poker tables and call girls—maybe not *exactly* like this one.

I gently pushed open a door. It was like a portal back to the life I might have lived.

The Portrait Room ambled away in front of me, a wide boulevard of a gallery connecting the north wing with the south. Guests used to traverse this arcade after dessert, strolling from the dining room across to the music room where coffee was served.

The first portrait, of my great-grandfather, was truly awful. It was the work of some Edwardian hack who slapped together a blurry likeness complete with a gloppy mustache. It was what John Singer Sargent would have done—if he were drunk. Shame that such a man should be immortalized this way when he was the one responsible for illuminating New York City.

Little known fact: Edison invented the light bulb, but my great-grandfather was the one who made it work.

The incandescent light by itself was no better than a circus trick. For electrical inventions like the light bulb, oven, or radio to be useful, the world needed the mass distribution of electricity itself. My great-grandfather, Thomas E. Mulcahy, did that part. He invented the entire infrastructure of commercial electricity: the first mass AC power stations, the transformers, junction boxes, fuses, domestic circuit breakers and even the light switch necessary to turn the light bulb off and on. His inventions connected the city like a giant central nervous system. He cofounded Consolidated Edison and started a company, the first of its kind, to manufacture electrical apparatuses for home and commercial use. It made him rich.

Next to my great-grandfather hung my grandfather and then my father. The portrait quality showed successive improvement, but the strength of chin was in clear decline. This aligned with family history. The men went from inventive to professorial; from bold to cautious; from self-reliant to dependent. They produced limited offspring and died young. Dad, as Grandmother discovered a few months after he passed, had been trusting his business manager, a college pal with reckless tendencies. That fellow plunged the family money into risky investments that failed.

Finally, there was me. The end of the line. I was meant to take over the family company, but Dad died before I was old enough. In the portrait, my chin was clear-cut with a determined upward tilt. The picture was appropriately museum-quality, painted by a Russian woman known for her presidents, monarchs, and heads of state. She was halfway through a picture of FDR when he died. This famous portraitist was Mom's pick, naturally.

The Russian required my mother to convene a collection of candidate frocks, hauled in by the armload from Saks and which Aunt Kathleen tugged one after another over my sweaty little body. She rejected a dozen until I appeared in the green. At which point she said, "Now we paint."

The painter had fierce talent. She wielded a brush with only two hairs to create the velvet luster of my dress and to execute each of my golden-red eyelashes.

In the picture, my eyes had the kind of optimistic sparkle that makes you want to say, "Poor little fool."

"What an adorable girl."

I was jolted from my reverie by a male voice behind my left ear.

"Can you imagine what her life was like?"

I spun around, still clutching my shoes in my hand. I had

not heard a single footstep or board creak. The man behind me was tall and tuxedoed. He had that medium-brown color of hair, which, post summer, seems to be every shade from blond to chestnut. He grinned. The chipped tooth immediately gave him away from his magazine picture. It was Peter Priest's competitor, Robert Goodman.

I froze, caught in the confusion of my multiple identities toward this man. I was a badge-less, possible call girl, wandering around the secure rooms of a foreign embassy. I was the new employee of his archrival. I was the daughter of his rent-controlled tenant. I was the girl in the portrait in front of us.

"Another world. Completely gone," he said, shaking his head at Portrait Me. He paused. "I'm sorry."

Yeah, me too, I thought. Sympathy, no matter how well intentioned, stung.

"Don't be," I said, an edge to my voice.

He looked confused for a moment, then squared his shoulders. "Maybe I need to start again. Hi, I'm Rob Goodman. I was just talking to an acquaintance, Angela Price. She said there was a woman up here I needed to meet."

New identity: Angela's ex-roommate and current matchmaking target. *This* was to be Angela's solution to my money problems.

"Oh, I...Angela must have given you the wrong impression." I primly put on my shoes.

Goodman watched for a moment. "This isn't going very well." He put one hand over another, cracked his knuckles, and stopped. "I'm not trying to pick you up..." He halted. "But I'm beginning to wish I *were* now that I see you."

"I think I'd better go." My shoes on, I started to make my exit.

"I want to offer you a job," he blurted out.

"Oh!"

"Not the line most men use?"

"First time, actually."

"You're so gorgeous, my best chance is probably the job offer."

I laughed. I liked self-effacing men—especially of the handsome and rich variety. I decided to be honest since he seemed to be a friend of Angela's. "Listen, I appreciate your coming to find me. I really do. But I already have an offer from Odyssey Capital."

He threw his head back with a big, "Ah!" He adjusted his stance. "Angela didn't say which firm. I bet Priest locked you in with his usual ploy. Twenty percent over any other offer, right?"

His lack of reverence toward the intimidating and enigmatic Priest made me like him more. "A bird in the hand," I said.

"At least allow me to *try* to persuade you to come to Hermes?"

"Well…" If he did make me an offer, I really *would* get more money out of Priest.

"Seriously. Visit me at my office on Monday?"

"Sure, but I'm being honest. If you make me an offer, I'll go to Priest for more."

"It's a date for Monday, or I'm not leaving."

"Okay. Yes."

"Good," he said. "I have to say, you don't look like Priest's typical hire."

"What's his typical hire look like?"

"Less…I mean more…"

"Male?"

Goodman laughed again. "Goes for all of us, I suppose." Goodman turned back to the portrait. "You know, I remember that family."

"You do?" I asked, amused he wasn't making the connection between me and the image in front of us. All grown up and all dolled up—with jewels, smoky eye makeup and vivid lipstick—maybe I did look like a totally unrelated person. For sure, on the inside, I turned out completely different from that hopeful little girl.

"My dad owned the building next door," Goodman went on. "Now it's mine. I remember that family moved out of the neighborhood. Late eighties I think. Not sure what happened."

"How about that."

"Can you imagine having parents who adore you so much? To have your portrait painted?"

Sure, I could. But then Mom shut me out, retreating into her own pain. These days she never thought about the portrait's subject (me), only its value and the fact that she couldn't get her paws on it.

"It *is* hard to find that kind of love anymore," I said truthfully.

"Tell you one thing, my father sure wouldn't have had a picture painted of me." Goodman gave a rueful chuckle and looked at me with intense blue eyes. "Had to do everything on my own from the time I was a teenager."

Such candor from this stranger was surprisingly moving. "Actually, me too."

Goodman pursed his lips and gave a quick nod of mutual understanding. "Well, I'm sure that girl also had her share of troubles, like any of us. I wonder where she ended up."

Chapter Eight

Όποιος πεινάει καρβέλια ονειρεύεται.

(The hungry man dreams of loaves of bread.)

—Greek proverb

I MET ANGELA the next day for lunch, before we went to see the apartment in her building. We sat at a posh Madison Avenue deli called San Macarius. There, the early morning power breakfasts between heads of multi-billion-dollar banks had long wrapped up. Now, at noon, private-school moms in Lululemon yoga duds lunched in the company of each other and their Birkin handbags ($20,000).

The place had the tiniest tables, pink-marble tops the size of Frisbees. Angela ate fresh berries and yogurt for twenty-four dollars, while I had the thirty-five-dollar turkey sandwich. I eyed a nearby handbag, which cost more than my first car. I was not a purse-carrying kind of girl, but I liked the idea of a VW dangling in the crook of my elbow. I would put my name on the Birkin waiting list. It was a year long.

I thanked Angela for the Rob Goodman intro. I told her it wouldn't go anywhere because of the offer from Priest. She shrugged. "You never know."

"I got the sense you didn't tell him who I was."

"Jeez, I thought he'd make the connection once he saw the portrait." I shook my head. Angela popped a blackberry in her mouth. "Men. They never notice things."

"Listen, don't mention it, okay?"

"Why not?" she asked.

"Mom."

"Your mom is great," she sighed, probably thinking of her own mother, a Jersey-accented and tracksuit-clad contrast to the woman Angela would have preferred as a mother.

"*Sure*, she is."

"Maybe if you were nicer to her." Angela knew my mother and I were estranged. She blamed me.

"You know Mom's a big rent-control cheat," I said. Angela's blind hero-worship of my mother was as irritating now as it had been at sixteen.

"I don't think that's fair." Angela clinked down her silverware.

So I told her about how Mom kept her apartment in Goodman's building from before she was married, how she wanted a payout, and how she bribed the super to say she lived there.

"So, all these years she's renting that apartment as Margot Conover?"

"Mmm." I didn't go on to remind Angela that wasn't her real name. Mom asked me not to mention her lease to anyone, and I let my exasperation with Angela get the better of me.

Margot Conover was Mom's *nom de guerre* as a model—à la Marilyn Monroe (Norma Jeane Mortenson), Joan Crawford (Lucille Fay LeSueur) and Lauren Bacall (Betty Joan Perske). It was the appellation most people recognized. Few—obviously including Angela—remembered Mom's actual maiden name was Margaret (Peggy) Condon.

Angela and I needed to get off this tired old argument about whether Mom was or was not an ideal mother. Whatever I thought of Mom, I didn't want to sabotage her payout.

"Mom doesn't want to risk *anything*. That lease is like a lottery ticket."

"Crazy, right?" Angela said. "I read an article about all this rent-control stuff in *New York Magazine*. They said some guy in the Lower East Side got $500,000 for his lease so the landlord could sell to a developer. But first, they did all kinds of things to poke holes in his lease, interviewed the super and the neighbors. In the end it was easier to pay him."

"Anyway, the point is Mom wants to avoid anyone nosing around, since she used to be rich and also doesn't stay there the required amount."

"Of course. No question. I would never mention it," she said with stack-of-Bibles solemnity. Angela longed to ingratiate herself with my mother so fervently, I was convinced she'd keep her word, more for Mom than for me.

"Thanks," I said.

"Good for your mom. I hope she gets the money. Your mom is the best."

I turned my head so Angela wouldn't see my eye roll.

A WHITE GLOVE opened the door to the Grandhope Residences, the former Grandhope Hotel. Stitched seams ridged the doorman's knuckles and converged at his wrist like the veins of a fan, disappearing into his suit cuff. The cuff bore three spectacular stripes of gold braid. The suit was that shade of profound midnight requiring at least a dozen passes of a lint roller to keep clean.

"Good afternoon, Mrs. Price." The white gloves clasped one another expectantly.

I wondered for a moment why Angela kept her married name. Because of her daughter, perhaps. More likely, after having finally achieved such an uber-WASP surname, she was reluctant to go back to Conti. That might have been the attraction to Mr. Price in the first place.

"I'll need the key to 6C."

The gloves didn't move.

"Miss Mulcahy is interested in 6C. She grew up in the house next door. The *embassy*." The gloves reshuffled, left over right. "Well?"

"That apartment isn't on the market yet, Mrs. Price. I don't think I'm authorized to let people up."

"Never mind authorized, José. I want the *key*."

Angela had certainly gotten comfortable ordering staff around. Back when she'd visited our mansion, she had gaped over the women in pale pink uniforms and scalloped aprons. Our swallow-tailed butler stunned her into such shyness, she could not speak.

"Thank you," Angela said, taking the key without even looking at the man attached to the gloves. We walked to the mahogany-doored elevators across a carpet so thick it sunk under my feet like dough.

Like the venues I'd seen with real-estate agent Sarah, the Grandhope was also a movie set. Its lobby was a library straight out of King's College, Cambridge, with faux-antique bookcases full of used books the decorator bought by the yard, arranged for attractive interplay of height and color, lacquered and glued in place.

⌒⌒⌒

INSIDE THE ELEVATOR, another set of white gloves was attached to another staff member in the same exceptionally lint-free condition. "We kept the elevator man," Angela said. "We even saved the old mechanism." The gloves levered a crank to set the car into motion. Doors closed, the chamber filled with the scent of furniture wax. Inhaling furniture-wax fumes is like sniffing markers. I wondered how the elevator man stayed upright.

"I don't know why we're doing this, Ange." I disembarked from the elevator and took a lungful of fresh air.

"Oh, hush." Angela stabbed the key into the lock of 6C. "The woman who lives here had a massive stroke. She's only in her sixties. No one found her for a day." Angela swung open the door. "She's on life support. They've set the date for pulling the plug. My cleaning lady heard it from her cleaning lady."

I learned the full scope of Angela's harsher side when we were away at Sorrows. There, Angela no longer had the protection of a rich best friend because I was no longer rich. Angela proved she could take care of herself, though. She cultivated rumors of her father's mobster connections and burnished her own gangster cred, boarding-school style. Mean girls soon discovered Angela had no reservations about putting laxative in their oatmeal or flushing beloved hamsters down the john.

Angela fished her mobile phone from her purse, and I walked across the living room, which was a movie set of Imperial China. Red brocade swathed the walls, and dragon figurines with faces like pug dogs emblazoned black lacquer furniture and pillows. Beyond the garish interior, a large window beckoned me like a doorway in a dream. I approached.

Through the window I saw directly into a third-floor room at the Greek embassy. Where there had once been a little girl's canopy bed, there were now putty-colored filing cabinets. In long slices between the cabinets, I could still see remnants of pink-rose wallpaper. That was the very room where Mom laid out portrait dresses and where Aunt Kathleen read me bedtime stories while Dad listened.

Angela spoke into her phone. "Sandy? It's Angela. I have a friend here. Delia Mulcahy. Yes. For 6C. I know, but she's about to die. Can you come up? My place. Ten minutes."

Odd semantics floated through my head. Something about Delia Mulcahy who was about to die. I couldn't really concentrate. I suddenly understood what Sarah said about your socks rolling up and down over a window. They say you can never go home again. I knew this lesson as well as anyone, since my old home was now the literal territory of another country. But this was as close as anyone could get—looking, every day, through a window into my past.

Angela came up beside me. "Kind of eerie."

"Yeah," I said.

"You like it?"

"I love it."

"Thought you would. Sandy will be at my place in a few minutes. He's the board president. What he says goes."

I felt the weight of coming disappointment. "You're really sweet, Angela. But I don't know why I'm even doing this."

"That attitude isn't going to get you anywhere." She crossed her arms at me. "You never know where it will lead."

❦

"WE'D BE LIKE roommates again," Angela said as we walked down the hall to her apartment, which was also on the sixth floor. There was 6C, the apartment "for sale" at one end, 6B in the middle, and 6A, Angela's, at the other end.

As we passed 6B, the door opened. A tall specter of a woman emerged. She wore dark glasses and leaned on a cane. Her outfit was of grays, whites and black. But she sported a pair of red shoes. Her plume of fluffy white hair reminded me of the tufts atop Muppets.

"Angela?"

"Hi, Judith."

"I thought I heard you. It's time to do my pills."

"I have a friend visiting right now. So, three o'clock?"

"Fine." Judith shut the door.

"Was that Judith Fisher?"

"The same. How do you know her?"

"I'm pretty sure that's Mom's art dealer. I remember her saying something about a Judith who lived at the Grandhope."

"She was the *one* hotel guest who stayed when it went co-op," Angela said. "She totally screwed us on this hall."

"Have to say, you don't look very screwed." The brass lighting fixtures glinted, and the hall table veritably preened under its coat of polish. Angela pursed her lips and ignored the comment.

"She *insisted* on staying. It's really hard to throw out a tenant in New York, especially if they're old or disabled or crazy. I don't understand all the laws. But the lawyers said it was better not to fight it because we'd delay the whole conversion. Judith wanted to keep her room exactly the same because she's nearly blind. She said she couldn't possibly adapt to a new environment. We built around her. Because of Judith, my apartment is three bedrooms instead of four. And 6C has two instead of three."

Inside Angela's unfortunate three bedroom, the décor was restrained preppy perfection. A pattern of English ivy twined over her living room couches and across the matching window valances. On the couches sat rose-colored cushions embroidered with hunting dogs. Lamps fabricated from floral ginger jars graced marble-topped tables. Silver picture frames contained photographs of a frolicking little girl in East Hampton waves. Angela's apartment was also a movie set. Of a home presided over by my mother, Peggy Condon Mulcahy. Angela had been Mom's most attentive student. I sank into a feather-stuffed cushion.

"That's Madeline," Angela said pointing to the little girl in the surf.

"She's adorable." Angela beamed at my comment. "Do I get to meet her?"

"Not today. She has gymnastics. Nanny takes her. Put that down." She took the picture from me. "*This* is what I want you to see." Angela handed me a copy of *Upper East Side Magazine*. It was dated March 2006, a few months ago. A photo from the 1970s ran full bleed on its cover. Was that Mom?

Yes, it was.

Mom with a dozen other gowned women on the mansion steps. That must have been taken at some society benefit. A headline above Mom's head said, *Memories of Old New York*. It wasn't just me then. A lot of people were obsessed with the past. I flipped pages.

The issue was devoted to a retrospective of famous New

York families in previous decades and centuries—Rockefellers, Vanderbilts, Astors, Roosevelts... and my family. There she was, Mom laughing at the Union Club, walking in the park holding my hand, striding down the street with shopping bags. Her caption, *Mrs. John Mulcahy, a former model, was considered New York's most beautiful socialite in the 1970s.* There was even a picture of me and Angela that said, "Electricity Heiress, Brigid Mulcahy, and a friend."

"I'm *the friend!*" Angela exalted.

"I can't believe people still care about this."

"Are you kidding? It's Camelot stuff. C'mere." Angela beckoned me into her kitchen, tastefully done in pure white cabinetry and pearlescent mosaic backsplash tiles. She led me into the butler's pantry.

Angela pointed to the electrical panel. Its face said MUL-CAHY.

That name was on every piece of electrical equipment in the city. After inventing the power grid, my great-grandfather started Mulcahy Electric, which supplied all electrical machinery to New York and beyond, commercial, domestic, and military. "When we renovated, we had to replace all the wiring. But I saved this and turned it into a spice cabinet."

"You save the *circuit breaker?*"

"The new equipment is hidden in a closet. Look!" Angela opened the Mulcahy breaker door. There were rows of small glass jars with orange tops.

Appropriate irony. A Mulcahy electrical panel with nothing but oregano and smoked paprika in it.

After Dad's death, the business manager-slash-college pal took over at the helm of our company. He was already gambling company assets in high-risk investments, which were failing. Next he doubled down, squeezing more cash out of the business by cutting corners and using cheaper parts.

A year into the college pal's tenure as CEO, Grandmother's attorney uncovered the fraud. We were nearly wiped out. It would take years to recoup, but it *could* be done. The college pal was fired, and Grandmother, then in her eighties, planned for a long climb back to profitability, running the company herself if she had to, with her trusted attorney's help.

Unfortunately, disasters tend to pile on. Just then, bits of the MTA caught fire, followed by several apartment buildings. A public scandal brewed. Ed Koch, shaking his finger at a TV camera, vowed to get to the bottom of it.

My grandmother's middle name was "honor." Making the front page, she announced Mulcahy Electric would replace every flawed product sold in the past three years, down to the last wire, switch, and fuse. The company would make good on its reputation for quality. To do it, she sold the house and liquidated all assets.

It was a grand gesture. It was munificent. It sacrificed everything in the name of honor. Including me.

Grandmother unwittingly taught me an important lesson: honor was for suckers. Aunt Kathleen taught me the corollary: so was love.

"Anybody home?" we heard from the living room.

"Here comes Sandy," said Angela. "Make sure you play up the family history thing."

I didn't get a chance to comment that a family bankruptcy might put a damper on financial negotiations between me and the co-op board president. In a moment, Sanford Roache crammed into the butler's pantry with us.

"That name meant quality," said Roache to the fake circuit

breaker. He was a fit type in his late sixties, with the thick neck of a former football player, sporting a mustache and wielding a titanium mechanical pencil. Over lunch, Angela told me he was a failed architect. Fortunately for him, the city enacted Local Law 11, an ordinance that required façades to be repaired every five years to keep bricks from falling on people's heads. Roache marketed himself as the façade guy and made a fortune. He paid off politicians to strengthen the law, and his name was emblazoned on banners on scaffolding all over the city. "Tell me something." Roache sidled up to me confidentially. "Is it true that your family lost *all* its money?"

People were always amazed by this. That so much money could be lost. Like when Donald Trump lost billions. It was as if they thought somehow the sheer *size* of someone's fortune made it impossible to squander.

"Sandy," chided Angela. "Of *course* not."

"Sorry," said Roache.

"Delia has a fabulous new job." Angela led us into the living room. "You have no idea how brilliant she is."

"I imagine it's in the DNA." Roache winked at me.

Angela leaned over and whispered something in his ear. His eyebrows went up. I wondered what number she lied to him. "But she's *just* landed her job, so…" Angela looked at him.

"So, what we have here is a liquidity problem," advanced Roache.

I nodded. Among many other things, liquidity *was* a problem.

"Tell you what." Roache took a little pad out of his breast pocket and clicked up a millimeter of lead in the titanium pencil. He wrote. He paused, looked at me, looked back at the pad. "We have never done this in the history of the building.

But with your background in the neighborhood—everyone has read that *Upper East Side* piece—you're like a flesh-and-blood princess returning. Here's what we'll do. We'll actually waive the 50-percent-down requirement. Get whatever mortgage you can. Okay?" Roache looked to Angela for approval.

"Mmmm," she said. Angela was tough.

Roache pursed his lips then grinned as if he were Santa Claus about to pull a gift out of his sack. "Okay, how about this? Instead of five million in assets, we'll accept three." Angela broke into a big smile. "Now I better leave before I give away the farm!" Roache said.

"SEE?" SAID ANGELA as she closed the door on a gratified Sandy Roache. "I can't even think of a building that's done that for anyone."

"I'm sorry, Ange. It's just not going to be enough." How could she not know this? Being rich skewed people's perspectives.

"You still have Rob Goodman to see." Angela fingered a throw pillow. "Maybe he can come up with a signing bonus or something. I hear they do that." Who ever heard of anyone giving an unproven junior quant a three-million-dollar bonus? But I zipped my lip. Angela had done what she could. She reached over and gripped my forearm. "I *so* want to make this work out for you. Make up a little bit for the past."

It was too sad. I would never have apartment 6C and its magic, sock-rolling window.

Chapter Nine

Don't steal; thou'lt never thus compete
Successfully in business. Cheat.
—Ambrose Bierce, "Decalogue"

W HAT HAPPENS WHEN you fall through the earth? They say you land in China. I spent a lot of time in the People's Republic of Despair. That first year at Sorrows, my days were drained of all color, all texture, even of all measurements of time. In bed at night, overcome with the exhaustion of simply having to live my life, I would fall apart into sobs. Day after day. Month after month.

I had lost everything. Dad was gone three years by then. In her own way, Mom was gone too. Having lost her husband, then her financial security, and finally her sister, Mom disconnected, turned inward, and retreated to a solitary life in Centerville. Phone calls with her were short, tortured, and monosyllabic—neither of us able give any comfort to the other. We had both lost everything, but I was the child and needed her. So I got mad. My anger contracted into a small, dark marble of resentment, cold and black as obsidian.

At least Mom had Bert, who circled her world like a protective knight. My champion, Aunt Kathleen, the one who said, "We'll get through this together," inexplicably jumped off a roof, leaving me with no one.

I was a smart enough kid to know the first phase of grief is denial and that it passes on to—well, whatever came next. With Aunt Kathleen, I never made it out of denial. No matter how much I thought about it, her death never made sense.

I scoured the newspapers looking for stories on suicides. I absorbed the details of every incident. I read about addicts, people with terminal illnesses, women with dead toddlers, husbands who gambled the mortgage, and people who, for no reason, floundered endlessly in a thick, black sludge of despair until deciding to end it all. I became an amateur expert on the causes of suicides. Still, when it came to Aunt Kathleen, nothing fit.

Within a few months of my arrival at Sorrows, the head-mistress, Sister Scholastica, learned of my weeping from the girls in the room next to Angela's and mine, Angela herself being no snitch. Sister insisted I go to the on-staff psychologist. This ex-priest hippie said I would never know a reason for Aunt Kathleen's death. He advised that I bury the hope of ever finding a reason along with Aunt Kathleen. That piece of advice made me feel as if I was down a well and someone just pulled up the rope.

Angela eventually told me her reason, but that came later during the incident that ended our "friendship" in Ohio.

Sophomore year, I expected Angela to request a room reassignment and wondered why she didn't. Papa Conti, I assumed. He remembered Aunt Kathleen was behind that first playdate. I think he knew his daughter wasn't the easiest "friend" in the world, and yet she was at our house, week after week. He inferred, correctly, our "friendship" had smoothed the path for Angela at Rosemont. The flowers Mr. Conti sent to Aunt Kathleen's funeral dwarfed all others. After mass, he put his hand under my chin and said, "Your aunt Kathleen was good to my girl. I'll never forget it." Packing Angela off to Sorrows to be my companion was the most concrete way he could help. Like it or not, Angela was stuck with me, just as I had once been stuck with her.

Then, junior year, something good happened. The ever-anachronistic Sorrows required two years of either archery or equestrian arts, and I chose riding. The school's lesson horses were a bunch of spiteful nags, expert in all manner of shying, bucking, balking, rearing, and dumping riders in the dust. While we girls hung on for dear life, our instructor, a Hungarian cavalryman, accustomed to training soldiers, shouted, "Keep zee heels down, zee hands together and zee elbows in!" The Hungarian whipped us into shape, training us to ride in tight formation like a phalanx of mounted Amazons. It was fabulous. I forgot to be sad.

Horses were like a flash of something bright—a warm day in the middle of winter. The donated school horses were all refugees from some other life—like me. Also like the riding master, who fled a communist crackdown in Hungary. I felt true compassion for those horses. I could do something for them, if not for myself. The animal world held a sort of love I walled off against humans.

As a new batch of lesson horses stepped off the van at Sorrows, the Hungarian would divide them into the "honest" ones and the "dishonest" ones. The terms had Tolkienian import to him. His mission was to bring equine hooligans to the side of the light—and to teach us useless girls something along the way.

There was no end of Hungarian lore regarding the dark and

light souls of horses. The bones of an honest horse could keep a piano in tune. Changing a horse's name turned him bad. Copper pennies in a water bucket cured moodiness in mares. A horse with white socks was sure to be bad. The worst kind of horse, though, was one where you could see the whites of his eyes.

The Hungarian's gnarled leather-stained hands were magical and gentle. Nothing could anger him quicker than a girl who sawed back and forth on her horse's mouth. It was like *zee rape of zee woman.*

We girls didn't jerk on horses' mouths to be cruel—we were scared shitless. Riding a bucking, rearing runaway horse is like sitting on a thousand pounds of erupting TNT. The animal's sides quiver in anticipation. Keeping a stranglehold on the reins was about simple survival.

The Hungarian demanded the opposite. To master the animal—and yourself—you didn't clutch or cling. You asked for more.

"Go! Go! Leg! Leg!" the Hungarian bellowed. "On through no-man's-land!"

I was the only one who could execute this kamikaze instruction. The Hungarian beamed and said I had "the heart of a soldier." I wasn't so sure about that. I just empathized with the washed-up mounts because I felt washed-up, too. Also, it helped that, at the time, I didn't particularly care whether I lived or died.

"In no-man's-land, you must just to think and your horse, he must do," the Hungarian commanded. For him no-man's-land represented no less than the boundary between good and evil. A zone of stalemate, where the two forces hung in perfect equilibrium. You had to have the nerve to breach it and tip the balance in order to defeat the powers of darkness.

The Hungarian drilled us on all forms of horsemanship, from dressage, to jumping, to riding in phalanx formation, to harnessing a buggy and driving.

By senior year, most of us were pretty good little soldiers, and I was the Hungarian's right-hand girl in turning stable nags into battle-worthy horses. I was also his lover. I was the one who pursued him.

I intuited he would understand my need for physical closeness with no strings attached. I had lost a lot, but he had lost way more. I knew he would be a strong, kind, and expert lover. In fact, the riding master's prowess in bed was still a tough bar for any of the other men in my life to hurdle.

THE HERMES OFFICES were only a few blocks from Priest's. An early-balding and stocky man met me outside the elevators. "Mitch Mitchell," he said, and led me across their trading floor, which brought to mind the *Vanity Fair* description of Priest and Goodman being different "to a Shakespearean degree." Priest's trading floor was solemn, monochromatic, and intense. Here at Hermes basketballs, whiffle balls, ping-pong paddles with the little rubber orbs attached all lay on desks, leaned against cubicles, and littered the floor.

Suddenly, a few bars of Nirvana grunge rock blasted from a speaker, then just as suddenly stopped. At this signal, one of the traders vomited into his wastepaper basket.

"That's our notice of a bad trade," said Mitchell. "A million or more."

Robert Goodman wielded a lacrosse stick as I entered his

office. *Flash.* The shaft of the stick gleamed, and his arm muscles flexed under the white business shirt. *Zoom.* The ball left the red-thong pocket. *Bong.* It glanced off the wall, leaving a small black mark, and *whoosh* Goodman cradled it again.

So that made two young, good-looking, rich men in one week. Neither encounter being about sex. Funny how things work out.

My goal here was singular. I was on this interview to leverage more money from Priest. Once employed by Priest, I guessed it would be fine to sleep with Goodman. But rejecting this guy's job offer was probably going to kill the mood.

"Welcome!" He finished a final thunk-and-swoop, propped the stick in a corner, and fell backward into his chair, swinging his legs on his desk, beaming his chip-toothed smile, and gesturing me to sit.

There was a tank with a Komodo dragon very close to the chair. Another tank seemed empty, but I thought I saw a pattern that could be the skin of a snake.

I hung back.

"Something wrong?"

"There seem to be a lot of reptiles around this place."

His laugh was infectious and triggered my own grin.

I sat. He regarded me with a lightly puzzled expression, as if trying to identify the woman he had seen at the party. As with Priest, I wore knotted-back hair, glasses, and just a tiny bit of lip gloss.

"You've met Mitch Mitchell." Mitchell took a chair in the corner in a way that told me that was where he always sat. He made a church steeple of his fingers, brought them to his lips, and propped his elbows on the arms of his chair. "He's my enforcer."

That sounded ominous. And perhaps vomit-inducing.

"Oh?" I kept my expression studiously neutral.

"It's a joke, Delia. He's my COO. My right hand, so to speak. Keeps things going around here. I let people get away with murder. I don't hire anyone without him."

"Thanks, but I explained to you about Odyssey."

"Sure. Sure." Goodman paused, then angled forward. "You must be good if Priest wants you."

"I am," I said. I thought I heard a snort from Mitchell. He had my résumé with my third-tier credentials. Places like this were all Stanford, MIT, and Ivy League.

Goodman shot a glance at Mitchell then brushed a few golden strands out of his eyes with freckled hands that spoke of yacht clubs and rudder handles. He sat back. "Let's talk about what you want."

"This really isn't going to work. Whatever you say, Priest will give me 20 percent more."

"Did I say money? I asked what you *want*." Goodman lowered his chin in expectation. I furrowed my brow. "It's great to watch the wheels start turning, Delia." He came around the desk and leaned his backside against it, crossing his long legs in front of him and pressing the palms of his hands on the edge. His feet ended in tasseled loafers, no socks. "I've learned people *want* things, and it's never just money. Money's always a part of it, but years of making deals taught me everyone's got a soft spot, and that's the place to negotiate. Right at the soft spot. I once made an investment in a crappy company just to meet my first wife."

"Rob," said Mitchell.

"Listen, Delia," Goodman continued. "The only thing in life that pisses me off is a person who won't negotiate. It's unreasonable. Now think for a moment and tell me. Other than money, *what do you want?*"

He folded his hands and waited. He looked completely comfortable and at ease with whatever I might say.

Well, if he was asking. There was something I wanted, and, strictly speaking, it wasn't 100 percent about money. I told him about my real estate predicament. The apartment. The financial requirement.

"Those co-op boards. More fun than a barrel of monkeys!" He sat down at his desk and looked at Mitchell. Their eyes met.

"I could buy a different apartment, in a few years when I've saved up," I explained. "But I want *this* one. It'll be sold soon. I saw it before it was even on the market." I decided to leave out the part about the dying woman. "It sounds childish, I guess. But you asked what I want, and that's it."

"Doesn't sound childish. Sounds like a trader's instinct. It's about timing. Timing is everything on Wall Street."

I noticed a glint in his eye. I went for it. "Is it something you can help with?"

Goodman laughed in a way that seemed to make all cares dissolve. "You and I will get along just fine, Delia." I looked at Mitchell the enforcer to immediately wet blanket the idea. His fingers remained in front of his lips. "You're about to see how much fun it is to be in charge of the books," Goodman said.

"IT'S THE OLDEST trick in New York real estate." Goodman glanced over Mitchell's shoulder as he struck keys, creating a dummy Hermes Fund investment account for me, spoofing the assets. He printed out an official report.

I wondered aloud if it was possible to get caught.

Mitchell looked at me as if I might be simpleminded.

"All kinds of shenanigans go on in buildings," said Goodman. "I should know. I own one! They're practically *expecting* you to do something like this."

"And that's it?" I held the statement, wondering if I could have done this myself with some online forms, a bad copier machine, and a bottle of Wite-Out.

"They call us to verify," Mitchell said, as if reading my mind. "I'll handle it. Consider it your signing bonus."

"What if they want to see my finances two months from now?"

Goodman chuckled. "It's a co-op board, not the Nine-Eleven Commission. If anyone asks, just say you gave it to the poor. It's a free country, and you're a generous woman."

It was my turn to laugh out loud—at his audacity. The freedom of it. That was *exactly* what money meant: freedom and joy.

It was genius. Goodman had found a way to beat Priest by offering me money that wasn't really money. I wondered if he'd cooked up this plan with Angela before our conversation in the Portrait Room.

The salary offer was not quite as good as Priest's, but I would have my apartment.

I considered, for an instant, going back to Priest and asking him to do the same thing. But I remembered what Priest said about his abhorrence of corruption. I doubted very seriously he was going to help me commit fraud. And it was too dangerous to ask. I recalled how Priest considered himself superior to other hedge-fund owners. He might even tip off Sandy Roache. If I wanted my apartment, with its window into my past, I couldn't risk it.

Did I personally have any qualms about the scheme? As I

believed I have mentioned, only the rich can afford ethics.

I sent an appropriate email to Priest, saying I'd decided to take another offer for reasons having nothing to do with money. Which was technically true.

⌒⌒

"DID YOU KNOW what Goodman would do?" I called Angela to crow. "Is *that* why you kept telling me to see him?"

"La-la-la, I can't hear you," she said, laughter in her voice. "I am a co-op board member and will not listen to your scandalous tale."

"Angela…"

"You'll be in your new apartment before you know it. They're pulling the plug on Friday."

"Wow. Did you have to put it that way?"

"You're not the first person to want someone dead over a New York apartment, and you won't be the last. It's not like *you* killed her. By the way, you need to offer two-point-two million. A similar apartment in the neighborhood just went for that. You want to make sure the family has *zero* incentive to put it on the market. Give them a top price out of the gate. I hear her kids are really strapped for cash."

It was really happening. All of it. There was a vast Times-Square-at-New-Year's-stroke-of-midnight celebration inside of me. I would start at a fabulous new job making buckets of money. At the same time, I would settle myself into my own apartment, like a perch, with a ceaseless view into my former kingdom.

As for Angela, I probably needed to remove her quotation marks.

Chapter Ten

But Satan is now wiser than of yore,
And tempts by making rich, instead of making poor.
—Alexander Pope, "Moral Essays"

"GOOD MORNING, MISS Mulcahy."
Miss Mulcahy. What a nice, princess-y ring that had.

The night elevator man cranked the handle. The car lumbered into motion. I tapped my toe and breathed furniture-wax fumes. One hippopotamus. Two hippopotamus.

Fifth Avenue was deserted and dark. I stabbed my hand into the October air. Three a.m. The Asia market was cratering.

I squinted for a cab like a birdwatcher on the hunt for a yellow-throated warbler. My father, who taught me birdwatching, would be impressed I remembered this species. A cab materialized out of the void. Inside, it smelled of air freshener. We swerved around Columbus Circle. I thumbed Mitch Mitchell my progress. He would be cruising down from Greenwich in his Maserati ($150,000). I alternated between refreshing my email and looking out the window. I was just two months into my job as a Hermes Fund quant.

Priest hadn't let things go at my email. He called me up. Actually, his secretary called and said, "Hold the line for Mr.

Priest."

I waited five minutes before his voice came on. "I believe we agreed on one round of negotiations." His voice was flat and confident.

"We didn't have an agreement." I was piqued at being made to wait and by his tone, which implied that I was *going* to work for him. "Those were just your terms."

"You are turning down my counteroffer, then. Twenty percent over Goodman's. I seem to remember money was your priority." Correct. Also, slightly accusatory.

"As I mentioned in my email, this has nothing to do with money." I made my best attempt to sound as neutral as Priest.

"I'm to understand you prefer the *work environment*?" Not neutral anymore. His voice crackled with sarcasm.

"Yes," I said, a bit pleased I'd ruffled Priest. There was no explaining the real reason. You don't just blurt out you are committing fraud, which was exactly what Goodman, Mitchell, and I were in the midst of doing. The co-op management agency had phoned Mitchell several times to provide details on my Hermes "accounts."

"Just so you understand, this will not be Goodman's first time of—as you say in English—mixing pleasure and business."

"Is that what you *think*?" I hated that my voice squeaked. I was outraged at the implication. Odd, I know. If he'd accused me of fraud, I would have taken it in stride. But I *never* had to sleep with a man to get an opportunity.

"Goodman doesn't have the capacity to appreciate your mind." I could hear Priest shifting the phone to his other ear in frustration. "I offer you 20 percent more and you go work for him? A beautiful woman? You tell me what it looks like."

"I don't *care* what it looks like." So he *did* notice I was beautiful.

"You're making a terrible decision."

"Thank you for your concern, Mr. Priest," I said, and the call was over.

Inhaling air freshener and thinking back on the call, I had to admit Priest arrived at a reasonable, if insulting, conclusion. Not that it mattered anymore.

The cab's tires shuddered to a stop on the cobblestones in front of Hermes. I shoved two twenties through the divider opening. "Keep the change." The meter read $27.50, so I was giving him a $12.50 tip. I didn't have time for change. I didn't need change anymore.

I strode along the banks of cubbies where the programmers worked. On day two at Hermes, Mitchell put me in charge of a team. I now oversaw the group that wrote trading algorithms. These were computer programs that exploited flaws in the market.

Hermes's software team in this new area of high-frequency electronic trading was weak and young. I was like their den mother, presiding over a bevy of cubicles accessorized in action figures, light sabers, and cans of Red Bull. I quickly mastered the firm's algorithmic trading systems and was now shoulders deep in topics like database architecture, code reviews, and latency metrics.

"Did you deploy?" I grilled Tina. She was my first hire and the only other female on the team. I needed another woman junior to me, so I wouldn't get stuck with *all* the shit work. Tina was young, pretty, and faced the same obstacles as me in the all-male worlds of computer science and finance, so she was immeasurably grateful for the opportunity. Mitchell assigned Tina to nights because she was female, and he knew she wouldn't complain.

Tina typed furiously, looking green with fear. If she had pushed out code to the production server without invoking the automated test scripts, we could actually be *causing* the Asia crash.

"I swear I didn't."

"Get up." I was pissed. If one woman made a mistake, the guys would think we were all incompetent.

Nearby, the other night traders were hedging our Asia exposure by hand. I had to check on all systems. Errors were like roaches. If there was one, you assumed there were millions.

From the flat screen in the corner, CNN Asia screamed the market was in free fall. It was due to some massive automated trade. Was it ours? With three monitors going, I ran diagnostics. Key stroke after key stroke, I launched scripts. Mitchell arrived and stood nearby, arms folded. The other programmers melted away. They were afraid of him. All kinds of Mitch-Mitchell urban legends circulated the office. I'd heard one about how he put himself through school with his winnings as a Golden Glove boxer, and another about how the guard dogs patrolling his Greenwich estate only understood commands in Dutch.

After twenty minutes, I had verified all our code.

"It's *not* us."

"You're all lucky it's not," Mitchell glowered. He did nothing to quell the urban legends. I suspected he started some. "So, what is it?"

"Who knows?" I said, stretching my neck from side to side. "But for sure it's machine-made." CNN started barking again. The activity in Tokyo was returning to normal. Whatever caused the flash-crash had disappeared. This was the danger with hedge funds like ours. These days the market was at the mercy of a bunch of greedy geeks and hackers.

"You're staying, I suppose." Mitchell turned to his office.

"Yep." I stood to stretch and get some coffee. Of course I was staying. I worked like a sled dog.

"Good job," he muttered and stalked away to the glassed-in fishbowl where he kept an eye on everyone. He would launch into his typical routine, combing over the previous day's trades, more than fifty thousand transactions on six screens.

My first two months had gone by in a blur. Hermes lent me two hundred thousand dollars for the down payment on my apartment. The stroke victim's kids pulled the plug on her, as predicted. Angela was right about them being cash strapped. They immediately accepted my offer. I moved in immediately and took over the maintenance even before we closed. I was just finishing the purchase process, which involved the two hundred thou down, a two-million-dollar mortgage, and my faked investment statements from Hermes showing three-point-six million in assets.

Colossal sums were just another day at the office for me now. Hermes, like other hedge funds, lived in a win-win-win world of stupendous money—hundreds of millions of dollars daily, hourly even. The great thing about hedge funds was that we made money on fees. Whether the clients won or lost, *we* won. We played with other people's money, in everything from distressed equities, to stocks, to derivatives, to my current area: high-frequency electronic trading. We took all of the benefit and none of the risk.

A 2-percent fee might seem like a small amount. Unless you're working with billions, which we were. We also got 20 percent of the profits. Investments that lost money? That was the client's problem. Fortunately, we didn't lose much money. Our record wasn't quite as good as Odyssey's, but it was good. We were printing cash. With my thesis idea, I was hoping we'd make even more. I hadn't had a chance to talk to Mitchell or Goodman about it, but I planned to. All the money we were making gave me a sort of amnesia about the impending crash. But we *had* to do something to prepare. It was almost 2007 and I wondered how much time was left in the bubble.

In the break room, I considered the individual gourmet coffee pods from France costing seven dollars apiece. The coffee maker expectorated noisily into my mug. I chewed a stir stick. Ironic how my great-grandfather started this all a hundred years before with the mass distribution of electricity. Today, money was just electrons zapping back and forth from one trading pool to another. It was *this close* to imaginary.

Through the break-room window, I saw Mitchell hunched over his terminal. Goodman had not lied when he said Mitchell ran the day-to-day. I hadn't seen Goodman in weeks. The coding boys told me that's how it always was. Mitchell "enforced" while Goodman was out making deals, recruiting new investors, and traveling to Europe and Asia. I tied my stir stick into a knot. I preferred talking to the handsome cheerful Goodman over bulldog Mitchell, but time was running out.

~~~~~

MITCHELL LOOKED SURPRISED to see me in his doorway. I put my thesis on his desk.

"That's why Priest wanted me."

Mitchell eyed the title and opened the cover. "What does it say?"

"Subprime bonds are…" I began. Mitchell held up a thick hand.

"I know what a mortgage-backed derivative is. Our investors can't get enough of them."

"What happens if the housing market crashes? It will sometime."

"That's the beauty of the subprime bond, Delia. It's *diversified*. Thousands of different underlying mortgages. They can't *all* go bad at once. That would be like an eight-deviation event. You *do* understand the meaning of the word *diversified*?"

Everyone knew "diversified" was supposed to mean "safe." Your risk was low because if one thing was bad, the others would be good.

Having scoured 130-page prospectuses for thousands of mortgage bonds and plowing through a copy of the Moody's database, I knew the trillions of dollars of existing subprime mortgage-backed bonds were neither safe nor diversified. They were colossal piles of shit.

Why? There was a wide-ranging conspiracy to give mortgages to people who could not afford them. The ticking time bomb was the teaser rate. People signed at 8 percent, but after two years the rate bounced to twelve, which the mortgage holder could not pay. My math said the first big swath of these teaser-rate loans was scheduled to go bad in 2008. And here we were, almost to 2007.

Mitch sat with his church-steeple fingers while I explained all this. "You know we're making a lot of money on what you're calling shit," he said.

"I'm not saying don't sell subprime bonds." Who did he think I was? Priest with his polar bears? I didn't give a crap what Hermes sold to unsuspecting clients. "I'm just saying we need to be prepared. Besides, we could really make a lot of money in a crash. It's all in there."

"Fine, I'll read it."

"Will you give it to Goodman?"

Mitchell looked at me in a way that called to mind the Golden-Glove-boxer story. "If I think it has merit, I'll *consider* showing it to Goodman. We're done."

I knew in both my math and my gut I was right. While millions of people went bankrupt, I would be richer than my wildest dreams. I just had to get Mitchell and Goodman to agree.

I paused in the doorway. "One more question." Mitchell's look said I was pushing my luck. I continued anyway. "You guys wanted me because Priest wanted me. Now I'm telling you why, and you don't seem very interested. I don't get it."

Mitchell threw my thesis onto his windowsill. "Rob just gets a kick out of screwing Priest."

I supposed being hired out of spite was one notch less insulting than being hired for my body. I sighed, reminding myself that it was about the money, not my ego, and at least I had my apartment.

Chapter Eleven

Much have I travelled in the realms of gold.
—John Keats, "On First Looking into Chapman's Homer"

THE EARLY MORNING spring sun shone in my window as I ate my thirty-eight-dollar bagel deluxe from San Macarius. It was Sunday, and I had a bit of a break. I would go to the office in the afternoon.

I hadn't heard back from Mitchell on my thesis for months. Goodman went skiing in Gstaad over the holidays with the daughter of an Italian count.

I opened my favorite, sock-rolling window, and a March breeze blew in. The air was losing its chill. On their knees, blue-jumpsuited building staff worked on our six flower beds. The beds edged the building and surrounded the sidewalk trees protected by little black iron fences with signs commanding, "Curb your dog."

The blue jumpsuits readied the soil for crocuses. Six weeks later, the still-fresh flowers would be yanked up and supplanted by daffodils in April, tulips in May, pansies in June, impatiens for July, begonias for August, mums for September and October, purple cabbage for November, yew boughs for Christmas, and birch stems for winter. Everything was replaced before it had a chance to fade, and the flower bill for the building was forty grand a year. Such costs, board member Angela informed me, were par for the course to keep a building like ours *crème de la crème*. Angela got that expression from Mom.

It was worth the money. I was finally *home*. Well, as close as I was ever going to get. I was here, at my beloved window with its view to the old fairy castle. My center. Like the hole in a doughnut, it provided essential meaning and identity.

Here was a surprise: Mom sent a housewarming gift! She needlepointed me a pillow. The pattern was of emerald-green parrots. When I took the pillow from its box, a piece of paper fluttered out. A news clipping about the strange phenomenon of a tropical parrot flock that somehow found a way to survive in central Brooklyn. Mom commissioned the pattern of these remarkable birds ($500). It probably took her a good two months to finish. I wondered, with a tinge of guilt, if Mom wanted to show she cared. Then I read her note at the bottom of the article. "I would appreciate the return of the Valentino dress at your earliest convenience." What Mom lacked in maternal instinct, she made up for in pure narcissism.

Mom aside, my new life was amazing. I was making money hand over fist; I was back to riding. I leased a horse, Cinnamon, the same hue as her name. She won the amateur-owner division at the Hampton Classic two years back, and the cost to lease her was $35,000 a year. I decided to lease rather than buy because taking full responsibility for another living creature wasn't my style. I paid $2,500 a month to board her at a fancy stable in Greenwich and bought an Audi A7 ($80,000) to get back and forth to the barn. I garaged it across the street ($875 per month).

I was looking out every day at my former castle; I even had

plans to renovate my apartment. The red brocade wallpaper needed to be ripped down. I dreamed of Costwolds-esque stoves, Canyon Ranch baths, and space-colony entertainment rooms. The possibilities were endless!

I had Angela to thank. She did all of this for me without asking for a single thing in return. This despite the fact that many years ago, I had unceremoniously and unilaterally broken off our "friendship."

⌒⌒

ANGELA AND I were a couple years out of college in the fall of 1995 when she came to visit me in Columbus. I was living in an apartment complex with flags flying out front saying, "Welcome Home!" and "Rent Today!"

Angela and I kept in touch just a bit during college. She was a commuter living at home, shackled to her trust fund, while I went away. Papa Conti sent me a Christmas card every year.

That evening Angela pursed her lips at the boxed wine container from which we were drinking, and she looked around my apartment with its pressed-board kitchen cabinets and thin carpeting of bought-in-bulk tan. "Do you ever think about the old times?"

"Yeah." I did think about it. All the time.

"Please don't let *this* become *you*. Dee, you need to remember *who you are*."

Angela meant the *who* who was an heiress.

But I didn't have the foggiest idea who I was. Such questions led invariably to Aunt Kathleen. If you don't know the person closest to you, how could you possibly hope to know yourself?

I babbled out some version of this to Angela. It must have sounded like a repeat of those sobbing nights at Sorrows. I ended with a phrase she'd heard a thousand times before. "If I only knew the *reason*."

That's when Angela changed it up. Instead of her usual—*I know, Dee. I'm sorry.* Or, *She was wonderful; I know you miss her*—she drained her wineglass in a single gulp, clinked it down and said, "I'll give you a reason. She did it because she was a dyke and couldn't stand herself anymore. Okay?"

"She was a…"

"I said a dyke. And probably a drunk," Angela added for emphasis. "That's why she left the convent. It happened all the time and the church just hushed it up." Angela splashed more wine in her glass and curled her lip. "They were all dykes, those stupid nun bitches. Especially that cunt Scholastica. Kathleen couldn't bear what she was, so she jumped. The end."

Dyke, cunt, drunk, bitches. The words were a barrage of slaps. "You don't have to say it like…"

"You wanted to know *why*, and I told you *why*. I was waiting for you to—I don't know—just figure it out."

The next morning, after Angela left, I knew I would never want to speak to her again. I couldn't bear hearing her describe Aunt Kathleen the way she had. Months later, as my feelings cooled, I realized I actually owed Angela a debt for that night, even if I couldn't forgive her for the way she'd delivered the news. She gave me a reason.

Being gay was a deep, dark secret—especially for a nun. It *could* be a reason for suicide. It was the only reason I ever heard that made any sense.

I was grateful to Angela for telling me. I might always be

bound in the chains of my past, but Angela hacked me free of the wall.

I never called her again.

Now, in our new Grandhope life together, we didn't talk about the Columbus incident. It appeared Angela forgave me for cutting her off, and I assumed Angela's opinions toward gay people had matured along with the rest of society's. She'd gotten me a job and an apartment, and all out of the goodness of her heart, since I had nothing to offer her in return. Altruism wasn't a character trait I associated with Angela—the old Angela, anyway. I guessed, just like with Aunt Kathleen, you never really know people.

I FINISHED MY bagel while the jumpsuits planted the doomed crocuses. Suddenly, one of the blossoms took flight. It took me a minute to realize it wasn't a flower flying, but another colorful entity. A parakeet, to be exact, yellow and green with a tiny touch of blue. He fluttered to the branches above the gardeners. Someone's escaped pet. People needed to be more careful.

I took out my notebook and did a quick sketch of the bird. Old habits die hard. My father taught me to do it. In a time before cell phones, a quick drawing of a bird with its markings was a go-to practice for birdwatchers.

Behind me, chimed an email arriving. I glanced at it. The *From* line popped out. *Robert M. Goodman.*

My mouse click was a pounce.

A brief two lines said he was arriving back in town today. He and Mitchell wanted a meeting. They would tell me when.

My thesis.

Good. I replied, *I was looking forward to it.*

Time to check my finances. My favorite hour of the week.

Salary per month: $50,000
Tax: Fica, NYS, NYC: $13,000
Monthly Income total: $37,000

On to expenses.

My payment was $11,356 per month on a $2 million mortgage. My total housing bill was closer to fifteen grand a month because my co-op maintenance—the New York version of a homeowners' association fee—was $3,500. There was also the horse, stable board, and car. But I was covering all my bills and still had money to spare, which I rolled back into the Hermes Fund using a somewhat questionable accounting trick to avoid taxes.

I felt rich. In relation to my neighbors, though, I was a pauper. Yesterday, I overheard a woman with freshly blown-out hair ($95) say into her cell phone: "I'm headed out to Teterboro so Ryder can do that birthday party on the Vineyard."

Teterboro was a regional New Jersey airport and code for *private jet.* Vineyard was, of course, Martha's Vineyard. And Ryder was three and a half years old. This was a world of Lear jets, personal drivers, and second, third, and fourth houses. These days, rich was a new, X-treme-sports kind of rich. I was looking forward to playing.

While all this richness roiled everywhere, Mom's next-door rent-controlled building remained stuck in time. Nicknamed *Number N* because of the faded awning, its mustard-colored brick seemed perpetually grimy. The edifice was barbell shaped, two apartments per floor facing each other, with a courtyard in between.

Number N was an asylum for the underprivileged and quirky. On the sixth floor, there was a yoga instructor who crammed students into her living room to contort as her radiator blasted steam. A former soap-opera actor lived on nine. He now starred in commercials for virility enhancement pharmaceuticals. A five-hundred-square-foot studio on four supported eight Koreans, the staff of a nearby dry cleaners. A village of Brazilians, the neighborhood dog walkers, lived on ten. The blinds of an apartment on thirteen never came up. The woman there ran a consignment shop above an expensive boutique on Madison. She was Mom's floor neighbor.

The old Irish super was a woman named Norah. Super-ships were like fiefdoms, passed down in families. Norah's predecessor was childless, so, when the end was near, he summoned a cousin from the old sod, and she came. That was in 1983. A woman super was an anomaly, just like women doormen, cabbies, or firemen. Norah made up for her gender with a mouth that could strip paint off walls. This now-sixtyish harridan beat pigeons off the sidewalk with her broom, a cigarette hanging out of her lips and a menacing, "Fuck off, you little fuckers."

Though Angela hated such a downscale neighbor as Number N, I thought it was kind of cool the place still endured, in all its eccentricities. It was odd that Goodman didn't do anything with it, since the rule for him was you never left money on the table.

My cell phone chimed a text. It was Angela.

Nanny sick. Must take Maddie to gymnastics. Help Judith? List on fridge.

Well that sucked. Sunday mornings I rode Cinnamon. I closed my laptop. I couldn't say no to Angela, my friend, from whom I had definitively deleted the quotation marks.

⤳

"DELIA MULCAHY. LET me see you." Judith put her face up to mine as if I were a store window and she wanted to look inside me. Owl-framed glasses overwhelmed her gaunt face and obscured a pair of cloudy eyes. A hairdresser had fluffed her coif to an extreme degree around her small skull. On her feet were a pair of orthopedic shoes in red below an outfit of gray and black. I was coming to know this look as her signature, the shoes like a spot of color on a sepia-toned photograph.

Judith touched my hair. "Hair like your mother's, and Kathleen's." That irritated me. Ancient Judith was a neighborhood fixture, so she knew both Mom and Aunt Kathleen. If Judith thought I was interested in a trip down memory lane, she had another thing coming. I was here to do a favor for Angela. I ducked away from Judith's hand.

"Yep. Same hair. Angela said something about your pills?"

"Your mother still sells through me."

"So, I hear," I replied, moving further into Judith's living room. Art covered every inch of wall—spidery silverpoint drawings, yards-wide canvases blotched with color, and tapestry hangings, thin and powdery with age. Overhead, ceramic fragments of an abstract mobile bobbed from wires. Across the room, a brass sculpture of dancers with balloon-like ass cheeks did the mambo on a gold-leaf Louis Quatorze commode.

"You're wondering how I still deal in art when I can hardly see."

"Not really." I had no interest in chitchatting with this woman who knew so much of my painful past. I looked around to start my task.

"I can still see the important things," she pursued. I doubted that. Mom said she traded only pieces she sold originally or knew intimately before she lost her sight.

"Is that the kitchen?" Angela's instructions were on the fridge. I was to put Judith's pills in little plastic boxes so she'd take the right medication each day.

Judith followed me, palming her way across her apartment, still clutching her cane. When she ran out of wall, she grasped the backs of chairs. She did it quickly, like a person navigating a rope bridge across a precipice, but one they knew well.

Her kitchen was still the small, efficiency style left over from the Grandhope Hotel days. Judith opened a drawer, extracting pillboxes, long and colored plastic, with compartments for each day of the week. Then she pawed her way through the cupboard, taking out amber prescription bottles.

Angela's instructions said, *Read dosage and put pills in daily containers.*

"I bet you're also wondering why Angela does all this for me."

No doubt she was going to tell me. I squinted at a pill bottle. Lasix. *Take one every morning with food.* I plunked seven in their slots. The next pill was an antidepressant. *Take one quarter, every night before bed.*

"I wasn't smart enough to buy long-term care insurance when I was younger, and Medicare only covers a nursing home. I pay for my own aide three days a week, so I can get out. I use some cheap quote-unquote agency, which means the women are definitely illegal and probably refugees. They can't read medication bottles or balance my checkbook. Evidently they are weak on subjects like math and reading these days in Somalia."

Judith looked at me as if she wanted me to be shocked.

"That's unfortunate," I said.

Judith sighed her disapproval of me as a conversation partner. "I have a question for you." She stroked the top of her cane. "In all of New York City, a metropolis with three-million dwellings, how many six-bedroom apartments would you say are currently available for sale?"

"Don't know." I quartered pills and counted them.

"Make a guess."

"No."

"Thirty-six."

"Huh."

"Huh?" Judith stamped her cane at me. "There are only thirty-four *Vermeers* in the *entire world*. Which means a big apartment in New York is practically as rare as a Vermeer." She cast covetous glances around at her collection, as if wondering whether she had missed any Vermeers.

"Why are we talking about this?"

"Because of our mutual 'friend': Angela." Interesting. I could hear quotation marks in Judith's enunciation. "The thing that girl wants most in the world is a big apartment."

"I've heard her say that." I halved a beta blocker. I thought back to my first visit when Angela said Judith had screwed up her chance for a four bedroom.

"Angela has a golden opportunity when I'm, shall we say, *finished* living here." Judith paused for me to react. She clearly didn't know I myself circled buzzard-like around my present dwelling, waiting for its owner to die. She went on, "Angela and I have what you call a symbiotic relationship. She helps me with things aides can't do, and in return, I have promised her first right of refusal on my apartment when I die. She won't get a Vermeer, so to speak, but she'll be able to expand. The arrangement allows me to avoid a nursing home. A situation I value as much as a Vermeer. Well, almost." Light glinted off the thick lenses of her glasses.

"Good to know," I said.

She paused again. "Are you finished with the pills?"

"Close." I put in the final tablets. One was to curb frequent peeing; the other was for blood pressure and the final one for cholesterol. Boy, old people took a lot of pills. I snapped the lids down.

"I have something else for you to do." Judith felt her way back through the living room and fingered papers on her desk until she came up with a small, green-encased portfolio. "I need you to write some checks for me and sign them."

"I'm sorry. I don't feel comfortable doing that." I didn't trust this woman. What would keep her from saying I stole money out of her checking account?

"Oh, for pity's sake. Angela does it all the time."

"Then let Angela do it this time. She's the one getting the apartment. You know, when you're *finished* with it."

Judith frowned in my direction. "I don't want to wait for Angela to do it. I like my bills paid on the first of the month, which is tomorrow. Can you at least add up the bills and calculate how much I should have in my account when they're paid?"

I sat at the desk and looked at Judith's various monthly bills.

"Read them out to me."

I read, "$149 in electricity, $99 for cable, $2,800 in co-op maintenance."

"Maintenance," she stamped her cane again. "It's robbery."

I read off a few more bills. Judith waved her hand, signaling enough. There was not even a calculator on the desk. I took up a pencil and paper. I summed amounts and looked in her register, which showed a balance of $15,567.67. I caught Mom's name in outgoing checks. The amounts were small: $250, $175, and $70. I was tempted to look further back, but didn't. Judith fingered the top of her cane as she sat in an armchair, her back to me.

"You know, Delia. I understand suicide."

I stopped figuring. "I suppose you think being old and blind gives you the right to say things like that to me."

"Now don't get testy. I was talking about myself. *I* contemplated suicide. The psychoanalysts say almost everyone does. Basic existential issues. You know emptiness, loneliness, senselessness."

"Narcissism, cowardice," I put in. While I accepted Angela's reason for Aunt Kathleen's suicide, I still blamed Aunt Kathleen for not being braver. Because I *needed* her.

"Depression is like torture," said Judith. "It's as if your blood is boiling inside you."

Aunt Kathleen never *seemed* depressed. I refocused on the checkbook. "Torture is like torture. Depression is like thinking too much."

Judith turned the side of her face to me. "I'm just telling you because if you ever contemplated suicide, you understand others in the same boat. About ten years ago when I lost my eyesight, I was ready to do it. It's really the easiest thing in the world. You barely have to do anything. A few pills. The right pills."

"Why didn't you?" Carry the seven.

"You could say I simply grew out of it. If you wait long

enough, time will take care of things itself. So, I've decided I won't. And once you give up the idea of suicide, you discover an intense will to survive."

I considered possible responses: *Glad it's all working out for you.* Or, *Mazel Tov.* I settled on, "Okay."

Next to me, my Blackberry chirped an incoming email. Thank God.

"You kids and your phones," Judith said. "They're always interrupting."

From: Mitch Mitchell

Meet now with Goodman. 450 West 37th Street, PH.

MM

Chapter Twelve

Every time a child says, 'I don't believe in fairies,' there is a fairy somewhere that falls down dead.

—J.M. Barrie, *Peter Pan*

I HURRIED OUT of the building. Number N's super, Norah, was outside. "Too much fucking rich garbage," she said to our bags set out on the street. Embarrassingly, the Grandhope had been identified by the health department as a rodent hot spot. It was a constant topic at board meetings, Angela said. We were on our third exterminator.

Rob Goodman lived in one of the vertiginous towers newly bristling the West Side. The location was once a wasteland of car dealerships, parking lots, and ramps feeding the Port Authority bus terminal. It used to be called Hell's Kitchen, but they were trying to get people to use the new developer-invented name, Clinton.

I stepped into his tremendous fifteen-million-dollar space of granite and glass and teak and stone surfaces with 290-degree views taking in the Verrazano and Statue of Liberty to the south, the gleaming new towers of Jersey City to the west, and the grand span of the George Washington Bridge to the north.

"Delia!" Goodman got up from a glass table by the windows upon which were two laptops and my thesis. Mitchell kept his seat. Goodman grasped my hand, and, for a moment, I half expected him to kiss it. It brought me back to our first meeting, when I stood barefoot in front of him, sleek-haired and gorgeous, while he wavered between asking me out and employing me. He was in especially good form today: tanned and athletic with chestnut hair hanging rakishly in his blue eyes. Without letting go of my hand, he guided me over to a seat at the table. "I don't pretend to understand half of what's in here." He gestured to my thesis. "Mitch has been walking me through."

I imagined Goodman really *did* understand, though perhaps not so well as the near-genius Priest. Goodman was rich, he was powerful, his apartment commanded a view of four of the five boroughs. He could handle a little advanced math.

Mitchell folded his arms and sat back, regarding the interaction between us. Feeling observed, I restrained my pleasure at seeing Goodman. "Take it from here." Mitchell pointed to a page about two-thirds in, the chapter entitled *Shorting the Housing Bubble via Credit Default Swaps on Mortgage-Backed Derivatives*. "Your insurance theory."

As Goodman sat forward, his elbows on the table, all energy and anticipation, I explained. I told him about the housing bubble, the impending crash, and my plan to buy a kind of fire insurance. Or polar-bear insurance. Tomay-to, tomah-to.

"Why haven't we heard about this before?" Mitchell asked. "You think you're smarter than everyone else?"

"Mitch." Goodman held up a hand.

"I'm just saying." Mitchell slumped back, but kept his gaze fixed on me.

"No, I don't think I'm smarter," I said. I was, but I wasn't going to say that. "It's just not so easy. It takes a long time and a lot of work. You have to know *which* bonds to short. There's a *lot* of analysis. The computations are nontrivial."

"I can see that." Goodman touched the appendix of my thesis, which was thicker than the thesis document itself.

Mitchell turned to Goodman. "Rob, you're not *really* considering shelling out millions to buy insurance? And paying the premiums for who knows how long? That's not what we *do*. Our investors won't stand for it."

Mitchell landed on the key objection. You had to actually *buy* the insurance and wait until the floating polar bears drowned before you could collect.

Goodman got up from the table and walked over to the windows. He gazed at the Statue of Liberty, who at that moment looked like a schoolgirl raising her hand too eagerly. "You're amazing, Delia," he said.

"I just did the work." Out of the corner of my eye, I tracked Mitchell's reaction to Goodman's praise.

"Work no one else thought to do." He turned around. "Mitchell has raised a key objection. We buy this insurance, keep paying the premiums on it. I have another. What if the market doesn't crash? What if it never crashes?"

"Never?" It was one thing to dispute the housing bubble, but an end to all crashes ever?

"There are some who think the market has achieved perfect efficiency. There is so much information, available in real time, smart algos trading electronically. With a market like this there *can be no bubble*. No more crashes. No more recessions."

I admired him for this viewpoint. It was utopian. Misguided, but utopian. "I've heard that idea."

"But *you* don't believe it."

"The market's bound to fail. Right now, it's like everyone's just clapping to keep Tinker Bell alive." Aunt Kathleen would read me this scene over and over. I loved it, the power of belief to animate that stupid fairy.

Goodman threw his head back and laughed.

"The Peter Pan market theory," Mitchell sneered.

"That's a good name for it," Goodman said. He approached me, now serious. "You say Tinker Bell dies."

"Yes. She does."

"And if she dies…"

"With my strategy, we make billions," I finished.

"And Priest was on board with it?"

I remembered Priest's strange reaction, disputing the ethics of my strategy and yet wanting to hire me at the same time. What *had* he been planning? I actually wasn't sure. But I wasn't going to tell Goodman that. "No one else would even give me an interview." This was an accurate fact.

"I find *that* hard to believe." The corners of Goodman's eyes crinkled. The small crows' feet and a few gray strands mixed in with his fair hair were the only things showing his early forties age.

"Priest is no idiot," Mitchell said.

"Idiot's the last thing he is." Goodman extended his arm and handed me out of my chair. "Thank you, Delia. Mitch and I are grateful for this tremendous insight you've given us. We need to think about it. Call a few more smart people. We'll let you know what we decide."

Goodman walked me to the door and held out my coat for me. As Goodman helped me into my coat, I could sense, with my acute male-libido radar, the electricity in Goodman's touch. I liked that. I often thought about how we met, with him saying he wished he was there to pick me up. I had plenty of opportunities with the rock-hard traders at Hermes, but I wasn't that interested in going to bed with them. If I could attract the richest, best-looking and (one had to think) rock-hardest, why would I settle for less? But Mitchell didn't need to worry. I wasn't sleeping with Goodman.

Men might do a lot for a pretty woman. Buy them jewelry. Buy them cars. Even buy them apartments. Girlfriend stuff, just in the billionaire lane. But they would *not* change their hedge-fund strategies for you or help you earn a fortune. I had to do that for myself.

I had made an excellent start.

The catch was I would lose everything if the market crashed.

⌒⌒

I WAS DRIVING back from the barn in July 2007 and got stuck in the mother of all traffic jams on the Major Deegan, a pileup of people coming back from the Jersey Shore on Sunday afternoon. I thumped the steering wheel in frustration. It wasn't so much about the traffic. I was really irked about the fact that I hadn't heard back from Goodman about my strategy in three months, and I was starting to doubt myself.

All the market signals were mixed. On the one hand, Merrill Lynch disclosed losses in its Q2 earnings due to a downturn in subprime. On the other hand, the Japanese and the Germans were inhaling subprime bonds like crack.

I was Hermes's top-notch quant, and my 2007 bonus was going to be $750,000. Minus the $200,000 down payment on my apartment, minus taxes, I might net three-hundred kay. Hermes offered an option to roll your bonus back into the fund. They did some fancy accounting and you only paid 15 percent capital gains. Meaning I'd net $425,000.

That certainly was terrific. Next year, 2008, given seniority and performance, I could get $1.5 million. That would be the true beginning of my new fortune. With that kind of money, I could weather a crash. I just had to make it to the end of 2008.

But what happened if the music stopped and everyone had to find a chair? My strategy of buying bond-market fire insurance was the only thing that would protect the firm and me from financial disaster.

My mind was swinging like a pendulum. What if I was wrong and there was no crash? Goodman was a smart guy, wasn't he? Tinker Bell would be perfectly fine if everyone just clapped hard enough, wouldn't she? Goodman, true to form, disappeared, flying all over the country. There was a rumor that he was still dating the daughter of the Italian count. Mom's article about his taste for aristocratic women came to mind.

I knew all the historical crashes by heart. The great tulip crash of 1637; the South Sea Bubble of 1720; the Florida Real Estate Bust of 1926; the Great Depression; Black Monday of 1987; the 1990s Asia Crisis. I also looked at yo-yos, pet rocks, the NordicTrack, high-leg bathing suits, fondue pots, and Billy the Singing Bass. The history of bubbles and busts showed one irrefutable thing: *afterward* everyone said they saw it coming. Every crash was absolutely inevitable and perfectly obvious to occur precisely when it did. The truth? No one really knew when a crash would occur. There were countless crashes that were *supposed* to happen but didn't. And there were crashes no one spotted. Pretty much everyone whiffed on 1987.

Right now, in the summer of 2007, there were only a few random financial bloggers who predicted a crash. They were openly mocked on the financial news channels. Yet, if a crash *did* come, people would teem out of the woodwork saying it was inevitable and they themselves predicted it all along.

A few weeks ago, I couldn't stand the suspense, and approached Mitchell again about my thesis.

"Priest thought my analysis…" I began.

"I…*we*…don't care what Priest thought," Mitchell snapped. "He was probably just trying to get into your pants. Who are you anyway? Some girl from Florida?" He put my thesis in his desk and slammed the drawer. "We'll get back to you when we get back to you. In the meantime, we gave you a job to do, now do it."

As I WALKED up the garage ramp toward my building, Norah of Number N, who also knew me from the past, fixed me with a good, long stare. Norah's look was the kind that would have prompted the Greek island women to spit three times and wave blue amulets. "Too fucking high and mighty to say hello," she said under her breath. Norah was the only person alive who said *fuck* more than I did, and I mostly said it in my head.

On the sidewalk, a clutch of people gathered, some with binoculars. Heads swiveled like prairie dogs. The attraction was the parakeet, perched in a sidewalk tree. From his markings, he looked to be the one I saw back in spring.

Across the street, a man in a khaki jumpsuit set up a tripod. He was one of the hawk paparazzi who covered the famous raptor clan colonizing the cornice of Mary Tyler Moore's building. Years ago, the first hawk, a light-colored specimen dubbed Pale Male, selected Fifth Avenue as a nesting site and caused a media frenzy. The co-op board tried to remove his aerie, and protests erupted. Ms. Moore herself stood on the picket line, and the event was covered around the world. They had to let Pale Male stay. Now postcards bore his image and guys with high-powered lenses sold glimpses of him to tourists.

"Someone needs to catch that parakeet," said a bystander.

Good luck with that. A lost dog strives to find its way home. An escaped tropical bird? He's on the lam for South America.

Norah opened the Number-N door. Judith emerged on the arm of a woman wearing scrubs, a headscarf, and a sweatshirt that said *Pink.* One of Judith's innumerate, illiterate aides. "What's going on?" Judith asked, sniffing like a dog on a scent.

"There's a bird," I replied.

"Delia!" Judith's head snapped to me. Drat. It was easy to forget she couldn't see. "Just the person I wanted to see. You can go back upstairs, Fatima," Judith said to the aide. "Walk me to the deli, Delia." Judith hooked her arm in mine and pointed forward with her cane. "I'm in the mood for a black and white," Judith said, naming the New York cookie iced in yin-yang half-moons of chocolate and vanilla. We shuffled a couple of steps, her red toes flashing. Then she stopped, as if forgetting she wanted to go anywhere.

"I just had my bi-yearly visit to Viviane on thirteen," Judith said, cocking her head to Number N. I vaguely recalled Viviane was the name of the woman who lived in the apartment next to Mom's and who owned a consignment shop nearby.

"Bi-yearly?"

"Viviane has something I want."

"Hemlock?"

"Very funny." Judith gave my upper arm a retaliatory pinch. "She has a spoon jar."

"A what?"

"A spoon jar. The kind you keep on your counter and put spoons in. It's just sitting in her kitchen. It's valuable."

"A valuable spoon jar?"

Judith stopped. "It's *lost treasure*."

The old woman really was a little cracked. "Just how did she find *that*?" I asked.

"How did she find it?" Judith repeated. "The Dead Sea scrolls were discovered by roaming Bedouin goat herders, and you ask how she found it?"

"Okay," I said. The bird took off, winging to another tree. The small group *oohed* and trailed after him.

"In my business, you hear these stories all the time," Judith continued. "A poor Anatolian farmer digs something up. A middleman finds out. He pays the farmer a small amount and gets the loot out of the country. International traffickers in Switzerland take over. The Swiss are really dirty," she asided. "With a little counterfeit paperwork, it's on to London or New York. Auctions, or museums, or *me*. I wouldn't be surprised if half the treasure of Troy is on the Upper East Side right now."

I positioned myself around Judith to see the bird better. "Are you saying Viviane was an Anatolian farmer? Or was it a Swiss smuggler?"

"She's a consignment store owner!" Judith stabbed her cane tip in the direction of Viviane's shop on Madison. "The spoon jar probably belonged to someone's dead mother, and the kids sold it on consignment without even knowing."

The parakeet banked down an alley and disappeared. People *aahed* with disappointment.

"What *is* all the commotion?" Judith asked, rotating her head.

"The bird flew off." I urged her forward. She resisted.

"If I could only convince her to sell it."

"You'll figure something out. Why wouldn't she sell it if it's worth that much?"

"She's a bit of a what-do-you-call-it... those people who never throw anything away. There's a television show about them... I hate being old... boarders?"

"Hoarders."

"A bit of one of those. Goes with her profession, I suppose. Landlords hate those boarder-hoarders. Can take years to evict them if they dig in their heels." The photographer folded his tripod as the other birdwatchers dispersed. "I enjoy chatting like this."

"That makes one of us." The aide got paid to tolerate Judith. Angela was getting her near-Vermeer-big apartment one day. I wasn't benefiting from this exchange in any way.

But Judith's single-mindedness about the spoon jar sparked a thought. Judith said she visited Viviane twice a year just to pester her. It reminded me—persistence was important. If Mitchell was against me, I couldn't just accept that. I needed to approach Goodman directly. Mitchell would be pissed, but I would do it.

"It's time to go, Judith. I'm busy."

Chapter Thirteen

There was a crooked man,
And he walked a crooked mile.
He found a crooked sixpence,
Beside a crooked stile;
He bought a crooked cat,
Which caught a crooked mouse,
And they all lived together,
In a little crooked house.
—Mother Goose

F OUR BLACK SUVs screeched into the intersection at 84th and Fifth, blocking seven thirty a.m. commuters. Traffic piled up like water behind a plugged drain. Dark-suited men carrying Kalashnikovs jumped out of the vehicles and trained their weapons toward the surrounding dog walkers, briefcase carriers, and school children in kilts.

Three of the dark suits raced to a small townhouse, where they extracted a gray-haired man and hunched him into an SUV. With loud *chunk-chunk* sounds, the doors closed, and the coterie sped away. At 7:33 a.m., all of us who had paused momentarily continued about our businesses.

"Who do you think that is?" I asked.

"Dunno," said Angela. "Can't keep them all straight."

Any number of nationalities came to mind: Iraqi, Israeli, Egyptian, Turk, Saudi. Our neighborhood was home to half a dozen extremely dangerous diplomats and dozens of average-danger-level personages, as evidenced by the very large number of private security guards and dark cars with inscrutable plates.

I was not usually out and about at this late hour of the morning. Normally by six thirty a.m. I was seated in my Nolita office reviewing code. Today, however, I was meeting Rob Goodman at San Macarius. I emailed him, with no Mitchell on the cc. A firing offense. But Goodman agreed to have coffee as soon as he was back from Italy in October.

When I mentioned my appointment with Goodman to Angela, she changed her Pilates class and decided to walk Maddie to school herself. She planned to pass San Macarius "as if it's natural." She wanted a word with Goodman because she was still looking for a deal. I owed Angela, so I agreed.

Six-year-old Maddie dangled from Angela's hand, looking up at her mom occasionally as if surprised to see her.

"So," Angela continued, "you're going to talk to him about your thesis thing-y?"

"Yeah."

"What's it about again? You keep telling me, but I never remember."

"The housing bubble. A way to short the market through a kind of insurance called a credit-default swap."

"Never mind!" Angela put a hand up. "Forget I asked."

Deals and dealmakers, bankers, hedge-fund owners, and VCs, all gathered inside the frilly pinkness of San Macarius as they did every morning. Men in expensive suits sat around the tiny, blush-marble tables where they had hushed conversations covered by nondisclosure agreements. Rose-coated waiters served them coffee in filigreed silver tureens. Great historian of saints that she was, Aunt Kathleen taught me Macarius was a fourth-century street merchant who sold candies and baked goods before turning anti-carb, becoming a hermit and ascetic. But he was still considered the patron saint of pastries. Today, all of New York knew him for the sweet and sticky pastries served to banking titans at his eponymous eatery.

"Delia!" Goodman disentangled his long limbs from the wrought-iron legs of his table. He leant in as if to kiss me. In midair, he seemed to decide that was too familiar and shook my hand instead. "Angela Price! What a nice surprise."

I looked for Maddie, but she'd been deposited by the cash register with a jam-filled croissant. "I was taking my daughter to school, and Delia and I bumped into each other. Thought I'd come in and say hi."

Goodman peered around Angela to see Maddie. "She's adorable." Goodman gave her an enthusiastic wave, but Maddie held the pastry with both hands.

"I haven't seen you in a while," Angela said.

Goodman dragged his hand through his hair. The locks fell back into his blue eyes. "Sorry. Travel. I love the foundation board but..."

"No worries," Angela soothed. "I just miss hearing what you're up to. You know, I'm *always* looking for an opportunity."

"Well." Goodman flashed that terrific chip-toothed smile. "There's still room in the fund."

"Mmmm," said Angela. "Hedge funds are not really my speed." What that meant was they weren't her father's speed. "I was thinking if you have another deal. Ground floor sort of thing. Real estate maybe? Doing anything with your building?" That would be just the ticket for conservative Papa Conti. Something for which he might authorize tapping Angela's trust.

"I'll let you know. And I promise I'll be at the next meeting." He pulled out a chair for me in a clear dismissal of Angela. She smiled smoothly. I watched her exit. Her face fell as she realized the croissant had oozed jam all over Maddie's school jumper.

Goodman poured me coffee from the silver tureen. "Your friend Angela. She sure is eager."

"I think she wants you do to something with your rent-controlled building, so she can invest in that," I offered.

"You know about that building?"

"I live in the neighborhood." I shrugged casually, remembering Mom's desire to stay on the down low. "So why don't you do something? The location is amazing." While Mom and I didn't have what you would call a normal mother-daughter relationship, I truly hoped she would get her payout. I planned to contribute to her monthly expenses after I got my bonus.

"It's a small building with no air rights. Not worth my time right now." Goodman took a scone from the basket of pastries in front of us. It glistened with a coating of egg wash and sugar. I knew air rights could be purchased from surrounding buildings, and I wondered if any in the area had them. I supposed Goodman would have already looked into that. "But that's not why you wanted to meet privately."

"No."

"Listen, Delia, I want you to know I think your research is brilliant. I mean obviously your paper is brilliant because Priest is no fool. But I'm not going to pursue this insurance strategy." Goodman munched his pastry and brushed crumbs off his lips.

"I know Mitchell is against it," I said, remembering his girl-from-Florida dig.

Goodman's smile faded, and he put down his coffee. "I know I like to say Mitch runs the show. But he's a good sergeant, that's all. I make all the big decisions at Hermes. *I've* decided against your strategy."

I felt that sting. I also got a glimpse of the steeliness beneath Goodman's boyish good humor.

"Okay. So why not?"

"I was intrigued because Priest was. This business is all about gaining an edge on your competition. I've recently learned Priest is *not* pursuing your strategy either. He got a look at your thesis, and he's a mathematician. Maybe his team wouldn't have been as good or as fast without you. But they would have done something similar eventually."

"How do you know he's not using the strategy?"

"I have lots of programmers working for me. Half of them used to be hackers. Let's just say I have access to certain emails that maybe I shouldn't."

A number of emotions hit me all at once. First, was surprise at the level of corporate hacking going on. Then I was surprised that I was surprised. Then, I felt embarrassed Priest had rejected my ideas. Finally, there was confusion about Priest inviting me to New York on the strength of my strategy and the new information he was doing nothing with it. Did Priest believe in clapping for Tinker Bell, too? Was it something to do with his ethics and the polar bears?

"Wow. I...I don't know what to say."

"Based on what I hear from Mitch, that's unusual for you." I laughed. Goodman leaned his elbows on the table, his smile and good humor returning. "You came up with a genius strategy. But Wall Street is all about timing. Your strategy might have worked at a different time. It's my opinion that the era of crashes is over."

"I suppose that must be true." How else could you explain the fact that the market kept rising when the fundamentals were so off? I was new to all this. There was probably a lot to the markets I had yet to learn.

"Priest and I used to work together, you know," Goodman continued.

I remembered Mom's story from *Vanity Fair* about their falling-out, but that no one knew the reason. "I heard that."

Goodman noticed my cup was empty and poured me some coffee. "Priest and I have a long history. Everybody wonders what happened. He'd just come here from Athens. Some break with his father. We met in graduate school. We got to be friends. We had a lot in common because I didn't get along with my father, either. Priest and I liked to play cards. I was the one who taught him to card count."

"Interesting."

"Yep. Made him unbeatable. Then, when he started Odyssey, a bunch of us joined him. We were making more money than any of us ever dreamed."

"So, what happened?"

"I just couldn't stand him being my boss. We're both competitive, you know. Full disclosure—I left and I took clients. I also took Mitch Mitchell. Was it wrong? Yes. Do I regret it? No."

"Thanks for telling me." I wondered why *Vanity Fair* couldn't get the story when Goodman was happy to sit here and narrate it to me. I liked his openness.

"You're welcome." Goodman crumpled his pink napkin

and tossed it on the table. He looked across at me steadily, frankly admiring me in the way confident men often did. "Do you remember that night we met at the Greek embassy?"

"Yes," I said. I liked that memory, too.

"One of my more awkward moments." He laughed. "Sometimes I wish we met under different circumstances." I stopped myself from saying *Me too*. As much as I could feel the interest of this hot billionaire, Goodman was my boss, and I was after my fortune. Goodman let his statement sit for a second, then said, "Listen, Delia, there's the big annual bond market conference coming up in Las Vegas. I was thinking since you're the resident bond expert with your thesis, maybe you'd enjoy it."

"Thanks. I would."

"I'll tell Mitch it's authorized. Just one other thing. Drop the credit default topic with him. It's kind of pissing him off."

Chapter Fourteen

Money often costs too much.

—Ralph Waldo Emerson, *The Conduct of Life*

A S A KID, I loved to play with Monopoly money. There were peppermint ones, strawberry fives, lemon tens, lime twenties, blueberry fifties, apricot hundreds, and orange five hundreds. I sorted the bills in all different ways: by denomination, by color, or simply to create rainbows. The dull hue of real money was a disappointment. Why didn't true legal tender come in even funner colors than play money, maybe with stripes or sparkles?

"How about some marbles?" Aunt Kathleen entered my pink-sprigged bedroom carrying a sack of clattering glass balls. She disapproved of my Monopoly money sorting. Nuns didn't like money; they liked stories about saints who gave up all their money.

I shook my head.

"You're what they call a tough customer, Delia." Aunt Kathleen clacked the marbles back into the bag. She went to the bookcase where there was a deck of cards. She shuffled expertly. Every Tuesday afternoon, Aunt Kathleen's day off, there was a rummy game in the basement of Number N among herself, the super, a neighboring doorman, and a lady named

Judith Fisher who lived in a hotel. When Norah came in '83, she joined the game.

"Wanna try?" Aunt Kathleen offered me the deck.

I concentrated on my small hands to get the shuffle right. Aunt Kathleen took the piles of colored money so we could use it to bet in gin rummy. Betting with Monopoly money was okay in Aunt Kathleen's book because *it taught you how to lose.*

Aunt Kathleen dealt. Ten cards were a lot to hold. I rearranged the shiny rectangles, looking for possible melds and sequences. I had two sevens, but also a six, which went with one of the sevens, and a four. I hoped for a face-up five, but the face-up card was a jack.

"What's wrong, kiddo?" Aunt Kathleen had amazing radar. I think that's why Mom and I depended on her so much.

What's wrong today was Angela. Being "friends" was hard. Angela was a chubby outsider from New Jersey with early-sprouting boobies and a testy temper. Today the cafeteria served pasta. It was an inspiration to Regina Maguire, one of the meaner girls.

"Look, it's Betty Spaghetti," Regina taunted Angela. Angela slammed down her tray on the lunch line's metal rods and stomped off. Before Angela, I was effortlessly popular. Everyone liked me because I had the biggest house. Now, I had to deal with things like this.

I stood for a moment in line, debating whether to do the "friend" thing. Finally, I went to find Angela. I searched for her in the locker room, but she wasn't there. I went to all her favorite toilet sulking spots, but still no Angela. I returned to the cafeteria where they were out of spaghetti and the other girls ignored me as much as they could without crossing the line that would get them uninvited to my upcoming tenth birthday party.

I narrated this to Aunt Kathleen, while I bet an apricot hundred and she saw my bet. I took a card from the facedown pile. It was the hoped-for five. I put down my four-five-six-seven meld.

"Good one," she said, taking the face-up jack and not discarding anything.

I had only five cards left. "Angela is like homework." Aunt Kathleen laughed.

"I'm glad you did your homework today."

I took another facedown card, a useless nine. "I can't wait until I'm grown up and I don't have to do homework anymore." Aunt Kathleen took a pad out of the pocket of her checked shirt, which was tucked into a nunnish navy-blue skirt worn with blue tie shoes. She opened a page and ticked a mark. She was tallying how many of my sentence started with the phrase, *I can't wait until I'm grown up and...*

"How many?" I asked.

"Four hundred and fifty-seven." I giggled. I wanted to jump up and ask her to prove it to me, but I was carefully fanning a hand of seven cards. The nine had just been joined by an eight, making use of the orphan seven. I put down my three-meld.

"Good one again, pal." Aunt Kathleen took another card off the pile and put down a pair of fours. Her hand was going badly, which could have been for real, or just because she was letting me get ahead.

Another life lesson: when you're playing with a beginner, you have to let yourself get behind to make it a fair game.

You didn't want to be *shooting fish in a barrel.*

Because that *wasn't sporting.*

"Some people keep doing their homework even when they grow up." I knew we were now talking about something other than homework.

"Why?" I asked.

She shrugged. "Why do you think?"

This was the part where I was supposed to say *for God* or *for love* or something similar, but I didn't.

I tattled instead. It was risky. A known informant, Aunt Kathleen would spill the beans to other adults when she thought they needed to know. But I was upset by the day's events, so while I took more cards, I told her.

After lunch was art class. Regina of the Betty Spaghetti comment was the best artist in fourth grade and her folder was filled with masterpieces. When she opened it, she discovered a pen—the kind with the liquid ink that stained your jumper—had bled its black payload all over everything.

It was, in military parlance, an asymmetrical response. A whole year's artwork destroyed over spaghetti. It was also my first real introduction to Angela's mean streak. Art teacher Sister Louise said Regina probably left the pen there herself. I didn't believe it for a minute. Neither did Regina. Neither did Aunt Kathleen.

Aunt Kathleen stopped playing cards. That meant it was serious, since Aunt Kathleen could have continued playing cards through a hurricane. She adjusted her expression in the way that said she was concealing a grown-up thought and readdressed her hand, discarding a five meld she'd clearly been holding.

We went a few goes quietly. Aunt Kathleen's pink seashell nails were light against the dark cards. "Friends change, you know." She reordered her hand. "It's healthy. Maybe next year you and Angela will get new best friends." Angela was now on thin playdate ice.

But it came to nothing. After that one big retaliation, Regina backed off. The Rosemont girls were soft. The Sorrows crew was tougher. There, full capitulation required laxatives and hamster assassinations. By then, Aunt Kathleen was dead, and there was no one to tell.

Ironic, how life worked out. Today Angela, not Aunt Kathleen, was the one remaining in my life. Angela searched for me and helped me get my apartment. She was my friend and neighbor without so much as a single quotation mark.

C—✺

IN MY APARTMENT, Angela shook her head at the wallpaper sample. It was November and we were planning the new décor for my living room. I was finally going to remove the bordello-red wallpaper and replace it.

"Wallpaper is a pain to remove," she said. As if to prove her point, through my beloved window, the rose vine pattern in my old bedroom still clung doughtily to its walls.

"Why would I remove it?"

"If you want to renovate again in a few years."

"How many times do you think I'm going to redo the apartment?" Angela shook her head at me as if I was a hopeless case. "Paint's cheaper, I guess," I added.

I *was* starting to get concerned about my burn rate. The renovation was costing me twenty-five kay. When I first moved to the Grandhope, I was like Dorothy entering the Technicolor half of the movie, delighted by my strangely vibrant surroundings, spending hand over fist. Now, I wondered if I should maybe throttle back. Perhaps give up the lease on Cinnamon for a while. Maybe help ride one of the misbehaved horses at the barn.

"You've convinced yourself about this epic crash."

"I don't know." Goodman didn't think one was coming. And, seemingly, neither did Priest.

"Have you ever thought you could be wrong? I mean it *has* happened before."

Angela meant that I had been wrong about Aunt Kathleen. That I hadn't known she was gay. Bringing up Aunt Kathleen was not exactly cricket since it was a painful memory. But no-quotation-marks Angela had been good to me, so I let it slide.

This dithering was ridiculous. I needed to get on with things. If no one was pursuing my short strategy, maybe I *was* wrong. Why was I so worried about money? Perhaps, I unconsciously absorbed Aunt Kathleen's values regarding money. She and Peter Priest could have had a spirited conversation about polar bears.

Tinker Bell was doing just fine, thank you very much, as we headed into the end of 2007. I only had to make it to December 2008, when my million-plus bonus would be a done deal. I'd pay down some of my ridiculous mortgage, bank a bit, and even give Mom a tidy sum. At that point, if a crash came, I could ride it out.

I had to act like a new-and-improved kind of princess in a new-and-improved kind of castle. I would buy that car-priced purse, maybe two. Renovate every three years, if possible. Someday, if I had a three-year-old, I would put her on private jets to birthday parties without batting an eyelash. Any reserve about money was to be obliterated. I was making tons now and on my way to making even more.

"This," said Angela, choosing a paint chip of the lightest, creamy lemon. "Your mother will love it. When is she gonna visit?"

"When are you going to do *your* kitchen?" I asked, changing the subject. Angela had been wanting to rip out her kitchen for a while. It backed up to Judith's, which backed up to mine so they could all share the main plumbing line. Papa Conti approved of these kinds of renovations. He believed in real estate, in contrast to hedge funds. Real estate was solid and an appropriate activity for his New York lady daughter.

"I'll get around to it," she said. "First things first. We have got to get this stuff off your walls. You are never going to have the time for it with your crazy work hours. Since you have this business trip coming up, the workmen have a solid week. I can manage it while you're gone."

"Why don't I do my kitchen too?" I congratulated myself on the idea. A kitchen renovation would be at least a hundred and fifty grand. It was justifiable as well, since the stroke victim woman had last done the kitchen in the eighties.

"Delia." Angela looked up from a book of fabric swatches. "You're like a pendulum. A second ago you wanted paint because it's cheaper. Let's pace things out."

"Says the woman who helped me get a two-million-dollar apartment with no assets."

"That was different. You *had* to."

I *did* have to. Daily, the view through my window anchored me and reminded me what this was all about. I was heading backward to the original me. Just a bit more time with my ridiculous salary and epic bonuses, I would be the *me* I was born to be, one in possession of my rightful fortune.

Chapter Fifteen

Μην τρέχεις γυμνός στα αγγούρια!

(Don't run naked into the cucumber patch.)

—Bawdy Greek proverb

I HADN'T FLOWN first class since the trip back from Athens with my spurned mother. The modern first-class cabin to Las Vegas had lovely enclosed little pods where you could stretch out. Around me, in other pods, nestled gamblers wearing silver neck slides. There were also blue-dress-shirt finance types headed to the same subprime bond conference as me.

I adjusted the pillow behind my head, tucked the quilted comforter around my legs, and took a sip of the pre-takeoff champagne. I reached into my white, lizard-skin Prada handbag ($1800)—still eleven months away from my twenty-thousand-dollar one—to dab some makeup around my bruised left eye and cheekbone.

Yesterday's riding accident.

The flight attendant rolled by with a cart of today's papers. I took the *Financial Times* and read the headline.

Frankfurt Raid Uncovers Trove of Art Stolen by Nazis

The over 1,200 artworks, including paintings by Monet, Rembrandt, and Titian, are estimated to be worth about €750 million, according to a preliminary analysis by authorities. The art, believed to be stolen by the Nazis, was unearthed in the clutter-filled apartment of an elderly Frankfurt woman, German authorities confirmed Monday. This spectacular find of lost treasure is reverberating across the art world.

Lost treasure found in the apartment of a hoarder? Sounded familiar. Maybe blind Judith was not so cracked about that spoon jar after all.

I set down the paper. A man in a nerdy, short-sleeved dress shirt on his way back to coach stared hard at my face as he passed, probably forming all kinds of stories in his head about the woman in first class with the abusive husband.

Cinnamon was *not* the culprit. In fact, she was the quietest horse I'd ever ridden. When I commented on it, the people at the barn said these days the horses were doped with tranquilizers because wealthy clientele didn't want to get kicked off.

I had finished riding and was rubbing down Cinnamon, when a commotion erupted in the indoor arena. A man named Eugene who worked as an HR manager for Bear Stearns had recently bought his daughter a new show horse. Even janitors at Bear got six-figure bonuses. The stallion of famous bloodlines was purchased ($115,000) and shipped in from Sweden ($43,000). Unfortunately, the horse had a hollow leg for tranquilizers. The vet recommended gelding. That didn't work either. It just pissed him off.

The horse had, once again, thrown his rider. She fled crying, and her father, Eugene, looked around helplessly for an instructor.

The horse pranced to the far side of the arena, snorting, his tail held high.

"I can hop on him." I stepped onto the turf.

"Would you?" It was a plea.

"Sure."

I approached. The red-bay horse threw his head back and rolled his eyes. They had rims white like hard-boiled eggs. Also, he sported not one, not two, not three, but *four* white socks, rising to his knees, no less. In Hungarian terms, this was the worst kind of horse imaginable.

Before he could bolt, I got my toe in the stirrup and leapt on. The horse took off, wheeled to reverse, and took off again. He reached the end of the arena and executed an acrobatic shy with three rolling bucks. Eugene stared open-mouthed. Unlike Cinnamon, this white-eyed fiend was as sensitive as a raw nerve. Every kick of sand or rattle of the aluminum sides of the arena caused a swerve, a twist, a spurt.

"Wow," Eugene said.

I laughed. It felt amazing. I was a-throb with adrenaline and power. I was the horse-riding me of days gone by. I was an excellent rider—as only the Hungarian cavalry could produce.

"Sometimes they just have to get the butterflies out of their system." The white-eyed horse took a few nice trotting steps. The Hungarian taught me that when a horse surrenders to a rider, the capitulation is complete.

I was considering a halt and dismount. Just then, the horse went for a desperate last-ditch move, The Scrape. It's typically performed against a tree trunk or under a low branch. Today, the horse threw himself against the side of the arena.

My head crashed into the wall. Twelve hundred pounds of horse writhed and thrashed against the aluminum, lunging away, and hurling himself again. A thought sprang up.

I could die.

Had I really not ever considered dying before? Was I that far into teen oblivion, grief, and despair? Or was that feeling of invulnerability just part of being young? Whatever the case, now at thirty-six, I tasted my mortality, tangy like the iron-edged blood in my mouth.

The horse prepared for a third attempt. I felt my body shrink up in terror. My thoughts jumbled together, my mind unhinging with the blows.

Go! bellowed the long-dead Hungarian in my head. *On through no-man's-land!*

With a surge of Hungarian training, I straightened my back and vised the animal's sides. He lurched forward, twisting and bucking. I jabbed him with my spurs. Vaulting and rearing, we did four rounds at eye-blurring speed, my heart pounding, my ears ringing, sweat dripping down my back despite the cold. On the fifth circuit, he threw three bucks. Round six, just two. By round seven he slowed. On round eight, he arched his back and took a gentle hold of the bit, snorting in the way horses do to say "uncle." Round ten was perfect. We'd acquired an astounded audience. They *oohed* and *aahed* at his world-class, six-figure movement.

I had done it—the very thing the Hungarian said might not even be possible: I'd mastered the white-eyed horse.

The ride was worth it, despite my throbbing face. I replayed the sensation of taming that magnificent devil all through our ascent to thirty-thousand feet.

DENIZENS OF THE bond world boiled through the gilt halls at the Las Vegas Venetian Hotel. Baroque urns overflowed with Little-Shop-of-Horror-sized blossoms. Somewhere in the distance, fake gondoliers plashed thin-prowed boats along a dyed-green Grand Canal under the dome of an indoor sky.

You had to pass through the casino to get anywhere, which was repeatedly depressing. Working in finance was a form of gambling, but we were professionals. Las Vegas attracted suckers who never learned Aunt Kathleen's lesson: *the house always wins*. On my way to the main session, I saw a woman, gray faced like she'd been up all night, bracing herself against an ATM.

The conference ballroom hosting today's sessions accommodated five thousand. Years ago, a bond conference would attract a mere few hundred. That was before the era of subprime and a trillion-dollar market created out of thin air.

I was grateful to Rob Goodman for sending me. I was surprisingly happy to get away from New York while Angela directed workmen around my apartment. It was a chance to sleep in a hotel bed, get room service, and take a break from my eighty-hour weeks. I took my seat, a strange combination of conference chair and ducal throne.

A nearby trader wearing a wedding ring he didn't attempt to hide ogled my legs, which were sleek in my new Barney's suit ($1250). He was good-looking, fit, and the dark type I found appealing. I made eye contact. He held my gaze. I didn't work for him or with him. Fair game. I ran a finger along my skirt's hemline, skimming my thigh. He shifted antsily in his seat. Maybe some fun of a nongambling kind was in order.

Our flirtation was interrupted by a man taking the seat next to me. He looked more like an engineer for an aerospace contractor than a finance professional, wearing a blue oxford shirt with nerdy short sleeves, a pair of brown slacks, and Rockport tie shoes. I wondered if he was from the Securities and Exchange Commission or one of the ratings agencies. They were the only badly dressed people at the conference.

I noticed his badge, which said Corning Equities. Probably some third-tier hedge fund. These days there were a lot of small investment companies made up of three guys, their trading terminals, and a golden retriever sleeping nearby. The man looked oddly familiar. As the session began, lights dimming, I pegged him as the coach-class guy who noticed my black eye.

The first session panelists all had "Global" and "Leveraged" in their titles. They discussed *exotic investment products* and the *securitization of contractual debt.* Their vocabulary was thick with words like net-net, billion, fourth quarter, euro, Deutschmark, trade imbalance, China, revenue, global flows, offshore, onshore, momentum, yield, inflation expectations, swaps, bonds, shorts, longs, puts, calls, buy, sell, hold, options, basis points, blue chips, capitalize, and an alphabet soup of acronyms: ETF, LIBOR, S&P, PE, CEF and EBITDA. It was a finance-world tower of Babel.

All confirmed Tinker Bell clappers. Anyone who questioned the looseness of current lending standards, speculative buying, or phantom liquidity, was shouted down with assertions that the US economy was never in better shape! That wealth had risen dramatically! That trade was freer than ever before! And that monetary policy was spectacular! Everybody was giving Tinker Bell a clean bill of health and a thump on the back.

The panel was a warm-up to the main event, a famous economist and Ivy-League business school dean. His Power-Point charts spun onto the Jumbo Trons, showing how much better off the average American was now at the turn of the twenty-first century. No longer at the mercy of credit card companies (red lines zipped high); the middle class could replace high-interest-rate debt with lower interest rate mortgage debt (blue lines and green lines cooled the graphs). It was a win-win-win. Banks won with fees. Investors won with new products. And average Joes won. More Americans than ever were getting cheap mortgages. "Thousands, millions of people have bettered their financial lives through the simple step of remortgaging their houses and taking the equity to pay down their cards," the dean said.

A fizzle and zap ended the PowerPoint slides. Next the dean was going to interview a new finance celebrity. A blue-suited figure with no tie strode onto the podium. Jin Soo Park was a first-generation Korean American. Park had become famous as one of the leading CDO managers in the country. CDOs were the newest and most exotic of exotic financial products.

"Five years ago, you were making a hundred and twenty thousand dollars a year as a salesman for MetLife," the dean said.

"Yes."

"How much last year?" asked the dean.

"Seventy-six million."

The audience roared.

Park was a charismatic guy who no doubt attracted money to his fund like iron filings to a magnet. He explained CDOs to the rapt audience. They rebundled existing subprime bonds so they could be sold all over again. Kind of like the way you spin sugar into cotton candy. The process created more supply for the seemingly limitless subprime demand.

"We're talking triple-A ratings and more triple-A ratings."

I typed fast on my laptop as he spewed details. One of my jobs here was to investigate CDOs for Hermes so we could buy these terrific things.

There was a change of guard on stage, another person added to the mix. Tall guy. Broad shoulders. Curly dark hair. His back was turned while an AV technician affixed the mic-transmission box to his belt. He pivoted.

Peter Priest.

Literally the last person I expected to join a conference like this, which was a cheering section for the most ethically sketchy, polar-bear-endangering financial products.

The dean bantered with Priest, referencing Plutus, the Greek god of money, who gave us the word plutocracy. Priest was patient with the dean, who clearly just wanted to show off.

"Now, Mr. Priest, your perspective on the CDO?"

"The collapse of the CDO market, subprime, and all of U.S. housing, is a virtual certainty." Around me people looked up from their Blackberries. The conference, which had become Groundhog-Day repetitive, was suddenly taking a turn.

Did Priest just say what I thought he said?

The dean was off-balance. Priest eyed him steadily.

Jin Soo Park sat forward, itching for a fight. "You're predicting the implosion of a whole class of investments, all with triple-A ratings?"

"Yes."

So, Priest *wasn't* among the Tinker Bell clappers. He *did* still think the market was heading for a crash. But, according to

Goodman, he wasn't pursuing my strategy to short the market. What did it mean?

The dean and Park looked at each other. Park pursued. "So, you're saying the triple-A ratings by all three agencies, Moody's, Standard & Poor's, and Fitch are worth nothing?"

"The ratings agencies are prostituting themselves." Priest folded his hands.

There was a discernable intake of breath from the audience. Park shook his head. The dean shifted in his seat.

"Your implication is the ratings agencies don't represent the interests of investors," the dean continued sternly. "That's a serious accusation."

"This is a case of, as we say in Greek, everyone trying to hide behind his finger. Or, in English, that the emperor has no clothes. Wall Street states the bonds are triple A-worthy, so the rating agencies give them triple-A ratings. The client is the bank, not the investor. It is difficult business to disagree with your clients." There were uncomfortable chuckles from the audience.

"Mr. Priest, it seems you are questioning the underlying assumptions of the entire market structure." The dean's tone was such as he would use dealing with a mouthy undergraduate. That was not going to go over well with Priest. "Voicing such opinions can do irreparable damage to faith in the financial system."

Priest's black eyes flashed. "Let me tell you how the market works," he said, soft fury in his tone. Everyone in the room leaned forward. "When banking ceases, lending ceases. When there is no lending, trade ceases. When there is no trade, the hospitals in the City of New York have only six days of penicillin left."

There was a silence in the room and on stage. It was shock tinged with resistance. I felt a chill.

Overhead, the PowerPoint advanced to a Q&A slide, which seemed like a broad hint from the offstage conference manager to *move things along*. The dean opened up to audience questions.

I found myself standing at the question-asking mic before I even knew what I was doing. *Was* Priest pursing my strategy after all, despite the email evidence Goodman had? I wanted Priest to tell me something—anything. It was a long shot—the idea he would reveal something substantive in this open forum. My advantage: I had him trapped onstage. Afterward, he would melt away, and I might never have the chance to ask him again. I just *had* to know more about what he thought of the coming crash and *what* he was doing about it.

A stage light shone in my face so that I could hardly see. The dean said, "Yes. First question from the young woman."

"If you are so certain about a crash, what is your fund's strategic position?" The stage crew readjusted the blinding light. Priest looked me in the eye. If he was surprised to see me, he didn't show it.

"Ms. Mulcahy." Around the auditorium heads jerked to look at me. Who was this woman Peter Priest acknowledged by name? "Always a pleasure to see you."

"What investment strategy is your fund pursuing to survive full market meltdown?" I pressed.

"That's proprietary information."

Behind me, the next questioner moved in for the mic, but I held my ground. "I've recently read about the use of credit default…"

"That's an arcane theory." Priest cut me off, eyes snapping

angrily. "As any junior finance associate knows, the *only* strategy is to reduce your exposure to these toxic products. Now." Toxic products? Hermes's balance sheets were stuffed with toxic products. I had already sent three emails from this conference to buy *more*. "You need to *protect yourself,*" Priest said. I felt the comment was aimed directly at me.

The guy behind me shouldered me aside and took the mic. The Q&A session continued while I exited the hall.

Chapter Sixteen

There are two times in a man's life when he should not speculate: when he can't afford it, and when he can.

—*Mark Twain, Following the Equator*

THE AFTERNOON TALKS ended at two, so conference attendees could go to investment-bank-sponsored activities like shooting-range excursions, paint-ball warrior outings, and invitation-only gambling. I wasn't in the mood. Priest's comments about the certainty of an impending crash chilled me, despite the desert heat.

A minuscule number of alarmist bloggers and pundits were voicing similar crash predictions and were scorned by the mainstream. This wasn't some fringe blogger, though: it was Peter Priest. He ran Wall Street's most successful hedge fund. He was smart. Brilliant, even. One of the few people I ever met who could go head-to-head with me on the math. I enjoyed Goodman. But I respected Priest.

I took a seat in the shade by a wave pool the size of two football fields. I was wearing a green bikini and a gold sarong around my hips—bought in my excitement about this work-slash-getaway. Now I felt ridiculous, as if I should get dressed and *do* something. What was there to do? Goodman had shut down talks about my short strategy. Would he care about

Priest's dire assessment of the market? Would I even be able to reach Goodman? I remembered something about a trip to Patagonia. I was sure Mitchell would call me "a girl from Florida" and tell me to keep my opinions to myself.

I just sat there in my bikini, sipped a daiquiri, and mechanically typed up my notes on CDOs.

"May I?"

I looked at the *may-I* man over my sunglasses. I was not in the mood to be picked up.

The coach-class guy again, now in khaki shorts and blue golf shirt. He was pale, thirtyish, with aviator-style glasses and a jawline that showed a case of old acne. He sat in the gold pool chair facing me before I gave him permission. Usually guys like him didn't have the guts to hit on me.

"You're Delia Mulcahy, aren't you? You asked a question during Q&A."

Well, that was a strange pickup line. "Yes."

"You're interested in credit default swaps, right? To short the market."

"What makes you say that?"

"You're in the footnotes."

"Excuse me?"

"I'm Gabriel." He put out his hand. I didn't shake it. He withdrew. "I'm interested in your theory," he continued hastily. "I've read some of the really complex stuff. And I saw a reference to some paper you wrote buried in the footnotes."

"Okay," I proceeded tentatively. If Priest found out about me, others could too, I supposed.

"But I can't find your paper anywhere."

"Ah, well." I closed my laptop, feeling stalked. "A couple of years ago I wrote my PhD thesis on the theory of shorting the market through credit default swaps. But it was never published. Maybe the title is on some list somewhere. I don't know."

Gabriel hailed a waiter in a red-striped shirt and straw hat and ordered a Diet Coke. "I was wondering if you'd be willing to talk to me about your theories. You know, any of your current thinking or more recent research."

I inserted my laptop into its sleeve, hoping he would get the hint. "Look…"

"Don't go. This market is going to crash and crash hard. Seems that guy on the panel today thinks so, too. He's some big shot."

"Peter Priest." I pushed back my chair.

"I quit my job at Merrill. I'm in charge of a new fund."

"*You*? Have a *fund*?"

"I have a partner. A backer. He's thinks the bubble is going to burst too. I've been looking at the swap angle, but it's just taking me way too long. I need to find an analyst. There are only three or four guys who even understand the short strategy. Three or four guys and *you*. You may have actually invented it."

I sat back down and took a sip of my daiquiri. The conversation was starting to make ominous sense. "You can't afford me."

"I know that," he said. "I also know that the guys at Hermes aren't listening to you. Goodman has a huge ego. He was on MSNBC last week. From what I can tell, Hermes has nothing, *zero*, in a short position against anything." I knew for a fact that was true. I felt the chill again.

"So, you want me to leave Hermes and work for… Who are you again?"

"Corning Equities." Gabriel handed me a card that was, to

my great surprise, professionally printed. "You don't really believe all this nonsense." He gestured to the wave pool and beyond as if to include the whole bond conference and all of Las Vegas. "That means you're terrified about what's really going to happen." Gabriel's eyes were like pale blue marbles. Above me, ten thousand gold-toned hotel windows glinted in the desert sun.

"Let's say that's true." The minute the words were out of my mouth, I knew just how true they were. I had spent months torqueing my mind in the opposite direction. After hearing Priest, now Gabriel, it snapped back like a bent tent pole. "You've already said you can't afford to pay me what Hermes does, and, frankly, I can't take less." I thought of my two-million-dollar mortgage, maintenance, horse expenses. I knew small funds like this guy's asked you to work for little or nothing on the chance they'd make it big.

"I have a deal to offer you," Gabriel interrupted. "And you can keep your job at Hermes."

⌒

IN THE NEXT ten minutes, Gabriel outlined his proposal. His backer was in for two hundred and fifty million. The idea was to build a one-strategy hedge fund, accruing as big a position as possible on credit default swaps, shorting the subprime market. It was a fund 100 percent about buying insurance. Gabriel needed an analyst and trader partner to help him do it.

Gabriel knew I couldn't leave Hermes. But he and his backer at Corning had devised a fascinating structure so I didn't have to. For my information and services as a consultant, Corning Equities would reserve a 10 percent position in the fund for me in an account I would control. They would front all the cash. I would provide a fast track to buy up swaps. To keep me under their control, they would only release the agreed-upon share to my account at the moment we jointly decided to sell.

If my calculations were right, the trade would be worth hundreds of millions of dollars, with millions or even tens of millions for me.

It was simple and brilliant. If the crash did come, I would be saved. The timing would have to be precise. Timing was everything on Wall Street. If we did it right, just before the market imploded, we would make oceans of cash.

"One question," I asked. "Who is your backer?"

"That's not part of the deal." Not surprising, considering how eccentric these guys were. "Now, I have a question," Gabriel said.

"Shoot."

"What happened to your eye?"

"My eye? It's nothing."

"I don't mean to ask anything inappropriate. But we're talking about a lot of money. My backer saw you and mentioned it." Gabriel's thin lips formed a line.

Gabriel's backer was here? Was he one of the people around me in first class while Gabriel sat back in coach? Perhaps. Also, today's sessions had been broadcast on closed-circuit TV, and I had been at the mic. The backer could be in Zurich for all I knew. "Jesus Christ."

"One of your Hermes bosses has a reputation."

Wow. Urban legends about Mitch Mitchell sure got around. "I got this injury from a horse. We're in finance, not Fight Club."

Gabriel shrugged. "I don't know. There's a lot of violence in our strange little world. Just not in the flesh. Most of it isn't anyway."

We finalized the deal on a handshake. No paperwork. The arrangement was so unorthodox, working for two companies at once, providing information in exchange for a position in the fund that would be earmarked for execution—who knew if it was even legal? My only risk was if Gabriel tried to screw me. But, in that case, I wouldn't be any worse off than I was now.

⌘

THE SECURITY LINE snaked around the Las Vegas airport, past more slot machines. People played Keno. Others ate unnaturally large cinnamon buns, pretzels, and cookies oozing out of oily paper sleeves. Queuing up, overweight men in their fifties wore tropical shirts. Their wives wore tracksuits, emblazoned with horses and rhinestones. How many of them had recently remortgaged their homes and used some equity for a trip to Vegas to gamble? I ran equations in my head. Twenty-six percent.

When the market crashed, these people would lose their jobs and would no longer be able to afford their mortgages. They would not be able to sell their homes because their houses would be worth less than what they paid. They would be foreclosed upon. Empty homes would drag down the value of other not-empty homes. And so it would go.

The Great Circle of Life! Now Playing at Luxor! aptly proclaimed a nearby billboard for *The Lion King*. I swished by in my first-class line thinking how lucky I was to run into Gabriel. And how much ever-loving money the disaster would mean for me.

Gabriel was right. In the back of my mind, I *had* really been worried. If the market crashed, my job would go with it. Without my six-figure salary and seven-figure bonus, I would be back to square one. Actually worse. I would be at square minus two million, the amount of my mortgage. I had been in denial, clapping up a storm for Tinker Bell. Hermes was on the wrong side. I didn't blame Goodman for his lack of insight. Finance celebrities and thousands of people around me at the conference all agreed with him.

I wondered how many weeks or months were left in the market bubble for Gabriel and me to amass the right short positions. I hoped it was enough time. I would *make it* be enough.

I picked up a paperback at a nearby bookseller. It was a murder mystery. I hadn't read one in years. Aunt Kathleen was never without an Agatha Christie in her bulging satchel. It took me until Chapter Six at the gate to remember I never actually liked murder mysteries, except when narrated by Aunt Kathleen. I resented the novels had such tied-up-in-a-bow endings, where the evildoer was punished, and the detective seemed to have known all along—or, at a minimum, from the halfway mark. I boarded the plane and stuffed the novel into the seatback pocket next to the vomit bag.

Five hours later, my plane, amidst dozens of others in the New York airspace, spiraled down on its landing route. It was as if we were simply the biggest species of bird in the giant aviary of the city firmament. Out the window, I saw the large vacancy at the bottom of the island. It reminded me of the other beings flying on that execrable day. Jet fuel, the papers said, burned at three thousand degrees, literally boiling the blood inside you. So, they jumped.

Boiling blood. Where had I heard that before? Oh, yes. Judith said her depression was like boiling blood.

All these years later—even after learning Aunt Kathleen's reason from Angela—I still could barely accept the ideas of depression, boiling blood, and suicide. Especially when it came to Aunt Kathleen. I knew it was childish to feel this way. Obviously, people *were* depressed and *did* commit suicide. Every day.

But how could *she* have done it?

We'll get through this together. Somehow, pal, we will.

Why did she say that, suspecting or even knowing she was *not* going to be there for me? How could she do it when I needed her most? She wasn't fleeing a burning building, after all.

Aunt Kathleen's broken promise changed me into the person I was today. I had given up on love, trust, honor, and other people. I was who I was, and there was no changing it now. I was me—with all my scars, cynicism, and hardheartedness toward polar bears and people in Las Vegas airport lines.

The *me* of today might not be very nice, but at least she was going to make a lot of money.

Chapter Seventeen

I think you are wrong to want a heart. It makes most people unhappy. If you only knew it, you are in luck not to have a heart.

—L. Frank Baum, *The Wonderful Wizard of Oz*

I CAME HOME to an apartment smelling of newly dried paint and a pleased-with-herself Angela. "With these colors it's like a blank canvas for whatever anyone wants to do next."

"Who's anyone?" I wondered if I needed to remind Angela that, despite handing her the reins for the previous week, the place was mine.

She gave me a wry smile as if caught being naughty and said, "I mean the decorators and architects, dear. When you decide to really *do* the apartment. But you'll never have time."

She was right about that for sure. As the early winter of 2008 progressed, I was monstrously busy. There was my normal work at Hermes, which had acquired a predictable, if frenetic, rhythm. Combined with that, my sideline work with Gabriel was overwhelming.

Gabriel and I communicated by a second cell phone, laptop, and private email account. Nothing could be accessible to the all-seeing eyes of Mitch Mitchell.

One of the urban legends about him was now confirmed:

Mitchell owned a gun.

While I was at the conference, a young programmer named Jake stole some core code from Hermes's proprietary trading algorithm. No doubt to sell it to a rival hedge fund.

Mitchell discovered the breach. I deduced he had sniffers to track everyone in the office, down to the keystroke. He went to the guy's apartment and forced him to destroy his copy of the code.

Mitchell told everyone the story the day I got back from Las Vegas in an emergency meeting of all programmers. Not the gun part, though. I learned that from Jake's roommate. Later, I heard an exaggerated version of the story in which Goodman was also there, waiting in the hallway like a puppet master while Mitchell did his bidding. This was how urban legends were born.

Speaking of stealing code, in the aftermath of the Jake thing, I heard more gossip about the history of Goodman and Priest. People said Goodman enlisted Mitchell to steal Priest's proprietary trading algorithm. Possible, I guessed. Takes a thief to catch a thief.

When Goodman showed up a week later, he was hale and cheerful, walking the trading floor and thumping guys on the shoulder, saying it would be a record year and asking what happened to Jake.

I wouldn't have blamed Goodman if he had stolen Priest's code. Who was I to judge? I was handing our customers recommendations for CDOs knowing full well they were a Ponzi scheme. I was optimizing algorithms to front-run trades through high-speed electronic mechanisms. I saw email chains laced with insider information and juiced our buy/sell algorithms based on them.

And I had my sideline with Gabriel.

Stealing code seemed kind of mild in comparison.

I did my mountain of work at night in secret. I threw my-self into the material with renewed rigor. I updated and combed through my databases and came up with exactly which classes of bonds Gabriel needed to buy insurance on. Then, based on my research, I advised which reinsurers to approach. AIG, SwissRe, Deutsche Bank, UBS.

It was slow and painstaking, peeling back layer after layer of the individual assets, applying my mathematical models, and deciding which assets were the most radioactive and which lenders had made the worst loans. Half the time, I was reading the fine print of hard copy material from investment houses. I heard Google had a new project to digitize books and periodi-cals. I wondered how long it might take them to get around to digitizing the prospectuses for subprime bonds.

I needed the answers to a key set of questions: how far did housing prices have to fall for the loans to self-destruct? Which Wall Street firms had created the most toxic bonds? What were the variables? Why, for example, was the default rate in Georgia five times higher than in Alabama? Why was it only 5 percent in California, when everyone knew those hippie-dippies were all leveraged up to their hair plugs?

Most nights, I got only three or four hours of sleep. Some nights I didn't sleep. For brief breaks, I went to the deli. The brisk walk in the freezing morning air gave me a second wind before I headed downtown to Hermes. At that hour, just before the winter dawn, the only ones out were bread trucks, limo drivers, and me.

One silent January day at five a.m., I spotted a familiar face behind the windshield of a town car idling on Madison.

"Bert?" I knocked on the window.

Bert rolled it down. "Deel-yer!" he said. "What are you doing out at this hour?"

"Coffee run. How about you? What's with the car?"

"I'm taking some extra work. Lotta cops do it. You know, bring in a little extra cash."

"Extra cash?"

"Who doesn't like extra cash?"

I was reminded of Judith's check register and its paltry entries for Mom. "No one, I guess."

Bert folded the *Daily News*, which he was reading on the steering wheel. "Don't worry, honey. I just remortgaged the houses. Take a little equity out. Value keeps going up and up. The banks have been banging down my doors for years. Money's practically free, they say. No reason not to take advantage of it."

That was love. Abiding, futile, and marked by acts of foolish nobility.

DESPITE ALL THE pressure, I scraped together a few hours here and there to go to the barn. I gave up the lease on Cinnamon so I could help Bear Stearns Eugene with his horse. The daughter switched to soccer, but Eugene kept the horse. I think he actually loved him. Great connoisseur of irony that I was, I called the horse Whitey, first for his white markings, and second for the gangster, Whitey Bulger.

As previously mentioned, the Hungarian gave a white-eyed horse slim odds. *Iz like very bad people. How many you know who change?* I thought I saw a chance for Whitey. With me as a

161

rider—and perhaps an exorcist. Truth be said, like soft-hearted Eugene, I was growing fond of that horse. He was intelligent, he was bold, and he was wicked. He just needed an opportunity to realize his full potential. Sounded like someone I knew well.

Aside from these brief, life-risking excursions on Whitey, I worked my ass off day and night. There were times when I could hardly believe what I was doing with Gabriel. I made a crazy arrangement with some guy I met in Las Vegas with an undisclosed backer and was providing information in exchange for some promised payout. It was nuts. On the other hand, given what I'd seen in Las Vegas and around Wall Street in general, "nuts" was a relative term. I wasn't depriving Hermes of my expertise. Goodman had made it abundantly clear I was not to bring up the short strategy again.

We amassed our position, and Gabriel's backer fronted all the cash to do it. He—or she—also paid the ongoing insurance premiums. Once we were fully invested and ready to sell, Corning would transfer 10 percent into an account for me. If we were right, the deal would pay sixty to one. My share would be worth tens of millions.

My work was tedious and unromantic. I was in hip-waders, slogging through the sewage of toxic assets. Saturated in the poisonous goo the financial industry had spewed out for a decade, it was impossible not to think of the implications of all of it. What I now called *The Polar Bear Dimension*, in a grudging nod to Priest.

Combing through data, discovering the flagrant criminality of the financial system, was awful and exhilarating in equal measures. The fraud was of an inconceivable dimension. There were thousands of examples of downright white-out-and-scribble-in falsification of loan documents. A whole category of people who worked in the finance industry had decided to imperil the economic wellbeing of the entire world.

Everyone was tainted—to different degrees. Take the Bear Stearns HR guy Eugene with the recalcitrant horse. He arranged the health benefits, disability insurance, and compensation packages of people like me. He was probably tainted less. Take people like me, planning to profit from all this malignancy—probably more.

As a mathematician, I knew the truth better than most. When the shit hit the fan, what Gabriel and I were doing would make things worse. When subprime exploded, the banks would go down. But we would pull down a whole 'nother sector of the economy: insurance. The insurance firms were on the hook to pay. But there was not enough liquidity in the whole financial system to make good on what would be owed. Everything would be sucked under because of us. The world economy would collapse. Just as Priest had said, as the ice floes were melting, we'd be turning up the heat.

I reminded myself that, while the situation would be cataclysmic from a societal perspective, from *my* perspective it was the opportunity of a lifetime. And, anyway, why should I give a fuck about the polar bears?

With the money I would make, I would at least be able to save one of the over-mortgaged masses—Bert, and, by extension, Mom.

We had to sell at just the right moment, when the price of insurance soared but before the whole system seized up and the market collapsed. As Goodman said, timing was everything on Wall Street. I'd heard someone declare this principle was also true for love—that you had to meet someone at just the right moment. Interesting idea, but I doubted it. And anyway, as I believed I have mentioned, love was not anywhere on my list of goals.

ONE TUESDAY IN February 2008, I decided to ring up Moody's, the ratings agency. Posing as a PhD student working on my thesis, I reached Colleen in Securities Research. I was curious about my adversaries, the way you want to see the other guy's hand in gin.

"What do you think the mortgage default rate is going to be in 2008?" I asked.

"Five percent," she said in a dull tone.

"What are you basing that on?"

"We're basing that on 5 percent." She sounded miffed.

"The models I'm working on show some different numbers," I advanced.

"Okay."

I offered her my email address. She probably took it down to get me off the phone.

I also called a mid-level officer at the SEC, the putative regulatory body of the financial industry. My conversation with him was shorter than the one with Colleen. I got the sense he didn't even grasp the basics. Maybe he didn't give a crap. He didn't take down my email address.

Why did I hint about what I knew and give them my email? I guessed it was Aunt Kathleen's card-playing principles. You didn't want to *be shooting fish in a barrel. It wasn't sporting.*

Chapter Eighteen

You will always be fond of me. I represent to you all the sins you have never had the courage to commit.

—Oscar Wilde, *The Picture of Dorian Gray*

T HE BARN WAS quiet when I pulled in one morning in early March, the sun just thinking about rising. I could hear the dull *shush-shush* of grain hitting feed troughs at the other end. Morning feeding was finishing up. The Hungarian taught me to wait half an hour after the horses ate to ride, which was fine. It gave me time to brush and tack. Today, I planned to do a little more work on driving. The stable had a light buggy and harness, which I had just gotten Whitey to accept. Driving is a tough one, because when you first hitch horses up to a carriage, they think the thing is chasing them.

I extracted my brush box from my tack trunk, custom-painted with my initials ($1500) and walked down the aisle with its stained and lacquered boards and gleaming brass name labels for each horse.

Who was that in front of Whitey's stall, head leaning on the bars?

"Eugene?"

"Hi." He turned to look at me. His blond hair was streaked with silver.

"Eugene, it's six thirty." He often came to watch me exercise Whitey, but on Saturdays. During daylight. "Is Whitey okay?" I looked over Eugene's shoulder. Whitey had his nose in his breakfast.

"I knew it was your morning to ride. I wanted to talk to you." In the glow of the fluorescent barn lights, the normally pale Eugene was printer-paper white.

"What's going on?"

Eugene grasped my upper arm and pulled me aside—even though the only ones listening were twenty equines. "I'm about to lose my job."

"How do you know?"

"I have a friend in accounting. Bear's going under. The whole thing."

"Bear. Whole thing?" I repeated. Despite what I knew, hearing Eugene say it out loud knocked the wind out of me. Bear Stearns was one of the oldest and most respected investment houses on Wall Street. They survived the 1929 crash.

How could I be surprised? I knew from my research Bear was a veritable printing press of toxic bonds. Eugene told me even worse: they also bought massive amounts of these same assets and held them on their own books. They were brewing poison Kool-Aid and also drinking it themselves.

"I have to sell Whitey." Eugene looked disconsolate.

"Come on, Eugene. Not right away. There are cheaper barns than this one."

"I wish I didn't have to admit this to you." Eugene's color now rose like a blushing child. "It's just…" He grasped the bars of the stall again and said the next part to Whitey, as if he were explaining to him. "With the kids in private school, and my wife not working, I've been living check to check. It sounds ridiculous, doesn't it? Without my job, I can't pay my mortgage. I don't know how I'll pay horse board."

I suppressed a gasp. Eugene had been at Bear forever. He told me fifteen years. He was making three or four hundred thousand a year, with bonuses on top of that. And *he* was living check to check?

I thought of all I had spent on horses and cars and redoing my living room. I decided it *was* possible. I didn't really have any savings either, strictly speaking. I paid back the loan I'd taken from Hermes for the down payment on my apartment. When I got my bonus, I rolled it into Hermes to avoid taxes. It was locked up. If anything happened to Hermes, all my savings went too.

"I'm sure you'll get another job." It sounded lame. But what else do you say?

Whitey, done with his breakfast, came over in search of a carrot. Through the stall bars, he played with the cuff of my jacket. Eugene shook his head.

"Delia, I'm worried what'll happen if I try to sell him."

He was right. No matter how much raw talent Whitey had, his future was dim. If the horse were younger, an expert rider might take him on as a potential international-level mount. A gelded, mid-career show horse who was un-rideable except by the likes of me? Horses like that ended up at third-rate hack barns—for example, at a boarding school called Sorrows. I knew from the Hungarian, the next stop for the horses if they washed out at Sorrows was the meat auction. It was one of the reasons we worked so hard to redeem them.

"Would you buy him?" Eugene's voice was plaintive.

"I..." Whitey's nibbling had proceeded up my arm and he was now playing with the hood strings of my coat. "I guess..."

"Please, Delia."

As much as I loved Whitey, taking full responsibility for another living creature? It wasn't really my M.O.

"Eugene…"

"*Please.* You're the *only* one who cares about him aside from me. You know he has a good heart in there somewhere. You bring it out. I can't bear to think where he'd end up if you don't take him."

"*If* it's necessary."

"Thank you." He practically collapsed with relief.

"A last resort," I reminded him.

"Understood." Eugene smiled.

Eugene left to go to his doomed job. I thumbed an email to Mitchell telling him he needed to unload our position in Bear.

I brushed Whitey and harnessed him to the carriage. As if to underscore Eugene's point, Whitey shied and balked with such deviousness, he might have killed another handler.

Bear Stearns failed that Friday, March 14th, 2008, sucked under by subprime.

⌒

AND ALMOST NOTHING happened.

Two days after Bear failed, the federal government bailed them out, assuming thirty billion dollars in Bear Stearns debt as a sweetener to get J.P. Morgan Chase to buy them. Pundits screamed about something called "moral hazard." Moral hazard, a term Aunt Kathleen would have liked, is what happens when people are let off the hook for their bad behavior—leading to more bad behavior.

I was glad for Eugene, who kept his job, at least temporarily. They needed an HR guy around to handle all the layoffs. I was also glad I didn't have to take on Whitey just now on top of everything else I was dealing with.

To wit—Gabriel and I grappled with profound confusion.

The thing was, our insurance strategy paid off *only* if the metaphorical house *actually* burned—not if it *started* to burn and someone poured water on it, as the government had done with Bear. What did this mean? Would the federal government step in and rescue *everyone*? Would they do it before or after we executed our trades? As certain as I was of the math and my analysis, I could not be sure of all the other capricious variables. Once again, the importance of timing overshadowed everything.

Everyone was shaken by the Bear collapse. At work, Mitchell disappeared for hours into Goodman's office. They looked serious.

No one knew the answers, least of all the people who said they did. I remembered my research about crashes. Afterward everyone said each crash was perfectly predictable and happened exactly when the numbers predicted they should have. So why didn't anyone *actually predict* them? I thought of the crashes that people predicted yet never happened. Were Gabriel and I false-crash Cassandras?

I was the analyst, so it was my job to recommend what we should do. Before the Bear failure, the price for "insurance" was rising, indicating the market agreed with us. There would be a crash. After Bear, prices for insurance fell. Which suggested no crash. We could liquidate our positions, but at the current price, and with what Corning had been shelling out in premiums, it was little better than a break-even proposition.

"We should wait," I told Gabriel, and he agreed.

"You think October?" he asked.

"End of September."

ACROSS THE COUNTRY, the crazy spring weather that year was a metaphor for the market confusion. There were heat waves, blizzards, tornados, ice storms, and out-of-season hurricanes. In New York, an unseasonably mild winter turned into an even milder spring. Balmy April days in the sixties turned into balmy May days in the seventies. It felt like we were living in a bubble.

My work with Gabriel went dormant. We had amassed our position, and now we waited and waited.

The lull left me with more free time on my hands than I'd had in months. Not that anyone working for Hermes can be said to have much free time. I'd still wake up before dawn, though, as if I had to get on my separate phone to Gabriel. I found myself idly staring out the window into my childhood bedroom, ruminating.

I think I was steeling myself for what lay ahead, girding my loins for what I was about to do. Funny to say I, of all people, needed to fortify my resolve. When it came to money, I considered myself a stone-cold killer.

Up till now, I happily participated in all kinds of Wall Street shady dealings—like acting on insider information and creating algorithms that exploited the market. Still, what I was about to do—it was of a magnitude geometrically different in scale.

Priest was right when he said, *When banking ceases, lending ceases. When there is no lending, trade ceases. When there is no trade, the hospitals in the City of New York have only six days of penicillin left.*

Our big-short trade would be monumental. It would be a disaster for millions of people all over the planet. Moreover, Gabriel was likely correct about one key detail: I *was* the one who invented the strategy that would destroy the global financial system.

Not to say we were alone as we prepared to sell insurance swaps that would cause worldwide financial meltdown. As Gabriel also noted, there *were* probably three or four other guys who knew about it. Maybe they didn't stop with the "footnotes" but approached my thesis advisor as Priest had done. So it was three or four guys and *me*.

I assuaged my "conscience" (quotes stet) by reminding myself I would be able to save a limo driver, a reclusive old woman, and a thug of a horse. But I was raised by Aunt Kathleen, so I knew, weighed against all the lives that would be ruined, this was not even a shadow of a justification for what I was about to do.

And still I resolved to do it.

⁓

JUNE MELTED INTO July, and I continued to wake up early and stare out my window. During one window-gazing session, I spotted the yellow parakeet on a parapet of the Greek embassy. How had that damn bird made it through the winter? Or maybe this was a new bird and the other one died of exposure. Exactly how many escaped parakeets could there be in New York? I wanted to compare from my notebook sketch, but he was too far away.

Little known fact: Central Park is one of the top ten places in the country for birdwatching. When I was young, I used my hand-drawn sketches to see whether the same birds showed up year after year. When I saw one I recognized, it felt like a small miracle.

Looking past the parakeet, my eye was drawn up to the skyline and the new billionaire tower poking up its head on the southern shoals of Central Park. In keeping with the bird theme, I called it the Blue Heron, because at night the construction lights turned the skyscraper all blue.

The tower was the newest of several herons stretching their necks above the skyline. I read a recent article about them, which explained that engineering advancements had made it possible to erect the needle-thin spires. Small lots, which in the past would never have hosted a skyscraper, could now do it. All you needed were sufficient air rights. Developers bought the air rights from as many surrounding buildings as possible to build higher and higher.

For many years, Jacqueline Onassis organized opposition to taller and taller buildings because they cast long shadows over the park. But she was dead, and billionaires really wanted these cloud-piercing apartments.

This new heron would be the tallest. Taller than the Chrysler building, taller than the Empire State, and taller even than the Freedom Tower that would replace the tragic twins. The Freedom Tower would be *officially* taller, but only because of its spire. The billionaire Blue Heron would have more actual floors. So, really, it won.

Sales were swift. In the tower at the corner of 57th and Seventh, the penthouse was in contract for eighty-seven million, and the rest of the building was 95 percent sold. Demand was hot, but even once fully occupied, these buildings would stay pretty empty. The apartments were tax havens and tools for money laundering. It was estimated 30 percent of the city's most valuable real estate was vacant at any given time.

People said the new Blue Heron might finally crack the hundred-million-dollar mark for a single apartment.

My musings about blue herons led me back to Rob Goodman and what he said that day at San Macarius regarding Number N and why he didn't develop it. He told me, since the building had no air rights, he could only build a structure of the same size, which was hardly worth the effort. I wondered for a second time if any of the surrounding buildings had air rights to purchase, then thought once again surely Goodman would have investigated it.

And yet it had taken *me*, "some girl from Florida" to perform the necessary deep dive into subprime to understand the market's impending disaster. City records could be as impenetrable as subprime bond prospectuses—buried in files at the department of buildings. I supposed it was possible Goodman or his father didn't dig or dig far enough. I would hate to think Mom's payout opportunity would founder because someone missed something decades ago.

It was worth a brief look-see. I'd check into it if the summer continued calm and I had the time to spare.

Chapter Nineteen

Cuius est solum, eius est usque ad coelum et ad inferos.
(Whoever's is the soil, it is theirs all the way to Heaven and all the way to Hell.)

—Principle of property law

E VERYONE REALLY DID mellow out after Bear. It was like a giant exhalation; the bullet had been dodged. The market stabilized. Business in the finance world resumed its usual pace. August arrived. The city emptied out, bringing the late-summer lull.

Was it really a lull? Or was it like riding a white-eyed horse, awaiting the moment of the diabolical spin? Or like waiting to see who will be the first to stop clapping for Tinker Bell? Or like playing a game of gin rummy with an opponent notorious for letting you get ahead then suddenly putting down her winning hand? I couldn't know.

Some financial writers were starting to say that it was just a matter of time. The other shoe would surely drop. Then, in conflicting news, it was reported that the famous "Wall Street Fear Index" hit an all-time low.

There was a big algorithm deployment at Hermes, so it took me until the beginning of August to get around to double-checking on the thing about air rights near Number N. In the future, I would be able to do the research from my desk. Mayor Bloomberg promised to put all city records online at the click of a mouse. But that project might not go live until 2013. Digitizing all of New York City's millions of records was a Google-level effort and one had to doubt whether it would ever get done.

For now, the building records could only be found in over-stuffed drawers in a downtown office. Fortunately, I wasn't afraid of filing cabinets. Eventually, I found a free afternoon and told Tina to cover for me. Since it was August, even workhorse Mitch Mitchell was out of town. Besides, Tina didn't give a shit. Speaking of Google, it was her last week working at Hermes before she took a job in their top-secret data initiative, that project on digitizing "all human knowledge." I was a little proud I was the one who gave Tina her start.

I trekked down to the department of buildings and finally got a clerk to pay attention to me.

"I'm looking for records pertaining to air rights," I began.

"There's no such thing as air rights." The clerk's elaborately braided hairdo piled on top of her head veritably tilted with irony.

"But I hear people saying, 'air rights,' all the time."

"No such thing. I can only look up *transferable development rights.*"

I asked her to please do that.

"On what building?"

"The buildings around Number Ten East 80th Street." I almost said *Number N* out of habit. That would really have pissed her off.

"There is no such thing as *around.* I need exact addresses."

She turned her back on me to stuff a manila folder in the center of a jammed "out" tray.

I wrote down the addresses adjacent to Number N.

Twenty minutes later, I had a printout for each of the buildings and was sitting in an orange plastic chair flipping pages, trying to make sense of all the acronyms. *DOB Special Place name, DOB Remarks, Landmark Status, SRO Restricted, UB Restricted, Environmental Restrictions, Legal Audit Use, Loft Law, TA Restrictive, Violations DOB, Actions, Plumbing Inspections.* It went on and on. The buildings department had as much jargon as Wall Street.

Finally, I found what I was looking for. Four pages into the printout on Number 12 East 80th Street, the building directly east of N, I saw an acronym: *TDR.* I deduced this stood for "transferable development rights." Next to it was typed NO. Okay, so no air rights in that building.

I looked next at Number 7 East 79th Street, which backed up to Number N. *TDR: NO.* I went to Number 9 East 79th street. *TDR: NO.* I flipped to the final property: 990 Fifth Avenue.

TDR: YES

The Greek embassy, my old house, had air rights.

⌒

BACK IN MY apartment, pages now drooping in my hands, my mind roiled with questions. I looked across at the embassy, the sky above it a vast vacant gold mine of air rights.

I was confused and enraged.

Our property had air rights! Never mind Number N. Why hadn't my grandmother sold to a developer rather than the

Greek government?

But she hadn't done it.

Had Grandmother actually been dotty enough to preserve the family house out of sentimentality? What possible reason could she have had for not taking advantage of what the property was worth?

It made no sense. I knew a lot about real estate, and yet, I had to admit, I knew nothing at all about real estate. I could quote mortgage rates and default rates and the float on a subprime bond, but, until a year ago, I didn't even know what a co-op board was or how you tricked one into letting you in. I had no idea how to answer all my questions.

Lucky for me, I knew someone who could.

"DELIA!" SARAH ITALICIZED at me over the phone. "So nice to *hear* from you, honey. How's that *window* of yours? You ready to flip?"

She didn't mean perform a backflip. She was wondering if I was ready to sell the apartment for a profit and use her as the broker this time.

Sarah didn't hold it against me that I made a direct buyer-seller arrangement for my apartment. True to form, Sarah said, "If I'm not in *this* deal, I'll be in your *next* one."

"Not yet, Sarah."

"I guess you're *right* to wait. You paid *top dollar*. So, you *really should* wait for prices to go higher." Sarah knew I paid above market value for my place, to make absolutely certain the stroke victim's kids jumped at my offer. Since I wasn't planning to flip it—pretty much ever—I figured it didn't matter if it took five years or fifty for my equity to go up.

"Listen, Sarah, I have a question."

I explained the history of my house, its sale to Greece, and the puzzle I'd now discovered—that it had air rights.

"What I can't understand is why didn't my grandmother sell to a developer?"

"You're *right* to wonder." I heard Sarah's keyboard clicking. "What was that address again?" Sarah kept talking while she was typing. "Ah I *see*."

"What?"

"Your old place, well, even with the garden and all, the parcel's actually *not* that big. Those tall buildings we have these days on small lots? Back *then* they didn't have the technology. *That* might be your reason. They probably *couldn't* do very much back then. I mean maybe not enough to mean good money for *developers*. They might have wanted engineering studies. Your granny was pretty old and in a hurry. All that takes *time*."

"That makes sense." So, maybe Grandmother didn't sell to developers because there wasn't enough space to build a decent apartment building. Or it would have been too troublesome and expensive to figure out. And she was under pressure to raise cash.

"My word! Look at *that*." I heard some more hard clacks on the keyboard.

"What *that*?" I asked, but I knew.

"Just *gorgeous*. I wonder *why* no one ever thought of *it*. The rental next door. Those two properties together? Look at that big, beautiful *perfect* lot. *That* would have been the *deal of the century*."

"Yeah," I said. "That was my next question. Number N."

"Beg pardon?"

"I mean Number Ten. The rental." I told Sarah what I knew. That the family who owned Number N always wanted to develop but lacked air rights. Grandmother had air rights but not enough space. It was a perfect opportunity, and yet nothing had happened. "It just doesn't add up," I finished.

"Well." Sarah paused. I could hear a pencil tapping. "It's possible for some reason the rental building wasn't *in the clear.*"

"Like how in the clear?" I asked. My skin started to tingle.

"Sometimes there's a problem with the *title.* Sometimes they find a *toxic tank* in the yard and the place might get turned into a superfund site. Buried *bodies*—figurative *and* literal. I've heard it all."

"I bet you have."

"There's one thing that used to be *real* common. Happens less now. Not a lot of people know about it."

"Rent control?"

"Why, you *got it,* honey. One rent-controlled tenant who doesn't want to budge? Won't take a payout to leave? That's the *whole* shooting match."

I hung up the phone, and an equation materialized in my head.

Deal of the Century + Someone Standing in the Way = Murder

You didn't have to be Angela Conti Price, daughter of a mobster, to figure that one out.

Chapter Twenty

The only thing that you absolutely have to know is the location of the library.

—Attributed to Albert Einstein. True source unknown.

AFTER MY CALL with Sarah, my world tilted on its axis. Aunt Kathleen's suicide was a turning point in my life and also Mom's. I gave up on other people and on promises such as *we'll get through this together*. Mom, her stalwart sister gone, drifted into an eccentric, reclusive existence in Centerville, leaving me with no one, except maybe Angela. In the aftermath of all of it, I accepted life on new terms. If Aunt Kathleen could abandon me like that, then I was fundamentally alone.

But what if *none* of that was true?

What if she *hadn't* deserted me—hadn't killed herself, but was instead murdered? Faced with this new information about the circumstances back then, I had to concede it was at least a possibility.

Such thoughts threw me into uncharted territory regarding Aunt Kathleen. I now saw the possibility she had been murdered.

At the same time, I also had to acknowledge it might all be a huge coincidence, and she really had killed herself.

I was entering a new Schrödinger's-cat stage, where I held both mutually exclusive realities, at the same time, together in my mind. The two Aunt Kathleens, dark and light, jumper and victim, known and unknown, yinned and yanged and danced together, sometimes whirling into gray.

I only had bits of the puzzle, and many more questions than I had answers for. The biggest one—if the real estate Deal of the Century was possible back in 1986, why didn't it happen? Was Aunt Kathleen the reason? Did she get killed for it? What about my mother and grandmother? What did they know?

And even more mystifying: once Aunt Kathleen was out of the way, why didn't the deal happen *then*?

It was maddening not to be able to pursue these questions. But with August vacations in full swing, and with Tina, the other female workhorse, now off to Google—my responsibility at Hermes doubled.

The market was twitchy, and I was forced to pay attention since I was actively playing both sides of the coin. On the one hand, I was trying to do my best for Hermes. I had gotten approval from Mitchell to short some bank stocks in case there was a crash. I think he was sitting on a beach in Southampton somewhere and just wasn't paying close attention to my email. Goodman and Mitchell were still deep in Tinker Bell territory.

I also tracked the market on behalf of Corning, i.e. me and Gabriel and our backer. The sources for the information I needed on that front weren't written down or broadcast anywhere. It was all about tuning in to rumors and gleaning the behavior of brokers who might be selling. Across my screens, I had constantly refreshing newswires, chat threads, Google alerts, and scrolling conversations.

The second week of August, Gabriel and I tested the market, trying to establish a price for our swaps. People were offering only a few percentage points above what we paid because subprime debt was still, even after Bear, triple-A rated. No one wanted to own insurance on a polar bear in a life jacket.

Another question that kept me up at night: what if something happened that caused the market to rebound?

That would mean all my work with Gabriel was for naught. I consoled myself with the thought that if the bet with Corning didn't pay off, I still had my job at Hermes. If the market crashed, the Corning side won. Either way, I was covered.

I tried to focus. Odd to say but reclaiming my fortune—which had been my central objective for so long—subtly shifted to the side, as the subject of Aunt Kathleen nudged its way center stage. I was so mentally distracted by the mystery of her death, I surprised even myself.

Nothing had ever diverted me from my quest for wealth before. Greed was the guiding principle of my life. Was it possible, I wondered, that there was something more important to me than money?

Maybe, there just might be.

I CONTINUED TO puzzle about Aunt Kathleen. A quick call to Bert revealed that getting a look at the police report from back then was a pipe dream.

"Old police reports?" he asked. "Whadja want them for?"

I wasn't ready to tell Bert what I was thinking. I was afraid I would sound crazy if I disclosed my suspicions out loud. Also, it's in the nature of cops to be skeptical. They like to tell you you must be imagining something.

So I lied. "It's this job, Bert. You know they have me researching everything. Half the time I don't know why."

"Jeez Louise. 1980s? I'm thinking there's a warehouse in Long Island City. But you tell those assholes you work for—excuse my French—that the NYPD isn't their personal librarian service. You need a lawyer with a warrant for that."

Frustrating, but Bert's use of the word "librarian" gave me an idea.

Second best to an actual police report, was the police-blotter section in the *New York Daily News*. The coverage was gruesome in the eighties. And Aunt Kathleen, lover of murder mysteries, used to pore over the *Daily News*, which was chock-a-block with stabbings and shootings and mobster raids. I knew just where to find a trove of periodicals stretching back to the Dutch.

I had to wait for a Wednesday, which was when the public library was open late. On Wednesday September 3rd, two days after Labor Day that year, I was heading out from Hermes at five p.m.

"Where the fuck do you think you're going?" barked Mitch Mitchell. *Shit.* He was back. I thought Mitchell, like the rest of the hedge-fund elite, would take the whole week off after Labor Day. Private schools didn't start until the following Monday. "Is this what happens when I'm on vacation?"

"Bathroom," I said.

"With your bag?"

"Lady stuff." He blinked hard, but turned around.

It would have to wait another week.

PATIENCE AND FORTITUDE are the names of the lions outside the main branch of the New York Public Library. They were given those monikers during the 1930s, as a reminder of the qualities that would be needed to weather the decade-plus of deprivation of the Great Depression.

You girls may be on duty again soon, I thought, mounting the library steps. Gabriel and I spoke briefly that day. The market was feeling more brittle, the rumor mill swirling. It might be just a few more weeks now. We reviewed the specifics, even though we both knew how it would work. He and I would decide to execute the trade together. Gabriel would transfer my position to me. We'd pull the lever at the same time. No one would get ahead of the other. It's what Aunt Kathleen called "honor among thieves."

Inside, I rushed through the library's vaulted foyer, with its historic floor plaque from an immigrant with no schooling who credited the public library for his entire education. Upstairs, I scooted up to a computer terminal, which seemed out of place amid the carved wood bookcases and painted ceilings. I keyed search terms. I was looking for the *Daily News* from April 21st, 1986, the day after Aunt Kathleen died.

They had the edition. Just as reams of paper did not intimidate me, I was undeterred by microfiche.

I snagged a green request slip from a box in the center of the research table and jotted the periodical's reference number on it. I checked my phone, since I had stopped wearing a watch. It said six p.m. I wondered how long it would take them to retrieve the spool. Would I have to come back? I could hardly wait for another Wednesday.

"We don't have it here," said the research librarian from behind her fuchsia-sided reading glasses. Her name tag said, "Janice."

"Do I have to go to another location?" There was a whole other collection housed in an office building across the street. I checked my phone's time again.

"Yes," Janice said. "California."

❧

I SAT DEFLATED on a stone bench outside the vault-ceilinged catalog room. Before dismissing me, Janice expressed amazement I was so ignorant of the biggest news in all of library-dom: Google's mass digitization project.

In 2002, the University of Michigan made a calculation of how long it would take them to digitize their collection of seven million volumes. They predicted a thousand years.

Larry Page said he could do it in six.

A consortium of universities and libraries signed on to the project, including the New York Public Library. Books, periodicals, microfiche, were all shipped off to a top-secret location on Google's Mountain View campus. There the material remained, as Google worked through it all, and had been for six years now.

Janice said there was no telling when all the material would be available again. Rumors said Google would go online with batches of stuff incrementally, starting in 2010. A short-term sacrifice in the availability of research materials for such a magnificent long-term goal—the digitization of all human knowledge!

I was defeated. The information I wanted was locked in a

warehouse in California. What would I do next? Did another trove of New York news microfiche exist somewhere? And where was that?

"Miss?" It was Janice, name tag now askew on one side of her tan cardigan, leaning over me as I sat on the bench. I looked up. "At least I can offer you this." Janice handed me a printout off a dot-matrix-style printer, long like an airline manifest.

"What is it?"

"It's an index for the edition you wanted. We used to log the headlines for the microfiche. I just remembered we kept these as a record of what we sent to Google. I was thinking it might help."

I took the printout from her, trying not to snatch. On it were the *Daily News* headlines from April 21st, 1986.

Palestinian held in disco bombing

Man falls off bridge to his death

Koch implicated in parking violations scandal

Gorbachev declares accord still possible

Man charged in murder of romantic rival

Suicide's death is a puzzle

Daughter of famed actor found dead at club

I finished and sighed.

Nothing.

Wait.

I followed my finger back up the list.

Suicide's death is a puzzle? That could be it. The language was pretty vague. A lot of people's suicides were puzzling. It could be anyone.

And yet on that very day.

"This one," I said. "Is there more information? Anything at all?"

"I'm sorry, no. The actual microfiche is at Google."

TINA RESPONDED TO my call at midnight. She confirmed that, yes, the secret "all human knowledge" data initiative for which she was hired was the project Janice described.

"I worked like a dog at Hermes," she said. "It's just as bad here. Maybe worse."

I didn't tell Tina that what I was about to say might sound crazy. We worked elbow to elbow on Wall Street for months. Crazy-sounding things were an hourly occurrence. I described the piece of microfiche I was hunting.

"I'm sure it's here somewhere," she said. "You can't imagine what it's like. Semitrucks pull up every day filled with books, and boxes and reels."

"You must have some serious technology shit going on."

"Top secret."

"I want you to find it for me, the microfiche of that edition."

"Are you kidding?" Tina detailed her eighty-hour weeks. "Now it's getting worse. We're racing against the clock," she said. "Because of the injunction."

"Injunction?"

Tina went on to describe the lawsuits that book and newspaper publishers had filed against Google. Even though many books were out of print, they were not yet in the public domain. Publishers, who were being crushed by Amazon, could theoretically make money off these titles, yet Google was planning to put them all up for free. Newspapers and magazines had a similar angle. They were also going out of business and hoped to make money off their archives, which they couldn't do if Google posted all their back issues on the internet.

The Justice Department was getting involved and everyone feared an impending injunction, which could happen at any time.

"We're all waiting for the word we've been iced. Could be any minute. In the meantime, it's balls to the wall," said Tina.

"What happens if you're shut down?"

"It'll be a fucking mess. I guess they'll have to send it all back. But no one here will give a shit what happens to it. No one will be left with shits to give."

Chapter Twenty-One

Μέτρα φυλάσσεσθαι· καιρὸς δ᾽ ἐπὶ πᾶσιν ἄριστος.

(Observe due measure, for right timing is in all things the most important factor.)

—Hesiod, *Works and Days*

THE FLIGHT TO California ate up all of Thursday, September 11th. Gabriel wasn't happy I'd be offline for seven hours. But, aside from that one plane ride to Las Vegas in January, it was the only seven hours since I'd started on Wall Street I'd been unavailable. I slept with my phone next to my pillow. I rode Whitey with a cell phone strapped to my leg, so I could grab it mid-buck. Surely, after nearly two years on Wall Street, these seven hours could not be the decisive ones in the market.

"All good, right?" I asked Gabriel when I landed in San Jose.

"You bet," he responded. I could hear the relief in his voice.

"Okay. I'm online from here on out." My return flight was the next day, Saturday, and the market would be closed.

I thumbed an email to Mitch Mitchell with an update on my "food poisoning" situation. "Still puking," I wrote.

Five a.m. on Friday the 12th of September, I beeped myself

into the Google Mountain View campus. Called the Goog-leplex, it had sweeping buildings that were part terrarium and part biodome.

I made a deal with Tina. She would have a "family emer-gency" and take a personal day, and I'd get her badge. I needed to do this myself since I knew what I was looking for, knew all the players involved, and could pursue threads Tina would never spot. The possibility I could find out the truth about Aunt Kathleen was worth the thirty-six-hour trip to California.

We were both pretty sure that Google's level of security wasn't so tight as to catch a person who was supposed to be off work using her security card.

I hiked to a warehouse on a back lot. Tina and I were ap-proximately the same height. But she was blonde, and I was a redhead. I wore a wide turban-style headband to cover my vivid locks, putting my head down to remove my sunglasses as I scanned Tina's picture ID card on a keypad.

The guard standing next to the metal detector didn't wear a suit, rather a royal-blue golf shirt with a Google logo. Nearby, his Google Security Segway waited for him to buzz away.

I grabbed my knapsack off the screening belt. "You forgot to leave your phone," the guard said, holding out a gray airline bin. He consulted his X-ray image. "I see you have two."

My phones?

Tina didn't mention having to leave my phones. But phones had cameras and the place was top secret. Keeping my sunglasses on, I looked at the guard's face to read his level of seriousness. High. I glanced inside the airline bin. There were a dozen phones in the well.

I quickly checked each device for activity—all quiet—then dropped mine in with the others: the Blackberry I carried for

Hermes, and the Nokia I used for Gabriel.

The finance world, which had been in a shaky holding pattern for months, would have to hang on just a few hours longer.

⌇

THE FLOOR OF the warehouse was lined with custom scanning stations. Books traveled in little cars with specialized devices to lock each volume in place. Above it all were millions of dollars of optics and lights, four cameras pointing at each book, and lasers to measure the convexity of the paper. A human operator turned the pages by hand and fired the cameras via his foot pedal.

Tina worked in the software shop, located in a separate area, which handled the next step. She and her team wrote algorithms to straighten and align the text, optical-character-reader applications to capture the words, and identification and separation routines to tell the pictures and text apart.

Tina told me where to find the periodical storage for the New York Public Library's collection. I beeped my way into room A-113. As expected, bankers' boxes packed the temporary shelving floor to ceiling.

Blessedly, the boxes were labeled. More blessedly, Tina told me where to find one of the three microfiche reading machines the project team kept in a back closet in case anyone needed to check the hard copies. And even more blessedly, I knew how to spool and read microfiche. Back at the NYPL, Janice's paper index would have been rubber-banded around each cartridge. But Google had no need of dot-matrix-printed indices because, once digitized and running on supercomputers, the microfiche would be infinitely indexable.

Step 1: find the right box.

Tina said the guys in logistics had the advantage of an RFID system to track box locations. All I had was a rolling sixteen-foot ladder. I went down the shelves, aisle by aisle, climbing and checking labels.

I lost track of time. Without my phone, I had to dismount the ladder and go into the hallway to find a clock. At nine a.m.—noon Eastern time—I made my way back along the vast hallways to check my phones in the lobby. I retrieved them from the guard, turned them on, waited. All was still quiet. Then they rechecked me through security, which had a line due to some smoker-break returnees. The whole exercise took forty-five minutes. I couldn't consume my one day here running back and forth through security checking my phones. I'd have to leave them alone for the rest of the afternoon.

I went back to the storage shelves.

I read hundreds of labels, penned at the New York Public Library by someone like Janice. Room A-113 was a bust, containing magazines from the 1980s and no newspapers. Room A-114 got me closer, with newspapers, but only through the 1970s.

As I mounted the ladder, deciphering the peeling labels on boxes, and looking inside at the cartridges of film, I was overwhelmed by the colossal physicality of all human knowledge. The internet was vast but abstract, like the universe spreading out to infinity. Here, I was *inside* information, surrounded by it, digging into it, like a miner pickaxing for a lump of gold.

Finally, in room A-115, I found a box that seemed like the one. It was labeled *Daily News* March–April 1986. I opened it. Inside rattled unlabeled cartridges of microfiche.

The storage closet with the microfiche-reading machine was a trip back in time to a trip back in time. I loaded the spools into spindles. The microfiche contained thousands of micro-photographs of newspaper pages. Tiny movements of my thumb sent dozens of pages flipping by. I had to use delicate motions, like driving a temperamental spaceship at warp speed.

Bits and pieces of the 1980s zipped past, from early and late in the decade, as I loaded the spools out of order. It was a grab bag of culture and news events.

Russians deny second meltdown at Chernobyl

Michael Jackson wins eight GRAMMYS

PLO Terrorists Hijack the Achille Lauro

Lady Di do biggest hit since Dorothy Hamill

Britain threatened by gay virus plague

Gandhi assassinated

New daytime star Oprah Winfrey racks better ratings than Donahue

St. Helens explodes

Donald and Ivana spotted arguing in Vail

Mixed in between were TV Listings and Dear Abby columns. Also, advertisements for Eastern Air Lines the official airline of Walt Disney World; Great Neck car dealerships running Buick LeSabre specials; Vidal Sassoon hair-product coupons; and lingerie sales at Gimbels.

I found the year 1986. January. The next spool had May. Then August. I kept going.

There! The headline flew past. My subconscious registered it even though my eyes didn't quite see it.

In tiny increments, I inched the dial in reverse, determined not to miss the article. I scanned each square on each page, slowly. Methodically. Painfully.

Finally, it appeared on the screen.

Suicide's Death Is a Puzzle

To friends and fellow residents of Number 10 East 80th Street, Kathleen Condon was generous, spunky, and "very strong."

They can't explain why Ms. Condon, 42 and a former nun, jumped to her death from the building's thirteenth floor roof on Wednesday. Her body was found in the garden of 990 Fifth Avenue, a private home where she worked as a nanny.

Tenants and staff remembered Ms. Condon Thursday and were puzzled over the contradiction between the woman they knew and her death by suicide.

A neighbor, who declined to give her name, said, "I thought everything was fine. And half an hour later she's dead." A bystander who identified herself as an art dealer said Ms. Condon was in a dispute with her landlord.

The owner of the building, Howard S. Goodman, could not be reached for comment.

An officer on the scene, Albert O. Brennan, said Ms. Condon's death was being investigated as a suicide.

My head spun and my heart thumped. I read and reread the article. The one hundred and fifty-seven words contained more information than I'd had in a lifetime. The story had no byline, but the reporter's opinion was clear: the suicide was fishy. I scrolled forward through the microfiche, looking for any coverage days or weeks later. I sat there for another two hours hoping the unnamed reporter had done a follow-up. But there was only Madonna's love life, Nicaraguan Sandinistas, and the Mets beating the Sox in the World Series because of Bill Buckner.

The world had moved on. It was a small news item, a weird death, and that was that.

I scrolled back to the original article, taking it down word-for-word in a pocket notebook.

As I made my way through the endless temporary hallways of the storage facility, a story took shape in my mind. Howard Goodman approached Aunt Kathleen and offered to buy her out. He explained she could make some money herself and clear the way for a larger price tag for the Mulcahy mansion.

But Aunt Kathleen turned him down.

Why?

One reason stood out above all others. Money never mattered to Aunt Kathleen. She frowned on Monopoly cash sorting. She read to me about saints who gave up their fortunes. She took a vow of poverty and spent years in a convent. She would have stayed a nun except for being kicked out.

What's more, right at that moment in 1986, she was witnessing the downside of money writ large. My family was falling over a financial precipice, and they were taking me with them. There wasn't anyone to right the ship. Grandmother was old and frail. Mom was no one's idea of a financial steward. And I was only fourteen. Maybe a big real estate deal didn't sound so great to Aunt Kathleen, given the circumstances. She might have wondered what gold-digging fraternity pal would show up to milk the profits this time.

Maybe Aunt Kathleen was reluctant to give up the one solid thing left—her rent-controlled apartment. For generations of

New Yorkers since World War II, nothing could be more of a sure thing than a lifetime lease on a rent-controlled apartment. It could even be passed down in the family. Aunt Kathleen was a card player, and she was holding the ace.

If Goodman had been angry with Aunt Kathleen over foiling the possible Deal of the Century, it was likely neither my grandmother nor Mom got wind of it. If you perhaps needed to kill someone, you sure didn't want to advertise it.

All those pieces formed a picture. But one big thing still didn't make sense. With Aunt Kathleen out of the way, her death ruled a suicide, what happened to the Deal of the Century? The rent-controlled apartment went to Mom, who would certainly have cashed in on it. Yet the deal died along with Aunt Kathleen.

The article left me with this and other questions. Who was the neighbor? It could be anyone. The art dealer—was that Judith Fisher? I needed to talk to her.

But my first conversation would be with the cop on the scene: Albert O. Brennan.

Bert.

I'd see him the minute I got back to New York.

I looked at the clock in the hall. It was two p.m. in California, five p.m. Eastern. Trading closed at four thirty in New York. I felt relieved, convinced I was in the clear. Irrational, I know. I had a kind of superstition that if anything major had happened in the markets, surely the very walls of the Googleplex would have vibrated with the impact, as if from an earthquake.

Chapter Twenty-Two

London Bridge is falling down,
Falling down, falling down.
London Bridge is falling down,
My fair lady.
—Nursery rhyme

I EMERGED TO brilliant beams of the Silicon Valley September afternoon streaming through the warehouse lobby windows. A headache stabbed my temples, springing from the intense light, library-box mold, and the fact that I hadn't eaten in hours. I picked up my backpack from security and scrounged through it for the last of the trail mix from my flight. The security guard handed me my phones.

I switched them on. The Hermes device, which was the latest Blackberry model, would boot relatively quickly. The Corning Equities low-end Nokia took forever. I was pushing it to its limits with news feeds, instant messenger, and market apps.

I rolled my bag through the parking lot to my rental car, watching the Blackberry wake up. First a circle, then a triangle, then the Blackberry logo of dots. A progress bar filled up, millimeter by millimeter, indicating the phone was loading the

OS.

The "desktop" appeared. *Plink, plink, plink.* Icons material-ized for email, phone, instant messenger, web browser. The screen remained stubbornly blank in the upper right, as the device searched for a cell tower. Nothing. Nothing.

I checked the Corning phone. It was still booting. Maybe it was frozen.

Back to Hermes. There. It found a carrier. Finally, cell phone bars appeared. Email connected.

One, two, three, ten, seventeen, thirty-four, forty-six. The email counter skipped over numbers as email flooded the phone. The messages poured in. They scrolled by so fast, it was hard to click one or to know which to click. I saw subject lines fly past. Hermes client names. A tsunami of message threads. One word kept repeating.

Lehman.

The Berry reached 213 emails when I heard a beep from the Corning phone. It had booted and acquired a signal. New Voicemails: sixteen.

Only one person had that number. Gabriel left me sixteen messages.

My head swam as I felt my blood pressure bottom out. The same kind of thing happened when Whitey was about to explode. I knew what came next. And it did.

A surge of adrenaline deluged my body, set my ears ringing, and lit every nerve on fire. There was no time to read email or listen to voice mail. I dialed Gabriel. I didn't even hear the ring on the other end.

"Delia! Where have you been?"

"I was in a warehouse. They took my phone away," I said.

"Uh." Gabriel paused for one confused beat because what I

just said sounded like a kidnapping. Then he plowed on as if even that didn't matter. "I did it. I sold Corning's position. I couldn't wait, Delia. You just disappeared."

"What? Why?" I stuttered. I had only been offline for five hours.

"I transferred your position to you first, like we agreed. But it may be too late."

"Gabriel, *what is happening*?"

"You don't? You mean? You haven't heard?"

"Heard what? What the hell is going on?"

"Oh, God, Delia. It's Lehman Brothers. The rumors are all over. They're on the brink. If they don't find a buyer by Monday, they won't make it."

"Monday."

"I transferred your position. Then I sold."

"Okay." It was what we'd agreed to. Now trading was closed. Surely, all wasn't lost. Monday morning was my next chance.

"The thing is, there's something else."

"What?"

"AIG."

Those three letters stood for the largest insurance company in the world with a market capitalization of $1.2 trillion. They were on the hook to pay all the swaps we had bought.

"AIG?"

"They're on the brink, too." Gabriel's voice was flat. "If they go under…"

Both of us went silent, well knowing what would happen if AIG went under. We were among a handful of people on the planet who'd developed the equations illustrating the cataclysmic outcome of just that scenario.

"Jesus."

"The treasury secretary called everyone to the New York Fed. The guys left standing, anyway: J.P. Morgan, Bank of America, Merrill."

I disassociated from the present, as you do in physical shock. I understood the facts but seemed to have no emotional connection to them outside of a cold, stunned, paralysis. Five hours had changed the world. I had a brokerage account filled with "insurance" that, this morning, was worth tens of millions.

What would it be worth when the finance world opened for trading on Monday morning?

My math-trained mind lined up the data. Lehman going under was bad. It would precipitate a banking crash not seen since the Great Depression. But AIG going under literally simultaneously? What Peter Priest and I had discussed years ago might actually be happening and with a precise synchronicity I never thought possible. My big-short strategy, now finally executed by Gabriel and, perhaps, a handful of like-thinkers, was going to pull down the whole economy. The global economy. Over a weekend.

My Blackberry rang. Mitch Mitchell's name flashed on the screen. "I have to go, Gabriel."

"Maybe you can do something Monday," he said. I hung up.

"All I can say is that you better be in the fucking ICU," Mitchell growled. "We're looking at a six-deviation event. It's all hands on deck. All weekend. Who knows who will be alive on Monday."

I SWUNG BY Tina's on my way to the airport. I could tell by her face, she'd heard the news. I handed her back her badge.

"I was going to go back to finance if this Google project gets shut down," she said. "Maybe I'll finish my PhD. God, it's in *classics*." She paused to take in my gray face. "I'm sorry, Delia. I hope your day was worth it."

I paid thirty-five hundred dollars for business class, so I could get the remaining seat on the jammed red-eye back to New York. Before my job on Wall Street, such a sum seemed like a king's ransom. It might seem like that again soon.

◯────◯

I ARRIVED AT the Hermes office Saturday, September 13th at noon. No one seemed to care where I had been or why. Even Mitchell appeared to have forgotten. Things had gone too far for that. Traders sat around watching news feed, typing into instant messenger, trying to find someone who knew something. We prepared to short bank stocks as soon as the market opened Monday morning.

On Sunday, September 14th, CEOs of all the major banks arrived at the Fed in New York. The government wanted someone to buy Lehman without government money to sweeten the deal. The Fed was not going to make the same mistake it had with Bear. No moral hazard this time. The treasury secretary took periodic breaks from negotiations to dry heave into a wastepaper basket.

Monday September 15th dawned. No deal. Lehman filed Chapter 11. AIG declared itself insolvent. The Dow fell 500 points. The world began to vaporize.

Tuesday the sixteenth. The Fed nationalized AIG. My

swaps were gone.

Wednesday the seventeenth. With AIG's failure, the big-short strategy I authored pulled the bottom out from under all of finance. With no federal bailout, financial markets would soon cease to operate. The Dow dropped another 450 points. Short selling was banned.

Thursday the eighteenth. AIG was delisted from the Dow.

The third week in September, Warren Buffet told Congress they were looking at the largest financial meltdown in world history. It would humble the Great Depression. The government, which previously refused to consider a bailout, was now desperate for Congress to pass one.

Monday September 29th. In a surprise move, Congress voted down the bailout. The Dow fell 778 points. The largest point drop ever.

Credit markets seized.

California and Massachusetts asked the federal government for billions in loans to continue emergency operations. Municipalities large and small could not access normal credit instruments to pay their firemen or police.

When banking ceases, lending ceases. When there is no lending, trade ceases. When there is no trade, the hospitals in the City of New York have only six days of penicillin left.

October 1st. A $700 billion bailout was passed. It wasn't enough and $600 billion was quickly added. Another $183 billion was pumped into AIG.

With the bailout finally complete, the world avoided a return to the financial Stone Age. But monumental damage was already done.

The second week of October, credit was in a deep freeze. All short-term lending stopped, and nothing the Fed could do, from injections of cash to dropping interest rates to zero, made any difference. US automakers were next in line to fail, pulled down by their credit divisions. The Dow kept falling, 500 points at a pop. By mid-October, the country entered a deep recession.

And me?

I tumbled along with the avalanche. It was if the entire finance world was dissolving like sidewalk chalk pictures in a heavy rain. There were no offers in the market for anything. The market simply ceased to exist. A giant void opened up, and I was in free fall trying to grab anything solid. The Lehman implosion was followed in quick succession by others. Fannie Mae and Freddie Mac were nationalized. Washington Mutual was seized by the Treasury. The federal government forced Bank of America to buy Merrill Lynch and Citigroup to buy Wachovia. Prices moved so quickly, you couldn't even track them on-screen.

Somewhere in the middle of it all, Hermes failed. The ban on short selling, combined with clients yanking all their money out, put vast numbers of hedge funds out of business.

Gabriel sold all Corning's credit default swaps on the very last day it was possible to trade them.

We predicted the trade would pay sixty to one.

It didn't.

It paid eighty to one.

Part II
HEART

Chapter Twenty-Three

Therefore those eager for glory will often secure a sorrowing mind in their breast-coffer.

—The Wanderer, Old English Poem

W HEN THE STORM finally spit me out, I crawled up onto the shores of a new reality. It was an outcome I'd never considered. I always thought there would be either Hermes or Corning. If a crash came, sucking Hermes under, my short strategy would pay off. If the market stabilized and no crash came, I had my job at Hermes. As it turned out, I had nothing.

I hope your day was worth it.

Tina's words seared me like a brand.

Who knew *those* five hours, that *one* day would seal my fate? I knew better than anyone. In the history of crashes, it's always just *one day*. In 1929, there was Black Tuesday. In 1987, Black Monday. A gold panic caused Black Friday in 1869.

Could have been any day. A Thursday the month before. Or a Wednesday six weeks later. But it wasn't. I had gone treasure hunting on Friday September 12th, which, for the Great Crash of 2008, was *the day*.

By late October, economists and finance writers were all saying they saw it coming and the crash was absolutely inevitable. Events were virtually preordained to happen precisely as they did.

Bullshit.

Gabriel and I predicted a crash, and up until the last minute, people thought we were fruitcakes. Now everyone was saying you had to be a fool not to see it coming. My theory was being validated. This knowledge only served to concentrate the intense brine of anguish, regret, and self-loathing in which I was pickling.

I hope your day was worth it.

What could *possibly* be worth losing your fortune just on the brink of having it? Losing it for the *second time* in one lifetime? Tens of millions of dollars slipping through my fingers. Was *anything* worth that?

My mind stuck on the question. What *would have* been worth it?

Saving a life?

Saving your own—definitely.

Saving someone else's? Only if they really mattered.

Had I accomplished anything even remotely in that category?

Aunt Kathleen's death changed everything for me. I gave up on all relationships, except the one with my bank account. If something in the microfiche proved she was murdered, then I would have known she didn't abandon me. She really had meant it when she said, *We'll get through this together.*

Recasting history that way was kinda like saving a life. Both mine and Aunt Kathleen's. Maybe also Mom's.

But that wasn't what I found.

What did the article mean, anyway? Did it really point to foul play? Or was the reporter just a muckraker, sensationalizing a suicide to sell papers? Who were the neighbors? What about Mom and Bert?

To summarize, I had risked and lost everything. All I had to show for it was a bunch of questions, and no idea if I would ever have the answers. For the record: *No, it was not fucking worth it.*

The consequences of my actions were so immense, they enveloped me like a suffocating fog. All the questions made the fog denser until I felt like I could hardly breathe. An answer, any answer, would feel like a gulp of fresh air.

AFTER HERMES WENT under, I had nothing but time on my hands. One day in late October, trying to escape the sensation I was being strangled to death, I walked to Midtown and got a table by the window in a deli. I watched finance people walk to and fro. Buy-side guys, sell-side guys, and investment bankers, going through the motions of showing up at their offices. They looked like zombies. How many of them would lose their jobs? What would happen to all the office space they occupied?

Down at Hermes, I heard Mitchell and Goodman were in a frenzy. Sure, Hermes was gone. But these guys were still rich. They had money in investments that had taken a beating but were still worth millions. The critical question was where to move it. Was anything safe? People didn't even trust money market funds anymore. They were buying gold and literally stuffing cash in mattresses.

I didn't have that problem. All my money disappeared with Hermes because it was locked up in the fund. I had a bit over fifty thousand dollars in a savings account. How long would that last? I was carrying a two-million-dollar apartment. How deep would the recession be? When would I be able to get another job? Six months? Surely within a year.

A vise-like force compressed my chest. It wrapped around my rib cage and squeezed. I managed a shallow inhalation and counted to ten. Then out—nine, eight, seven, six. In on ten, out on ten until the panic attack passed.

I had to get a grip on myself. I needed to think clearly. I was living the oldest story on Wall Street. The market made fortunes and wiped out fortunes. If you couldn't stand the heat, you needed to write software for an automated call center in Minneapolis. I had awesome skills. I could begin again. Hedge funds would rise from the ashes.

Wouldn't they?

My breathing eventually eased. I would have this same conversation with myself tomorrow and the day after, just as I'd had it with myself yesterday, and the day before. Maybe eventually it would stick.

I had to hold on at least until the dust settled. I took a swig of my coffee. It was bitter and cold.

I needed to do *something* other than wait.

❧

I DROVE OUT to Centerville. My plan was to turn in my Audi and take the train back to the city. The car barely had ten thousand miles on it and was in mint condition. But the dealer in Lynbrook was already drowning in luxury cars traded in by petrified finance people. They said I might get twelve grand of the eighty I paid. I told him I'd think it over and be back later.

"Delia." Mom looked up from her stitching of herons with great craning necks. "It's not like you to come…unannounced."

Mom inserted a pause between *come* and *unannounced*, implying that it was not like me to come at all.

True enough.

She sat in her "conservatory," a badly screened porch pulling away from the house. Through the plastic winterization, I saw Bert raking leaves. He pushed back his Mets baseball cap, wiped his brow with a handkerchief from his back pocket, and continued to work. That was good. It would be a two-fer. First Mom. Then Bert.

"It's important," I said.

As Mom basket-wove, I told her what I'd found out. The air rights of the mansion. The possible deal of the century. Then I took out my notebook and read her the article about Aunt Kathleen's death from the *Daily News*. When I finished, she did not look up.

"Well?"

"I must remember to cancel my subscription to the *Daily News*." Her needle pierced the canvas.

"Mom." I put my hand over her work. "Did you know the story?"

"Bert!" Mom called out.

"Mom," I demanded. "Did you hear any of this? You were her sister. What did you know?"

Bert appeared in the doorway, a leaf falling from his pants.

"Bert," Mom said levelly, "Delia needs a ride back to the train station."

I continued addressing only Mom. "You must have thought about it. Did you have doubts?"

Bert looked from me to Mom and back again, trying to read the situation and failing. "Sure, Peggy. I didn't even know she was here. Right away." He readjusted his cap. "C'mon,

Dee."

"I'm not going anywhere. I have a right to know. If you knew the story, how come you never told me?"

Mom's eyes were flecked with sparks of green. "Bert!" There was a hint of panic in her voice. "She'll miss the three fifteen."

Bert, eyebrows going up, took my arm. I jerked away. "I found an old article in the *Daily News*," I said to him. "It read like Aunt Kathleen didn't commit suicide. It said *you* were on the scene." Bert's eyes got wide and he regrasped my upper arm with much greater force this time, reaching around to grab me on the other side as well. I felt the guy who'd cuffed and frisked and muscled his way to retirement. He was actually going to remove me, bodily if necessary.

Manhandling me across the living room, Bert got me through the door and out of the house. He released me on the porch.

"Sorry about that, pal," he panted.

I rubbed my arms. "Jesus Christ, Bert!"

"I know you're going through a lot, Dee. Losing your job and all. But I can't have you upsetting your mother like that."

"Upsetting *her*! Aunt Kathleen died twenty-two years ago, and I have to learn from an old newspaper clipping that maybe she didn't kill herself? And *you*! You were there on the scene! You never told me? What the hell, Bert?"

"Bert!" Mom sounded frantic, calling from inside the house. "The *three fifteen*!"

Bert stood. Obviously, I wasn't getting anything out of anyone today.

"Never mind. I drove myself." I brushed off my jeans.

THERE WERE TWO people in front of me at Lynbrook Audi with trade-ins. So, the process took the rest of the afternoon. Long Island Railroad chugged me back into the city, just as it had years before. I took a train and a crosstown bus to get home, feeling sweaty under my fall coat and exhausted by the time I reached the crisp Grandhope awning just after seven o'clock.

A limo idled out front.

"Miss Mulcahy," said the doorman. "Your car is waiting for you."

I peered into the smoked window of the limo. Rosary beads hung from the rearview mirror. A figure in a Mets baseball cap was reading a paper propped on the steering wheel.

Bert had followed me into town.

"Hiya, Dee." He got out and held open the door to the back seat, just as if I were an actual customer. I got in and we drove three blocks to the Parthenon deli.

The cacophony from midday had ceased, and the deli was just small clinks and murmurs. Greek music emanated from a dusty CD player.

I scooched into a booth across from Bert. He opened the binder-sized menu and addressed himself to it as if it were the morning paper. He motioned for me to take up mine. I already knew I was going to have a plain turkey sandwich. Everything upset my stomach lately. I waited for Bert to decide.

I took a deep breath, trying to arrange my thoughts. I knew I probably seemed irrational to Bert—dredging up a decades-old death. But finding out if it all had been *worth it* was not irrational to me.

In the background, I heard the radio playing something in seven-eighths time on Greek *laouta* and *bouzoukia*. I recognized the song.

It was a classic. Whenever it came on that Aegean summer, the net-mender and pistachio-sheller belted along. I learned all the lyrics, finally getting them perfect, though not understanding a word. I was particularly proud when I nailed the refrain, a complex juxtaposition of consonants.

I sotiria tis psychis einai poly megalo pragma.

The day I got it right the net-mender and the pistachio-sheller applauded.

"So what does it mean?" I asked.

"It signifies," the net-mender began, index finger to the sky, "the salvation of the soul amounts to..." He stopped. The net-mender's English was more scholarly than the pistachio-sheller's, but he sometimes petered out after a few words. He looked to his companion for help.

"It means—" the sheller took a last drag on his cigarette and threw it to the ground "—the salvation of the soul is a really big deal."

The salvation of the soul is a really big deal.

Aunt Kathleen would have liked that, I thought sadly.

As I recognized the music from long ago, I felt tears begin to sting.

"You okay, Dee?" Bert asked.

"Fine," I said, picking up my menu.

A waiter showed up with thick-lipped mugs. He sloshed coffee into one for Bert. I asked for tea. He waved at a woman who tinged down a metal pot, too hot to touch; a tea bag scalded inside.

Bert ordered a burger with bacon and fries. I got my sandwich.

"So?" I began. "You wanted to talk?"

Bert sighed heavily. "That thing you read in the news—it's a story, Dee. Nothing more. No witnesses. The suspicion about Howard Goodman, as far as the police were concerned, there was no proving anything."

"I'm not asking about the police. I'm asking about Mom. About you. What did you think?"

Bert shrugged and shook his head. "Howard Goodman is dead. Talking about it ain't gonna bring Kathleen back. What does it matter?"

"What does it matter? What does it *matter*? That Mom never talked to me about it? God, I hate her sometimes."

Bert looked like I'd punched him in the gut. "Don't say that." He took my hand and gave it a squeeze. I looked at him, unmoved. He let go of my hand. "I'm sorry. I can see how it would matter to you."

"And it doesn't matter to *Mom*? She was her sister."

Bert folded his hands in front of him, elbows on his knees. In that moment, I saw an eighteen-year-old boy, soon to be a cop, sitting in a pew that was too small for him. "Delia, here's the thing. Your mother doesn't understand what a wonderful person she is."

"Good grief." He really was hopeless.

"She's never known it. Not at seventeen. Not at twenty-seven, not at seventy. Some people—they don't think they're good enough. No matter what. That's how it was with your mom. Marrying your father made it worse, him coming from all that money." I saw a flash of fifty-year-old jealousy. "People like your mom have a hard time thinking they're good enough even to be loved. They think they'll mess it up. Especially when they have a beautiful little daughter."

A waiter bustled to the table. There was a clinking of plates on the tile surface. The edges of the bacon poking out of Bert's burger still sizzled. My turkey sandwich on white bread was accompanied by a lonely pickle.

"Whatever about Mom, Bert." I wasn't in the mood to psychoanalyze her. "What does Mom's inferiority complex have to do with anything?"

Bert took a solemn bite and chewed. "In a way, your mom blames herself for Kathleen. She thinks that she wasn't a good enough sister. That she somehow should have stopped her sister dying like that."

"Maybe that's true."

Bert put down his burger and made a frustrated fist on the table. "I'm trying to explain why your mom never told you. She doesn't know what to say. Talking about it is too much for her." I wanted to say, *Everything is too much for her,* but I didn't. "I'm not a priest or a shrink. I can't say it any better than I am."

"Okay, Bert. Fine. Maybe you're right about Mom. I still want to know *what happened.*"

Bert made a motion like trying to push his chair back, but the booth didn't budge. He folded his arms instead. "You want me to be a cop, I'll be a cop. Here's what goes on with a suicide. The landlord phones up and says, 'So and so committed suicide.' And *that* defines the situation. From that moment on, it's a suicide."

I told him what I'd learned about the real estate deal, and how Aunt Kathleen might have been standing in the way. His shoulders rose and then fell.

"I'll tell you one thing, if Goodman had a motive like that, nobody knew it at the time."

"A neighbor said Aunt Kathleen was in a dispute with her landlord."

Bert drew a hand across his head. "*Everyone* in New York is in a dispute with their landlord."

"But you didn't even try to investigate?"

"Jiminy Cricket! It was 1986! There was crack and gangs and three thousand murders a year. Three thousand, Dee. The cops didn't have time to worry about maybe a suicide's not a suicide when the landlord says it is. Then you got Goodman telling us she's *that* kind of woman."

"*What* kind of woman?"

Bert looked side to side, then uncomfortably ate a fry. "She was..."

"I *know* she was gay, Bert." His brow furrowed for a moment, and I could tell he was wondering how I knew. Then it smoothed out and I could see he was deciding it didn't matter.

"I'm not saying it was right, how everyone thought, but that's just how it was. It was a big deal back then. Someone says a woman who used to be a nun is secretly a queer? You line ten people up and they would say she was a degenerate, and that's why she committed suicide."

"So her being gay made it so the cops didn't care at all? What about you? You *knew* her!"

"I did, Dee." Bert shrugged, looked out the deli window, then back at me. He took a deep breath as if deciding something. "Your mom always thought she drank a little too much."

I felt lump in my stomach. I thought she drank a little too much, too. Bert took a moment to polish off his burger. My sandwich sat untouched.

"Look, Dee." Bert wiped his face with a napkin. "Could it

have been murder? Something with that real estate thing? Sure. It could've. I'm not saying it's not. But here's another thing I learned on the job. You never *really* know anybody. Never. Later, when I was a detective, I investigated suicides where it turned out they were really homicides. But there were also plenty of times where everyone swears they could never have done it. That the person was always whistling a happy tune. You know what? Turns out they really *did* kill themselves."

"Wow."

"And *that's* why you and me never had this conversation before. Because I can't *give* you an answer. Could it have been Howard Goodman? Sure, it could have. Could one of the cops have missed something with Goodman saying she was *that way*? Yeah. Did *I* see anything? No. You have to have a *reason* to investigate someone. Life isn't like the crime dramas and murder mysteries where there's always an answer. Unless Saint Peter rides down here on a bolt of lightning and says, 'Howard Goodman did it. It was him,' you got nothing. Why bring it up to you? Especially then. You were a little kid. You'd've been thinking there's maybe the guy out there who killed Kathleen and you couldn't do anything. Thank the Good Lord Howard Goodman died when he did. The truth died with him."

"God, Bert." It was all too hopeless. I suddenly felt spent.

"I'm really sorry, Dee." He reached across the table and patted my hand. "It's no use torturing yourself, and especially not your mom when she's made her peace with it. Better to believe what your heart tells you. Or, just forget it and say, 'God rest her soul.'"

We were silent for a few minutes together. Bert, a man with two underwater mortgages, put his hand over the check and hailed the waiter.

"How are you doing, Bert?"

Bert wrapped both of his big hands around his coffee cup. "The art market is way down. None of your mom's stuff is moving. She uses that for her pin money, you know."

Pin money was code for *what-she-lives-on*. "I know."

"Fares are way off, too. None of the finance guys are going to the airport in limos anymore."

"I wish I could…" I started. Then I didn't know what I could say.

Bert reached across the table and tugged on one of my red tendrils as if I were ten years old. "You're a good girl, Delia." *Deel-yer.* "You got your own problems. Tell you one thing, though. I'm glad you're out of that Wall Street mess. I gotta buddy in the white-collar division. They're under a lot of pressure to go after people who had their fingers in all that funny business."

Chapter Twenty-Four

It's no use going back to yesterday, because I was a different person then.

—Lewis Carroll, *Alice in Wonderland*

I COULDN'T SLEEP. Before dawn the next morning, I made my way up through Central Park to the North Woods. The best bird migration times were around Tax Day in the spring and fall. Since it was now late October, I could catch the tail end of the fall season, scores of birds taking a break from their many-thousand-mile journeys, stopping to hang out in the strip of green down the center of Manhattan.

I knew dozens of species by shape and flight style. There was the sharp W of seagulls as if just off the tip of a calligraphy brush; the anxious wing beat of ducks; the gangly herons with legs trailing like unretracted landing gear; the gruesome-eyed cormorants; the raptors with wings ending in thick splayed fingers. I could identify any number of woodpeckers, finches, mergansers, warblers, and buntings. This morning, I spotted a nuthatch and a couple of red finches, all on their way south. I jotted them in my notebook.

No one really knew why my great-grandfather fixated on birds. They were a source of endless fascination for him. Maybe it was because he spent so much of his time underground, in tunnels and transfer stations. Maybe it's that all humans dream of flying. In any case, ornithology became part of the family tradition. Some families are nautical, alpine, or horsey. We were birdy.

Aunt Kathleen thought it was important to reinforce one's heritage, so she boned up on birds. She taught me about the intelligent avian mind and how, unlike dogs or cats, birds are never truly domesticated.

These musings reminded me of the parakeet periodically fluttering through the neighborhood. I had found my sketch to compare him and, indeed, it was the same parakeet, somehow surviving, from the very first time I spotted him. He was lost, stuck out of place and out of time.

Which was a little how I felt.

I came to the park as a distraction, but thoughts of the escaped parakeet and a cold mist of rain turned my mind to its now-habitual dark course.

My conversation with Bert left me despondent.

During those first weeks of September, researching the threads about Aunt Kathleen, I experienced a kind of elation. It was a sensation I could hardly remember having since I was a child. A spark compelled me to board a plane to California, identify the warehouse, find the truth. This impulse felt different from my drive toward money. It felt like hope. Hope in what? I hardly knew. I had a conviction it would lead somewhere. If Aunt Kathleen were redeemed, might a different Delia be possible? One who was *worth it*?

Bert shut the door to that fantasy.

You never really know anybody. Never.

I had asked him to be a cop, and he had been a cop. No research about Deals of the Century, or trips to Google, or

spelunking through microfiche would give me what I wanted—
to redeem Aunt Kathleen. Howard Goodman was dead. Saint
Peter wasn't riding down on a bolt of lightning with a dispatch.
I would simply never know.

*Believe what your heart tells you. Or, just forget it and say,
'God rest her soul.'*

Could I forget it? What choice did I have? I had given up
my fortune for nothing. And that was that.

If misery loved company, I had plenty. In swaths of gleaming Midwestern Toll Brothers developments, in adobe-tinted
Nevada ex-urbs, in tidy Tudor New England cul-du-sacs of
newly renovated basements and kitchens, in Kentucky trailer
parks, Miami sky rises, Alabama golf-and-lifestyle developments, and of course, in Centerville, Long Island, where a
knight of a man mortgaged two houses to support Peggy
Condon Mulcahy—everyone was ruined. The extent of the
crisis was still unfathomed. Economists predicted it would take
until 2018 for a full recovery. A decade.

On top of everything, I knew I helped to cause it all. This
knowledge joined all my other bleak thoughts as I walked
through the dreary North Woods.

Reading the news now, I understood that there were, indeed, just a handful of people—those three or four guys and
me—with the same idea. Did they find my idea, like Gabriel,
in the footnotes? Exactly how many thesis copies had my
advisor sold? Or did we all act simultaneously like migratory
birds? It didn't matter. I was, without question, a mother of the
catastrophe.

The fact that I hadn't profited from it was a mere detail. I
couldn't claim any moral high ground. If I had returned a day
earlier, I surely would have cashed in on my brainchild. Gladly.

No question. Given the chance, I would probably do it again.

The future was both inexorable and commonplace. If millions of others had the courage to face it, I certainly could, too. I would be just another person who cut her losses, surveyed the wreckage, and decided how to begin again.

It was either that or take up needlepointing.

OUTSIDE THE GRANDHOPE a blue jumpsuit ripped up purple mums for October and replaced them with winter cabbages for November. I wondered why we were replacing purple with purple. We usually went for a color change. Angela would have something to say about this. Norah, the super at Number N, smoked a cigarette while watching them work.

I got on the elevator. Nearby, the woman with the jet-setting preschooler was talking into her cell phone.

"I usually spend a hundred with Elena for fall clothes." Elena's was the posh boutique below the consignment shop. *A hundred* meant $100,000. "Not this year. I *can* afford it, but you can't be seen with shopping bags *now*."

Inside my apartment, I took off my coat, and removed my binoculars. "Knock, knock!" Angela poked her head in. "Can I come in?"

"Sure." I sank into a chair, purchased during my Las Vegas trip by Angela, and ran a hand along my windowsill, looking out to the rose-wallpapered bedroom of my childhood, filled with embassy filing cabinets.

"I've got the documents." I took the folder from Angela. "You're lucky," she said, and I glared at her. "I don't mean lucky *that* way. What I mean is, the board *could* have said no.

We just turned down another sublet."

I sighed. I'd asked Angela to clear it for me, renting out my apartment. I couldn't support the maintenance and mortgage. I couldn't sell it either. Like every other homeowner in America, I would never get back what I paid for it.

"They're nice people," Angela said. "He's been relocated and they couldn't get their son into private school. You know how *that* is. I hired a consultant for Maddie. Anyway, these people needed a place close to P.S. 6, which is almost as good as private. They'll take it furnished."

Subletting would keep me afloat for a little while. I was keeping a spreadsheet to calculate how long I had left before my money ran out and I would be broke. According to co-op rules, I could sublet for two years.

"You're a good friend, Ange."

Angela smiled sympathetically. "Look, it's only for two years. That's plenty of time for things to turn around." I thought of the 2018 date predicted by the finance news.

"Have you figured out where you're going to live?" Angela tried to keep a smile on her face.

"I have an idea." It was one of two upcoming visits of supplication I wasn't looking forward to.

First Peter Priest; next Mom.

Chapter Twenty-Five

Only that which cannot be lost in a shipwreck is yours.

—Al-Ghazali

SEEING ME, PRIEST'S face registered a level of puzzlement that left me puzzled. For one thing, I had an appointment. Next, he must have known Hermes's fate. I was sure he kept track of his nemesis Goodman the same way Goodman kept track of him. He must have guessed I would come crawling back to him for a job.

Priest gestured to a chair as he had two years before. Behind him, the soft surface of the suede walls was blurry like stone under water. He looked thinner and seemed even more world-weary than in Las Vegas. Which didn't make sense. Odyssey had survived. Since Priest was one of the few who'd anticipated a crash, he'd amassed all the right positions against banks and housing. Even if Priest hadn't pursued my fortune-making big short, he was one of the last men standing. He should have been triumphant.

I sat. Priest did not. I tried to read him. Did he still hold a grudge that I'd rejected his job offer? Would he laugh me in the face when I asked for another chance?

"Thank you for seeing me," I said. He nodded, then went to a display case. It had coins, pumiced with age. He took one out and tossed it to me. I caught it.

"From my very first treasure hunt," he said. I fingered the medallion, which looked as if it had spent a thousand years on the sea floor. "In my day, all us boys in Greece knew how to dive."

Small talk wasn't really Priest's style. But, at least it was an opening. What's more, I had something to contribute on the topic.

"I know," I said. "I went diving with a Greek boy once."

Priest's eyebrows went up. Then he folded his long frame into his expensive chair and looked at me with intense interest while I described the summer I spent on a Greek island. I told him about the two village men who commanded the young *palikari* to take me scuba diving. A strange expression crossed his face. "Sounds crazy, I guess. I'd never been diving before. Then I just went off with some kid I didn't know."

"Did you find anything?" Priest focused on another coin from the collection, flipping it between his fingers, the way players in Las Vegas do with their chips.

"A little stone statue," I said, holding my thumb and fore-finger a few inches apart. "But the village men wouldn't let me keep it."

As it happened, the net-mender blasted my diving compan-ion with a caustic stream of Greek. I narrated this detail to Priest, using the Greek word *malakas*, "jerk," and got a rare laugh. I remembered how I'd enjoyed talking to Priest. He would have been about the same age as the *palikari*. Priest put the coin down. He leaned forward on his forearms.

"Old-timers don't like people poaching antiquities. Some think the objects should go to the national museum. Some don't trust the government at all and think they should be left where they are. Some just believe it's bad luck. The old man might have let you keep one of these." He gestured to the coin. "They're, if you'll pardon the expression, a dime a dozen." It was my turn to chuckle.

"Looks like you did a fair amount of diving." I tilted my chin at the collection of objects.

"All of us did. The Aegean is littered with artifacts. My island in particular attracted treasure hunters because there was a local tale of an ancient shipwreck."

"Oh?" I folded my hands on the desk in a gesture that said, *I'm waiting for the story.* If he liked chatting with me, he might be inclined to let bygones be bygones.

Priest leaned back. "According to legend, during Homeric times, a ship was traveling to the temple of Apollo on our island. Carrying riches from its home city as tribute to the god. Pirates attacked it. The ship sank. Centuries later, sometime in the 1970s, a few of the objects turned up on the black market."

"How did they know the objects were from that particular ship?"

"Scholars in Egypt discovered a cache of ancient writing around the same time. One account described a ship that left Asia Minor with a list of all the treasure. The items matched the description exactly."

Priest was a good storyteller. As he talked, his deep voice low, he conjured an epic world. The triremes etched in the office glass around us came alive. I remembered what Judith said, that the buildings of New York harbored half the plunder of Troy. "Poachers must have descended on your island."

"For a while. But no one ever found anything more. Our grandparents used to say they hid everything in underwater caves. Only the oldest villagers knew where the treasure was."

"And a maybe grown-up boy or two?"

Priest turned to replace his coin, and I couldn't see if he was still smiling. He swiveled back, his face now serious. "We are both treasure hunters of a kind."

So that was the point of the story. "That's true." I handed him my coin.

"I admired your particular treasure hunt."

"How do you know what I was on the hunt for, in *particular?*"

He ran his hand down the lapel of his jacket, checked cashmere across broad swimmer's shoulders and covering long arms. "You forget to whom you are speaking. Reclaiming a glorious past is one of humanity's oldest desires. I come from a culture that has been trying to do that for centuries. Since the fall of Constantinople."

Maybe Priest *did* understand. "I never thought of it in those terms."

"And I never thought I'd actually see you in my office again." Priest's tone indicated we were done with the chitchat.

"Yet, here I am."

"You'll forgive me for noting the irony in that."

I supposed I deserved that. There was nothing to do except plunge into the deep end. "I thought you might have a position for me."

Priest tossed his Blackberry on his desk. It hit the leather surface with a thunk of frustration. "Tell me this. Where's Goodman? Why isn't he taking care of you?"

"I don't know where Goodman is. Hermes folded. Why would Goodman take care of me?" I stammered. Then my mind caught up with his implication. I remembered the phone conversation with Priest after I rejected his job offer. Priest accused Goodman and me of mixing *business and pleasure.*

"You spotted my talent," I said quickly. "What makes you think he couldn't?"

Priest let out a scoff. "Because I *know* Goodman."

"We were never involved," I said. "Goodman was *not* interested in me," I added determinedly, though his attraction had been obvious.

He laughed under his breath. "You're not a very good liar, Delia. How things ended with you and Goodman is none of my business." He was clearly not buying the story Goodman and I weren't lovers. "However, what happened in September *is* my business."

"How can you say…?" I started. But Priest was on his phone, talking over me.

"Then *find* him," he finished into the receiver, slammed the phone down, and looked at me as if he wanted to say more. After a silent moment, he left the room.

It was all too jumbled. The banter about scuba diving, his enthralling legend, his quick change of attitude, his seeming obsession about me and Goodman. It reminded me of a phrase Aunt Kathleen liked. About jealousy, but I couldn't bring it to mind just now. My male radar didn't seem to work with Priest, leaving me to wonder—was it possible *he* was attracted to me?

I had no idea what would happen next. I was not getting a job; that seemed obvious. Or was I? He didn't tell me to leave. Who was Priest so urgent to find? I sat and waited, bewildered.

The door opened, and Priest re-entered with a man behind him. His companion was wearing a short-sleeved button-down shirt, brown tie shoes and aviator glasses.

As he had when we first met in Las Vegas.

Chapter Twenty-Six

For when the One Great Scorer comes to write against your
   name,
He marks—not that you won or lost—but how you played
   the game.
   —Grantland Rice "Alumnus Football"

"GABRIEL!" I GASPED. I looked from him to Priest, my
mind grappling for understanding.

"Go ahead," Priest directed Gabriel. "Tell her."

"I'm sorry, Delia." Gabriel shifted uncomfortably. "Mr.
Priest didn't want you to know."

The years 2007 to 2008 telescoped in my mind. Gabriel
introducing himself to me at the Las Vegas conference. His
extensive knowledge of me and my work. The unknown
backer. The overriding need for me and only me. The completely unorthodox financial arrangement. It made perfect
sense. I was blind to the obvious.

Goodman had Mitch Mitchell as a henchman. Priest had
Gabriel.

It was so beautifully and diabolically simple. When I turned
down Priest's offer, he found another way to "hire" me. Clever.
Brilliant even.

"You used me," I said, stating the obvious. "I suppose I was an easy target."

"I was trying to *help* you!" Priest's deep voice barked so angrily I jumped. His black eyes glittered. "I *knew* Goodman didn't get it. He would never appreciate what you discovered. I formed Corning as a separate trading group. I told Gabriel to find you."

"You talk like *you* didn't get anything out of it." I thought of all the effort I'd put into Corning and all the money Priest must have made.

"It was a fair exchange," Gabriel put in, palms up. "You had *no* risk. We got the benefit of your knowledge, and you would get..." Gabriel stopped. "I don't understand. You left *millions* on the table. You just disappeared. Why?"

Priest was the last person on earth to whom I would explain why I'd disappeared—my foolish trip to California in search of the truth about Aunt Kathleen. I felt duped and defeated.

"I guess," I said bitterly, "you were able to overcome your *ethical qualms*. You know. The polar bears and all."

"I did *not* overcome my objections." Priest slapped a palm on his desk with a *thwack*. "I did it anyway. *For you.* It was your idea and you deserved to profit off it. Because..." He dragged a frustrated hand through his hair. "You were going to be ruined at Hermes."

Was Priest actually trying to convince me he wanted to help me out of the goodness of his heart? People didn't act that way. Moreover, Wall Street people didn't act that way. "Bullshit," I said.

Priest pressed both his fists on the desk in a clear effort to keep from pounding it. "When I found your thesis, I *knew* what it meant. What the consequences would be. I was planning to hire you and take it *off* the market."

I sucked in a shocked breath. "You were going to buy my work and do *nothing*?"

"It sounds naïve now. Like trying to put the genie back in the bottle. You were right when you said I was deluding myself that I could avoid the corruption in this business. There is no way to avoid it."

"So, then, Corning?"

"I couldn't stand the fact that you were working for Goodman. As I've told you, I know him well. You—with all your ambition, your dreams, and your brilliant idea. It was all going to be wasted. Worse. I knew you wouldn't be able to convince him to do anything to prepare for the crash. He's too cocky. I thought you deserved a chance. *That's* how I justified my hypocrisy. I formed Corning, knowing that..." He looked out the window. I could see he understood the enormity of what he'd unleashed with the power of my idea.

"You must have made a fortune."

I ran quick math in my head. At eighty to one, Priest made billions.

Priest looked at me fiercely. If I were a guy, I thought, he'd probably slug me right now. "*Trianta argyria,*" he spat, leaving me to figure out the Greek.

My brain stretched for the words. It came up with *thirty pieces of silver.*

"I'm liquidating Odyssey," he said.

My job hopes evaporated.

Priest walked back to the windows. Gabriel stood silent and serious, looking at his hands.

My head hurt trying to process it all. Dissolving Odyssey. I could hardly fathom it. In fact, I couldn't fathom anything about this strange, inscrutable man. Even if I understood, though, there was no point. My objective with him was finished. "I'll leave then," I said.

"One moment." Priest turned to Gabriel, telegraphing something Gabriel understood.

"Here." Gabriel handed me a card. It said, *Vista Equities*. "That's where I'll be going. A new fund. Forming now. You can call in January." Gabriel looked at Priest and he gestured dismissively with his hand. "I'm sure Mr. Priest will provide a recommendation. With that, they'll be eager to interview you."

Chapter Twenty-Seven

When sorrows come, they come not single spies,
But in battalions.

—William Shakespeare, *Hamlet*

BACK AT THE Grandhope, my mind churned as I went back and forth over my strange interlude with Priest and Gabriel. Tide in. Tide out. Thoughts lapping to and fro like waves, working the edges off stones, breaking them down into sand, and buffing ancient coins into worn discs.

Priest was exotic and unreadable. How could I make sense of him and his motives?

There was no denying he was a money man. And I was a cynic. These basic facts reinforced the theory that Priest and Gabriel had simply run a con on me. Priest wanted my specialized knowledge, and he came up with a clever plan to get it.

But Priest had seemed sincere when he said he admired my quest. I remembered his palpable concern for me in Las Vegas when he said, *Protect yourself.* I had to admit it was possible Peter Priest tried to save me.

I also had to concede there was some *thing* between us. I'd felt it from our first encounter. Our conversations took unexpected turns such as those involving polar bears and treasure hunts. Whatever this *thing* was, it was a different kind of thing from my pattern with men. Goodman's style of electric arousal and frank appreciation—I was more accustomed to that. Priest admired me in a way I hadn't experienced before. What did it mean? Maybe he envisioned other possible outcomes, such as Corning making me rich, Priest disclosing he was the author of my fate, and the spark between us turning into a flame.

If that was what he'd planned, it had failed. My foolish quest to California on the day the news came out about Lehman had been the wildcard. As I left his office, Priest made no effort to suggest any future connection. Was he disappointed in me for my failure at the critical moment? Was he disgusted with me for prompting him to execute a strategy that violated his own moral code? Or was he simply burned out and exhausted by Wall Street and everything it stood for? Whatever the case, as I left, Priest turned away as if he were sick of the sight of me.

At least I had a job prospect. A new hedge fund, where, with Priest's recommendation, I was a shoo-in. It wouldn't be Hermes-style money. Nothing would be for a long while. But I could pick up the pieces and go on with my life. Perhaps, by spring, the crash would feel like a massive setback but one that could be overcome. I let the sense of relief wash over me, soaking in it like a warm bath after backbreaking work.

A few days went by when Angela called.

"Your subletters contacted me. They haven't heard from you and their kid needs to start the term in January. What's the matter, Dee? It's not like you to forget."

It really wasn't like me to forget. Maybe, like Priest, I was experiencing my own burnout. I would have loved to just bury all the fall's events, pick up at another hedge fund, and pretend like nothing happened. I remember feeling that way when we lost all our money and Aunt Kathleen died—wanting things to magically go back *to the way they used to be.*

But, as confident as I was that the job at Vista Equities would materialize, I didn't yet have an offer. I hadn't even met them. I needed to act. I had ready and willing subletters approved by the co-op board. Before I signed the arrangement, however, I needed to make that second unpleasant trip of supplication.

I told Angela I would contact the subletters in the morning, after I went to Centerville. This was a tough one, because I hated asking Mom for anything.

"Hmmm," Mom said as she wound embroidery yarn into loose skeins. "That's an interesting idea. I could get a break from paying rent. Art sales have been dreadful since the downturn."

Living in Mom's Number-N apartment was the ideal solution. Her rent was frozen in time, inching up just the tiniest percentage (controlled by law) every few years since 1969. The ample two-bedroom now stood at $419 a month. Apartments in Birmingham, Alabama, were more expensive.

"Your mom is really happy to be able to help." Bert handed me a Coke and looked at Mom as if willing her to say something nurturing. "You'll get back on your feet soon." I wondered how Bert's feet were doing, with two mortgages now deeply under water.

"I hope so." I didn't mention the January job prospect. For one, I was a little superstitious, and didn't want to jinx it. For two, Bert said he was glad I was getting away from Wall Street. And for three, the disclosure might decrease the sympathy factor, now in my favor, for moving into Mom's apartment. After all, the place *was* empty.

Mom made a neat knot in a piece of yarn binding a skein. "I'll also be happy not to pay the electric bills."

"Great," I said. Bert, of course, was the one footing the bills.

Mom put her yarn down and looked at me. "I really don't want to bother with any paperwork. I'll call Norah about the arrangements." Mom was protecting her own interests. My name on a sublet would start a ticking time bomb.

It was that quirk in the rent-control law, the rule on succession rights. After some time in residence, a first-degree relative—husband, wife, sister, brother, son or daughter—could make a claim on the lease. Which would complicate any potential buyout deal. Mom didn't trust me. In her weird, reclusive world, she probably didn't trust anyone, other than Bert.

"Fine," I said. "No paperwork."

⌒⌒

I STOOD FOR a moment outside Number N. The rim of the awning frayed like a hobo's cuff. The entrance was dimly lit. The floor was black-speckled stone, and the walls were painted the color of skin, that creepy, peachy institutional hue of hospital halls, high school gyms, and mental wards.

The elevator had a circular porthole window with wire mesh behind the glass. I pressed B for basement, and the carriage clunked into motion. The basement hallway smelled of Clorox, and black boxes of rat poison lurked in all the corners.

Norah's office door said, "Superintendent." Under this title was a long poster, produced by the City of New York entitled, "Know Your Rat Facts."

Know Your Rat Facts

Myth: Cat-sized rats live in NYC.
    Fact: Most rats weigh no more than two pounds.

Myth: Subways and sewers are rat havens.
    Fact: Most rats live in buildings at basement level.

Myth: Rats are immune to poison.
    Fact: Rats choose not to eat poison because of the supply of residential garbage.

Myth: Cats, dogs, and hawks control city rats.
    Fact: Only people can make the difference.

Was the city trying to make me feel better or worse about rats? I knocked on Norah's office door.

Her lips were bright with pink-orange lipstick and her hair was dyed the color of fox. She wore a fuchsia blouse and sat at a long, slanted draftsman's desk. Her floor-to-ceiling shelves were stocked with plungers, spare doorknobs, hammers, boxes of screws, light bulbs of all imaginable sizes, window screens, and dozens of paint cans, drips frozen on their sides.

"Well." She swiveled to look at me, taking a sizzling drag on her cigarette. "The apple doesn't fall far from the tree." She squinted into the smoke. "But sometimes it does. Then it rolls into a fucking ditch."

"Meaning what, exactly?" I waved away her smoke.

"Meaning I hope you and your Wall Street crowd all go to shagging fuck the way you fucked the whole fucking world." Norah flicked ash at me.

"I'm wiped out too." I toed ash off my sneaker.

"Who gives a fuck about you? You made your fucking bed. Now we all have to lie in it. One good thing: it'll bring us back to good old days, like '78 when the city went bankrupt. We didn't have all these fucking billionaires. You appreciated the little things then, like getting through a day without being mugged." Norah ground out the cigarette in a ceramic ashtray that said O'Neill's Pub around its chipped edge.

"I lost the point of this story. Was the crash good or bad?"

"Wouldn't you fucking like to know?"

"I'm just here about the apartment."

Norah took a set of keys off a pegboard that hosted dozens of them. "I know why you're here."

I explained about no paperwork. Norah snorted and flicked her hot-pink lighter. "Isn't that lovely? Your mother thinks you'll try to claim the lease. You're a pair, the two of you."

That was the opposite of true. Mom and I weren't a pair in *anything*. "As long as we're clear," I said.

"Fine with me. Why should I give a fuck?"

"No reason."

"I'm not doing this for you or for your mother. I'm doing it for Kathleen. She was a good woman. A great hand at cards. None of you deserved her."

I couldn't argue with that.

Norah handed me the key to 13B, and, with a flick of her Zippo lighter, sent me on my way.

THE CREEPY SKIN-COLORED paint extended down the thirteenth-floor hall and wrapped inside apartment B. A scratchy red tartan couch. A rocking chair with a light blue floral seat cushion held on by bows. A wingchair in purple and pink chevron. A painted yellow bookcase with religious books inside and a tribe of Saint Francis statues on top. The décor, left by Aunt Kathleen, was rectory parlor, circa 1976. Pea-green-and-orange medallions embossed the linoleum kitchen floor. On the bookcase, I spotted the spine of a familiar chartreuse volume, my favorite saint's story as a child.

Aunt Kathleen's presence hit me like a tangible force. I veritably smelled her scent—a combination of cigarettes and L'air du Temps. The sensation was nostalgic and excruciating. I would probably never be able to resolve *who* she was, the Aunt Kathleen who committed suicide, or the Aunt Kathleen who was murdered. Still, whoever she was, it was imprinted on me as if I were a bird hatched in her nest.

The décor and the smell—real or imagined—cast me back into my memories of this apartment as a child.

Aunt Kathleen prepared peanut butter and jelly, while I played a game of finding animal shapes in the lurid linoleum. She packed our sandwiches, and we went to a hallway where there was a door leading to the roof. Aunt Kathleen swiped down a key from the lintel and unlocked the door.

The roof was another world, forested by great water towers, TV antennae, and air-conditioning equipment. Aunt Kathleen arranged two web-and-aluminum lawn chairs on the tarpaper surface, and we ate our sandwiches admiring the view over the rooftops and into the mansion garden below. She liked to come up here on her own, even after dark. With the livid mercury lamp, it was bright enough to read, she said. I used to look out my window for her in her lawn chair. It felt like she was watching over me.

After our Number-N roof lunch, we returned home to the

mansion. I went to my room to retrieve cards for gin. Coming back, I heard a whispered argument on the stairs.

"She's spending too much time over there," Mom said.

"Don't be silly, Peggy. It's just lunch."

"Delia is *my* daughter, and she lives *here*."

"Okay, Peggy. Okay," Aunt Kathleen soothed.

"Good." I saw Mom peck Aunt Kathleen on the cheek, then click down the stairs in her heels.

"What's *she* so mad about?" I asked, catching up to Aunt Kathleen.

Aunt Kathleen raised her eyebrow at my tone but decided to let it go. "Well, Delia, jealousy isn't the best way to show love. But it *is* one way." I looked at her, puzzled, and she tweaked one of the plastic-balled elastics tying my braids. "Your mother loves you. That's all." I shrugged. I knew Mom loved me in her own weird way.

I recalled Mom arranging silverware at my doll tea parties and the special care she took with my clothes and hair. This was her parenting comfort zone—fussy, particular, and related to looks and entertaining. It was as if, in this rarefied atmosphere of my father's social class, she forgot her instinct on how to mother. Mom might have been quite comfortable raising a brood in a two-family home in Flushing Meadows. But she had given birth to an heiress. Sometimes she acted as if she were a little afraid of me.

Aunt Kathleen was immune to any considerations of money and social class. She had an unerring sense of everything a child needed. Whatever gaps Mom left, she filled as easily as water flowing into void spaces.

After the argument between Mom and Aunt Kathleen on the stairs, I spent less time at Number N. The memories of the place never faded, though. I would be living here now, and I would need to get used to Aunt Kathleen's presence all around me.

I raised the blinds of 13B with an emphatic *zzzip*. The living room window was large, multi-paned and needed a good washing. It looked over empty window boxes. They were illegal—due to the same law, Local Law 11, that made co-op board president Sandy Roache rich. Ad hoc façade attachments were prohibited. But, since no one cared about city codes at Number N, the window boxes stayed.

A flash of green and yellow caught my eye once again. The green boughs of the alley tree were autumn golden, so it took me a minute to spot him. The parakeet fluttered amid the tree branches of the Number-N courtyard, then swooped and landed in the window box.

I noticed there was an air exhaust vent from Aunt Kathleen's stove pointing at the window box. That explained how he'd lasted all this time. The story about the parrots on Mom's needlepoint housewarming gift was that they escaped from a pet-store shipment in the 1960s at Kennedy Airport then nested in Brooklyn telephone poles because the transformer boxes kept them warm. This parakeet, like the Brooklyn ones, had found a small microclimate made by a window box and a stove vent. He blinked at me with his harlequin face.

Looking past the bird, through the boughs of the leafy tree, I saw directly into the living room of apartment 13A. As with many apartment buildings, Number N was shaped like a horseshoe, a courtyard separating the two ends, apartments on either side facing each other as in the movie *Rear Window*.

In 13A, a dark-haired woman with hazel eyes and a small blond child peered back at me. Cardboard boxes rose around the pair like stalagmites. I only had a second to take in the scene. The woman, startled to see motion in the long-dormant 13B, grasped the cord of her own blinds and spun them closed.

That was the hoarder Judith talked about. I remembered her saying hoarders could cause trouble for landlords if they wanted to get them out. The 13A neighbor could be a real hitch in Mom's buyout plan.

That is, if Rob Goodman himself ever wanted to redevelop. Without the air rights, he could only rebuild on the same footprint, which, he said, wasn't worth it. My old mansion, the only adjacent building with air rights, was now an embassy. Acquiring its air rights would involve no less than a treaty with the EU.

I wondered what Goodman would do next. I thought of Vista Equities. Hedge funds would again rise from the ashes. Maybe Goodman himself was contemplating a new one. He might call me. Even if he did, it was a better idea to make a fresh start at Vista.

I took one last look around at the place, which emanated Aunt Kathleen from all of its fibers, then locked the door to 13B and returned to the Grandhope, thinking it was a good thing I didn't need to move until January and reminding myself I was lucky to have a near-certain job.

❧

SINCE IT WAS November, I had a pile of mail including holiday catalogs, year-end appeals from museums and foundations, also two Christmas cards. Even two was a surprising number, since, other than Angela, I didn't really have friends. One was from Mom, in Bert's handwriting. The other was from my dentist.

I opened my door, and, with my arms full of mail, couldn't close it behind me.

"Hello, Angela," I said, sensing her presence as I put the mail down. Angela hadn't returned my key from the renovation she'd supervised.

"I'm not stalking you." Angela was ensconced on the tan microfiber couch she'd picked for me. She drew her hand over it as if admiring how practical it was.

"Yes, you are."

"I was finished at Judith's early, so I decided to wait for you." Angela also had Judith's keys, making her like the *gaoler* of the sixth floor.

"I'm amazed how you keep that up with her." I grew weary of Judith after a few minutes. She was such a conspiracy theorist, always posing questions like whether you thought a pharmaceutical cabal was secretly in control of the soda pop industry. I never did ask her whether she was the one quoted in the *Daily News* article. After my conversation with Bert, it seemed moot.

"I *want* her apartment," Angela said. "She and I have an agreement."

"Right," I said, trying to ignore how vulture-like that sounded. It was one thing to *have* such an agreement; it was another to advertise it. One day, the walls would reverberate as Angela broke through to Judith's. As I absently began sorting mail, a question occurred to me. "Why didn't you buy *this* apartment when it came up for sale? Then, when Judith's gone, you could have had three together." What a Vermeer that would have been!

"Couldn't," Angela said, picking up my mother's needle-point pillow of the green parrots and admiring it lovingly. "Co-op rules. Someone has to *live* in the apartment if you own it. I can't very well live in my place and another one at the end of the hall."

"Mmm." Judith really was a wrench in her plans since Judith's place was in the middle. "I assume you have the papers." I gestured to the folder in Angela's hand that contained the two-year sublet agreement authorized by the co-op board. The renters would pay me ten grand a month, which, stratospheric number that it was, did not quite cover my monthly nut of mortgage and maintenance, a sum approaching fourteen thousand.

"Yep."

I sliced a finger on the envelope of a credit-card offer that was ingeniously disguised as results from a medical lab. "Ouch." I sucked on the paper cut. Angela passed me a tissue.

"But."

"But what?"

I nearly threw away another letter, thinking it was a scam disguised as certified mail. It *was* certified mail.

"But the subletters really want to move in sooner," Angela finished.

"I don't know about that, Ange," I said. Less than an hour ago I was at Number N. With all the memories the place held, I needed to gird my loins to move there in January. "Didn't you say there's a kid who has to finish the school term?" I was now distracted by the certified letter. The doorman had signed for it.

"It's the dad," Angela said.

I succeeded in prying open the certified mail envelope and left a fingerprint of blood on it. The letterhead said Drucker & Garrett. A law firm. Why was their name familiar?

"What about the dad?" I asked reflexively while scanning.

"He's commuting up from Richmond. It's killing him."

"Uh-huh." I remembered Drucker & Garret was the Hermes law firm.

"He wants to move here ahead of the family." Angela's voice faded as I separated a cover letter from a thick accompanying form. The form said, "Settlement Agreement."

My eyes latched on to phrases. *SEC violations, improper practices,* and *trading ban.*

"He'd like to be here next week."

"Right." I turned cold and read on.

Dear Ms. Mulcahy,

Hermes Fund LLC has reached an agreement with the Securities and Exchange Commission and with the Attorney General of the State of New York regarding allegations of improper trading practices at Hermes including, but not limited to, insider trading, dealing on advance information, commonly known as front-running, and other illegal activities. The agreement, which requires acceptance of its terms by Hermes Management and senior trading staff, contains the following stipulations:

- *That managers Robert M. Goodman and Mitchell J. Mitchell each pay a fine of $2 million dollars.*
- *That all senior staff members known to be implicated in the alleged activities, Rafael X. Acosta, Tyler D. Broadhead, Athina G. Brooks, Jan W. Feltre, David L. Greer, Brigid M.C. Mulcahy, and Matthew P. Preston accept 2-year bans on trading and other financial-advisory and financial-management activities.*

The agreement is attached for your signature. Our office may be contacted for questions.

Angela put her hand over the letter. "You're not listening to me, Dee." I could feel my color returning and my body flooding with heat as my heart sped up. "I'm afraid if you don't agree, they'll lose interest and go looking for a sublet somewhere else. Lots of Wall Street people can't afford their apartments now."

I looked at Angela and felt as if the rotation of the earth had stopped. "Tell them yes."

Chapter Twenty-Eight

"The only way not to think about money is to have a great deal of it."

"You might as well say that the only way not to think about air is to have enough to breathe."

—Edith Wharton, *The House of Mirth*

I WENT TO Number N that very afternoon, wandering over blindly from the Grandhope. In my panic and confusion, I couldn't think what else to do. Alone in Aunt Kathleen's apartment, trying to calm myself, I sat on kitchen floor looking for animal shapes in the linoleum. My mind spooled through thoughts, like a computer cron job run amok. There would be no Vista Equities job in January. There wouldn't be any finance job in January. Or the next.

In on ten. Out on ten.

I used the contact number for Drucker & Garrett. An associate seemed prepared for my call. The SEC investigators, she said, had subpoenaed emails and trading records. There was incontrovertible evidence of insider trading. Hermes management immediately offered to make a deal. Negotiations were swift. I could, of course, engage my own attorney and try to strike my own independent agreement.

Sure, I thought. *With what non-existent money?*

I remembered Bert telling me about his buddy in white-collar crimes who was under pressure to get indictments. I thought of all the insider-information emails I'd seen and the ones I'd sent—like the one to Mitchell telling him that Bear was going under. Of *course,* there was incontrovertible evidence. We had done everything alleged and worse. The associate said the feds weren't going after the big banks, because they were in bed with the government. She told me I was lucky. There could have been a lifetime ban, or fines for the traders, or jail time. She seemed proud of the work they had done to negotiate this "favorable" settlement.

I was sure she was right.

But what would I do for two years? How would my money hold out? I needed to go back to my spreadsheet, which I hadn't looked at since my visit with Priest. How far under water was my apartment? Would I have to declare bankruptcy? What would that do to future job prospects? The media was reporting companies now required a credit check before hiring you.

My breath growing shallow, I opened my laptop to do financial projections.

The crash wiped out the half million dollars in bonus money I had in Hermes when the hedge fund went under. I went down to twenty-three thousand stashed in savings. Then I sold my car, which brought me back up to thirty five. Which was all I had to ride out the storm. Subletting my apartment would slow the bleeding but would not stop it.

The math was inexorable. The subletters were covering ten grand of the Grandhope expenses, leaving another four thousand. There was $419 a month in Number-N rent, a couple hundred in electricity, the same in food. That meant my total monthly burn was just under $5,000. As for income, after a bit of poking around, I signed up on eLance for some helpdesk and website gigs at $27 an hour. My calculations suggested I might piece together freelance income of about $1200 a month.

I clicked the button to graph what the future would hold.

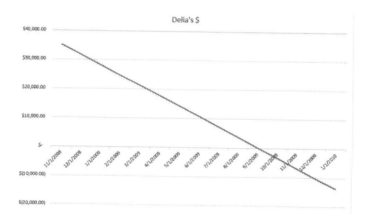

I would be dead broke by Labor Day 2009.

I tapped away, working the numbers. What if I got more freelance work? On the income side, I factored in another $300 a month. This squeezed a few additional weeks out of my resources, not the years I needed for my trading ban to expire.

I picked up the phone to call Sarah, feeling nauseated.

"Two million," I said after a few preliminaries. "I'll sell it for that." I had paid $2.2 million. But, in my situation, I had to lowball right out of the gate. This amount would pay off my outstanding mortgage and I'd be out from under the apartment.

"I might get you one-point-eight," she answered.

"Oh my God." If I was only getting one-point-eight million for the apartment, I was two hundred thousand dollars under water. Where would I ever come up with that money? "But I can't sell at one-point-eight. That doesn't cover my outstanding mortgage."

"Welcome to today's real estate market."

"Everybody's saying New York real estate has held up well," I objected.

"It's frozen up like the Arctic." Sarah's once-chipper voice had the tone of a burnt-out emergency room nurse. "And it's gonna stay that way for a good long time. Buyers won't pay prerecession prices when houses in Florida are going for ten grand. Sellers are insulted at the offers so they won't sell. People will just sit and wait. Of course, if you've got an apartment for twenty million, things are great. There are still bidding wars."

"What do I do?"

"Try foreclosure."

"But if I went into foreclosure, the bank would probably only get one-point-eight at auction anyway. It's *the same.*"

"Doesn't make sense, now does it?"

"Isn't there any other option?"

"Join a protest." Sarah paused. "Listen, Delia," she said, tone changing. "Understand one thing: you will *not* get the two-point-two million you paid for that apartment. You will *not* get two million. Maybe—*maybe*—I could get you one-point-nine if someone, for some crazy reason, wants *that* specific apartment. Someone in that situation might pay a *little* more." It was a bit of the old Sarah, the one who had been so italic about everything. "I'm not sure *who* would pay above market or *why*, but *you* did."

I felt the sting of that. "Yeah."

"All I'm saying is I'll keep my eyes open."

I hung up. The bird in his window box gave me two mechanical blinks.

My next call was to Telefony, the call center outfit in Minneapolis. The HR woman, sounding beleaguered, told me their VC funds had dried up and the thirty-something CEO was working on a plan to reinvent the firm. She advised me to check back, maybe next summer.

My thoughts swirling, I moved from the floor of the kitchen to the floor in the living room and numbly read spines on the bookcase, landing on *The Lives of the Saints.* This uplifting anthology was full of martyrs who were stoned, crucified, bound to moving wheels, flayed, immolated, scourged, branded, dismembered, disemboweled, de-toothed, buried alive, and boiled in oil.

There was also the thin chartreuse volume, the saint's story I'd liked as a child.

On top of the bookcase Aunt Kathleen's Francis statues paraded as if mocking me. Francis was heir to a family fortune, but he'd given it all up for a life conversing with birds. Unlike me, Francis had done it voluntarily. The avatars were small, cheap, and uncanny-valley, as if made by Madame Tussaud. One of them looked like a drag queen.

The blinds of my across-the-alley neighbor, Viviane the Hoarder, were closed tight. She was clearly hating the fact that I would now be in residence. With Mom "living" here (quotes stet), there was no need for Viviane to guard her privacy. As I watched, fingers appeared around the edge of the blinds, and a section of pale face, hazel iris and dark hair peeked out. Our eyes met. She disappeared.

I sat there as dark descended. I didn't turn on the lights. After a while, I heard a rustling at my door. I opened it and looked right and left. Then I saw there was a piece of notebook paper taped to the peephole. It was scrawled in Magic Marker and said, "Eat the Rich."

So, it began. On top of everything else, while at Number N, I was to be the poster child for the 1 percent. The author of the note could have been any of the tenants. Viviane the Hoarder, the yoga instructor on six, the former soap opera star on seven, the second-floor Korean woman from the nearby dry cleaner's, or one of the fifth-floor Brazilian dog walkers.

But it was probably Norah.

I lay on Aunt Kathleen's single bed, with its cream chenille bedspread, the sort I last saw on a Catholic school retreat. The bedroom window had views into the garden where Aunt Kathleen landed.

I fell asleep eventually, slept fitfully, then woke easily in the early morning.

A frantic restlessness enveloped me before I was even fully awake. It's like the day after you are fired, when you decide to call up everyone you know. Or how, on getting a dire diagnosis, you visit doctor after doctor, just to feel like you are *doing* something about the situation when, really, there is nothing you can do at all.

I opened eLance and put in some bids on some jobs. Then, rather than stare at the screen, I went to the Grandhope to pack.

As I was packing, I had an idea.

⌒⌒

AN ARROW POINTED up to *Viviane's Consignment*. I carried the sartorial bounty of my now-past hedge-fund days: six pairs of shoes, each costing over a thousand dollars; a suit from Barneys that originally retailed for thirty-five hundred; a cocktail dress, designed by a favorite of Kate Middleton, which set me back six grand; and the $1,800 Prada handbag. Since Viviane was my new neighbor, consigning my clothes with her was a way of raising some much-needed cash and extending an olive branch at the same time.

Elena, the proprietress of the dead-quiet ground-floor boutique, stood in the back among racks of clothes; she wore an expression that simultaneously conveyed both boredom and terror. Customers were lacking in all the street-level Madison Avenue shops, even as the holidays approached. In contrast, the upper-floor consignment shops were thriving, as post-crash Wall Street wives consigned their practically new Hermès handbags and consorts of Russian oligarchs snapped them up. I clambered up the stairway, lugging my shopping bags. A bell tinkled my entrance. Carousels arranged by color created spectra of skirts, dresses, blouses, blazers and slacks. White tags with handwritten prices dangled from sleeves.

"Be right there!" Viviane called from the clothing thicket.

I looked around, wondering what the consignment price was for size-nine Christian Louboutin boots. At least, with consignment, I could get some money back for my clothes. Not so for all those thirty-five-dollar bagels, leased show horses ($35,000), car-garage expenses ($875/month), and sushi takeout ($183—just for me).

She of the hazel eyes, dark hair, and mountain range of boxes emerged between the clothes racks, a tagging gun in hand.

"Oh!" Viviane stopped short. "Hi." The greeting landed with the splat of a sodden tennis ball.

"Gucci, Prada, and Loro Piana." I removed ostrich skin

loafers, a calfskin satchel in scarlet, and a cashmere sweater-coat so creamy you could eat it.

"Sorry. I'm not buying Italian just now," Viviane said.

The racks around me were dripping with Milanese wares. Viviane must have received the memo from Norah that I was persona non grata. "It appears you are," I countered.

"Last year." Viviane smiled steadily.

"I must have *something* you're in the market for."

"I don't think so." Viviane squeezed the grip of the label gun, and a plastic strand pierced a blouse cuff.

I folded the sweater-coat. My skin remembered the lush nap. Thousand-dollar clothes really *did* feel different from mid-priced togs. "Just so you know, I'm wiped out, too."

"Am I supposed to feel sorry for you?"

"You're supposed to run a business." People's hypocrisy amazed me. "Everything in here was bought with Wall Street money."

"Wives." Viviane wrote $300.00 on the label for a silk blouse with *Bergdorf Goodman* inside its collar.

I guessed everyone had to make a stand somewhere, drawing an arbitrary, uncrossable line. I left for her competitor down the street.

⌒

BACK AT AUNT Kathleen's apartment, I plugged $1,450 into my spreadsheet—what I would receive for my clothes *if* they sold. The consignment shop down from Viviane seemed optimistic about the handbag and textiles, less so about the shoes.

Next, I scanned my eLance dashboard. A physical therapist

had a website contact form that needed debugging. I claimed the job and spent the next ninety minutes picking through bad phone, address, and email validation code. After that, the physical therapist wanted me to update their appointment sign-up form. Four hours later, I had made $108.

As the day waned, I looked out the window. The bird huddled in a corner of the window box, head tucked deeply into his wing. It was November now, with temperatures in the forties. He looked cold. That was sad.

As the apartment darkened, my frenzied energy began to drain away, as I knew it would, leaving behind a dull apathy laced with fear. There was nothing to do but wait and wait some more. Ironically, that's what I thought last summer, before the crash. Back then, I was anticipating a huge triumph and the restoration of my fortune.

Now?

I had no idea what the future held. How bad would the recession be? Would Telefony have a job for me next summer? At the moment, the call center was my only prospect—my best-case scenario. I would leave New York and move to Minneapolis. It would be as if I'd wound the clock back to when I was living in Florida, in bed with Eric, planning to take the Telefony job in the first place. Except now, I was two million dollars in debt and had utterly failed at redeeming my past.

What if my finances gave out and my apartment went into foreclosure? With that on my credit record, any and all job prospects would evaporate. Would the Telefony opportunity come through before that happened?

My breath started to shorten again. I controlled it more easily now, like a passenger on a thrashing ship who gradually becomes immune to seasickness. My cell phone rang. I was so focused in my bodily restraint efforts, I answered it without checking the number.

Eugene.

Shit.

Right after my meeting with Peter Priest, I'd planned to call him up and tell him the good news. With a job in January, I could take over Whitey's board! Now, I had nothing to offer.

Eugene sounded at the end of his rope. Since the crash, his wife had started divorce proceedings. "Whitey's all I've got," he said. "But I have to sell him."

"I'm broke too, Eugene." I told him about the trading ban.

"I wouldn't even want any money for him."

"Eugene, you're not listening. I can't."

He paused. "You know so much about horses, Delia. Do you have any ideas on how I can make money with him?"

"Eugene…"

"I was thinking how you were teaching him to drive."

"You can't be serious."

"It's just I can't bear…" His sentence trailed off. But I knew what he couldn't bear. The headlines in equine websites were grim. Horses, from fancy show mounts to backyard ponies, were being dumped on federal land to starve. If these animals were being abandoned, Whitey had no chance. He was gelded and had homicidal tendencies. The most humane thing to do would be to euthanize him. If I had come to this conclusion, so had all the other horse people around Eugene, and they had told him so.

"I'm sorry, Eugene. I have to go."

I hung up the phone and let my head sink into my hands. The Hungarian effort I'd put into redeeming that cursed beast—it seemed like the only thing I'd done in the last two years that mattered. But magnificent Whitey would soon be put down. This was the thought that broke me. I shattered into tears.

I sobbed and sobbed, crying myself to sleep in a way I hadn't since Sorrows.

Chapter Twenty-Nine

It's no use crying over spilt milk; it only makes it salty for the cat.

—Anonymous

THE SUPER PIONEER grocery store on the Grand Concourse in the Bronx was running a special on chicken. The round trip took me three hours, rolling my wire cart through the slushy March streets and onto two different trains, but it saved me thirty-five dollars.

Walking from the subway toward my block, I heard hubbub on 81st Street. A movie shoot. New York was a perpetual film set, and spring TV production was in full swing. White trailers lined both sides of the street. Each week from now until summer, they would clog up streets and avenues at night, taking up parking spaces, and filling the sidewalks with long buffets of fruit, kale, and quinoa for the cast, crew, and nimble-fingered Number N-ers.

I stopped to see if I could recognize any stars. I saw a woman who sometimes played the mother of murder victims. Other times she was the perpetrator.

I collected my Number-N mail and got on the elevator. The thirteenth floor clunked into view. Another message dangled from my door. It had the cut-out lettering TV shows use for ransom notes. It said,

WHeRe'$ mY bAiLouT

Norah was still at it. I ripped off the note. Inside, I threw the envelopes down on the kitchen counter, a freckled Formica surface with a metal edge. I shrugged out of my coat and pulled off my boots.

Four months had passed since I moved to Number N. I was calmer now. What choice did I have? I could only put one foot in front of the other and get used to the new normal, a day-to-day pattern of low-level freelance programming punctuated with abuse from my Number-N neighbors.

The Number N-ers were all suffering impacts from the crash, such as scarcity of yoga students, lack of business shirts to dry-clean, and the fact that unemployed people were now walking their own dogs. Also, Viagra's new Spanish-speaking campaign required Latin actors. It was an unrelated event, but the actor on nine still blamed me for it.

The notes pinned to my door reminded me I was a pariah. They included slogans like, "We are the 99%," "Ban Corporate Greed," "Democracy Not Plutocracy," and "No Bulls, No Bears, Only Pigs." Or sometimes, simply, "Whore." Residents kicked my package deliveries into dark corners of the lobby, and the actor timed his toilet flushes for when I turned on the shower.

Number N's anger was a mere echo of how the rest of America felt for the way they'd been screwed. Everyone knew the actual perpetrators didn't suffer in the crash, except for an unlucky few like me. The trillion-dollar TARP program took all the bad debt from the big banks, so they didn't have to deal with it. Citibank got a few hundred billion, and when that wasn't enough, a few billion more. Bonuses were getting paid on Wall Street. And on time.

As for the rest of the country, millions of people were without jobs. Other millions' homes were foreclosed upon. I read the crash-related blogs every day. Just this morning I learned of an illiterate cleaning lady in California with a mortgage just readjusted to $5,700 a month. A downsized Minnesota man with no health insurance couldn't afford the surgery to replace the battery in his pacemaker and died like a metronome running out of steam. There was also Bert, now under water on not one but two houses.

The cause for outrage was so immense, it seemed only a matter of time before people would be flooding the streets. Governments would be overthrown. Leaders would be locked up. It would be a kind of Bastille-storming, Bolshevik-uprising, Fidel-taking-of-Cuba, Basque-separating, Shah-overthrowing, Tiananmen-square stand-offing, and Tibetan-monk-self-immolating all rolled into one.

But none of that was happening. A few hundred people camped out in a small downtown park. Those protesters couldn't even decide what they were agitating for or against. The topics included bank regulation, unemployment insurance, healthcare, education, leash laws, unwanted gentrification of Brooklyn, insufficient cell phone bars, high-fructose corn syrup, genetically modified vegetables, free trade coffee and overly long lines at the Apple store.

They also included a fringe group agitating on behalf of horses. The Public Advocate wanted to ban carriage rides because PETA helped finance his last campaign. Norah joined that protest because the carriage drivers, many Irish, were her countrymen. I spotted her in some blurry YouTube footage waving a placard.

People were perplexed about what to do. The evil that had been perpetrated was too deep. It involved math. And everyone knew Americans were no good at that.

Thank God for Number N, with my $419 rent. I was in a low-rent lifeboat, just off billionaire row. I was certain I had the best deal in the building because Mom's place was the rare rent-controlled variety, which only applied to leases before 1971. I had no idea what others paid. In New York, you always hold your lease deal close to the chest, in case yours is better than the other guy's. Still, given the motley population, it was obvious everyone in the building had some below-market arrangement.

The others here might be covered by rent-stabilization laws, which were much weaker than the gold-standard rent control. There were dozens of ways for landlords to subvert rent stabilization, including costly renovations that brought apartments up to market rate. From what I could tell, none of that ever happened at Number N. The only explanation seemed to be that Goodman really didn't think the building was worth his attention.

What was Goodman doing these days? Like me, he was banned from a finance job. Probably waiting out the recession at his condo in Vail. As for Number N, he ignored it and turned everything over to Norah, who seemed to have free rein to run the building as she saw fit. Norah kept expenses low with her institutional paint and veritable hardware store of fix-it-yourself supplies. If she needed a hand, she hit up her superintendent cronies in the neighborhood and even Nikos, the security guard at the Greek embassy.

I pared an apple and set it outside for the bird. I named him Frankie, in homage to Aunt Kathleen's hideous St. Francis statues. I built a bird shelter directly in the stream of the stove vent and kept the fan running all the time. Just because he'd made it through one winter, didn't mean he'd survive a second. I used New York deli cups for his little house, so the exterior of his hut had blue and white Acropolis columns. Viviane's window shade now hovered at an acquiescent six inches so her daughter, Natalie, could watch the colorful parakeet.

The winter had been mild, and now it was warming up. So Frankie would be okay. At least I'd helped one animal. I never did find out what happened to Whitey. I assumed the worst because I never heard from Eugene again.

As the months went by, my distaste for Number N faded, then dissolved entirely. Sure, the neighbors abused me, but it wasn't like I'd *ever* had friends. The apartment was roomy, and the décor brought back nice memories. Sometimes it felt as if Aunt Kathleen had just left, shutting the door behind her, wafting a trace of cigarettes and L'air du Temps.

Ironically, this place *was* a kind of legacy. It belonged to my mother and my aunt. Theoretically, it could be passed down to me, and I could pass it down to my own offspring. The net-mender and pistachio-sheller would have given their stamps of approval. Of course, no one was leaving me this apartment. Mom and Bert needed the money if there ever was a buyout. And Mom wasn't the bequeathing kind.

Thinking these thoughts, I longed for a legacy of my own as much as ever. I had been deprived of my inheritance as a child, and the idea held me in its grip. Being left something, especially something as tangible as a home, was proof of love, proof of family, proof that you mattered to someone—even after they were gone. Maybe that's what my quest had really been about all along. But it wasn't ever to be. Sometimes you just don't get what your heart desires.

⁓

A FEW WEEKS later, in early April, I was sitting on the scratchy tartan couch with my laptop propped on the faux colonial coffee table. A sharp rap on my door startled my mouse hand and I accidentally deleted a row of data. "Shit."

Clack, clack, clack.

I undid the error, went to the door, and flung it open, expecting to find a sign telling me to occupy something. Instead, the specter of Judith leant on an ivory-topped cane with one arm hooked to her aide. Owl-framed glasses obscured her cloudy eyes.

"I just finished my semi-annual visit to Viviane, so I decided to pay you a social call." Judith let go of the aide's arm. "You can go, Fatima. Miss Mulcahy will see me home."

"I will?"

Judith caned her way to me, taking my arm and proceeding further into the apartment. "What do you have to drink?"

"Water," I sighed. I guided her to the purple chevron armchair.

"On the rocks, please."

Normally, I would have found Judith barging in annoying. But today I was feeling especially isolated, so even Judith was better than being alone. Maybe Number N was making me soft. Also, I'd never asked her about the *Daily News* article.

I brought Judith her water, then sat opposite on the red tartan couch. Her outfit today was the color of fog, with her signature red shoes, and she looked imprecisely in the direction of my face. She took a sip. "Ah. Bloomberg's finest." She set the glass down. "Nice place." I knew she couldn't really see it, but she probably remembered it from the past. "Planning to move here full time?"

"No. I'm just temporary."

"Aren't we all?"

"Listen, Judith, I've been meaning to ask you something. A few months ago, I found an old *Daily News* article. About…"

"Kathleen's death."

"Yeah. Were you the art dealer quoted in the article?"

"Of course, I was." Judith stamped her cane. "I said it before, and I'll say it now. Kathleen Elizabeth Condon did *not* commit suicide."

I paused and reminded myself of Judith's conspiracy-theory tendencies. "What makes you so sure? The police ruled it suicide."

"The police!" Judith scoffed, and turned her head as if looking out the window. Parakeet Frankie cocked his head at her.

I took a big inhalation. "She drank."

"Sure, she drank. Who didn't in those days?"

"And she was probably gay."

"Also true."

"Well, maybe those were the reasons she killed herself. She had a deep, dark secret. And maybe a drinking problem."

"Let me tell you something, Delia." Judith leaned forward, fixing on me with her impotent eyes. "If every alcoholic in the City of New York jumped off a roof, they'd need a separate sanitation department to clean up the bodies. And that's if we're only talking about the gay ones."

I sat back. *A separate sanitation department.*

Judith went on. "Your old house had air rights. Has, I suppose is the correct verb. Don't you just love the term? *Air rights.*

It's like putting a price on nothing. When your house went up for sale, Goodman senior had the opportunity of a lifetime. Join the two properties. Interesting how a *single* rent-controlled tenant can block the plan. Next thing you know Kathleen turns up dead. Howard Goodman was the one who called the police. You can imagine what he said. You said it yourself. She drank. She was *that* kind woman. The cops in those days…"

"So, you *really* think Howard Goodman did it? You're convinced?"

Judith thumped her cane affirmatively. "Who else had a reason? Certainly not Kathleen. I knew her. *You* knew her."

I looked at Judith's smoky lenses, considering. It was so tempting. It would mean Aunt Kathleen really *was* the person I'd always believed her to be. I remembered Rob's obvious dislike of his father. But even an asshole father is a long way from a murderous one. Besides, there was a whole part of this story that made no sense. "If all that's true, why didn't the tower actually *get built* with Aunt Kathleen out of the way? Number N and the embassy are still here to this day."

Judith waved a dismissive hand in the air. "Oh, there were lots of possible reasons for that. Maybe Howard Goodman thought he went too far and needed to let things cool off. There was the crash of '87. That really took the wind out of everybody's sails. Then the Greeks swooped in and bought your house, ruining the plan to join the properties. Howard got sick pretty soon after. It could have been a thousand things."

"Sun spots, maybe."

"Believe what you like. She was *your* aunt."

"What about Mom? Why didn't she ask these questions?"

"Your mother believed the police. People believed the police in those days." Judith crossed her legs; a vermillion toe tapped in the air. "Kathleen loved you like a daughter, and you won't even give her the benefit of the doubt. You can believe me or not. It doesn't really matter anymore. Howard is dead. One day, Howard's son will finish the story, so to speak. That's the one you worked for, right?"

"Yeah." The way Judith said *finish the story* sounded ominous.

"Change of topics," Judith declared, with a light cane stamp. "I have an idea for you."

"What kind of idea?" I was beginning to feel my more customary emotions toward Judith: grumpiness and impatience. She didn't have anything to add on the *Daily News* subject, leaving me no clearer than Bert.

"Remember what I said about that Viviane girl and the spoon jar?"

"Sure. I remember thinking you were cracked."

"I'm not *cracked*." Judith pursed her lips. "I told you it's worth a lot of money."

"So why don't you offer to buy it?"

"I did. Three times. First, I offered fifty. She said no. Then I offered her seventy-five. Then a hundred."

"Exactly how much is that spoon jar worth?"

"Maybe six."

"*Six hundred thousand dollars?* And you offered her fifty thousand even though you knew it was worth over ten times that?"

"I'm a businesswoman."

"I guess you are."

"Viviane's precise words were: 'I want to keep it. It's a really great spoon jar.'" That sounded like Viviane. "The object is described in a fragment of ancient writing. About a tribute vessel that sank."

Wasn't that like what Peter Priest said? Could it be the same? "Homeric writing?" I pursued. "Headed to the temple of Apollo? Only a few pieces of the treasure were ever found?"

Judith's murky eyes sparkled. "Yes! Exactly! The ship was from a city probably somewhere in Asia Minor being overrun by barbarians. The legend goes Apollo promised to save them if they would send the greatest treasures of the land. Otherwise, their city would fall. But the ship went down somewhere off the coast of Turkey."

"So, what happened to the city?"

"It fell to the barbarians. Or something. No record of the place exists. Maybe old Apollo hit them with a lightning bolt when the stuff never made it. A few pieces matching the description turned up on the black market. It was back in the seventies. I saw the items. When I could see. They were glorious."

"Were you involved in selling them?"

"None of your business." Judith paused. "But I'd like to handle this one. I could use the money. For better aides. I hate relying on refugees. And Angela."

"What's this got to do with me?"

"*You* convince Viviane. If you can get her to sell, I'll cut you in. Say a third for Viviane, a third for you, and a third for me."

Two hundred thousand dollars. I could get out from under my mortgage.

"What would keep me from just walking off with the thing?"

Judith smiled. "You can't just waltz into an auction house with that kind of object. You'd get arrested. You need to know the sort of buyer who isn't too fussy about provenance."

"I don't know how I would ever convince her," I mused, more to myself than to Judith. How could I succeed when Judith had been trying for years? "Viviane hates me."

Judith leaned forward on her cane. "You'll figure something out. That shark Rob Goodman hired you for some reason."

Chapter Thirty

Listen, my children, and you shall hear
Of the midnight ride of Paul Revere.
—Henry Wadsworth Longfellow, "Paul Revere's Ride"

APRIL WENT BY and May arrived. Intervals grew longer between the notes on my door. I couldn't tell if that meant Number N was starting to accept me, they were simply running out of slogans, or they'd just lost interest in the abuse-Delia game. The actor was scalding me less with his toilet flushes. I think he was in a better mood because suddenly he found himself in high demand. Silver-haired WASP types were needed to portray evil Wall Street CEOs, because series like *Blue Bloods* and *Law and Order* were incorporating the crash into plot lines. In the early morning, as filming was wrapping, and people headed to work, it was often hard to tell the real CEOs from the doppelgangers.

But, Viviane hadn't even budged in her regard for me. Despite the fact that the crash had actually *benefited* Viviane's business, she continued to cold-shoulder me in the laundry room, and her blinds hovered at six inches above the sill so Natalie, her daughter, could watch the window-box parakeet.

I was sure my care for the parakeet was a small notch in my favor, but Viviane's frostiness thwarted any conversation about her spoon jar. After months, I could hardly elicit more than a nod from her when I said, "good morning." Unless I were willing to actually break into her apartment, somehow identify a spoon jar amidst her hoarded piles, and steal it, Judith's opportunity was a lost cause.

As predicted, my funds were running out. The $1,500 a month I made freelancing had stretched the timeline somewhat. My graph now showed I'd be broke somewhere in the middle of September this year. Before then, I would stop paying my mortgage. According to the crash blogs, after a month of missed payments, the bank would begin foreclosure proceedings. Soon after that, my apartment would go up for auction.

One thing was for sure: I needed to land a job before any of *that* happened. Else, I would spiral into a cycle of chronic unemployment and debt.

I held out irrational hope that something miraculous would happen to save me. It could, couldn't it? Something from out of the blue? Then I remembered the gray-faced down-and-out woman I'd seen in Las Vegas leaning on an ATM back in January 2008. Luck will never show up for that woman. The reason it won't appear is precisely because she needs it so badly.

⸻

"GREAT TO HEAR from you again, Ms. Mulcahy." The Telefony HR woman's voice was more chipper this time. She explained Telefony was shifting business into robocalling for the mortgage-foreclosure industry. "We're getting ready to hire. Probably after Labor Day. Since you made it through our previous interview process, I think you are a solid candidate."

"Great." I took a deep breath. Robocalling for the mortgage

foreclosure industry. *If you are calling about losing everything, press one.*

"We *do* need to repeat the reference check. We've also added a credit-check process. Because of…everything."

"Right," I said.

She advised me to touch base again at the end of July.

Deep down, I understood if I got this position, I would be so much luckier than so many people. I would have an income, an apartment, a job writing robocall software.

Still, it was sad. I would lose my Grandhope apartment, with its prospect into my old bedroom, like a magical doorway into that other life and that other person I was supposed to be. Adding to the sadness, I was now attached to Aunt Kathleen's apartment. It was totally unexpected, but I sincerely wanted to go on living here. I was further surprised to find myself admitting I might even prefer this apartment in shabby Number N to the Grandhope.

Whatever my personal sadness, it was a pale shadow of the misery the crash unleashed on the country and the world. I continued to read the crash blogs and today I learned several thousand people, hundreds with master's degrees, showed up at a McDonald's hiring fair for ten available jobs. Another post was from a woman who'd been slowly selling her jewelry to make ends meet. "My wedding band went today," she said. "I got forty dollars. To me, it was a million-dollar ring." Whole countries who'd bought subprime investments were now teetering on default. Greece was most deeply in trouble. But there was also Spain, Italy, Ireland, and Iceland.

Compared to this, my concerns were narrow and egotistical.

I felt shame.

A perverse part of me was a tiny bit glad I had been sanctioned by the SEC. It was expiating, in some way, to know I was paying some form of restitution. Aunt Kathleen would have approved.

I was also oddly relieved that my funds would run out before the two-year trading ban was up. If I actually made it to the two-year mark, I knew I would be tempted to join one of the new hedge funds, rising from their own ashes like demon Phoenixes. Even now, with a full appreciation of the evil that had been unleashed, I probably would not be able to resist the money. No one learned from the crash of 2008; no rules had really changed, virtually predestining it to happen again.

These thoughts drew me to the chartreuse volume on the bookcase, my favorite saint's story as a child. I hadn't read it in decades. I took it out and sat on the couch while Frankie, in his window box, enjoyed a spring sunbeam over my shoulder.

I was eight when Aunt Kathleen and I stopped into the church gift shop to buy a mass card for a distant cousin who died. There was a small book section, and Aunt Kathleen picked up the tiny volume.

"Hey, now," said Aunt Kathleen. "You can almost never find this one. I think you'll like it. It's just the ticket." I didn't ask the ticket to where. Since it was a saint's story, I pretty much knew the destination.

The cover was a picture of Joseph and the Technicolor Dreamcoat. Except the person in the rainbow outfit was a girl. The title was *The Cloak of St. Brigid.*

My name.

There in the shop, we flipped the pages.

Brigid, a first-century Irish girl, was born a pagan and a slave. After hearing Saint Patrick preach, she converted to the new religion and spent all her time looking after the poor, the sick, and the elderly. Dozens of girls joined her.

That was standard-issue saint stuff. The next part was what hooked me.

Brigid and her band of do-gooders needed a home, so she approached the king of Leinster to give her some land. She asked for a piece of property with forests and lakes and fertile fields.

The king roared with laughter. Did she think he was crazy? Give her his best land for nothing? He was just about to banish Brigid from his sight when she asked, "Will you give me just as much land as my cloak will cover?"

She laid her little shawl on the ground.

"Why not?" said the king, who was up for a joke that day.

Brigid called four of her girls, and they each took a corner of the cloak. One walked east, one walked north, one walked west and the other walked south. The cloak unfurled. It stretched and scrolled, rippling with rainbow colors like a flock of tropical birds. When the cloak was done, it covered all the way to the horizon.

The king fell to his knees and converted. Brigid got her property.

Now *that* was a good saint's story. It was about *getting stuff,* not giving it up. On top of it all, Brigid was a good con artist, with that tricky cloak of hers. I endorsed the book, and it went to live on Aunt Kathleen's bookshelf.

As I reached the end, I felt a bulge between the last page and the back cover. It was a plump envelope. Inside were folded sheets of onionskin letter paper written in a vaguely familiar hand that I could not immediately place.

∽

I WAS DREAMING of birds carrying letters penned on onionskin when the jangle of my cell phone shattered the early morning dark. I lurched awake, scattering actual onionskin sheets everywhere. I scrambled for clothes and laptop, thinking I had to get to Hermes. Then I realized I didn't get hedge-fund calls about market meltdown in the middle of the night anymore. I picked up my cell and noticed two things. It was three thirty a.m. and the caller was Eugene.

I forced myself to ascend to consciousness. "What's wrong?" This was precisely the hour horses chose to colic. I spent many a night taking turns with the Hungarian walking a distressed animal up and down the stable aisle. If Whitey was, by some improbable chance, still breathing air, he might be sick.

"There was an accident. I can't catch him."

I struggled to understand. Clearly, Whitey had not been put down. Eugene, or someone, was riding him and got bucked off. Now the horse was loose. But why was Eugene calling me in New York to help him catch a loose horse in Connecticut? Moreover, why was he riding at three in the morning?

"I'm sure one of the people at the barn can help you. They should be around to feed in a little while." I pictured Whitey in full tack, stirrups and reins dangling, grazing on one of the manicured lawns around the posh riding facility under a waning moon. He'd be fine as long as he was away from the road. "Where is he?"

"In the park?"

Maybe I wasn't as awake as I thought. "What park?"

An anguished response: "Central Park."

Minutes later I was banging on Norah's door.

"Fucking building better be on fucking fire!" she bellowed.

"It's about my friend and a horse."

She opened the door to this unorthodox statement, and I blurted out the emergency as fast as Eugene had narrated it to me.

Inspired by the start I made teaching Whitey to drive, Eugene had gotten himself a livery license. Turns out, under city codes, passing an exam was all it took to drive a carriage. Eugene decided this was the way to support both himself and the horse.

Norah: "If you're fucking mental enough to want to drive a fucking carriage through fucking Manhattan with no fucking experience, then fucking good luck to you!"

Today was Eugene and Whitey's first day on the job. They made it all the way to evening without incident. Eugene suspected the livery stable manager might have medicated Whitey to a degree not previously attempted.

Norah: "The lads gave him a fucking elephant tranquilizer."

At eight p.m. the previous evening, Eugene took on his final passengers, a group of tourists from Beijing.

Norah: "Too many fucking tourists. Always asking for fucking directions."

Then Whitey's high wore off.

Realization dawned. He was in traffic, surrounded by buses, taxis and trucks. He started to jig. Then he started to jog. Then, an ambulance invoked its siren.

The horse bolted, barreling pell-mell around the park's

southeast pond, running, lurching, and thrashing in his harness. The carriage, with Eugene driving and the tourists clinging for dear life, passed Wollman Rink and careened up the Mall, scattering park visitors. The equipage reached the precipitous staircase at Bethesda Fountain. Eugene thought they were going over, when Whitey swerved violently, tossing everyone overboard, and disappeared into the wooded ramble, carriage and all.

The tourists had lacerations, but they could walk. Eugene was pretty sure. On second thought, all but one. It was hard to tell the extent of the injuries because they couldn't speak much English. Eugene didn't wait to find out. He ran after Whitey.

Norah: "They'll learn one fucking English sentence by morning. *We sue city.*"

Eugene chased Whitey all night.

"Now they're up by the museum," I concluded.

"The *museum*? I thought you were going to tell me they crashed through our fucking back alley. Why the fuck do I care about a runaway horse up by the museum?"

I had to whip Norah into action. I nearly redeemed Whitey once; now I had a chance to finish the job. He was my effort and my responsibility. Schooling that unschoolable horse was the one concrete good thing I'd accomplished in as long as I could remember. Maybe ever. "Can you imagine what this will do to New York carriage drivers?" I asked, leveraging her pet cause. "That horse is out of his mind. God knows if the tourists are dead or alive. It's the worst possible thing to happen just now. They'll say all of them are dangerous!"

THAT WAS ALL it took to get Norah on board. Next, I called Bert and asked him to check his police scanner. Yes, he said, there was a report about some injured tourists and a runaway carriage horse. One of the tourists was in the hospital. Park precinct cops would be on the lookout for horse and driver, who were both missing. If the horse looked dangerous, they had instructions to shoot him.

"What's going on, Deel-yer?"

"I'll call you later," I said, and hung up.

It was curtains for Whitey if they found him before we did. But no one could find a horse in a pitch-black park when they didn't know where to look. We had until dawn.

Chapter Thirty-One

Be strong, saith my heart; I am a soldier.

—Homer, *The Iliad*

A S NORAH RUMMAGED in her closet for emergency supplies, I headed out in search of the overnight TV production set. Among the milling cast members, I spotted the unmistakable silver pate of the actor. He wore a dark gray suit as if he had just finished playing J.P. Morgan CEO Jamie Dimon. I explained the plan.

The actor was rounding up extras when Norah arrived, placards and poles protruding from the small wire cart she used to shop for groceries.

"Do you have the shoe polish?" I asked her.

"Of course I have the fucking shoe polish."

"Here we are." The actor returned with the ten others I'd requested. "You said fifty bucks each?"

"Right," I said, "There's an ATM at the deli. I'll be right back."

"You don't have a pot to piss in." Norah pulled a wad of bills from her own pocket and counted out the money.

We made our way to the park. As we passed, Norah waved at Greek embassy guard Nikos. He saluted back. We crossed Fifth Avenue.

A pre-dawn bus glowed like phosphorescence. It was now four fifteen. Over the course of the next ninety minutes, the sun would rise, and rush hour would begin. In the light of day, tens of thousands of eyes would spot the horse.

How long could it take us to apprehend a loose horse in Central Park? I remembered chasing horses for hours on end back at Sorrows in small, muddy paddocks.

Central Park was 847 acres.

Our destination was the Great Lawn around which Eugene had been unsuccessfully pursuing Whitey since three a.m.

WE HUSTLED UP the hill north of the museum, passing a sleepy jogger trotting in a daze. An enthusiastic golden retriever tugged on his half-awake dog walker.

We arrived at the lawn, a fifty-acre oval of enough lush grass to satisfy a herd of horses. It was still too dark to see. We curved south to the shores of Turtle Pond beneath Belvedere Castle. A rump suddenly came into view. The ornate carriage was still attached. With the plume on top of Whitey's head, the gilt-and-white bridle, and the castle in the background, the only thing missing to complete the fairy-tale scene was a knight in shining armor.

If things had happened differently for Whitey, if he hadn't been purchased with Wall Street money as a mount for a spoiled girl, then tranquilized and gelded, he would have been competing in the Pan American games, maybe heading to the Olympics. Yet here he was in a ridiculous storybook getup. For such a magnificent horse, it was an undignified and desperate attempt at survival.

Eugene, posture slumping from being at it all night, approached the horse. He got within a few yards. Whitey bucked, thrashed his head, and spurted off to a safer distance. Pearly lather covered his neck. Eugene sighed, and prepared to advance again. The scene had been repeating for hours.

"Like pissing up a rope," said Norah.

"We're here, Eugene," I called.

I gathered the shoe polish and a bag of carrots. Norah took charge of the actor and the extras. We didn't have much time. I looked at the sky. Still dark but starting to change from velvet black to charcoal gray.

"Hey, boy," I said.

Eugene withdrew as I approached. Whitey's ears flicked my way. I knew he would remember me, the one rider who could control him. Horses always do. Whitey's sides quivered. Sweat, white and soapy, streaked his neck. Foam dripped from his mouth and coated his forelegs. His white eyes rolled everywhere. He looked like a rabid dog. Whitey not only looked dangerous—in his current state of mind, he really was dangerous. Maybe for anybody but me. I tried to remember something Hungarian.

The last time I saw the Hungarian was the morning of my Sorrows graduation. We had just finished our final lovemaking session. "My girl," he said, stroking my hair. "I tell you something even though you never ride again." He rolled over and lit his pipe.

By then, I was older, and I had some perspective on the Hungarian. I knew how sweet he was, and kind. And also that he belonged to another time, with all his lessons about battle on horseback. He was determined to pass on that knowledge to me, as if I might someday find myself in a post-apocalyptic world where combustion engines were extinct, the cavalry reconstituted, and Sorrows alumna called up for duty.

That graduation morning, the Hungarian was particularly earnest. It was as if he was trying to say something of great importance, entrusting it to me because he himself was at the end of his career training warriors, of his virility, and of his life.

"The horse, he goes into the battle for love of *you*. This how it is possible to cross through no-man's-land," he said, as he stroked my hair.

In 1998, an alumni mailing announced the Hungarian had died.

Thoughts of the Hungarian calmed me and shaped my resolve. "Here now," I said to Whitey. I cracked a carrot. He flinched and pawed with his front foot. I stopped. "It's me." His ears pointed my way. He went back to grazing. I needed to get close enough to touch him. If he accepted my hand on him, it would be game over.

I stepped forward. He stopped masticating. "Here's the thing, buddy." His radar ears tuned. "You're coming with me, or you're not getting out of here." He began chewing again. Slowly, I closed the distance. Whitey stayed firm, sometimes chewing, sometimes stopping to watch me, his ear always cocked. I continued my approach, inch by precarious inch.

After many minutes, my palm rested on his shoulder. Wet with sweat, it was sleek, perceptive and warm. I stroked my way up his neck and took hold of his bridle. He shook his head and pulled away. I gave a firm jerk back. He stomped, then blew a surrendering exhalation. Capitulation.

"Whosagoodboy?" I asked.

He munched the carrots noisily, and I beckoned to Norah. She took his bridle. "Stupid fucking donkey," she said to his face.

I dropped to my knees with the black shoe polish. A bay is red brown with a black mane, black legs and black tail, with the occasional splash of white here and there. Whitey's four knee-high white stockings and snowy forehead blaze made him distinctive. Those markings had to go if this was going to work. I got busy with the waxy tins and a cloth. I couldn't do anything about his noble bearing, which no amount of shoe polish would cover.

Joggers were now circling the lawn. There was a shroud of early morning fog. I spread polish fast to beat the dawn, sweating inside my sweatshirt and feeling the dewy air clammy on my cheeks. Whitey stood still while Norah softly cursed him out.

Gradually, the monochrome of night gave way, and the scene developed like a Polaroid. I finished with a touch of cordovan polish to the star on his forehead. The only white left were the rims of his eyes. Only someone like the Hungarian would spot that.

"Step back," I said to Norah.

In a quick motion, I took the reins, placed a foot on the running board and hopped onto the driving seat. Thank God for the Hungarian and his anachronistic buggy-driving notions of horsemanship.

Whitey threw his head and bolted into motion. He executed a buck, back feet hitting the carriage running board, cracking it. He swerved left and right. "Easy, boy. *Easy!*" If I didn't get control, we'd be careening up to Harlem Meer, a suicidal Whitey charging into the water, the two of us disappearing under the surface, green as asparagus soup.

He popped up and down between the shafts. "Whoa, boy."

He pranced. "Get on, now!"

"Hey," said a jogger running in place. "What's going on?"

Norah wheeled to face the runner, taking her attention from me and jigging, thrashing Whitey to execute her role. "What does it look like? It's a fucking protest!" She lifted a placard that said, *Horses Not Hedge Funds!*

The actor raised his sign. "Save New York horses!" He cued the extras who animated instantly, yelling "Barns over bailouts!" and "Equity for equines!" and "Don't steal our steeds!"

Whitey reared. The carriage tipped backward to a fulcrum point. We could both go over. I cracked the reins down hard on his back. The slapping sound was loud with the width of the leather on the wet of his sweat. He surged forward.

The sun rose. Joggers, dog walkers and stroller-pushers stopped and stared. Bicyclers braked and held their cell phones high. I managed the reins, all four of them, threaded through my fingers. Whitey dropped his head and took hold of the bit, muscles rippling in his harness.

"What do we want?" Norah called.

"Jobs for horses!" the actor responded.

"When do we want them?"

"Now!" the extras intoned. A few unrelated bystanders took up the chant.

"That's right!" called one woman, who held the hand of a little girl in a private school kilt. "I can't imagine New York without horses!"

"They're sending them all to the glue factory!" declared Norah, which wasn't true. For anyone except Whitey himself. The little girl started to cry.

Whitey's bridle jingled. I felt his tension in the reins. He was surrounded on all sides by people waving signs, bicycles swerving, mothers pushing carriages, and dogs barking. It was more chaos than he'd ever known, yet he forged on. It was as if he recognized his own mortal moment.

"Hah!" I urged.

A crosstown bus roared by on the 84th Street transverse. Faces plastered to the window. I saw Whitey's white eye grow wide as Fifth Avenue was nigh upon us. I tried to slow Whitey before we reached the oncoming traffic. He snorted and pranced, pulling hard. I braced my feet on the splintered running board and my biceps began to ache. Sweat streamed between my shoulder blades.

"We're taking a right! Keep up!" I shouted back to Norah. We only had to make it four blocks south to my intended destination. A startled cab driver squealed to a halt as I merged Whitey into traffic. Whitey shied. "Get on now!" I urged. The extras were gaining energy from the audience and ad-libbed generously.

We careened onto Fifth Avenue, trotting briskly in the bus lane. Norah and the others broke into a run. Crisp clanks shot from Whitey's shoes.

Behind us a veritable legion of rush-hour buses, M1, M2, M3, and BxM rumbled and lurched and crawled along like heavy artillery. Guerilla yellow cabs darted in and out as drivers took pictures. A distant jackhammer rat-a-tatted. The buildings of Fifth Avenue formed a canyon around us, with the airy command posts of billionaires towering above. Down dark side streets, anonymous officials of dangerous countries lurked in heavily curtained townhouse bunkers.

It was a bizarre and dreamlike no-man's-land. In that moment, every basket-case horse that ever arrived at Sorrows was subsumed into Whitey, and I was each schoolgirl turned soldier. It was as if I was being forced to play out the Hungarian's crazy chivalric battle fantasy. Yet here I was. I threw myself into the role.

On through no-man's-land!

Whitey broke into a valiant canter, leaving the others behind. It didn't matter. Our destination was in sight.

"Good boy!" I cried. I could hardly count the number of cell phones raised.

We reached 80th Street where Nikos, the guard, held open the embassy gate.

Chapter Thirty-Two

God forbid that I should go to any heaven in which there are no horses.

—R.B. Cunninghame-Graham, in a letter to Theodore Roosevelt

A MIDMORNING SUN shone on Bert and a fortyish police sergeant of the mounted force. Bert had called in a favor, and a police horse van quickly arrived. It disgorged necessities like a halter, lead rope, water bucket, and hay bag. On Bert's instruction, Norah hustled Eugene away. As they left, she cast a look over her shoulder and stabbed a thumbs-up over her head. I had crossed the Rubicon with her. The gesture said that for whatever time I had left at Number N, there would be no more notes on my door.

Seamus Rivera was the sergeant on the scene. He was the nephew of an old cop friend of Bert's named Seamus Byrne. Byrne's sister married a fellow named Pedro Rivera. The couple gave birth to Seamus Rivera who referred to his nationality as I-Rican.

Outside the gate, Rivera and Bert stood in identical arms-folded poses, looking forward. They made occasional comments and might have been watching a kid's soccer game on Staten Island, instead of a show horse munching hay from a bag hanging off a decorative fountain in an embassy garden.

The guard, Nikos, and I sat on a wrought-iron bench and drank thick, Greek-style coffee while we monitored the horse. Nikos had bushy eyebrows, a mustache, and Balkan-avuncular demeanor. The only thing missing from a scene long ago was a bag of pistachios, a pile of orange nets, and a battery-powered radio playing popular Greek tunes.

"This territory of Greece," Nikos said. He had been making the same comment approximately every fifteen minutes since we arrived for the benefit of the NYPD outside the gates.

A second cop, who couldn't have been twenty-two years old, looked in. "When you're done, can I get my hay bag back?"

"Sure thing," I said.

"You may need this." The young cop passed a pitchfork through the bars, looking cautiously in the direction of Sergeant Rivera as if the pitchfork might be a bridge too far.

"*Akrivos*," said Nikos, with a suspicious glance at Whitey's hind end. *Exactly.*

"We gotta figure out another way around this, Rivera," Bert said.

"They can't just harbor this horse here. People got hurt." The tourist had a broken arm and several busted ribs.

Bert shrugged. "All I know is—" he pointed through the wrought iron "—that over there is the sovereign territory of another country. If you want that horse outta there, you're gonna have to call the UN."

They crossed their arms again. The standoff continued.

I rolled my shoulders and sighed. I was proud of Whitey, no matter what happened next. He proved himself a true soldier of a horse, and the Hungarian would have been proud of us both. If Whitey could get through that Fifth Avenue no-man's-land, he could get through anything. My eyes traveled to the upper windows of the embassy, where faces filled the panes like fish at the surface of a pond, mouths gaping like carp.

"Aren't they going to kick us out eventually?" I asked Nikos.

He shook his head. "We mad at America for teach us make financial problem." Greece was billions in debt due to a subprime pipe dream foisted on them by American banks and made worse by their own rampant corruption. Unless Greece received a bailout, they'd be kicked out of the EU. "If America says no horse, we say *yes horse*."

Whitey chewed loudly. Another face appeared at the window with black eyes and curly dark hair. Peter Priest's eyebrows shot up with undisguised astonishment as he recognized me.

Thinking of nothing else to do, I waved and shrugged. He smiled and gave a disbelieving shake of his head.

"That man," I said to Nikos and looked up at the window. He followed my line of sight. "What's he doing there?"

The guard nodded. "He knows about money and is advising the government. He says Greece must sell."

"Sell? What?"

"Acropolis. Parthenon. Islands. Port of Piraeus. To people like Russian and Chinese. So Greece can pay debts."

"Oh."

Bert's and Sergeant Rivera's voices grew louder.

"Just say you lost him. The horse got away," Bert offered. "He galloped across the Madison Avenue Bridge and is lost somewhere in Yonkers."

"They have pictures!" Sergeant Rivera gestured in my direction. "With her! Driving down Fifth Avenue!"

"That was a totally different horse. Completely different markings," Bert asserted. "Two horse problems in one night is just a coincidence." The black shoe polish was already fading from Whitey's legs. Norah promised to come back with hair dye. Sergeant Rivera looked to the sky for help. "Different horse," Bert repeated.

Rivera sighed, took off his cap, and scratched his head. "She did a good job though," he said. "Galloping down Fifth in the flippin' bus lane."

Bert beamed. "She did, didn't she?"

"Where'd she learn to do that?"

"Peggy says some old cavalry guy at her finishing school." Bert hitched his belt. "Hungarian, I think."

"Did you say Hungarian?"

❧

TURNS OUT OUR Lady of Sorrows wasn't the only employer of Eastern European horsemen. A Czech taught riding to the NYPD mounted force for forty years and was a legend in the department. To demonstrate hot pursuit on horseback, he once rode a horse off a pier into Jamaica Bay. "Dove in like Esther freakin' Williams," Bert said.

The Czech trained Sergeant Rivera, Bert, and every mounted cop since the Johnson Administration. In later years he admitted, "I am good. But I am nothing compared to a Hungarian."

The Czech died the previous October at age ninety-six. Which meant the mounted force lost their key instructor and right when the police commissioner wanted them to expand operations. Those in emergency management thought it was just a matter of time before the anemic crash protests gained momentum and the Bolsheviks, Fidelistas and Bastille-stormers arrived. Since nothing was better than horses in a mob situation (Bert: "We learned that in the seventies, with the riots.") more mounted cops were needed. (Rivera: "Homeland is in full support.")

"Hungarians are the best. That's what our guy said. So, she must be good," Sergeant Rivera observed, and he and Bert negotiated a plea deal.

It was agreed that for my crime of driving a livery outside an authorized carriage zone without a license and in a bus lane, I would perform community service teaching a summer course to New York mounted police. There would even be a small stipend.

Rivera called his captain to clear the deal. "Cap'n says okay, and how much do you want for the horse?"

$$\sim$$

THE NEXT MORNING, there was a knock on my door. When I went to answer it, I saw Viviane's dark hair disappearing into 13A. On my doormat, she left a copy of the *Daily News*.

Splashed across the front page was a cell-phone picture of me and Whitey trotting down Fifth Avenue.

Horse Protest to Public Advocate—Don't Be an Ass

A woman driving a livery carriage led a protest in the bus lane on Fifth Avenue yesterday morning. The demonstration began around the Great Lawn and proceeded to Fifth Avenue, ending at 79th Street. The unidentified woman and approximately two dozen demonstrators called for an end to the public advocate's proposed carriage-horse ban.

Said one woman in the protest, "Wall Street billionaires have already screwed all of us. Now it's horses. What next?" The woman used a different expletive.

The jump page had a small sidebar story: "Horse Runs Wild, Dragging Carriage, Injuring Tourists."

A carriage horse broke loose in Central Park at approximately eight p.m. Tuesday, shaking up a group of tourists and injuring one, who was listed as stable at Mount Sinai Medical Center. Witnesses said the horse ran amok from 59th Street to Bethesda Fountain, where the carriage overturned. The driver was charged on a misdemeanor and released. The horse has not been found, but has been sighted in Yonkers, police said.

My fifteen minutes of fame.

I lay the tabloid on the coffee table. It would be a nice souvenir. Something to look back on during long winter nights in Minneapolis, after my shift programming aggressive robocall scripts for mortgage-payment delinquents. Parakeet Frankie approached the window as if he wanted a better look.

Across the alley, very casually, as if she did the same every morning, Viviane hiked up her blinds. Natalie, her daughter, arms folded on the windowsill, comfortably watched the bird. I smiled. It felt good to be recognized for something right I had done. It wasn't a feeling I often had.

From the bookcase, I took out the Saint Brigid book and removed the envelope from the back cover to re-examine the letters. These were the letters I'd fallen asleep reading before being awoken by Eugene. The familiar handwriting was not Aunt Kathleen's but Sister Scholastica's. Thin, exacting, and perfectly correct, it was a graphological representation of the woman herself. No matter how quickly she graded test papers or wrote your crimes on a detention slip, her penmanship was prim, nunnish perfection.

I always understood she and Aunt Kathleen somehow knew each other. That was the whole reason I was sent to Sorrows to begin with—because Aunt Kathleen trusted the headmistress. Some story about how they belonged to the same order and had once taught school together.

There was only one side of the correspondence to work with—Scholastica's—but the letters revealed—well, everything.

In most of the epistles, Sister Scholastica was responding to Aunt Kathleen's humorous reports of life outside the convent, events around New York; or, most particularly, of me.

Your Delia sounds like a delightful little girl! I look forward to meeting her someday.

The letters were signed *RMF.* Those must be the initials of her actual name, I thought.

The correspondence went on for years, though I had just a sampling in my hand. The earliest one described my first day of school. The later ones arrived just before Aunt Kathleen died. Perhaps these were the letters Aunt Kathleen decided to save.

One thing was for sure: They were far better friends than I ever knew.

I guessed they were more.

I was convinced I would never discover what really happened to Aunt Kathleen, whether she had abandoned me or not, but, with these letters in hand, I realized I *could* find out more about who she was as a person. I tucked away the letters in the book and mulled a plan to do just that.

Chapter Thirty-Three

"Beauty is truth, truth beauty,"—that is all
Ye know on earth, and all ye need to know.
—John Keats, "Ode on a Grecian Urn"

"T HAT'S VERY PRETTY, Natalie." The picture crayoned by Viviane's daughter might have been of SpongeBob, or camels, or spaceships.

"These are the babies," Natalie said.

We sat in Viviane's living room, which could best be described as a very full storage space belonging to a diligent and tidy pack rat. Stacks of magazines and newspapers grew like stalagmites from the floor. Rainbows of sticky notes protruded from the tied-up bundles sorted by type—*Glamour, Vogue, Lucky, Times, Post, Daily News, USA Today*. Shopping bags held folded textiles: baby clothes in one, doll clothes in another, blankets and dishtowels in a third. Bags, deteriorated with time, were inserted inside newer, crisper bags. The one free surface, a coffee table, smelled of Pledge. Her windowsills were white and soot-free. The visible patches of carpet smelled freshly vacuumed. Only the halos of dust around the stacks' perimeters hinted at the length of their tenure.

When Viviane and I bumped into one another in the laundry room that morning, she invited me for coffee, and I readily agreed. It had been three weeks since my carriage adventure with Whitey, and there was a palpable thaw at Number N. No more notes or timed toilet flushes. My packages appeared promptly outside my door. Norah fixed my doorbell, which had never worked. Viviane's blinds came up and stayed up. I was becoming a full member of the Number-N community, and I was truly enjoying it. Uncharacteristic for me, I know, inveterate loner that I was with only one no-quotes friend, Angela.

Viviane's invitation was just the spoon-jar opportunity I'd been waiting for. But now, as I sat with Natalie, I realized I didn't feel so great about cashing in on a black-market antiquity. A thought like this was also unlike the normal, ruthless me. Maybe I'd been living at Aunt Kathleen's too long, reading too many saints' stories. Whatever the cause of my mixed feelings, I *really* needed the dough. It was the only thing that would keep me out of bankruptcy. Even if I got a job in Minneapolis, which was far from a done deal—my experience with Vista Equities was a harsh reminder—the salary was not in the same universe as at Hermes. It would not support my Fifth Avenue mortgage. A sale was impossible; recent calls to Sarah revealed the real estate market was the same, or worse. Job or no job, foreclosure was a certainty. The spoon jar was the only way to avoid it.

If only I could get Viviane to agree.

"Are these deer?" I gestured to some four-legged entities on Natalie's paper.

"It's dogs," Natalie said with impatience.

"I'll go help your mom," I said.

In her kitchen, Viviane placed a pot and cups on a tray. The kitchen contained multiples of items you usually have just one of: Cuisinarts, bread makers, food scales, blenders, panini presses, coffee grinders, salad spinners, knife blocks, teakettles, and espresso machines. Above two stacked toaster ovens, was a shelf of cooking utensils. I spied the spoon-jar suspect, orange with black-robed figures around its circumference, spoons sticking out of its throat.

I paused. The object was beautiful, its background a glowing orange, with the dark shadows dancing around it. I had to admit, it was also the perfect size for spoons.

Naturally, I didn't take Judith's word for the spoon-jar story. Veteran that I was with Janice at the public library, I did my own research. Peter Priest's and Judith's stories of the ancient shipwreck were comprehensively corroborated by antiquities scholars. The Homeric text, the description of the treasure, the appearance of a few items on the black market, the subsequent arrival of poachers on a small Dodecanese island, and the fact that no more treasure had ever been found—it was all factual. International law mandated return of such objects to Greece. For kicks, I searched for the island Mom and I visited that summer. It was indeed in the same region as the wreck, a mere six kilometers to the south.

"How about you make Miss Delia a picture of the yellow birdie? Maybe do it in your room so it'll be a surprise." Viviane raised an eyebrow at me. Natalie looked delighted at the assignment and zipped away, weaving through canyons of boxes.

"She's sweet," I said.

Viviane's hazel eyes shone emerald in appreciation. "That'll be good for about twenty minutes."

"Clever," I said, taking a sip of coffee and pretending everything around me was just as it should be.

"I'm just sorting through some things," Viviane said with a wave of her hand, as if she understood it was necessary to say *something*. I wondered if she expected anyone to buy that there was nothing wrong when there clearly was. I understood by an aura she emitted like a pheromone one must not talk about this. Whatever it was, was literally unspeakable.

"Your apartment is the same layout as mine," I said casually.

Viviane's shoulders relaxed as she detected I was going to go along with the sham that everything was normal. She stirred her coffee. "I'm sorry I wasn't...nice at first."

"I didn't take it personally."

"Norah said you were from Wall Street."

"Used to be."

"What's your lease arrangement?" Viviane, like most New Yorkers, was endlessly fascinated by people's housing situations. "I used to see an old lady talking outside with Norah. I thought the apartment was hers. I figured she was one of those rent-control people who keeps the place but secretly lives somewhere else."

"I'm subletting from her," I said. "Temporarily."

"I wish you were here to stay." She sipped her coffee. "I don't have many friends."

"Me either."

Viviane hesitated as if she thought she might be going too far. She was sweet, if more than a little eccentric. I felt strange talking with her about friendship—of a kind clearly meant to lack quotation marks—knowing I had designs on her spoon jar.

I decided to be straightforward with Viviane. It was a big step for her to invite me into her home, so I was not inclined to be underhanded. This impulse was also a novel one for me: the insider-trader and mother of economy-destroying big shorts. But, at the moment, I really didn't have any underhanded ideas.

"Listen, I want to ask you about something."

"My spoon jar?"

"How did you know?"

"I figured Judith would talk to you eventually."

"Did you know she would give you two hundred grand?"

"I knew it was very valuable." I never saw such a sum of money make so little impact on anyone in my life.

"Well it is."

"It must be really important."

"It was part of a famous shipload of treasure. It was supposed to go to a temple to save a city. But there was a shipwreck."

"Oh." Viviane looked out the window toward the bird and my apartment. I didn't tell her Priest's story about the people from his island hiding artifacts to prevent further looting. That seemed the wrong message for Viviane just now.

"Where did *you* get it?"

"Some grandkids selling their grandmother's stuff." Just as Judith said. "I guess they didn't know what it was. I end up with a lot of nice things that way."

"I bet you do. Are you willing to sell it?"

"The thing is I get…attached to things. You mentioned about a shipwreck. It's kind of like that."

"Doesn't sound very auspicious."

Viviane laughed. The tone was like bells. "Actually, it's lovely. You know, when a ship goes down? After a while, little amoeba or whatever stick onto it, and eventually, it becomes a coral reef. That's how things are to me. They get important that way." Viviane looked over the stacks, all different heights, like a mini skyline of Manhattan, or, yes, like a coral reef. "Of course, I have to sell things because of my business. Which keeps me—" she paused "—in practice. But certain things I just want to keep." It struck me Viviane could as soon have cut off a limb as sell a possession she was attached to. "Some things aren't about the money," she said with finality.

"I understand." In the past, this statement would have felt like an utter absurdity. Now, I felt the most infinitesimal glimmer of comprehension.

"And anyway, what would I do with that kind of cash?"

What a strange question. "Use it to buy a nice apartment? One that could really be yours."

"*This* apartment is mine." Viviane put her cup down with force. I saw a glint of what Judith described, the difficulty of dislodging a hoarder from her nest.

"What if someone offers you a buyout? You know, a sum of money to leave?"

"I won't take it."

"It could be as much as the spoon jar."

"Absolutely not." Viviane started to look agitated, wringing her hands. "I can *make* them let me stay here. Because of my *circumstances.*"

"The way you live," I euphemized.

"Yes. Like how they let Judith stay at the old hotel. People with certain *circumstances* are protected."

All you had to do was substitute "hoarding disorder" for "circumstances." She was right up to the edge now of admitting her problem. I didn't push her any more. With her veil starting to fall, I could see Viviane's state of mind was itself as fragile as a coral reef. If I persisted, she would suck back into herself as rapidly as a sea anemone. The blinds would *zzzip* down and I would never see her again.

I left without the spoon jar.

⚮

I WENT HOME, feeling discouraged. The spoon jar was a long shot, but I had held out hope. In the background, Aunt Kathleen's battery-powered radio was broadcasting a finance program. These days the news reported constantly on joblessness at 10 percent and surging foreclosure statistics. Today someone was saying, "The massive de-leveraging of Southern Europe will continue, possibly for decades."

I went to flick it off. My hand on the button, I heard the accent of fishing nets and pistachios. Peter Priest was commenting on the situation in Greece.

"It is catastrophic. All self-induced, as is our situation here in the United States. But the reality in Greece is of pensioners who will no longer have enough to live on, and of young people who will never find a job. We will lose a generation. Perhaps two."

"The Greek papers say you are advising the government to sell off property," the host said.

"I am advising the government to consider the sale of assets, yes." It seemed Priest was keeping himself busy after closing Odyssey.

"Are we talking about things like the Parthenon and the port of Piraeus?"

"The world will know what is for sale when it is for sale."

"There are reports the Greek embassy in New York will soon be on the block and that you have been involved in the matter."

I turned the volume up.

"The embassy building is in a prime location, and the diplomatic staff can take space in any number of office buildings in the city."

"Can we consider that an announcement?"

"If you like."

"All right. The famously tight-lipped Peter Priest. With no confirmation on the sale of the Parthenon, but acknowledging the Greek embassy in New York will soon be on the market. In other news..."

That's why Priest was at the embassy the day I drove in with Whitey. My old mansion would soon be up for sale once again. I wondered if Rob Goodman knew, and if he didn't, how long it would take him to find out.

Would the Deal of the Century happen for real this time, just twenty-three years later?

Chapter Thirty-Four

ἐν ταῖς ἀνάγκαις χρημάτων κρείττων φίλος.

(It is better in times of need to have friends rather than money.)

—Ancient Greek proverb

THOUGHTS OF MINNEAPOLIS jobs and former mansions for sale had to be pushed aside as I arrived for duty at the NYPD mounted training facility at Pier 57. This job, in addition to providing some dearly needed cash, also neutralized the criminal charges against me.

Sergeant Rivera gave my hand a hearty shake, standing proudly outside of a stall inhabited by Whitey, his new mount. "Whatta horse!" he said. After our triumphant ride down Fifth Avenue, Whitey had definitively come over from the dark side and was allowing other riders, specifically Seamus Rivera, on board. "Moves like butter. Needs a little more street work. You gave him a great start." Whitey had a new home, and reportedly the department paid handsomely for him. Eugene visited every few days with a bag of carrots.

"What the Czech fellow did was teach the feel," Rivera said. "The feel. Can you do that?"

"Sure," I said, because I could.

The class was six midlevel riders. Rivera joined out of curiosity. They all sat, reins too loose, hips cocked to one side in a way the Hungarian would not have tolerated for ten seconds. Except for Whitey, the horses looked sleepy.

They weren't going to like this. The Hungarian's method required weeks of plain walking, because *Zee simple is zee hardest*. I got them all going in a large circle. I asked them to call out their horses' footfalls. "Right hind, right fore, left hind, left fore," the six riders intoned, as they revolved around me like cuckoos on a Bavarian clock.

To keep their minds occupied, I said, "Let's talk about no-man's-land."

THROUGHOUT JUNE, MY three-time-a-week riding instruction gave a rhythm to my life and a welcome distraction from the moving-to-Minneapolis sands draining quickly through the hourglass. Rivera's class did well, and Whitey was thriving. I told them all the Hungarian's stories—that they were part of a tradition of ancient soldiers—just as he told us Sorrows girls. It was probably all romantic notions, but it did inspire great riding.

"Ancient soldiers, huh? People think we're just for parades," Rivera said.

Frankie jungle-gymmed at my window one morning just after the Fourth of July. One long wing plume was broken after a recent rainstorm. I wondered if he were lonely and if a parakeet colony could happen here at Number N. It seemed unlikely. The Brooklyn flock escaped together from one pet-store shipment. Frankie would get a friend only if, by some crazy circumstance, another stray parakeet found its way to the back of Number N. Fat chance.

I left Frankie a cube of apple spread with peanut butter.

My cell phone rang, showing *Angela Price*. I didn't spend as much time with Angela after I came to Number N. She didn't like visiting me because she had to pass Norah in the lobby. And I was ashamed to enter the Grandhope, where the door-men looked at me questioningly and the other residents pretended they didn't know me. Now Angela was in the Hamptons for the summer. As I picked up, I could hear surf in the background.

"I sent you a link. Did you see it?" she asked.

Angela was forever sending articles I didn't want to read. Like "Six Ways to Deal with Curly Hair." Or "How Thirty is the New Twenty." The only links that had anything to do with what might be called the "real world" were articles about apartment prices.

"Just a sec," I said.

I opened my email and found her link.

Dutifully, I clicked it.

A headshot of Rob Goodman flicked on my screen.

Hedge Fund High Flyer Makes Foray into Distressed Real Estate

Robert M. Goodman, former CEO of Hermes Fund, a hedge fund that closed in 2008, has announced the launch of Hermes2, a real estate investment firm.

"It's a great market out there for real estate investors. We're buying up distressed properties all over the country," Goodman said.

Does Goodman plan to do anything with his famous rent-controlled property at 80th Street and Fifth Avenue?

"Never say never," he said.

"Huh," I said. A real estate venture didn't violate his trading ban. Also, it seemed Goodman was weighing opportunities with Number N. Did he know about the embassy sale?

"Thought you'd be interested." Angela's voice was smug. "That's *just* the kind of thing my dad would like. He believes in real estate. Can you connect me with Rob Goodman again?"

"I haven't spoken to Goodman since the crash." We had no reason to be in touch after Hermes failed.

"It would be perfect. If I invest some of my trust money, I can put the profits into an account I control." Financial independence from her father—it was one of the two things Angela wanted most. The second was her big apartment. "It sounds like Goodman's finally gonna do something with your mom's building. That would be great for her. Do you think she'd move back to the city?" I could see the fantasy taking shape in Angela's mind: she and Mom, shopping at Bergdorf's buying *crème de la crème* stuff together.

"He's got more than Mom to deal with." I told Angela about the complication Viviane presented. Goodman probably had two buyouts on his hands. Mom was easy. As for Viviane?

"Don't be silly. People'll do anything for enough money." I didn't argue with her.

I hung up, convinced the timing of Goodman's announcement was no coincidence and that he knew about the embassy going up for sale. The dominoes were lining up to recreate the same moment as two decades before when the Deal of the Century was possible. It was probably a good thing I would be gone from New York soon. I would not be around to see both my homes-slash-legacies—the mansion and Number N—razed for a billionaire blue heron.

I ARRIVED BACK home from the NYPD barn around six o'clock one Wednesday in mid-July. My T-shirt stuck to my back with sweat, and sand grit from the arena clung to my face. There was someone standing under the Number-N awning. It was a young woman in strappy sandals and a floral dress.

"Excuse me," she said.

"Yes?"

"Are you this woman?" She held out the weeks-old *Daily News* article about me and Whitey.

"I…" I halted. Was it wise to say anything? Whitey was living in a kind of witness protection program. What could anyone do about it now? Besides, I was building a pretty big fan club at the NYPD. "I am," I conceded.

"The people at the deli said your name is Delia Mulcahy," she asserted.

"That's right," I confirmed.

"Which means you are also this girl." Out of her messenger bag, she took the popular old issue of *Upper East Side Magazine* from March 2006, the same one Angela treasured. The strappy-sandal girl flipped to the photo spread. Me in front of the Mulcahy Mansion. Me walking hand in hand with Mom. Me with Angela outside Rosemont.

"Yes," I said. "That's true." I guessed I wasn't the only one who could hit up Janice at the public library.

"This is awesome!" The woman broke into a big smile.

"I'm sorry, who are you?"

"Rebecca Shapiro," she said. "*New York Times*. Lifestyle section. One more question. This one's a long shot." She pulled out her phone and flicked her finger on it. "Is *this* you?" It was a New York society website. There I was at the 2006 Wall Street Poker Night. Someone had snapped a picture of me coming out the embassy door followed by Rob Goodman.

"Yep."

"Fabulous!" she said. "A once-heiress, now protester, living in a rent-controlled building and dating hedge-fund bachelor Robert Goodman!"

"Stop right there." She was jumping to the same conclusion as Peter Priest. "I am *not* dating Rob Goodman, nor have I ever. I worked for him at Hermes Fund."

"And he didn't know *who you were?*" She gestured to the sepia-toned magazine spread of days gone by.

"No." That night, Goodman stood in front of my portrait and didn't make any connection. "There is no *who I am* anymore. Bottom line, I *worked* for Goodman. That's it."

"Even without the Goodman-dating angle, it's still a super story. *You*, living *here* in this Hotel-Chelsea-type building, next to your old mansion and protesting against the 1 percent." She tucked away her phone and papers. "Can I please come upstairs with you? Just a few questions and a couple of pictures?"

"Actually, no."

Rebecca Shapiro readjusted her bag on her shoulder and shrugged. "If you don't, I'll just hang around. You have no idea how persistent I can be. Look, it's no big deal. I'm just pitching. They probably won't run it. Letting me upstairs for five minutes is the quickest way to get rid of me."

REBECCA SHAPIRO GAPED at the interior of Aunt Kathleen's apartment.

"How big is this thing?"

"Two bedrooms."

"Do you mind if I ask how much you pay?"

"Yes."

"This couch looks like it came from eBay." She touched the red tartan.

"I call it church rectory furniture."

"That's funny." She wrote in her notebook. "Can you pose on the couch?"

I sat. In my peripheral vision, the bird appeared over my left shoulder looking for more apple and peanut butter.

"Is that a parakeet?" Rebecca framed us in her lens to take a picture.

"Is what a parakeet?"

⌒⌒

IT WAS EIGHT thirty and dusk by the time I led Rebecca Shapiro out of the building and watched her until she was out of sight. She seemed like the kind of reporter who might scale the embassy fence for more pictures.

Norah was outside, dressed in jeans and a bright pink cowboy hat. She was standing next to a man I didn't recognize. At their feet were four small Jack Russell terriers. She handed the man some bills. He passed her the leashes of the little dogs.

"Thanks." The man saluted Norah and hopped into a beat-up white van.

"What's going on?" I asked.

"Rat catchers. He says these dogs'll do thirty a night." Norah had an empty black garbage bag at her feet.

"Don't you have enough traps and poison around? Do we

really need dogs?"

"Can't have poison with you keeping that shagging bird." Norah had softened immeasurably toward me since the Whitey episode. The coverage had been a big boost to the carriage horse crusade. She lit a cigarette. "Rat catching with dogs is a new sport downtown. You let them loose in the alley and the fun is on. Dead rats flying everywhere." She left a bright orange lipstick print on the speckled paper of her fag. "Do you need any money?"

"Excuse me?"

"Do you need any fucking money? Because I can lend it to you."

"I need so much money, you can't imagine."

"Quarter million or so?"

"About that."

Norah took a steep inhalation. "Fuck."

I sighed. "It all seems so crazy now. My coming back to New York. Trying to... Hell, I'm not even sure what I was trying to do or why."

"Something was left to you and you got fucked out of it. Countries go to war over bollocks like that." Norah streamed smoke out her nose like a dragon.

"Yeah."

"Why don't you stop paying rent? Goodman will never know. I'll make it up somewhere else."

"Thanks. But I pay Mom and she pays the rent. She'd make me keep paying *her* even if you said she could skip a month or two."

"Sounds like your mother."

"Why is she like that?"

"Your mother?"

"Yeah.

Norah sipped the last few millimeters of her smoke. "Your mother never thought she was good enough." Funny. Bert said the same thing. "It made her afraid things would be taken away from her. Then they were. So, I guess she was right." Norah ground the cigarette under her heel. I thought of all the years I'd spent resenting things that were taken away from me. "Kathleen was another story."

"Yes," I said. "I suppose you were right saying I take after my mother."

"I called you a whore. That's different." Norah toed the butt into the gutter. "Well, you saved the horse. That'll be one thing you accomplished with your life."

Chapter Thirty-Five

Don't put on grand airs. The time for that sort of thing is past. You are not a princess any longer.

—Frances Hodgson Burnett, *A Little Princess*

I WAS EXCHANGING emails with Telefony now. It looked as if this job was really going to happen. As the calendar edged toward August, with Labor Day in sight, they were finalizing hires. I supplied them with updated references and résumé—trying to make my freelance work fixing websites' video players sound more important than it was. I gave them permission to do a credit check, which I would pass. For now, anyway.

My newly fixed doorbell chimed. "It's me," Judith's gravelly voice rattled.

Today she was wearing voluminous gray palazzo pants with the red shoes. Her hand rested on the silver hilt of her cane.

"I have liquor this time," I said, as she dismissed her aide. My small NYPD stipend allowed me to indulge in a few luxuries, like a ten-dollar white wine and a bottle of Johnny Walker Red.

"Is it after five?" She looked at the clock she could not see. It said four fifteen.

"Yes."

"Scotch."

I poured the amber liquid into a glass with ice. Judith's head continued its motion, like the radar on an airport tower. "We're in for a nasty hurricane season," she said.

The weather people were reporting that. I thought it was all a little alarmist. The blizzard they predicted in January turned out to be a drizzle. "So they say."

"There. We've covered the weather." Judith swirled the ice in her glass. "I hear there has been a *rapprochement* between you and our local hoarder."

"Yes." I sighed. I had failed in my one try at getting the spoon jar. Judith, no doubt, was here to pressure me to attempt another. I wasn't sure I could manage an actual break-in. Judith looked out the window toward Viviane's tapping her red toe.

Here it came.

Then, it didn't.

"So, about that Angela," Judith said.

"What about Angela?"

"You realize the moment I die her whole *plan* comes together. The one to get a big apartment."

"So you've mentioned. Repeatedly. She gets your apartment."

"Not just my apartment. She gets *your* apartment."

"*My* apartment!" Did Judith do nothing but spin conspiracy theories?

"Yes!" Cane stamp. "Ask yourself: why did she do cartwheels with the co-op board so *you* could buy that apartment? Why did she help you find a subletter? Because she needs you to hang on to it until I die."

"Oh, good grief!" I said. "If Angela wanted my apartment, she could have just bought it when it came on the market in 2006." Then I remembered her saying she couldn't.

Stamp, stamp. "What about the co-op rules? You have to *live* in an apartment if you own it."

"Okay, fine. But why did she want me specifically to buy it? Anyone could serve that purpose."

"Not anyone! Think, Delia! You showing up was the answer to her dreams! What could be better than her best friend occupying that apartment? Especially one who would owe her! You would be like a caretaker. Remember how she didn't want you to renovate your kitchen? She doesn't want to have to rip out a lot of new cabinetry. She waits until I die, then buys mine, then yours. One, two, three. Before I'm cold, Angela'll be at your door with an offer you can't refuse. I can hear it now. After all she's done for you...you wouldn't stand in her way...she'll find you a better apartment...*la la la.*"

"Huh." I supposed anything was possible. I was grateful to Angela for all the ways she'd helped me, but I was also realistic about who she was.

One thing was indisputable. If Angela did want to join all three apartments, events had to go in a specific order. Judith's first, then mine, or both at once.

"Getting my apartment, oh, well, that's okay. She gets a four bedroom," Judith went on. "Getting my apartment *and* your apartment—that's six bedrooms at least."

A Vermeer.

"Just you wait. You'll see. I won't be around to say I told you so. But I'll be saying it just the same. I just hope that day doesn't arrive *prematurely.*" She gave her cane a final dramatic stamp. "I plan to live to a hundred and six."

"You won't have the pleasure of an I-told-you-so, in the flesh or otherwise. I'm leaving. Probably in another month. The apartment will go into foreclosure. I have no choice. Angela's grand scheme, if there is such a thing, is not going to be revealed."

"Does she know?"

"Not yet," I said. Though I knew I would have to give her a heads-up soon.

"Oh, well," Judith said, clinking her ice. "Then we'll never know one way or the other, now will we?"

"Guess not."

"By the by." She reached into her pocket, pulled out a card, and handed it to me. It was simple, black and white, with a 212 number and the name Martin Norton. "I want you to have this. I'm no spring chicken, you know. I certainly intend to live to a hundred and six, but if I don't, or if *other forces intervene*, and you do happen to acquire the spoon jar, call Marty. He's the only one I trust to move it if I am no longer *in residence*."

MY SOMEWHAT TROUBLING conversation with Judith left me considering my friendship with Angela once again. Was Judith's theory possible? It would mean that back in 2006, when I first arrived in New York, Angela spotted the opportunity to get me in that apartment. She then waited, like an alligator blending into the surface of a pond, for her moment to strike. Were my childhood punctuation marks right after all? That kind of years-long planning would require more than quotation marks around the word "friend." It would need diabolical asterisks and footnotes.

Since a foreclosure was certain, I wouldn't find out, and I was honestly happier not to know.

Plotter or not, Angela needed a heads-up about the foreclosure. I had to tell my subletters, and Angela would find out from them anyway. Someone needed to inform the co-op board before an auctioneer arrived.

I really wanted to avoid the conversation. Saying it all out loud made it real, and part of me was still hoping for a miracle. Saving Whitey had seemed impossible. But here he was: horse employee #1 at the NYPD. There was also Frankie surviving in my window box. Maybe something good could happen—like an enchanted stretchy cloak creating a space for me.

I knew in my heart this was what they called "magical thinking." I steeled myself and dialed my cell phone. When Angela answered, I heard the voices of children playing in the background.

I told her about my financial situation, my timeclock, and the fact that I would be leaving after Labor Day.

"I can't believe it's that bad!" A seagull cawed, matching her alarmed tone. That bad? It was the worst recession in two generations. Sometimes I wondered what planet Angela was living on. Then I reminded myself it was the planet where three-year-olds flew on private jets to birthday parties, where the neighbor-lady spent a hundred kay a year on her fall wardrobe, and where consignment stores sold handbags considered dirt cheap at eight grand.

"Yes, Angela. It's that bad."

"But you're so *busy!*" she exclaimed. "I thought you had like three jobs. All that contract stuff." I felt a bit of Angelo Conti's frustration with his daughter—that it was necessary to explain how a few freelance jobs at twenty-seven bucks an hour would not, in fact, support a two-million-dollar apartment.

"It's just not enough." I told her I'd talked to Sarah, that nobody would pay more than one-point-eight million, and that

I needed the full two million to get out from under my mortgage.

"You have to hold out. You just *have* to."

"Actually, Ange, I don't *have* to."

"It's so frustrating I can't buy it," she said, and I felt a little hurt she was thinking about that rather than me having to relocate for a soul-killing job and face life after foreclosure. Angela sat for a moment in silence. "When?" she asked. "Exactly."

"September." I told her it would probably take another month before the foreclosure proceedings kicked in. My Telefony salary could potentially extend my mortgage payments another couple of months, but what was the point? The only reason to keep paying at all was to secure the Telefony job. If the apartment was going to be foreclosed upon, once I was safely in Minneapolis, why keep paying?

"The board is gonna hate that," Angela said. *"Anybody* could buy the apartment at auction."

"Ange."

"Okay. I understand," she said.

Th e calendar flipped to August. It felt as if time stopped, partly because August was so empty on the Upper East Side. All of senior-level banking and finance took the month off, European-style. You could cross Park Avenue without looking for traffic. Gridlock transferred to downtown East Hampton, where it took an hour to drive six blocks.

One Sunday morning, I was looking at the pile of newspapers in front of the Parthenon deli when I heard an unmistakable cry from Angela.

"Dee!" She came trotting down the block. She wore lime-green pants leaping with pink frogs.

"What are you doing in town?"

"Business." That was strange. Angela never had business. "Never mind that," she panted. "Did you see this?" Angela flapped the *Times* lifestyle section in front of my nose.

"See what?"

"Oh my God, Delia! Sometimes I think you live under a rock!" She opened the paper.

The headline read:

Rent-Controlled Princess. The Riches to Rags to Riches to Rags Story of One New York Heiress

Rebecca Shapiro had written her story and the *Times* ran it.

UPSTAIRS IN MY apartment, Angela spread the article on the kitchen counter. The photo editors had even unearthed pictures of my great-grandfather. He was standing next to a newly built power station, Waterside Number One on 14th Street. Under him the caption read, "Mulcahy progenitor, the inventor credited with electrifying New York." There was my grandfather and grandmother at the family factory, a wall of circuit breakers behind them. "Most pre-war buildings in New York still have Mulcahy electrical components. The company was forced into bankruptcy in 1986 due to quality-control issues."

Next came society pictures from the seventies and eighties. There was a stunner of Mom during her modeling career on the cover of *Harper's Bazaar*. Then Mom and Dad at their wedding reception, one greeting a Kennedy and the other a Vanderbilt. The caption read, "The third generation, Mr. & Mrs. John Mulcahy. Their union was the wedding of the decade."

They'd found a shot of Mom in the green Valentino and did a side-by-side with me at Wall Street Poker night. The caption read, "Two generations in Valentino. Mrs. John Mulcahy, the former model Margot Conover, and daughter Brigid ('Delia') Mulcahy at her former home."

Mom and I looked like twins.

Finally came the *Daily News* pictures, of me piloting the carriage down Fifth Avenue ("Mulcahy takes up arms against the one percent"), me on the tartan plaid couch ("Mulcahy at her rent-controlled home"). The yellow and green parakeet was clearly visible behind my head, looking directly at the camera as if he too wanted fifteen minutes of fame.

I quickly scanned the article copy.

Brigid ("Delia") Mulcahy, 38, lives at 10 East 80th Street, popularly known as Number N, a place ranking with the Hotel Chelsea as one of the few remaining rent-controlled buildings in the city. Her apartment looks directly out over her former home, the soon-to-be sold Greek embassy.

Before losing her job during the 2008 financial collapse, Mulcahy worked at Hermes Fund. In an ironic coincidence, Robert M. Goodman, former CEO of Hermes Fund, owns the rent-controlled building where Mulcahy now lives.

We moved to the living room with our coffee cups. "I just *love* this!" Angela flopped into the rocking chair and pointed to the picture of me in the Valentino next to Mom in the Valentino. "I already mailed a copy to your mom. I knew you wouldn't."

As I faced the back of the couch, across the way Viviane raised her coffee cup to me in "good morning." Viv looked up to the sky and shrugged a question mark. I twiddled my fingers to indicate it was going to rain. She smiled, disappeared out of sight, and popped up, umbrella in hand. I gave her the thumbs-up.

"Who's that?" Angela asked watching the pantomime.

"Neighbor," I said.

"Look at all that stuff," Angela leaned over and squinted to see into the depths of the apartment where stacks rose from the floor. At that moment, Viviane caught sight of Angela, and the blinds came crashing down. "*That's* the hoarder!"

I suddenly regretted telling Angela about Viviane and worse—bringing her upstairs without a thought to Viviane's privacy. "Oh, I'm starting to think that's all an exaggeration," I said.

"Exaggeration?" Angela gasped. I had gotten used to the coral reef of stuff, but I remembered what a shock it was when I first saw it.

"You know she runs that consignment shop above the old boutique. It's probably inventory for the store."

"Huh." Angela's eyes remained fixed on the window. "I hear that store has a great stock of Birkin bags," she said distractedly.

Sounds clattered in the hallway: the little girl's babbling about shoelaces and elevator-button pushing. In addition to Natalie's voice and Viviane's, I heard an exclamation of "Bollocks!" from Norah.

My doorbell chimed and I left Angela veritably caressing

the *Times* article.

Norah peered around a giant orchid. The stems were two feet tall.

"You just got this fucking plant," Norah said. She pushed by me to set the orchid on the coffee table. The wood creaked heavily. The stems bobbed. The blossoms had petals like yellow-speckled tongues. The bird hopped onto his coffee-cup shelter to get a better look. To Frankie, it must have been like a flower from home.

Angela glared at Norah. Norah glared back. Norah referred to Angela as "that mafia bitch." I was sure she'd done it in Angela's earshot.

"Aren't you going to open the fucking card?" Norah asked.

"Okay." I reached between the rain-forest stems to extract the card.

To the princess who got away!

Great to finally know where you are.

Dinner?

—RMG

Chapter Thirty-Six

Yet hear me, people, we have now to deal with another race ... and the love of possession is a disease with them. These people have made many rules that the rich may break but the poor may not.

—Sitting Bull

A NGELA REACHED FOR the card; Norah snatched it first. "Wanker," she said, flung the card down on the table and left.

Angela retrieved it. "Oh my God, Delia! He wants to have dinner."

"Apparently he does."

"I mean think of it. This is *today's* paper. It's not even ten a.m. He read about you then immediately sent you an orchid!"

"Yeah." I sat next to Angela, taking the card and fingering it.

"He seems really interested."

"I don't know." Goodman had a certain kind of interest; I was pretty sure of that.

"Relationship kind of interested." Relationship seemed a little extreme for one orchid. "It makes sense, a guy his age. See the way things work out!"

"What do you mean work out?"

"Whadda you mean what do I mean? Just when the chips are down, this rich guy appears! It's the perfect solution."

"Oh, Ange." She was nothing if not consistent.

"Don't *oh Ange* me." She stood up and put her hands on her hips. "You still have two months before they start the..." Angela could not bring herself to use the word *foreclosure*. "That's plenty of time to wind him around your little finger. The way you always do with men. Once you're his girlfriend, he'll help." I sighed. Only Angela could be disconnected enough to believe any new beau would instantly offer two-hundred-thousand-dollars' worth of "help." I would never accept financial help from Goodman or any other boyfriend, but I wasn't going to argue with Angela about it. "You are going to go to dinner with him, aren't you?"

"Yes," I said, because I did want to have dinner with him, and I wanted what would come after. I deserved some fun before I left for Minneapolis. "I *will* go to dinner."

"That's a start," said Angela, sitting down, smiling. "And while you're there, will you *please* remind him the princess has a *friend*? One who is *dying* to invest in his real estate deals?"

I agreed.

I went to bed that night in my nunnish single bed. Ironically, I had been living like a nun for a long while. I had been too busy for a fling during my hedge fund days. Now I was here in Aunt Kathleen's apartment with the chenille-covered single bed and bookcase of religious books.

I fell asleep and had startlingly sexual dreams, waking up wet and in need of release. Maybe, a date with Rob Goodman would put an end to my time of abstinence.

ENGLISH IVY TWINED up potted topiaries in perfect spiral cones at the entrance to Daniel. The plants seemed to say, "We are not average ivy. We are prima donna ivy." I wore the Valentino, which I never returned to Mom.

Corinthian columns vaulted me into the dining space. I approached the table where Rob Goodman sat. He stood up. I could see the instant impression I made on him. I still had my catnip-to-men quality, penniless or not.

"The princess arrives," he said with his chip-toothed smile. Tousle-haired as ever, he wore a custom-tailored linen jacket ($3,500).

The captain pulled out my chair. Another white-coated waiter adjusted Rob's seat for him. A third took Mom's Chanel bag and placed it next to me on its own miniature velvet stool. It was an enchanted forest of attentiveness where staff materialized like wood elves.

The sommelier apparated, greeting Goodman like an old friend. He presented a phone-book-thick wine list and poured two glasses of champagne from a bottle with a label curled by age. "With our compliments," he said, and evaporated.

"To the future," Goodman said as we clinked flutes. "May it turn out more profitably than the past." He raised an eyebrow and grinned.

"I'm sorry how everything ended."

"Easy come, easy go." Goodman waved his hand, reminding me of how much I liked his nonchalance with money. "It was an eight-deviation event. Besides, I made out okay in the end. Not as well as a guy like Priest, but better than a lot of the poor bastards out there." A waiter appeared. Goodman ordered caviar. Turning back to me, his eyes widened as he realized I was one of the poor bastards. "I'm sorry. It was stupid to say that."

"It's okay."

"It must feel like the second time around for you. Based on what the paper is saying." His grin was sheepish. I smiled back, telegraphing that it really was okay. He exhaled. "I can't believe I stood right next to you that day with your portrait in front of me, and I didn't see it."

"It's not important. Ancient history."

He shook his head. "Then you rode a horse? In the bus lane? To the Greek embassy."

"Amazing the skills you learn in finishing school."

"You realize you were breaking like ten laws?"

"The horse did seem to have an expired inspection sticker."

He threw his head back and laughed. A menu was put into my hands. Oddly it had no amounts on it. The captain leaned in. "Only the gentleman sees the prices."

Goodman tilted his menu down tauntingly and then back up. "Chivalry is not dead." He winked. "At least in menus."

I felt my pulse under my collarbone. A waiter appeared at that moment to pour more water. A wisp of annoyance crossed Goodman's face as if a fly landed on him.

"You like caviar?" Goodman asked.

"I adore caviar."

"I can always spot a woman who does." He tilted his head suggestively.

The dish arrived. Black pearls of beluga caviar glistened at the apex of an ice-filled crystal bowl. It was enough to fill two sewing thimbles. Two eensy tortoise-shell spoons rested on the edge of the bowl. The accoutrements included tiny blinis snuggled in a silver tray, the napkin swaddling them as if tucking them into bed, chopped egg white, egg yolk, capers, onions, and crème fraîche, the literal *crème de la crème.*

I had no menu to inform me, but I guessed the single dish cost $500. I chose a warm blini and dipped my spoon into the nest of eggs. Goodman watched me. "It's amazing how much you look like your mother in those old pictures. Margot Conover? Is she still alive?"

Mom really had managed to stay off Goodman's radar. When she got famous, everyone knew her as Margot Conover. But it was the Condon sisters, Peggy and Kathleen, whose names were on the lease.

"Yes," I said.

"Where does she live now?"

"On Long Island. She's just a regular senior citizen."

We finished the caviar and champagne. A great ceremony of choosing and tasting wine ensued. The next dish was a napoleon with *foie gras* between the layers. The dish was so beautiful it was as if it aspired to be something other than food.

"That green dress you're wearing belonged to your mother?" Goodman leaned over to get a better look, eyes pausing on my legs. "I also read that in the paper."

"Enough about me in the press," I said, encouraged by his lingering look. "I have some questions about *you.*" Rob himself was a source of information about the past, but I had to tread lightly.

"You're going to bring up that old skeleton in my closet? Living at Number N—I'm sure you heard rumors."

"I heard something about your father."

"I thought so."

"What do *you* think happened?" My heart beat faster, but I couldn't let on how much this mattered to me. Goodman didn't know my connection to Mom; therefore, he didn't know my connection to Aunt Kathleen.

Goodman shook his head. "I guess it's *possible* my father really did push that woman off the roof," he said with incredible calm. "She was complicating a huge real estate deal. My dad, well let's just say we never really got along."

"I get it." I remembered in our first conversation he said something about having to do everything himself from the time he was a teenager.

"Dad was trying to join our building and your old house, which came up for sale around that time. Just like today. Ironic how everything comes around. It would have changed *everything* for my family." Goodman set his glass down emphatically. So, he too had a lost kingdom, of sorts. "The police said it was a suicide. I guess she had problems. In the end, whoever knows anything about anyone?"

"I agree about that."

"It could also have been a tragic accident."

"True." Goodman had no more information than anyone else. I sighed. Then an idea occurred to me, "Now that it's for sale, why don't you buy the embassy?"

Goodman guffawed. "I'm flattered by your assumption. But I don't have *that* kind of money. I've heard a few shell corporations are circling. I'll be phone-call-number-one for whoever does buy it. Everyone knows the deal that needs to be made. Both buildings gone. A new tower on the corner. There'll be a joint venture or partnership. I just need to know who I'm dealing with."

"Makes sense." I sipped my wine. White, French, and probably $300 a bottle.

"I'm preparing. I have a couple of tenants to negotiate with before I can do anything." A *couple* of tenants. So Goodman knew he had to deal with Viviane. "One is this Mrs. Condon. That's the one you're subletting from?"

"Yep," I agreed, giving a mental tip-of-the-hat to Rebeca Shapiro for identifying Mom as *the former model Margot Conover*.

"I've never even laid eyes on her. How do you know her, by the way?"

"Family friend. On my mother's side." Mom had the right to sublet her apartment and doing so had a side benefit. It masked the fact that she otherwise didn't live there. Rent-controlled law required tenants to be in residence six months out of the year.

"Frankly, I'd be happy if everyone were a Mrs. Condon." Goodman finished off his wine. A waiter rushed over to refill it. "I hear she's eager for a buyout and, frankly, I'll gladly pay her. Someone who's hung on to a rent-controlled apartment for that long, since 1969—I can do business with a person like that. My only problem in life are people who have no price. It really presses my buttons." I recalled Viviane's comment that *some things aren't about the money*. "I become like a different person. It's not what I like to say about myself. Especially on first date with a beautiful woman, but there it is. Do you think that's awful?"

Awful? Who was I to judge? I had a side deal with Corning while I was employed by this man; I had contemplated selling an ancient artifact on the black market; and I was currently concealing the fact that "Mrs. Condon" was actually my mother. "No. It's not awful."

We were quiet for a moment. The lamb chops arrived, tiny as elves' hockey sticks. When we were finished, there was a graveyard of eensy bones.

The waiters removed our plates and bushed crumbs off the table with small silver-handled brooms. "I've been wanting to talk to that friend of yours. I haven't seen her in a while. I dropped out of a bunch of boards after the crash," Goodman said, wiping his mouth.

"Angela?"

"I've heard her father can be an aggressive real estate investor."

"I can give you her number." I looked for something to write on, and Goodman flagged the captain, who presented me with a blank card and gold pen.

"Before you ask—no, it was *not* the reason I invited you to dinner. At least two respected *New York City* news organizations have confirmed I can't resist a princess."

Dessert was tiny custards served in hollowed out and painted eggshells.

As we sat sipping brandy brought from a vault, Goodman ran a finger down the outside of my arm, which rested on the crisp, white cloth. A thrill traveled along my skin. "You can't believe what a temptation you were. I had to keep it professional because Mitch would have killed me. I stayed away from the office just to avoid your effect on me." Goodman repositioned his napkin in his lap, grinning devilishly.

The bill, when it arrived, was presented in a folder worthy of a private-wealth-management portfolio. I guessed it was north of two thousand dollars.

I felt like an older version of myself when, as we stood up, I said, "Let's go to your place." He put his hand at the curve of my back and the electricity of desire traveled through the tips of his fingers.

A photographer snapped our picture as we left. Goodman

courted the press and they courted him back. He smiled broadly and made a triumphant gesture as if to indicate he found the errant princess.

I STEPPED INTO his tremendous fifteen-million-dollar Hell's Kitchen apartment for the second time. We were hardly in the door before his arms were around me, unzipping my dress in one quick motion. He backed me into his windowed living room, high and open as a falcon's nest.

The effect of gazing from a New York skyscraper at night is similar to the sensation of new love. There is amazement, exhilaration, a kind of admiration bordering on disbelief. Today, with nothing but a pane of glass between us and the air, we hovered on the edge of beyond. I felt my dress slip off my shoulders and his audible sigh.

The facts of the vista, exhilarating and vertiginous, sharpened all bodily sensations. We sank to the floor in front of a convenient ottoman, so he could take me in a position where we could both see the view.

As I expected, he was a fabulous lover. He penetrated, hard and purposeful, relishing getting what he wanted with a satisfaction that was classic Rob Goodman.

Chapter Thirty-Seven

Money can't buy love, but it improves your bargaining position.

—Anonymous

WAS I SURPRISED that Rob Goodman wanted to go out with me again and just two days later? Not in the least. The sex was great, and men were like that. It was one of the things I appreciated about them so much in the past. Goodman brought out the previous version of me, which had been waning since my move to Number N. It made perfect sense. *That* Delia was an excellent match for him. I was happy to let her have full run of things for a while. She was strong and hard-shelled, weather-proof and clear about her needs. She deserved her time in the sun.

On our next date, we ate downtown, high-end sushi this time, rare fishes flown in that morning from Japan, with a bill of only $1100. The sex after was slower, more purposeful, and even hotter—if that were possible.

A second orchid arrived, and a third.

Norah set the new one on my windowsill. It was small with spiky leaves and primordial blossoms fringed purple and green.

"You're just fucking him, right?"

"Yes." It was a tad more complicated than that, I thought.

But, then, not really.

"Then you'll leave and break his heart?"

I didn't peg Goodman as the broken-hearted type. On the other hand, he was showing some unusual persistence. I recalled again Angela's comment he might be looking for a relationship. But I was going to Minneapolis. "Maybe a little bit."

"Good."

I didn't tell Goodman about my Minneapolis plans on our second date. I didn't want to disrupt the fun. Eventually, I would need to be honest with him.

The growing orchid collection on the windowsill fascinated the bird. It was as if a tiny bit of his rainforest home had arrived. It made for a funny scene, Frankie on the outside looking in at the tropical foliage within.

⌒⌒

I WAS DRINKING tea in the morning and watching the bird, savoring titillating memories of my third date with Goodman, wondering where he would take me for our fourth, when my cell phone rang. Co-op president Sandy Roache's name lit up the screen. I winced. Angela must have said something to the board about my pending foreclosure. I didn't blame her. She had to keep living at the Grandhope, and she needed to prepare the board for what was about to happen. Maybe she also wanted some extra pressure on me to start a relationship with Rob Goodman. Angela did have that side to her, too.

I had forewarning he would be exceptionally cranky. Angela gossiped he'd inadvertently sent a porno email around to the whole board. Several old ladies experienced loud videos taking complete control over their computers, multiple windows spawning, all containing sexual positions and practices they had no idea even existed. Roache's presidency, which he'd held for twenty years, was now in jeopardy.

"You know, Delia," he said. "The reason we *have* financial requirements is so shareholders can carry their apartments through a downturn."

I was about to retort to Roache *he* had been the one to waive key aspects of the financial requirement, when I thought better of it. "Yes. I know that."

"A foreclosure at the Grandhope is unthinkable."

"Right."

"I insist you reconsider. What you do affects all our values."

"Is anyone in the building planning to sell anytime soon?" Most of the people at the Grandhope were rooted there like oak trees.

Silence on the other end of the line. "No," Roache said finally. "It's the idea of it. No one likes to *see* their values dropping." Wow. He really *was* the façade guy.

"You can't force me to keep my apartment," I said. "It's a co-op, not Hotel California."

He was not amused. "Not good, Delia. Not good. I can't believe you and Angela put us in this position. You need to find a solution. That's what people do in these situations. They. Find. The. Money."

⌒⌒⌒

DINNERS WITH GOODMAN weren't the only repercussions of the *Times* article.

A few days later, I got an email from a guy running a blog called Gotham Bird. They received hundreds of emails about the parakeet behind my head in the article. The guy said I should be flattered my bird attracted his attention. Gotham Bird was number-one in bird-related web traffic in the city, with hundreds of thousands of visitors each month. The site featured a map of the five boroughs where a team of his best birdwatchers posted their sightings. They tracked the feathered celebs, like Pale Male and his descendants, an egret in the boat pond, a family of owls in the North Woods, and a Cape May warbler that appeared around Tax Day in April. An ornithologist and an avian vet wrote for Gotham Bird.

According to these experts, parakeets were hardier than people thought. The site received sightings of escaped pet parakeets all the time. Another member of his species might find Frankie. If another famous gaggle, *a la* Brooklyn, was about to form, Gotham Bird wanted the scoop.

He asked me to blog about the bird, for free.

I told him *free* was a non-starter.

I added up what he must be spending on avian vets and ornithologists. My technical knowledge could come in handy here. "Instead of a blog, how about I install a webcam and send you a feed?"

"Wow. That would be awesome! Traffic will soar."

"You pay for the hardware. Then, I'll install it and keep it running. I'll send you the code to update your site. For a hundred bucks a month."

He agreed.

The money wouldn't put a dent in my foreclosure fate. But a hundred bucks was a hundred bucks.

RETURNING HOME FROM an NYPD riding lesson the next day, I went to Best Buy for a webcam. It was wireless, weatherproof, and ran on batteries with backup solar power. I installed it, and Frankie approached the lens, tilting his head from side to side, greeting his public.

What would happen to him when I left? The thought stabbed my heart. I knew Norah would feed him and make sure he had shelter for a while. But what about when they tore Number N down? I imagined the bird in the path of a wrecking ball, colored feathers flying.

Then I remembered there were no wrecking balls anymore. They now disassembled a building from the inside out, stuffing it all down the elevator shaft, making the edifice seem to digest itself.

When all of that happened, where else would the bird find a perfect microclimate mash-up of illegal window box and stove vent?

I WAS STANDING on the afternoon coffee line at the Parthenon the second week in August. Steam billowed from the cauldron-sized coffeepots. Suddenly, I felt a tap on my shoulder. I turned around and was enveloped in a bear hug.

"Mr. Conti!" I muffled into his shoulder.

"Angelo, please." He let me go. He wore a silk paisley tie and prominent gold cuff links. How Angela liked to play up her father as a mobster to the girls at Sorrows! It terrified them. Who was he now? Clearly a successful businessman. Maybe one who could call on fellas from the old neighborhood in a pinch.

"Long time no see, honey. Angie tells me about you. How *are* you?" His question told me he knew but wasn't going to say it.

"Good. Good," I lied.

"Okay, okay," he said. "It's thanks to you Angie brought me a bona fide business opportunity."

"I'm glad," I said. "She's been really good to me these last couple of years."

"What goes around comes around. I'll never forget how kind Kathleen was to her. God rest her soul. If this real estate deal works out, my daughter may get off the payroll yet."

"That would be great," I said.

"This guy with real estate fund. He your new boyfriend?"

"Yeah," I said.

"Better be good to you or he'll hear from me." I smiled and let Mr. Conti pinch my chin the way he used to when I was ten.

⌒

THE NEXT TWENTY-FOUR hours were busy. I was out early to teach riding. Rivera knew I was leaving and was packing in their last lessons. We were up to trotting. It was a magical transformation, horses and riders operating as one.

"It's like he can hear me think," said Rivera, after a beautiful ride on Whitey.

I stopped at home to change, then off to my fifth date with Goodman, high-end Indian for $1300, followed by Hell's Kitchen after-dinner sex. I was thinking more and more that maybe Angela was right about his relationship kind of interest. I wanted to be honest with him because I actually liked Goodman. I always had.

"Listen," I said rubbing my hair with a towel. "I'm having a wonderful time. But you need to know I'm not in such a great place."

"The trouble with your apartment?" I was slightly surprised at that, but then thought Angela probably told him to lay the groundwork for an appeal to help me out.

"Yes, that." I could have told him right then and there I was moving to Minneapolis. But something else was more at the heart of the matter. "And other things."

"Like?"

"Like I've never been a relationship kind of girl. I've always been, I don't know, out for myself."

"That sounds like your version of: *it's not you, it's me.*"

"It really *is* me, Rob."

Goodman took a sip of brandy and put down his glass thoughtfully. The boyishness dissolved.

"What if I said I'm not going to go away?"

"I would say it's a free country, that I've told you where I stand, and it's not going to change. I've been this way all my life."

"Maybe you'll reconsider—if I send you enough orchids." Rob reached out, cupped the back of my head with one hand and ripped away my towel with the other, ready for another round.

I LEFT THE next morning to teach another lesson, dodging Goodman to get out the door because my leather-seated riding pants turned him on. I used my hurry as an excuse to avoid, once again, mentioning my impending departure. I knew I was procrastinating, but I let myself off the hook. Rob's reaction wasn't going to change things, so why ruin whatever time we had together?

He might believe he was brokenhearted for a bit, but he would get over it and move on to another princess. The Jet-Setter website said Charlotte Casiraghi of Monaco was planning her fall shopping trip to New York.

When I got back to the apartment at three, I cut some apple for the bird, then collapsed on the red tartan couch to watch him eat it. I was exhausted, sexually sated, and sad in equal measures. I had survived leaving New York before. I would do so again. I recalled the feelings from decades ago, losing my home and my world. Then, it was a mansion, a family, and a fortune. Today it was an eccentric bird in a window box and a place, furnished with rectory furniture, which had somehow become dear.

Across the way, Viviane entered her apartment and flung her purse down. I remembered her mentioning a meeting at school. I assumed it was to meet Natalie's teacher this year. Evidently it had not gone well. I waved to get her attention. I turned my palms to the ceiling and shrugged *What's up?* She looked back with a wet blotchy face and twisted a tissue.

Chapter Thirty-Eight

The petty thief is imprisoned, but the big thief becomes
a feudal lord.

—Zhuangzi

"WHAT'S GOING ON?" I asked when she opened the door.
"Oh...I...I...I can't even say it." In the low light,
her stacks looked ever more like formations on the sea floor.

"Just spit it out."

Her hazel eyes were browner today, and they fixed me in
stricken wordlessness.

"Is it," I ventured, "something to do with your *circumstances?*" She nodded agreement with the familiar euphemism, and
two tears broke over her lower lashes. "Were your *circumstances*
the reason for the meeting with the school?"

She took a few quick steps across the room to straighten a
stack of magazines, repositioning the edges so that the fluorescent sticky-note tabs lined up. "Someone made a report.
About...*my circumstances.*"

"Who made the report?" I asked. But a candidate came instantly to mind.

"They're not allowed to say. The school called child protective services." I felt a chill. "They already interviewed Natalie."

Viviane stopped. Both of us were picturing Natalie chattering to the social worker, innocently describing how they lived.

"Oh, Viviane."

"I've heard...they could take her away. A social worker is coming here."

"When?"

"Tomorrow."

BY TEN P.M., I'd organized a crew. I'd enlisted all the dog walkers and dry cleaners from the second and first floors, men and boys scurrying in and out with dollies. There was Norah, in a pink tank top, with her preternatural strength, cursing at the actor to put his back into it. His patrician face glistened with sweat.

Boxes, bags, crates, and cartons were all staged in the hallway, loaded on the elevator and ferried out the service entrance. Across the alley, Nikos, the embassy guard, directed traffic through the garden and down to the basement.

Viviane stood in the middle of the frenzy wearing the half-mad look of an animal trapped in a fire.

"That mafia bitch. I'll fucking kill her," Norah hissed as she hauled shopping bags. "I'll send her a box of dead rats."

"There's no way to know it was her," I said.

Norah was right, of course. From our time as schoolmates, I knew the lengths to which Angela would go. Now she and her father were Goodman's investors. Viviane was complicating the deal, which was now *her* deal. Angela would see no purpose in Goodman making offers and counteroffers. Instead, she took things into her own hands.

So did I.

I didn't care about business deals today, boyfriend or no boyfriend. There was only the prospect of a little girl being taken away from her mother. I knew how that felt. Other events of the past might be destined to repeat, but that one wouldn't. Not if I could help it.

I went to check out the kitchen, where I'd assigned the yoga instructor. She was putting the toasters into a box and writing "toasters" on it with a Sharpie marker. She picked up the spoon jar, dumped out the spoons and paused to examine it.

"I'll take that." I grasped the neck of the spoon jar. The yoga instructor looked at me but let go of the jar. I acted on reflex; just an urge to rescue a priceless artifact from a Sharpie-armed yogi. I slipped next door to my apartment, hid the spoon jar under my pillow, and returned to Viviane's.

In a few hours, my neck and back aching from strain, I went to the embassy basement to take stock. The basement was a many-chambered warren with wires, pipes and conduit snaking overhead. There was an old-style DC generator, which, I imagined, could still be fired up.

A line of switchboxes last updated in the sixties said Mulcahy, Mulcahy, Mulcahy as if to remind me my DNA was wired into the grid of the city.

Nikos drew his sleeve across his forehead. "*Polla.*" *Too much.*

"It is."

Black marker-scrawled boxes said, "kitchen, living room, bedroom one, bedroom two." To anyone who knew Viviane's apartment, this method of labeling was utterly absurd. A thing at Viv's only had meaning in relation to other things. A magazine halfway up the stack in the living room might mean,

"A fashion magazine from the time I was interested in hats, related to my hat-craft phase, which is in the shopping bag to the right." Now, the towers were disassembled, snapping these delicate associations. A whole world had shivered into a thousand pieces.

By three a.m., Viviane's apartment was clear of all boxes and bags, and she looked as if she had been flayed alive.

Norah vacuumed the carpet, trying to erase the gray haloes where each stack had been. The yoga instructor brought a few articles of furniture from her apartment, a fluffy batik futon, a poster, an area rug.

Norah stomped her foot at the stubborn gray marks. She left and returned with a bucket and a scrub brush.

I got into bed at four and took the spoon jar from under my pillow. Across its orange surface, black shadows of women processed, all carrying their own vessels, painted with women, to the seat of the gods. It was like an infinity mirror. I myself was no Judith, but even I could see the thing was exquisite. I replaced it under my pillow and fell dead asleep next to it. The lump of pottery was deeply comforting.

THE SOCIAL WORKER arrived the next day, a pudgy, middle-aged Latina in a brown suit and large hoop earrings. Viviane's blinds were drawn up so emphatically they seemed to imply they would never close again. The bird fluttered to the tree to look, as surprised as anyone at the change of scene.

The social worker didn't seem to notice the wide-eyed amazement on Natalie's face at the apartment's new orderliness. Norah's scrub brush had done its trick. The carpet was clean, if a little damp in spots. Heroically, Viviane preserved a calm smile. After about an hour of discussion, the social worker left. I managed to be conveniently on my way to the garbage when she exited.

"Seems fine," she said to her cell. "I don't know why someone reported her. Children have imaginations. And rumor is the landlord wants people out of the building." The social worker's tone implied that real estate might be at the root of a thousand schemes against a person.

Space. In New York, it really was the final frontier. The bodega stock boy cramming the contents of an entire grocery store into three hundred square feet; the nail-parlor ladies scooting through traffic jams of bodies; the burger flippers in closet-sized alcoves serving meals like human vending machines; the alternate-side parkers, repositioning their car every few days; the aspiring musicians, painters, and actors, packed into flats like pups in a pet store window; the quarter million people waiting for a spot in public housing; the child living in a 500-square-foot homeless shelter room with her parents and seven siblings; a hoarder surrounded by her coral reef; and a strange tropical bird in a window box. Everyone just wanted a space in which to survive.

Unfortunately, space was a zero-sum game. If you occupied a place, someone else, by definition, did not. This fact underpinned all of capitalism and every war ever fought.

LATER THAT NIGHT, I reconvened the team to bring all Viviane's things back. We asked her where she wanted them. "It doesn't matter," she said. We stacked papers, bags, and boxes in corners of the rooms.

Norah patted her shoulder. "You'll be at sixes and sevens for a while, then everything will be fucking fine. You'll see."

I woke up the following morning still exhausted and looked into Viviane's apartment. All her stuff remained where we'd left it and seemed like it might stay that way. The spoon jar rested under my pillow, a veritable gift from the gods.

A FEW DAYS later, I saw Angela on the street and tried to avoid her, but she spotted me. "Delia!" she shrilled, pivoting on her heel and storming down Madison to confront me. "How *could* you?"

"How could *I*? What about how could *you*?"

"There's a child living there!"

"It's not about the child and you know it."

Her eyes snapped. "After all I've done for you! You can bet that's the last you'll hear from your boyfriend, screwing up his deal like this. He was your only chance to stay in New York and clean up the mess you made."

I hadn't seen the worst of Angela's temper since high school. She could really be a bitch when she wanted to be. "That's a pretty harsh thing to say to a friend."

"Friend? Really? You always did this funny thing with that word when we were kids. You said it like *friend*." Angela's voice squeaked. "I can't get it right." She shook her straight dark mane in frustration. "It doesn't matter. I understood what you meant. So, don't talk to me about friends." She stalked off.

ROB NIBBLED MY neck. "I may like this one even better than the other," he said, as he pushed a shoulder-bearing vintage Halston down my arms. Mom had sent a few more of her dresses to me, care of Bert. It was an odd gesture, like the needlepoint bird pillow. It had me wondering *what's the catch?*

"I suppose Angela called you," I said.

"Mmm. Easy access," Rob growled and reached down the Halston's front to cup my breasts, pulling them out, and bringing them to his mouth. I saw stars, which could have simply been the sparkling skyline above Hell's Kitchen. "Angela does what Angela does," he said. Then, abandoning the delicate foreplay, he pulled up my dress, pushed me down, unzipped himself and thrust deep and hard. Angela was wrong about Rob not wanting to see me. I could have predicted that. Business was business. Sex was sex.

Connoisseur of the act that I was, I knew a man's style in sex revealed things about him, almost like palm reading or astrological signs. Rob was forceful, a ravisher in a way belied by his boyish smile. This proclivity to take what he wanted explained his business success. I was so ready for him that the sex was always fun. As time went on, a guy like this could get too aggressive. Crossing the line, as it were. I predicted Rob's passion would likely mellow into the satisfied-rich-guy kind of lust. With that thought, it suddenly struck me that I had just looked to a possible future with Rob. Must have been the giddy-making effect of the spoon jar under my pillow.

Afterward we finished, Rob poured us eau-de-vie. "Angela was just trying to do me a favor," he said.

"I'm sorry if…" I didn't finish the sentence. I had ruined a perfect opportunity for him to be rid of Viviane. But I wasn't really sorry.

Rob put a finger under my chin. "You just wanted to help a friend. That's natural. Everything will work out. In a few months, we'll all look back on this and laugh." He drained his glass. Rob was also looking to the future.

"And Viviane?"

"Like I said. That'll sort itself out. Things always do in the end."

I drank my own brandy, thinking of the truth of that and the spoon jar abiding under my pillow.

Chapter Thirty-Nine

With audacity one can undertake anything, but not do everything.

—Napoleon Bonaparte

THE THIRD WEEK in August, moving vans ringed the Greek embassy. Priest must have found them a new space. It made sense to relocate all the personnel and office furniture now, before the diplomatic season in September.

It was still unclear who would buy my old home, though I imagined all kinds of possible deals involving shell corporations. Priest was handling things on the Greek side. I wondered if he and Goodman, the two nemeses, would up end at the same negotiating table. Goodman had taken off for a week-long business trip to the West Coast. He was talking to development partners, he said, in anticipation of a reboot of the Deal of the Century.

As for me, I was caught in an eddy, with the spoon jar still resting under my pillow. I hadn't talked to Judith yet, but I would. I wanted to enjoy the jar for a little while, almost as if I was pretending it was mine. I could indulge myself for a few days. Probably, no one was around in August to buy spoon jars anyway.

Emails from Telefony came. There was a final job offer and

HR documents with their relocation process. Spoon jar or no, I would be leaving for Minneapolis. The jar proceeds would only serve to rescue me from bankruptcy. I still needed a job to live, and Telefony was the only offer I had. Rob was not the type to take on a dependent girlfriend, and I was not the type to be one. It was good, in a way, that I would not be in New York to see both my legacy homes—the mansion and Number N— conclusively erased.

Across at the embassy, men rolled in and out with dollies on which were objects shrouded in moving blankets. Doors and gates stood open. It could have been a scene from twenty-three years before.

Frankie and I were watching the activity when the name *Bert* flashed on the screen of my cell phone.

"Deel-yer. I think you should get over here."

"Here where?"

"Next door."

It was the great circle of life, where everything that happened before seemed determined to happen again.

"WHERE IS SHE?" Bert held open the embassy gate for me.

"In the parlor. They caught her on the way out," Bert said.

We went into my grandmother's yellow front room, where gaming tables had once been set up for Wall Street Poker Night years ago. Two dark-suited, silver-tied men stood with hands clasped behind their backs, European-gentleman style. One was tall and graying. The other younger and tan skinned. Mom, in an impeccable linen suit, hair newly coiffed, lipstick perfect, sat on a chair. Leaning against the wall was an object wrapped in a mover's blanket. From one corner, peeked a gold-filigreed frame and a swatch of painted green velvet.

Portrait Me.

Nikos appeared carrying a glass of water with a lemon slice floating raft-like on top. His mustache twitched at me sympathetically. He gave the glass to my mother. Even red-handed, Mom got great service. Bert stood beside Mom. Behind me, I sensed a fourth man enter. I knew it would be Peter Priest. Neighborhood gossip said he kept an office here.

"Delia." He greeted me, drawing curious looks from the two embassy men as to how we knew each other. "I'm glad you're here. It appears your mother is experiencing some confusion."

Embarrassment and anger made me feel hot. "Confusion," I repeated. Of all the things Mom was at the moment, confused was not among them.

"Yes." Priest extended his hand, and one of the men presented him with a green file folder, soft like fabric on the edges from having been rolled back and forth in a drawer for years. He opened it and took out papers. "Apparently, when this property was sold to Greece, your..." He turned to Mom to clarify, "I believe it was Delia's grandmother?"

"Paternal grandmother," Mom confirmed, taking a dainty sip of her water.

"Your grandmother arranged certain paintings would stay with the house." Peter consulted the papers and looked at Mom again who nodded. He closed the folder. "So, it appears your mother made the assumption if the house were sold again, the agreement regarding the paintings would..." he paused, as if searching for a word "...expire. The art would be up for grabs, as it were."

"Exactly," Mom said.

"I'm obliged to admit," Priest continued, "a resale of the building was not contemplated in these documents."

"You see," said Mom to the dark suited men and passed her glass to Nikos.

"From a legal perspective," Priest continued, "we don't know whether this particular painting—" he gestured to the *corpus delicti* "—is to be sold with the house itself, or if it belongs with the possessions of the Greek embassy, and therefore must move with them."

Mom sat straighter. "I would say the painting belongs to the possessions of *my family*!" Priest didn't seem to hear her. He was speaking in Greek to the other men. After some back and forth, they seemed to reach a consensus, marked by emphatic head nods and utterances of, "*Nai. Nai. Nai.*" *Yes. Yes. Yes.*

"So," Priest continued to us, "these gentlemen have consented that the portrait should stay with the house based on your grandmother's original wishes."

"Now see here…" Mom's voice was stern. Priest held up his hand to her, a thing I'd never seen done in my life, except by Grandmother herself, and he spoke again to the men in Greek.

But Mom was not to be silenced, even by the likes of Peter Priest. It was as even a match as I could imagine either of them ever having. "Young man," she pursued, as the two other men and Nikos left.

"Peggy." Bert put a hand on her shoulder. She shook him off.

"Yes?" Priest gave her his attention.

"I understand, Mr. Priest, they are going to tear this house down and build a big high-rise."

"And from where do you understand that?"

"The news."

"I see."

"I heard that too," Bert offered. "How can the painting stay with the house if there's no house?"

"And what on earth is the new owner going to do with a portrait of *my* daughter in his possession?"

"All interesting questions," Priest said, his smile enigmatic. "Perhaps for another day. The fact is I'm not selling this house."

"*You're* not selling this house?" I asked.

"That's right," Peter said. "I bought the house, and I'm not selling it."

"My God. Why?" I gasped.

Peter's eyes looked ferocious as he answered. "Because Rob Goodman doesn't get to have everything. The house, the deal, the money, and," he finished fiercely, "you."

"You?" Mom sounded a bit hurt, but not very surprised. There were daughters who called their mothers to tell them about their boyfriends. She was not that mother, and I was not that daughter.

"I guess you were right in the end," I said to Priest. "About me and Rob Goodman."

"You and Goodman were not the topic I wanted to be right about." Priest turned away and set the folder down on a side table.

"I don't follow," Bert interjected. "Is something wrong with this Goodman fellow?"

Priest squared his broad shoulders to Bert in a man-to-man fashion that excluded me. "Goodman stole from me once. He's capable of a lot of things."

"Huh," said Bert.

"He doesn't deserve Delia," Priest added.

"What are you doing, Peter?" I asked, stepping in between him and Bert, increasingly bewildered. What did he mean by any of this? Why had he bought the embassy? Was it possible he bought it—for *me*?

Priest looked down at me. I was tall and accustomed to looking at men eye to eye. But Priest was taller. His frown softened. His hand moved as if he were about to touch my shoulder, but then he stopped, as if realizing there was nothing like that between us.

He sighed. "I admired you from the moment I met you. When you showed up in my office that day—it's like you were on fire. You don't accept that you're fundamentally different from Goodman. You're decent, honest, *good...*" It felt as if he were heaping on me the weight of things that had once been possible. "And Rob Goodman..." His voice trailed off, both bitter and sad.

In that moment, standing close enough to kiss him, I could feel same connection I'd experienced before. I wondered—was something ever possible between the two of us? If there weren't other people around—Bert and Mom, with Nikos and the two embassy men still hovering outside—I might have found out. Or maybe that time was already long past. In any case, we weren't alone and something else was on the line just now.

"Peter." I placed a hand lightly on his arm, which gave a surprised twitch at my touch. Locking my eyes with his, I gestured with my head to Mom for a significant second. The joining of the two properties meant her payout. It would save her and Bert from financial ruin. "Sell the house, Peter. Make a deal with Rob. *Please.*" Priest looked stubborn for a second, but he followed my gaze, his sharp mind adding things up in an instant. Recognition crossed his face. Then defeat. "Just let it go," I said. "Let's not pretend things can be different."

⌒⌒

OUTSIDE ON THE steps of the embassy, I caught my breath and wiped my eyes. It would probably be the last time I would ever cross that threshold. Mom hooked her arm in mine to walk down the steps. Bert followed.

"Stealing from a friend," Bert said to the park. "Takes a certain kinda person to do that." Bert's father-like concern was kind of sweet. And naïve. I myself had just stolen a spoon jar. Bert held out Priest's business card as he walked. Peter had written his private cell number at the top. "I said to that Priest fella I'm former NYPD, and he could call me anytime. We exchanged cards." That implied possible side-bar discussions between Bert and Peter about me and Rob. Bad idea. I took the card from Bert.

"You like this Rob Goodman fellow," Mom said, making it a statement. "The one you worked for—from the cover of *Vanity Fair*."

"I do."

"Good. Because I never wanted you to have to make a choice like I did." I looked at Bert for a reaction to this—it was the first time I ever heard Mom admit she married for money. She loved my father in her own way. But maybe the real love of her life was Bert after all. If Bert had a response, he didn't show it. We walked on toward Bert's car.

"Thanks, Mom," I said. "But it's not serious."

"Mr. Priest seems to think it is," she said. "Interesting fellow." My mother gestured lightly with her hand, toward the embassy. "Reminds me of something Kathleen used to say."

"What was that?"

"Jealousy isn't the best way to show love, but it *is* one way."

AFTER MOM AND Bert left in Bert's limo, rosary beads swinging from the rearview mirror, I sat on a bench in front of the Metropolitan Museum. The plaza here would soon be torn up and rebuilt. A philanthropist donated the money. The same philanthropist who ran an energy empire and denied global warming. But he supported the arts. Things were just mixed up that way.

My brain buzzed with what had happened. What does a billionaire get to impress a girl? In this instance, the answer appeared to be the Greek embassy. Was it possible? Could Priest have bought the mansion as a sort of gift to *me*? I thought of our last meeting—when I also felt a *something* between us. I remember thinking I hadn't had that sensation with a man before. Something different. Something, perhaps, of the realm of magical cloaks and improbable birds.

I continued to replay the scene in Grandmother's parlor. Priest's unaccountable act of buying my family mansion, seemingly as a grand gesture toward me. His stated admiration and concern, and even outright lobbying of Bert. His words reverberated. *Rob Goodman doesn't get to have everything. The house, the deal, the money, and you.*

What also reverberated, and just as strongly, was Priest's vindictiveness. Goodman and Priest were nemeses long before I showed up. If Priest's purchase of 990 Fifth Avenue was a gift to me, it was also a way to spite Rob, but good.

Maybe Aunt Kathleen was right about jealousy showing love—but only up to a point. Mom's jealousy years ago showed she loved me. But my experience with Mom taught me that kind of love wasn't enough. There needed to be *more*.

A love of the kind of magical cloaks and birds? It would definitely require more than what I saw in Peter Priest: admiration mixed with jealousy. I wasn't even certain what that *more* kind of love would look like. But if there were love of the cloaks-and-birds caliber, I was sure it had higher standards. The bigger question was: did I even believe that kind of love was possible?

There was a Delia who might have thought so. She was the person who would have existed if not abandoned by Aunt Kathleen. This cloaks-and-birds Delia had revived briefly at Number N. That *me* seemed like a lost straggler from an exotic, ancient species. For a brief season and a brief flight, she took wing. She was bright, fragile, and unable to survive very long in the world as it was. She had briefly eclipsed the other Delia, the one who thought things like love were nonsense.

Number N may have had the power to temporarily reanimate the idealistic Delia, but Number N was doomed. What Delia would emerge from its wreckage? I was pretty sure I knew. For now, though, the person who sat on this bench was a mixed-up, in-between Delia. The one who would never have answers about Aunt Kathleen and who hid a spoon jar under her pillow.

The recollection of the spoon jar shifted my thoughts. Leaving the events with Peter Priest behind, I began to focus on what I would do next. I was right all those months ago. Faced with a choice, I would go for the money. Rather than endure a foreclosure, seven years without credit, and rebuilding my life inch by inch, I would sell the spoon jar.

I marshaled a dozen rationalizations to justify this action. Surely, Viviane owed me for saving her daughter from going to a foster home. Moreover, the spoon jar shouldn't have been with Viviane to begin with, but rather in a museum in Greece. At Viviane's, the jar wasn't doing anyone any good. It wasn't even holding spoons anymore. If the jar could benefit me, why shouldn't it?

I set those excuses aside. If I was going to do this, I would look it in the face. I knew exactly what would happen to the jar: it would end up in a ninety-million-dollar penthouse paid for with Russian mob money, sitting under a painting last seen in Vienna in 1938.

⌒

NORAH WAS IN the lobby when I came back. The floor smelled of a recent mopping with Clorox. She stood there, smoking, as if she'd been waiting for someone. It seemed as if that someone was me.

"You're needed in the basement." Norah turned and descended the steps.

The limestone tomb of Norah's office smelled of cigarettes mixed with paint solvent. A small street-level window let in a bar of light. Viviane stood next to the shelves, playing with a box of washers, stacking them on her fingers.

"I have something to say you." Viviane twirled the washers. Norah folded her arms.

"Okay." I suddenly felt the chill of the spoon jar under my pillow.

"I'm leaving Number N."

So, she did have a price. "Was it a good amount of money?"

"Shagging fuck," said Norah.

"I'd burn the money if I could." Viviane's voice was gritty. "I wish I could live here forever. I just *can't* stay."

"She's lost her only leverage," added Norah.

The pieces clicked in my head. Viviane really had planned to dig in her heels, using her hoarding disorder to fight eviction. But after she'd been reported to child services, that strategy went out the window. To keep her child, she had to prove she was *not* a hoarder. It was a choice—her apartment, or her child.

Viviane put two more washers on her fingers and looked at me, her hazel eyes with yellow flecks radiating betrayal. "And it's all because of you. That woman Angela. Your *friend*. She used Natalie to get at me." Viviane said "friend" in a way that conveyed I was responsible for bringing a viper to Number N.

"I'm sorry," I said impotently.

"I was starting to think you were a nice person. But Angela's your *friend*. And Rob Goodman's your boy*friend*."

"The two of them won't fucking stop until they get what they want," Norah said, and I couldn't disagree. A lone woman had no chance standing in the way of the Deal of the Century. Maybe she never had. "Who the fuck knows what they'll do next?"

"Maybe it was inevitable, me having to leave," Viviane said. "But you know the worst part?" Viviane's eyes were so angry, I could barely look at her. I knew what was coming.

"You took her fucking jar!" Norah jumped in.

I had been a fool to think Viviane wouldn't eventually open

boxes and inventory every single item. Her possessions were children of a different kind. In addition, the yoga instructor probably ratted me out.

"I thought you were my friend!"

"I just… That night… I just wanted to keep it from breaking," I stammered.

"It's been over a week," Viviane said.

"I *really* need the money," I admitted.

"You could have come to me," Viviane said. "You could have explained."

"You would have said no."

"Because it's *her* fucking jar!" exclaimed Norah.

"I said it wasn't about the money," Viviane said. "But you *made* it about the money." Viviane dropped the washers off her finger. "I don't want it anymore. You can keep the jar. I'm done with it, with you, with everything." Viviane turned her back, dismissing me from the basement as if I'd ceased to exist.

Chapter Forty

Perhaps the only true dignity of man is his capacity to despise himself.

—George Santayana, *The Ethics of Spinoza*

I SHOULD HAVE felt relieved. I had the spoon jar, free and clear. With Viviane's—you might even say—blessing.

So why was I despondent and nauseated with self-loathing?

I watched lonely Frankie cock his head, trying to make friends with the insect-eyed webcam, and realized I too was deeply lonely. I had probably always been and was just feeling the pain of it now. I understood I had definitively lost Viviane's friendship. At the same time, I fully appreciated what that friendship had been worth. It was a true no-quotes relationship. Perhaps the first one I had ever had. No strings attached. Ironically like the status of the spoon jar right now.

On top of it, I lost Norah's friendship. With barely a question, Norah had helped me save Whitey. She had changed her note-pinning opinion of me. She'd even made a sincere offer of money.

One thing, above others, made these realizations even more bitter. The way Viviane and Norah stood in contrast to Angela. Her "friendship" toward me had always been laced with ulterior motives. As a child, Angela had wanted to be friends because I was rich. Now, as an adult, she'd used me to get close to Rob for deal opportunities. Another possible drive behind her "friendship" was to have me act as a kind of placeholder in apartment 6C, so she could eventually get all three apartments. At first, I thought this the height of conspiracy theories. Now, it seemed not only possible, but probable. What Angela'd done with Viviane, exploiting Natalie to advance a real estate deal, gave me a renewed appreciation of the lengths to which Angela would go.

If Angela had played me, it was my own fault. I had been duped into removing Angela's punctuation because she helped me get what I wanted. Because of my own greed, I became blind to the person I always knew she was, from the time we were girls.

Despite all these thoughts, my external reality had actually improved. My path was laid before me, and the plan was simple. I would call Judith and tell her I had the spoon jar. She would find a buyer on the black market. I would sell my apartment for a million eight and make up the underwater piece with the proceeds from the spoon jar. With Viviane out of the picture, there would now be spoon-jar profits left over— six hundred thousand split two ways instead of three.

That extra hundred grand with no foreclosure looming extended my timeline. I might even have enough money to decline Telefony, stay in New York, let my trading ban expire, and take a job at a reborn hedge fund. I felt a certain disappointment in myself at this thought. Projecting into the future, I saw the idealistic Number-N Delia fade from view. I knew all along that, given the chance, I would not have the strength to resist hedge fund money.

I called Judith, who cackled with glee. Shame it was August, she said. I had been right about it being a lousy time to move a spoon jar. Her prospective buyer would still be yachting off Dubai. Give it a week or two, and he'd be back.

"I'll call the homecare agency today," she mused. "Tell them they're fired. I'll fire Angela too! I'm about to get myself some high-class help. I'll live to a hundred and six in style!"

Eventually, Angela *would* get Judith's apartment. In the meanwhile, I would sell mine to someone else. It gave me a satisfying thrill of revenge to know that at least I would keep Angela from achieving her Vermeer-iest apartment.

I CALLED TELEFONY the next day to stall. I told them I needed to finish the current contract I was working on. "They asked me for another two weeks, and I hate to leave anyone in the lurch."

"We admire that at Telefony," she said. "Employee integrity."

"How's mid-September?" I had no idea how long it would take to move the spoon jar, but that seemed like enough time. It might also give me an opportunity to suss out my future options with a New York hedge fund.

The Telefony woman agreed.

As I hung up, a text arrived from Rob. So much had gone on in the last week, I forgot he was due home today.

RMG: *Meet me on the roof.*

Dee: *What roof?*

RMG: *The one above your head.*

Up the small flight of stairs, I stepped onto the gravel-textured, tar-paper-covered Number-N roof where Aunt Kathleen used to sit, read, and drink. I looked out over a vista of water towers and air-conditioning machinery. Rob leaned against the perimeter roof wall, his legs crossed in front of him. On the ledge, sat an ice bucket, its cubes half-burying a bottle of champagne. He held two crystal glasses.

Rob extended a champagne flute in my direction.

Taking the flute, I put on a smile. "What's the occasion?"

"The embassy's been sold!"

"That's great," I said, feigning ignorance. "Who bought it?"

"Don't know yet. Just heard the transaction went through."

So Priest hadn't contacted Rob yet. This made sense. He wouldn't be eager to talk to him. "A quarter billion. Whoever it is will be calling me anytime now. After all these years, this is really going to happen!" Rob reached his glass for me to clink. "You'll be happy to know that woman Viviane agreed to leave. I told you things would work out."

"Right," I said. My champagne stuck in my throat.

"I haven't been able to reach Mrs. Condon, though. I keep leaving messages."

I shrugged. Mom was probably waiting for all the pieces to be in place, to solidify her negotiating position.

Rob went on, not leaving me an opening, excitement pouring off him in waves. He gesticulated. He grinned from ear to ear. He detailed plans—the potential architect, the materials, the permits, the timeframe. There would be a huge marquis condo. Maybe they could get Bob Stern, or Frank Gehry to design it. The sales of the units would be in the high eight figures. The penthouse itself might even break that legendary hundred-million-dollar mark. It was the Deal of the Century redux. The ultimate result would redefine *crème de la crème*.

Rob gave a big sigh, finally spun out. "Okay. Enough about business. Let me look at you." He put his hands on my hips to draw me to him, saw my face and frowned. "Hey."

"Hey," I said weakly.

"What's going on?"

I inhaled. He was so happy. "Nothing."

"God!" he exclaimed. "When a woman says 'nothing!'" He took my champagne flute and set it down. He propped his leg up on the parapet. "So?"

I searched a minute for what to say, looking out at the void of the park and the windows flashing like gems on the West Side. What could I say? I wasn't going to tell him about the spoon jar. Or Peter Priest. Or my sadness over the loss of Number N and its version of Delia. I opened my mouth and found myself recounting how I'd been so wrong about Angela, and that I'd allowed her to victimize Viviane. For now, that would just have to represent everything else. It kinda did, anyway.

Rob rubbed his chin. "I'm sorry, baby."

"Me too."

He reached over and took a curl of my hair. "I've gotten to know Angela a little." He wrapped the curl around his finger. "Could you just tell yourself that she hastened the inevitable with Viviane?"

"Well, that's one way to put it." I knew he was trying to make me feel better about my "friend," but it sounded like he was justifying what she had done.

"Eventually, I would have had to get her out," Rob said. "It would have been long and painful. Maybe it's better this way."

Rob's *eventually get her out* sounded ruthless. But he was right. Viviane herself said the same thing. In the real world, you can't just let one woman hold up a Deal of the Century. As for ruthless, there was me and the spoon jar.

"Rob…"

Suddenly he took me by the waist and dipped me—like the move dancers make at the end of a tango. My hair dangled over the edge of the building. He had an intense, playful look in his eye. "No, you don't…" He released his hold, so, for a split second, I had the feeling of falling. Then he caught me again. "I get to say something now."

I laughed. It was a reflex reaction, impossible to resist. The cry as you crest a roller coaster. Release. Catch. Laugh. Release. Catch. Laugh.

He swooped me away from the edge. "I'm gonna make this deal. And I want you to be happy. I love you." I gasped. All the sensations together were too overwhelming. The roof. The vertigo. The words, *I love you*. How long had it been since I'd heard anyone say that? Decades. Who said it to me last? Aunt Kathleen. My head spun and my heart throbbed as if I'd just snorted cocaine. "I know you've been struggling. You're so proud. Let me make it all go away for you. I have a surprise."

Out of his breast pocket, he produced a small velvet box. He popped it open with one hand. Inside was a glinting pink diamond the size of a watch face.

It was devil-may-care, impulsive, and extravagant. It was classic Rob Goodman.

∽

WHEN I SAID yes to Rob, he shouted his joy to the surrounding rooftops. Yet, even as I basked in his "I love you," I knew it was a compromise. I was no Cinderella, and he was no Prince

Charming. But he was rich, and I was tired. And he used the word "princess."

Didn't I deserve—*something*?

In that moment, and for the very first time, I felt I could understand my mother marrying for security. Life was hard. Rob offered to make it easier. I was acting with my eyes open. I was never after true love in the past. I'd barely had a long-term relationship. Peter Priest entered my mind for a moment, but I came to the same conclusion as before. If there were ever a concept that belonged to the fantastic realm of magical cloaks and fanciful birds, true love was it.

I might have been reluctant to say "yes" if I thought Rob himself was genuinely in love. But I heard the distinct quotation marks around Rob's *I love you*, though he himself was not even conscious of it. Rob's "love" was a fusion of bravado, enthusiasm, and lust. He still got credit for saying it, though. No one had done *that* for years.

The truth was, I was honestly fond of Rob and thought we could have a kind of contentment together, quotation marks and all. As for Rob's motivations, Angela was probably right about that one. With an enormous fortune in the offing, he seemed to have decided it was time to pick a princess.

Was I kidding myself? Finding a way to justify getting married? Maybe so. I was certainly not the first woman to indulge in that delusion. I probably wasn't even in the minority. Agreeing to marry Rob was a kind of surrender. The old Delia, hard-nosed and practical, would win the day, as I always knew she would. After all, she was the one who was a perfect match for him.

To celebrate, Rob and I left the rooftop, with dinner reservations already made at Daniel, as on our first date.

"I was going to rent out the whole place for tonight, so it could be just the two of us. But it seems more like a celebration with people around."

"And less expensive," I added.

"I don't think you get it yet." He played with the ring on my finger, rocking it back and forth so it caught the gloaming light on the roof. "How rich I'm going to be. Fifty grand for an evening—it's nothing."

Rob beamed as the Daniel staff congratulated us, and other diners craned to see. We went to his Hell's Kitchen apartment afterward, where the sex was spectacular, even by the standards of Rob and me.

When I objected, briefly, to the size of the ring and even the need for people to marry these days, Rob waved it off. "Buying that ring was the most fun I've had in years. You can't imagine the ruckus I caused at Cartier. Just think of the party we'll have!"

Immediately he started to name venues. Maybe when he made a deal with the purchaser of the Greek embassy, we could arrange for the wedding there—before it was torn down. What an appropriate end that would be! "The press will go crazy!" We would live in the new building once it was finished. It was all perfect.

Rob would not be risking his soon-to-be-new fortune by marrying me. We both knew better, though neither of us touched the subject. I believe I mentioned that rich men want ironclad prenups. I would orbit his life like a small moon. It was fine; I'd tried to make a fortune of my own and failed.

Fair was fair.

Chapter Forty-One

I Tiresias, though blind, throbbing between two lives,
Old man with wrinkled female breasts, can see.
—T.S. Eliot, *The Waste Land*

A WEEK PASSED after my engagement. Rob's Hell's Kitchen place transformed into a Deal of the Century command center, with Mitch Mitchell in attendance helping field call after call with developers and financiers. Mitch Mitchell was not my favorite company. So I spent most of the time back in my N apartment.

I also wanted to be at Number N as much as possible. It was the way life worked that I discovered far too late Viviane's principle of the coral reef. Things became important through a gradual accretion of meaning.

The Thursday following Labor Day, Aunt Kathleen's kitchen radio was yammering about a hurricane in the Atlantic. It was supposed to meet up with another hurricane predicted to form soon. I wasn't sure how that could possibly happen, but the weather people were pretty hysterical about it.

I resolved to reach out to Gotham Bird and ask them if I should do anything with Frankie to prepare. While I was at it, I planned to get their advice on catching him. When I first moved into Number N, I didn't consider the bird my problem.

He'd been in residence before I arrived and survived a winter on his own. As I'd felt when Eugene asked me to buy Whitey, taking responsibility for another living creature wasn't my M.O.

Not till now, anyway.

Frankie's magical microclimate was about to be wiped off the face of the earth. Could he find another? Or was my window box unique? It probably was. If I succeeded in catching him, how would Frankie like living in a cage in a billionaire tower? I figured he'd hate it, but at least he'd survive.

Across the way, Viviane's apartment's blinds were firmly shut, reflecting the renewed hostile atmosphere at Number N. Word had gotten around about me. No one put up notes, though. They were past that. It was as if they decided I was beneath even that attention. I wondered if Number N-ers were looking for new accommodations or if they, like the bird, would stay until the place was torn down around them.

As for the jar, while waiting for Judith's buyer to return, I kept it in my bedroom. Judith's apartment wasn't safe. She was blind, with aides trouping in and out. Not to mention pill-stocking Angela who had a key. With all that traffic at Judith's, we agreed the jar was best with me.

I went about life with it gradually sinking in that I would marry Rob. He was more excited about our wedding than I could imagine a man being. While I demurred, saying we had plenty of time, he hired a wedding coordinator. She called me to set up an appointment. Her tone indicated I should be more appreciative of my fiancé, a rich and desirable man, who had been forced to call the wedding planner *himself.*

It would be a fine life, I told myself. I would stay in New York after all. I would live in the billionaire tower, on the footprint of my two old homes.

The Telefony HR woman was, naturally, pretty pissed when I ditched them for a second time. I burned that bridge, but good.

Sarah had a different reaction.

"*Delia!*" Sarah's italics penetrated the phone. "Good to *hear* from you."

"How are you?"

"Oh, *fine!*" I knew that couldn't be true. Sarah didn't work in the world of Russian oligarchs and eight-figure apartment purchases—the only real estate that was doing well these days.

"You think you can do it? One-point-eight?"

"You *say the word*," she said.

"I have something to sort out first," I said. "When that's done, how long will it take, to get a buyer?"

"A few weeks. The co-op won't be happy. Values dropping in the building. They could reject a buyer out of spite. I've heard a few cases."

"The board'll be fine." Especially when their alternative was a bank foreclosure.

I never considered asking Rob for the needed two hundred kay. He was a money man, eye always on the bottom line. *Why make up two hundred thousand dollars on an apartment that was only worth one-point eight?* he would ask. Why not default; let it be the bank's problem? As for my credit rating, what did that matter when I was marrying *him*?

I would have to take care of myself in this, which was fine since I had the spoon jar.

IF ROB WANTED to see me, he sent a car to Number N. Deals aroused him. What with the building deal and the wedding itself being a kind of deal, he was insatiable. Two weeks after our engagement, I got in the car to go across town and found him there in the back seat, fully erect and pulling me down on him. He didn't seem to care about the driver on the other side of the privacy screen. "I'm rich enough. I can fuck when I want and where I want." Shameless? Yes. I had pegged Rob as a ravisher, and it was true.

Who was I to cast aspersions? I myself had screwed a provost on a campus quad at night and in a classroom during broad daylight. I was the one who criticized my former lovers for becoming too tender too soon. Rob was entitled to his master-of-the-universe phase, which would abate when the novelty of his billions wore off.

A week after Labor Day, Judith called to say her anonymous buyer was back from Dubai. She set an appointment with him the following week. I was to stand by for the jar hand-off.

I asked Sarah to list my apartment. It popped up on StreetEasy that afternoon.

JUDITH'S MEETING WITH the anonymous buyer went swimmingly. I dropped off the jar for inspection and collected it afterward. Judith said to expect a short lull, as procedures for money transfers were prepared through frontmen. I had no idea which oligarch, drug lord, or American CEO was the potential buyer of the ancient artifact.

Nor did I wish to.

The pause in the jar deal was like the calm in the eye of the storm. Speaking of storm eyes, the news media continued to predict an increasingly powerful hurricane ten days out.

A FEW DAYS later, I woke to the sound of a giant loon. Then I realized it was an emergency siren. The caterwauling got closer, a body-thrumming noise. I listened for a pitch change as the vehicle turned down Fifth. But the siren cut off. Whatever the emergency was, it was happening on our block.

By the time I got to the street, Norah was already there. As were other doormen and supers. Whether for a parking-space dispute, fender bender, bike accident, or ambulance appearance, people always gathered to gawk.

Norah ignored me. No surprise there.

"What the fuck is happening?" she demanded of the owner of the Parthenon deli.

"Maybe heart attack," he said.

The ambulance and a fire truck were in front of the Grandhope. The ambulance disgorged a gurney and three EMTs, who hustled into the lobby.

"Wonder who it is," the actor said to Norah.

"That mafia bitch?" Norah speculated. "Wouldn't that be lucky? Probably one of those old rich fuckers though. It's like a nursing home over there."

Norah was right. Judith might be the oldest, but the Grandhope had plenty other senior citizens. I was surprised we hadn't seen more emergency vehicles during my tenure on this block.

Other pedestrians stopped, wearing entrance tags from the museum. The sidewalks were getting clogged. I stepped into the threshold of Number N.

It seemed a long time waiting for the EMTs. That meant no real emergency. Maybe it was the woman on the third floor who was prone to falling. A broken wrist, maybe.

On the other hand, a long delay could mean the opposite: that there was nothing anyone could do.

This theory grew stronger as the police arrived on the scene.

Suddenly, people gasped and pointed. It was Frankie now perching on the Grandhope awning. Another time, I might have been amused. Today, in the heat of summer, I felt a shiver. Because I now understood what was happening.

Dread rising, I strained to see into the Grandhope lobby, where a gurney slowly exited the elevator, escorted by police and EMTs. The figure on the gurney was covered in a sheet.

Police held out their forearms to part the crowd. I got a glimpse of a formless shape being rolled onto the street. Someone was on the stretcher. And that someone was clearly dead. The EMTs lifted the gurney into the ambulance and I peered between the shoulders of the crowd.

A toe peeked out from the edge of the sheet, still wearing its signature red shoe.

Chapter Forty-Two

The bird of vision is flying towards You with wings of desire.

—Rumi, "Mystic Odes 833"

I N MY HEART, I understood ruthlessness was fundamental to humanity itself. Civilization required savagery. How else could you conquer continents and build great cities? A certain kind of barbarism probably underpinned all immense achievements and fortunes, even my great-grandfather's. Perhaps early man kindled these traits in his very nature just as he learned to spark fire. This fire, this tenacious human brutality, allowed man to pull himself out of the muck, walk on two legs, and surpass all other creatures on earth. Those of us who lost these traits would go extinct, the line of Aunt Kathleens dying out as surely as Neanderthal.

The coroner ruled Judith's death an accident. She'd taken the wrong pills, too many pills. She was blind. Her death was a mistake. The coroner noted it was also possible she committed suicide. Echoing Bert, the police said they couldn't really know.

This time, I did know. Judith was dead, murdered over an apartment. The person who killed her was my best "friend."

And I myself set in motion all the events leading to her death.

With the spoon jar sale nearly done, I'd placed my apartment on the market. This forced Angela's hand. If my apartment sold, the new owners might never agree to sell to Angela. They could keep it for fifty years. She had a narrow window of opportunity to get all three units, but *only* if Judith were out of the way. It was her one chance. In the end, Angela weighed Judith's life against the value of a Vermeer-big apartment. The Vermeer won.

Once again, I had stupidly and naïvely underestimated the lengths to which Angela would go. Judith herself told me, and I didn't take her seriously. I felt responsible. I should have prevented this. I could have done something, monitored the pillbox, filled the cases myself, called Bert. Something, anything to protect Judith.

I felt as if I would suffocate in the black ugliness of it all. Because of my quotation-marks friendship with Angela, and my own act of spoon-jar theft, I had lost Viviane's and Norah's true friendship. That was bad enough. Now, another friend was actually dead. *Judith* was dead. The sightless but shrewd dealer. The imperious order-giver. The spoon-jar spotter. The *separate sanitation department* phrase-coiner. The relentless author of conspiracy theories—all of which turned out to be true.

What could I do? There was simply no way to take up arms against the world as it was, in some great conflict between light and dark as the Hungarian imagined. The Hungarian himself had not succeeded in such a battle. In 1956, he faced off against Soviet tanks and lost. As thousands were executed, and the iron curtain slammed down steelier than ever, he fled with a quarter-million refugees and ended his life training useless girls on broken-down horses at a second-rate finishing school.

What could anyone do in such a world where good and

bad, actions and their consequences were twisted, braided, and knotted to a crochet of confusion?

Yet, it was necessary to do *something*. I went with the first thing that came to mind.

I grabbed a dish towel from the kitchen, as Gotham Bird instructed. I stalked back and opened the window. Frankie blinked and smiled. I breathed in and out, preparing. He preened a feather, suspecting nothing. I leaned out. He looked at me for a piece of apple.

I threw and hit my mark. Frankie tried to take off under the towel, but it was too heavy. I lurched and grasped, my body half out the window. There was a violent flapping. I closed my fingers on the fabric, drawing back inside. Frankie folded his wings and grew still, the way a tackled zebra mutely surrenders to the lion holding him by the neck.

With my toe, I nudged over the newly purchased birdcage from beside the yellow bookcase. I sank to my knees and uncovered the bird's face. Frankie looked at me, smile painted on. It was probably just my imagination, but I thought I perceived his heart, impossibly small and fragile, in my hand.

No. It wasn't my imagination. It was true. And the heart-beat was a plea. There, under my fingers, thrummed a clear drumbeat of entreaty. It was as if I could literally feel his heart's desire. The bird-dream pulsed with earnestness and was colored in every rainbow shade of improbability. His heart told me he wanted to be free—to live right here in the Number-N window box.

I wanted to answer the bird and tell him how hopeless it all was. That Number N would be destroyed and he would die.

The bird's heart heard me and replied such concepts had no meaning in the bird's worldview.

I stood up and put my arms out the window. In a flutter of lime green against white fabric, he was gone.

My empty hand continued to pulse with the bird's tiny heroic heartbeat.

It was an inspiration.

Chapter Forty-Three

Forgive us our debts, as we also forgive our debtors.

—Matthew 6:12

I HAD NO black dress appropriate for Judith's service, and I was strapped for cash. Rob would have bought me any dress on Madison Avenue, but I didn't feel like asking him or, for that matter, like shopping. So, I called Mom to see if she had something and Bert offered to drive it in for me. I went down to the curb to meet him and was startled to see Mom in the passenger seat.

"Hello, Delia. You're not looking very well." Bert held the door for her and handed me the garment bag.

"Tough week," I said. "Are you planning to go to the service?" Mom and Judith had a purely transactional relationship, but they still knew each other.

"No. I have some paperwork to take care of." Mom carried a manila folder, papers leaking out the sides. "There's something you need to sign."

I knew what it was. Mom was no fool. After the run-in with Priest, she would close every loophole and squeeze caulk into every crevice. I was her daughter and had been living for a significant time in her apartment. It gave me a claim to the place. Mom would want an attestation releasing any rights to a claim. Nothing would jeopardize her payoff. I imagined the other papers in her folder were affidavits for Norah and other Number N-ers to aver Mom resided the required 183 days a year. For a hundred bucks, I was sure Norah would sign. The others would do it for twenty.

"We have to do this right now?"

"I want to make sure things are in order, and everyone is clear, so that there is no subsequent confusion." Mom opened a packet of stapled-together pages with tightly packed type. A fluorescent flag, the color of my bird, marked a spot. "Sign here, dear."

I sighed. What did it help to feel hurt? I had simply gotten the mother I had gotten. I took Mom's pen.

"Aren't you going to read it?"

"I know what it says."

Mom looked somewhat disappointed as she turned to go, as if she expected me to admire her handiwork.

Back upstairs, I zipped open the garment bag and extracted a black silk sheath. There was more stuff in the bottom. A package of new hosiery in onyx, black Chanel pumps, a toiletry bag with a tube of lipstick, compact with foundation, and a palette of eyeshadow.

I probably needed to add "grooming and style consultation" to the list of insufficient ways to show love.

Dutifully, I dressed and applied the makeup. In the background, I heard my phone chime. It felt distant. Everything felt distant right now. Absently, I checked the screen. It was an alert. From Gotham Bird.

No. That couldn't be. So much had happened. I must be confused.

I went to the window.

It was true!

Someone spotted it on the webcam. A second yellow-green parakeet pecked at my window box, maybe blown here by the brewing hurricane currents.

The new bird fluttered to a nearby tree branch. Frankie stayed put. Together, they blinked at me with little clown faces at once comic and anciently serious. They were bright and enigmatic, like a sweep of highlighter pen on a sentence in a language I could not read.

I checked my phone again. The birds were trending on Twitter.

I sighed. The birds were a victory of sorts. I believed the term was *pyrrhic*. A Number-N parakeet flock might be forming just before the building was torn down. It was nice to know such a thing could happen. In theory, at least.

IN THE GUEST-BOOK sign-in at the funeral home, I saw the name Martin Norton.

"Mr. Norton?" I approached a man I thought was likely him, eyes twinkling above a white beard. With his diminutive stature, round middle, merry eyes, and neatly trimmed white beard, the only thing missing was the eight tiny reindeer.

"Marty," he said.

"Judith gave me your card," I said. "I thought you'd be here."

"I am so sorry for our mutual loss." The cheer in his eyes dimmed. "How did you know Judith?"

As he ladled me a glass of too-sweet punch, I explained that Judith had instructed me to contact him in the event of her death. That, hypothetically speaking, he might be the person to approach regarding an ancient artifact that had come into the possession of a friend. That Judith was pursuing the placement of that object when she died.

Marty finished ladling. "I think I know the special person Judith might have been speaking with. The one who was interested in…what did you call it…a spoon jar?"

"Yes."

"I will contact him."

"That's not exactly what I'm asking."

"Ask anything, my dear. Anything."

For the second time, I was going to walk away from a fortune. I was not reckless this time, off on a Google goose chase through all human knowledge. Nor was I emotional, confused by the two different Delias. I was cold and weary and resolved. I was out. I was done.

"My friend doesn't want to sell this object. She wants to take it back."

"Take it *back*? What do you mean?"

I told him.

It was an ambitious idea—to return the spoon jar where it belonged. I would buy a ticket to Greece, locate the Dodecanese island of ancient legend, find a *palikari*, don scuba gear, and transport the jar to safety in an underwater cave.

It needed to be done.

Because didn't all evil begin with theft?

I was no theologian, but even I could see Eve's apple for the great metaphor it was. The act of stealing encompassed every malevolency: theft of property, theft of freedom, theft of life, theft of hope. Also, simply the taking of more than your fair share of earth and sky, no matter how convenient or technically legal.

I could see it clearly, a chain of evil beginning with that biblical fruit. It assembled itself, link by link, through all of human history. It stretched back to ancient times and the brutality that founded civilization. Through later centuries, its links were forged by insatiable empires. The links of the twentieth century turned war into genocide and bombs into weapons of planetary annihilation.

In the new millennium, the chain was harder to discern. It was comprised of ice floes melting on uninhabited poles and drowning bears; of human beings trafficked in secret as easily as spoon jars; of babies anonymously starving to death in war zones; and of the illicit billions zapping along fiber optic cables financing it all.

Amidst everything, a bewildered humanity could no longer even tell what was and wasn't evil.

The chain had to be snapped, as far back as possible.

I couldn't make it all the way to the apple. But I could go back to antiquity with a spoon jar.

I didn't tell Marty the details about my scuba dream or the chain of evil. I simply asked him the logistics of transporting the jar.

Marty's cheery eyes turned hard. He nudged me away from the punch bowl. In low tones, he explained they called the black market *black* for a reason. If you were found with treasure in luggage, no matter what your intention, the artifacts would be confiscated, and the bearer arrested.

"You can't take it back. There is never any 'back,'" Marty said and left me with my punch.

I had one more thing to try.

I MOUNTED THE sweeping white steps, the small indents in the marble palpable through the soles of my shoes. There was no movement in the any of the windows as the new Greek embassy offices were downtown.

I approached Nikos, the guard, who was still there. He waved me past without even checking my bag. Nikos witnessed me driving a horse and carriage into the garden and gave safe harbor to the entire contents of Viviane's apartment at my request. What could he possibly have to say about my trespassing now?

The green-and-white lattice marble of the entrance hall floor intertwined underneath my feet, the grand staircase spiraled upward, and the pony-sized crystal chandelier cast small rainbow shards on the walls of the rotunda. All those rainbows, and not a single pot of gold, except the one I was carrying.

Great-grandfather's study nested behind the sumptuous yellow parlor, its windows overlooking the park. Carved birds decorated every inch of the mahogany wood paneling. In my childhood, the room shelved countless leather-bound Audubon print folios. Priest stood in this study, apparently in thought, looking across Fifth Avenue.

"Delia," he said, taken aback. Naturally, he was surprised. I waltzed in as if I owned the place.

"I'm not here to ask for a job again." I laughed weakly. "So, you don't need to worry about that."

"To what do I owe the pleasure, then?" There was a bit of pleasure in his enunciation of *pleasure*. He was glad to see me. But the atmosphere in the room was unmistakably melancholy.

This billionaire, this hedge-fund wizard whose every touch turned lead into gold, was not happy. I understood why, because I felt the same way. So much had happened. Priest and I shared a kinship made up of world-weariness and regret. He was brilliant as I was brilliant, but all that brainpower hadn't brought either of us any joy. We were two sides of the identical coin, as it were. Only there was more money on his side of the coin.

I took the spoon jar out of my bag. The orange glowed. Dressed head to toe in black from Judith's funeral, I might have joined the processing women on the jar. I set the object on Priest's desk.

His eyes widened. He picked up the vessel and turned it. "*Where* did you get this?"

"A consignment shop." Which was more or less true.

He looked bemused for a moment, glancing from the vase to me and back again, eyes questioning. "Why have you brought it to me?"

"You were the last option I could think of."

"I see." He bristled, shoulders stiffening.

I instantly wanted to take my words back. What I'd said was true. Priest *was* the only alternative to get the jar back where it belonged. But I didn't want to offend him. Priest felt almost like a friend. Maybe the only thing even approaching a friend I had left. I stepped forward and softened my tone. "What I meant to say was—I'm hoping you might be willing to take the object and return it."

Priest leaned against the desk, the treasure in his hands. He turned the jar for a long time, making the women march around and around. They, like me, must be bone-tired by now.

"You could get a lot of money for this object." His black

eyes met mine with significance. "May I ask why you're giving it up?"

I decided to explain.

I told him about the chain of evil, and how I wanted to break it. He nodded and actually seemed to understand. Then I told him about another dream I had. That maybe, if the chain were broken, one day in the distant future there could be magical cloaks again—colorful and of immense stretchiness. Iridescent tropical birds would grasp the cloak's corners and fly off to the horizons, winging on and on, as far as it took to envelop the earth.

I stopped, and there was silence between us as if neither of us knew where to go from there. What I'd just said sounded weird and mystical, chattering about cloaks and birds. So, I changed to Greek.

"*I sotiria tis psychis einai poly megalo pragma.*" *The salvation of the soul is a really big deal.*

His smile was sincere. "*Akrivos.*" *Exactly.* He gestured to a chair. We both sat for a moment and looked at each other.

"Someone told me a story once," Priest said after a while. "About a fisherman ordering a boy to return an object to the sea."

"I remember." I smiled, thinking how I had made him laugh with that story.

Priest took a key out of his desk and went to the bookcase. Familiar with this study, I recognized the key and its destination. He unlocked a panel and opened the safe inside. Crouching down, his broad back obscured what he was doing. When he straightened and turned, he was holding something in his palm, presenting it to me. It was a small stone statuette of a woman, approximately four inches high.

My eyes grew wide, and my jaw dropped.

"It was you?" I gasped. "*You* were the *palikari?*"

"I was," he said, putting the statuette on the desk between us. "I always felt guilty I didn't do as the village men told me, but I kept her. I think I wanted to remember a redheaded American girl, one who was so pretty I was afraid to speak to her in English."

I felt the warmth of his compliment, remembering the tall tan boy in cutoff shorts, a few years older than me, communicating silently through gestures. I understood him perfectly then. And, anyway, you don't speak under water. I touched the worn surface of the statue. "I can hardly believe it."

Priest shook his head with a soft chuckle. "When I saw your portrait in the embassy, I was struck how much it resembled that girl from long ago. I wasn't sure, until you told me your story. Then I knew you were the same girl, grown up and still beautiful and brilliant."

Peter looked at me intensely, and I knew he was searching for some sign—an opening into a different future for us both.

But in that moment, I had none to give.

Math taught you that a line slanted by even one degree will end thousands of miles off course if you extend it far enough. I was like that line. Things had progressed too far; my own chain of evil still bound me and, today, was growing too heavy to bear. I had just come from Judith's funeral, a death I bore responsibility for. I didn't feel as if deserved an alternate future.

I would pay a high price for my decision to take back the jar. My apartment would go into foreclosure, and I would be personally bankrupt. Staying in New York, I would look for a job and likely find one at another hedge fund. So, life would go. Returning the spoon jar had taken a lot of strength, and I simply had no more left to challenge the course of fate.

Waiting for a response, Peter seemed to know my heart. He sighed in a way that implied he, too, was giving up. "While I'm at it, I might as well return them both," he said, touching the stone statue.

"Can you do it? Do you have a way?"

"I do." I pictured a sequence of events. A bribe to an international customs official. A series of couriers, first on planes, then on boats—ferry boats, motorboats, and a small sailing skiff—culminating in a wizened old villager, nodding knowingly, taking possession of the parcel and handing it to a boy in scuba gear.

"Thank you." I stood to leave. "That's it, then."

I took a last glance around. What a shame about the beautiful woodwork in here. There were birds at rest, birds in song, birds in flight. It would all be torn down just like Number N. I moved to the door.

With two long impetuous strides, Priest blocked the threshold. "You're getting married." He gestured to my ring. "To Goodman."

"Yes, I am."

Apparently, he was not going to allow me to leave quite so easily, at least not without bringing up the subject of Rob Goodman one final time. I braced for Priest's scolding. I didn't want to endure his opinions about Rob or hear that I was "too good" to marry him. I didn't feel too good in any way. Only in this singular matter, the spoon jar, was I able to find the high road.

Hearing Priest's view on my personal life was too much just now and turned my weariness to incipient anger. After all, Goodman said he loved me. What had Priest done except save a scuba-diving memento, buy an old mansion, and criticize my choice of boyfriend? He was obviously jealous, but jealousy really *wasn't* enough. There really *did* need to be more.

"I wish you wouldn't," he said simply.

"Peter," I began irritation in my voice.

Priest went to take my hand, then, as if recognizing there was a ring on it, stopped. He was close to me, and I could smell the cologne of my Greek summer. I could sense, once again, his desire to touch me. The sensation was so strong it was as if he *were* touching me.

"There is a saying in ancient Greek. 'A crow is always found near a crow.' In English it is much prettier, and I always felt it rather fit us. We are birds of a feather, you and I." The corners of his eyes crinkled, and I wondered if he was also familiar with my Gotham Bird fame.

"In a way, that's probably true," I admitted.

"The two of us haven't had a chance." He did take my hand this time and looked down at the ring as if he hated it. "It's not too late."

There it was. The *more*. A beginning of it, at least.

But what could I say to that now? My logical mind lined up the facts. I had an actual relationship with Rob. The first real one with a man I'd ever been in. There was a ring on my finger. Wedding plans. A wedding *coordinator*.

What was there between me and Peter Priest? I barely knew him. It was crazy, to walk away from everything I had—for what? A potential? A birds-of-a-feather thing? It seemed timing really could be as important in love as it was on Wall Street.

Still, I might have been persuaded. I *had* told him about the cloaks and the birds, and he *had* understood. I might have given it a chance.

Except for what he said next.

"Goodman is not marrying you for *you*, Delia. He has an ulterior motive."

"Excuse me?"

"Think about it. He comes back into your life. Suddenly there's a ring. I don't know what his motive is, but you probably do, if you think about it. Ask yourself, what does he want? What can he get by marrying you?"

There it was. The animosity toward Rob, not feelings for me—it was always uppermost for Priest. This enmity was turning him into a Judith-level conspiracy theorist.

"I'm not having this conversation with you."

Now Priest looked as if *he* would like to take his words back. "I'm sorry, Delia." He let go of my hand. "Even if I never see you again, I care about you and I don't want anything to happen to you. I don't trust Rob and you shouldn't either."

"I appreciate your concern, but I'm leaving now." I touched him on the arm. "I'll always be grateful for your help with the spoon jar."

He looked quizzical at the term *spoon jar*. But I was already gone.

After I left the embassy, I went to Hell's Kitchen. I was barely through Rob's door before he was pulling me toward him, hand up my skirt. His cell phone's ring interrupted him. He looked down at the screen. "I'll be damned," Rob said. It was Peter Priest. When the call was done, he proceeded to strip me. The two old nemeses were now in the Deal of the Century together.

Chapter Forty-Four

Whatever we had missed, we possessed together the precious, the incommunicable past.

—Willa Cather, *My Ántonia*

THE MEDIA FRENZY about the approaching storm was escalating to outright mania. Weather maps showed the destined combination of the two storms. A hurricane hooking up from the south was to join with a tropical depression coming due west.

As the days passed, it became increasingly clear the storm would make a direct hit on the city. Adrenaline-pumped weathermen enumerated the possibilities: the breaching of sea walls and flooding of subway tubes, a weeks-long power outage, looting. Sergeant Rivera called to ask about Whitey's behavior in high water. The mounted force was gearing up to patrol the parks and for search-and-rescue in places vehicles couldn't reach.

The mayor told citizens they better get where they were going because he was prepared to close all the bridges and tunnels. There would be a full travel ban to keep idiots off the roads. In my neighborhood, the queues of double-parked luxury SUVs idled in front of awnings. They were stuffed with Dean & Deluca grocery bags, high-end baby strollers, and startle-eyed Weimaraners. Everyone headed to Westchester, New Jersey, and the Hamptons, which might also be decimated. Still, no one liked the idea of being trapped on Manhattan island with all egress blocked.

Rob planned to stay. His ultra-luxury building had a generator, parked on a barge in the Hudson. In the lead-up to the hurricane, he was ferociously busy. The impending disaster of the hurricane presented even more opportunities in distressed real estate. He was on the phone hour after hour with Angelo Conti, now his principal investor. I holed up in my apartment to sip my last dregs of time at Number N.

I told Sarah to take the apartment off the market. I would not pay my October mortgage. By Halloween, the place would be in foreclosure. Angela would be at the auction, raising her paddle the highest.

Sarah understood. Said she was very sorry for me and gave an italicized sigh.

⌒⌒

I SCRAPED UP batteries from an almost-empty shelf at a hardware store on Second Avenue to power Aunt Kathleen's old radio. Gotham Bird's editor emailed me to batten down the webcam. The pair of birds was generating record-breaking site traffic and people would be watching them through the storm. The avian vet said my second bird was female, so I instantly christened her Francine. The birds' webcam had solar backup, so I didn't need to worry about power. Just bought some zip ties to secure it.

As for the human element—me—Nikos planned to fire up the old DC generator in the embassy basement and Norah intended to tap into it. With a long cable, Number N would have one working elevator and the water pump. No lights or fridge. After my hardware run, I went to the nearly fully plundered grocery for peanut butter, a couple of cans of beans, and bread.

Coming back from my errands, I retrieved my mail.

There it was. The letter I'd been waiting for. At long last.

THERE WERE VERY few people at noon mass. Especially today, with a hurricane looming. Just a scattering of cleaning women, old men, and a homeless person who wanted a place to sit. I sat in the back of the small downtown church, so I could spot her.

Maybe you do just speak the religion you're born into. I knew the rhythm of the mass so well that I could stand up, sit down, kneel, sing, and intone all the required responses without conscious intention. It allowed my mind to wander, tracing my incredible journey from a Florida graduate-student apartment to Wall Street and a Fifth Avenue co-op, to a carriage ride through no-man's-land, to residency at Number N and Rent-Controlled Princess fame, to corruption and finally murder. I'd lost friends I barely recognized as friends. I was actually engaged to be married. I thought wistfully of all the missed opportunities, and there had been many—starting with the crash of 2008 when I might have regained my fortune. Wistfulness turned to regret when I considered Norah, Viviane, my misguided "friendship" with Angela, and Judith's death. I was at fault for so much.

Alongside all this was a pang for the missed opportunity with Peter Priest. I would never know how that might have ended. Maybe, if we'd had more time, he might have shown his feelings for me outweighed his enmity toward Rob Goodman. But playing *what if* was likely to drive me insane. What if I'd never been in the news and Rob never found me? What if I hadn't gone in search of the truth about Aunt Kathleen in the Google archives? What if I had believed Judith about Angela? It could go on forever.

There were things to be happy about. For example, I arrived at a conclusion regarding Aunt Kathleen. It developed over time, slowly, imperceptibly, while I was busy with carriage rides in bus lanes, spoon-jar plots, and losing both "friends" and friends. I think the idea surfaced into my conscious mind the day Judith died, when I spoke to the heart of the bird.

Suddenly, I just knew. *She didn't kill herself.*

And that was that.

I believed. It was simple and complete. I had allowed the two Aunt Kathleens enough room to dance, and finally one bowed and walked off stage. Aunt Kathleen had not killed herself, though there was no proof and there would never be any. The idea was like a buried treasure. It always existed. I just never had the strength to dig it up.

I didn't definitively conclude she was murdered. Her death could have been an accident. A bit tipsy, on learning the identity of a killer in one of her Agatha Christie novels, Aunt Kathleen gasped and toppled backward over the roof railing.

Given recent events, though, I thought it most likely her landlord killed her. My experience with Angela taught me not to underestimate what people were capable of. But the *how* mattered less to me now.

In the world's view, my conclusion about Aunt Kathleen, without any proof or facts, probably sounded crazy. But Bert said to listen to my heart. His advice didn't make much sense at first. Then I heard the bird's heart speaking plainly. When I listened to my own, I realized it, too, had something to say.

Sure, there were dimensions of Aunt Kathleen I didn't know. She did drink. She was gay.

You'd need a separate sanitation department.

I was grateful to Judith for that observation. Maybe I'd light a candle for Judith after mass. Once I'd accomplished what I came for.

Some months ago, when I discovered the packet of letters from Sister Scholastica, I made a resolution. I decided while many things about Aunt Kathleen would remain unknowable, I *could* learn more about her as a person. Scholastica was the one who could tell me.

My inquiry went first to Sorrows and was forwarded to the order's provincial. But Scholastica had left the convent, and it took a while to track her down. When she finally replied, she said she was overjoyed to hear from me and apologized it took her so long to respond. She gave me details of her life. She was living in New York on the Lower East Side where she'd grown up. She still attended noon mass every day at the Church of the Nativity. She made a joke about old nuns not being able to learn new tricks. She gave me her address, a phone number, and an AOL email that she said she didn't check very often.

She signed the letter, "Scholastica," in quotes.

I'd read the letter standing there in the Number-N mailroom after my hurricane hardware run. Looking at my watch, I'd realized I had just enough time to make it downtown by noon.

The service ended, the lugubrious organ reverberating through the small temple. I saw her before she saw me. She was maybe a few years younger than Mom, with short gray hair and wearing a green raincoat. Her face was pink, pale, and wrinkle-free, like all old nuns.

"Sister Scholastica?"

Recognition lit up her face. "Delia Mulcahy!" She laughed and held out her arms in a gesture of *look how you've grown.* "Clever girl. You found me."

"You mentioned about noon mass in your letter. I don't want to intrude."

"Don't be silly." She slid into a nearby pew and patted the seat. "Sit. It's not Scholastica anymore, though. Or Sister. I left the convent in '93. Call me Rosemary."

So *that* was her name. Rosemary.

"I thought if anyone would keep being a nun, it would be you."

"Everyone thought that. Tell me, how are you? Are you still in touch with your old partner in crime, Angela?"

"Yes." It was sorta true.

"What a little demon she was." Rosemary's inflection on the word *demon* was short of humorous. "I hope she's improved. Your aunt Kathleen would have been surprised the Contis sent her to school with you. Disappointed, too. She wanted you to make new friends."

"How did you know Aunt Kathleen?"

"We were close. In the novitiate together." Rosemary leaned back. "It's why Kathleen asked your grandmother to send you to Sorrows. Even though it was an awful place. She knew I'd look out for you like no one else."

"I'll say," I said, remembering all the detentions and her rapping on our door late at night. "You sure targeted us."

"I targeted *you*," she corrected. "Angela was collateral damage." Rosemary laughed and patted my hand.

"So exactly why was that?"

"Kathleen was gone. And I knew she would want me, above anyone, to take care of you." She paused. "I was special to her."

So, it was true. "I found a few letters you wrote her. They gave me that idea."

"What you don't know is that *I* was the reason she left the convent."

"You?"

"One of us had to go. That's how the provincial put it. Or both, they didn't care which. Funny how Kathleen and I accepted it all back then, so convinced we couldn't love each other and God at the same time. We both loved Him very deeply. Kathleen left. Her gift to me. She wouldn't hear of it being any other way. She loved me that much."

"*Sister.*" I felt tears burning.

"Rosemary," she corrected. "Ah, the letters we wrote each other! It was our joy and the one little sin we allowed ourselves. She was such an entertaining writer. She told me all about you." Rosemary looked to the flickering candles on the aisle. "I kept my promise to look out for you at Sorrows, didn't I?"

"Yes!" I agreed, a little too emphatically.

Rosemary smiled, then her face grew serious. "I had some doubts about that Hungarian riding master I hired. There were rumors he had an eye for you. I hope he never tried to take advantage of you."

"He did," I said.

"Oh, heavens!" She looked genuinely alarmed.

"I took advantage of him right back."

Rosemary laughed again. "At least Kathleen's not alive to hear *that*." She placed a hand on my knee. "I was sorry I never got the chance to write her all those letters I planned to send about you. I would have had such wonderful things to say."

She found a set of rosary beads in her raincoat pocket and began to finger them backward. "It was hard to leave the church. I felt like I wasn't honoring the sacrifice Kathleen made. But I decided things change. If Kathleen were alive, I think she'd understand."

"I know she would have."

"I never believed she took her own life, you know." Rosemary took my hand and squeezed it. I squeezed back.

"Me either," I said truthfully.

I couldn't say anything more for a minute, and we sat holding hands.

Rosemary gave my hand another squeeze. "Nor I."

I smiled. "Nor I," I repeated.

"Proves we taught you something, other than how to avoid curfew and sneak out to the stables. By the way, where are you living now? I bet you're married with your own kids." Rosemary winked. "Please don't send them to Our Lady of Sorrows."

"No kids. Believe it or not, I'm living in Aunt Kathleen's old apartment at the moment."

Rosemary threw her hands in the air. "God works in mysterious ways, doesn't He? When things started to look bad for your family, Kathleen wrote how glad she was she had that apartment. 'Delia will always have a place to live,' she told me. She loved that it was rent controlled. You know, she planned to leave it to you one day."

Chapter Forty-Five

The north wind doth blow,
And we shall have snow,
And what will poor robin do then?
Poor thing.
—Nursery rhyme

A S PEOPLE RUSHED around, the two birds were fascinated by all the commotion and took up a sentry position on the façade of Number N to watch the waves flee before the hurricane. People left for high ground farther inland. I saw Viviane depart with Natalie and remembered something about an aunt in the Poconos. In the surrounding buildings, there were fewer and fewer lit windows at night.

Sarah called. She didn't plan to leave the city and invited me to lunch. It seemed odd, going to lunch with the emergency situation unfolding. But what else was there to do?

"Hi, Sarah." I let her hug me, then adjusted my stool closer to the pink marble Frisbee. The restaurant had a giddy feel, as people who were staying behind charged the atmosphere with expectant excitement. I looked at the menu, blanched at the prices, and set it aside. I wasn't eating with Rob next to me, and my bank account was on its last gasp.

Sarah pushed the menu back in front of me. "Don't worry. *My treat.* News like mine deserves *a splurge.* You'll *never believe it!*"

I started to speak, but Sarah held up a peremptory hand. "We have an offer."

Oh, no! "Sarah, I told you. Things have changed. I can't sell at one-point-eight."

"I took it off the market. I swear. But *they* called *me.* All cash deal, the buyer's broker said. They want to move *fast.* We could be in *contract* this week."

"Cash or not…" I started.

"Don't worry, honey. Let me tell you *the incredible* part." Sarah bubbled, and the tiny table teetered. "The offer is *not* for one-point-eight. *Not* for one-point-nine. But for *two million dollars.*"

Two million.

Who else could it be but my former "friend?"

Why would she pay two million when the auction price would be one-point-eight or even lower?

The answer was classic Angela. She didn't want to bid against others at auction. What if a random buyer had a hard-on for my apartment? She wanted to lock up her Vermeer. A full two million dollars, in cash—the exact amount of my outstanding mortgage—would guarantee the sale. Just as my overpayment had done years before.

Her father would have no objection. It was axiomatic in New York real estate that the whole was *always* worth more than the sum of the parts. The final value of her six-bedroom apartment, when all three apartments were combined, would be immense.

I had been rescued from bankruptcy by Angela's covetousness.

"I wish I could take credit, honey, but this *literally* landed in our laps!" Sarah put on purple leopard reading glasses. "I hear the lady next door died. *Perfect* timing. Gives your neighbor on the other side the opportunity to join all three apartments. And may I tell you, *that* kind of situation doesn't come up very often." Sarah flipped through a notepad. "Oh, yes. One more thing. The buyer's broker asked me to ask you if you would be willing to sell some of your furnishings. Specifically, there was interest in a hand-needlepointed cushion?"

THE NEXT DAY, the hurricane blew in with all the ferocity predicted by the news and more. The storm surge flooded all of downtown, lower Brooklyn, and a good piece of Staten Island. The Jersey shore was virtually wiped away. Sea walls were breached. Floodwater charged into streets, changing them to rivers so quickly people were trapped in homes and caught in the act of fleeing. The number of drowned would be uncounted for days or even weeks.

Electrical wires and gas lines snapped, sparking explosions. One entire neighborhood in the Rockaways burned to a cinder. No one could get there to help. Where electricity was not knocked out, it was purposely shut down to control fires. Elderly were trapped on high floors with no elevators and no water.

Harbors were wrecked. The harbor closures immediately triggered a gas panic. No tankers were able to get in to deliver supplies. There were riots at filling stations and a stabbing. Manhattan garages, where the wealthy kept their cars, hired extra guards against gas-siphoning thieves. No one knew when the situation would end or how long city reserves would last. The city had concerns about fuel for police cars and police boats. The mayor announced motor-powered help was reserved for true emergencies only.

With fuel in question, horses were essential. They forged through chest-high water loaded with supplies for stranded residents and evacuating the sick. Troops of mounted police ringed gas stations, bringing order. Whitey was called out by name: the bravest horse, who would go anywhere. He was a press darling.

Because of all the pictures of Whitey, the Chinese tourists reappeared. They fingered him in online forums as the runaway horse that injured them. The *Daily News* retaliated with: "Foreign Interests Attack Hero Horse."

Since my neighborhood was on high ground, the only effect on us was minor: wind, puddles, downed branches, and no electricity. The birds, sheltered in the Number-N courtyard, looked only as if they had gotten a good spritzing.

The Upper East Side was a ghost town. Everyone who had a second home, which seemed to be everyone, was gone. There were blocks of boarded-up stores with long strips of tape over their windows. The few stragglers like me huddled inside apartments listening to battery-powered radios. In most buildings the elevators weren't working. Anyone left above the fourth floor avoided going out. An eerie quiet settled in. Trains weren't running. Buses weren't running. Bridges and tunnels were closed. We were cut off.

Eventually, everyone's cell phones died. The radio reported phone-charging queues blocks long around places with generators. The only person I knew with a working phone was Mom.

The heavy, retro-style handset in Bert's house got the tiny bit of power necessary off the copper line itself. At Number N, on the floors above the basement, we only had water and one elevator from the lone cable tapping into the embassy generator, but no lights. I let my phone die.

Peter Priest must still be at the embassy, I thought. I could see the small lamp glowing in my great-grandfather's office.

Rob was taking nonstop calls from his generator-powered perch in Hell's Kitchen. He was fielding constant check-ins from Angelo Conti and other investors. The devastation presented him with opportunities to buy property from those who would be wiped out.

ON DAY THREE of the storm, the skies still roiled with the curl-tailed hook of the hurricane. My radio was on. There was a report about bloated bodies washing up on the far reaches of Long Island.

I turned it off and left for a walk. The park was closed to keep people from being hit with flying branches. Across the boroughs, falling trees had killed six already. High barriers at park openings were lashed with plastic-zip-tie handcuffs. Beyond the barriers, I saw trees cracked open, their creamy insides revealed. Detritus—coffee cups, shopping bags, a sneaker, someone's hat—lodged in bushes, caught in light poles, and tangled in iron railings, as if everyone's life had been blown to bits.

I thought I heard a clip-clop in the distance, mounted police on patrol. Or maybe I just hoped it.

On my way back into the building, I saw Norah's cigarette

glowing under the awning. I was pretty sure she and I were the only ones left at Number N.

"Here's what I want to know." She paused, taking a long drag and exhaling. "How surprised were you?"

I let out a sigh. At least she was talking to me. Maybe she heard about the sale of my Grandhope apartment. "About Angela?"

Norah blinked quizzically then said, "No. About your mother."

"What about her?" My mother was always an odd combination of surprising and utterly predictable.

"Who would have thought Peggy Condon would turn out to be so beneficent?"

"Norah, I'm not going to talk to you if you won't make sense."

"One thing I'll say, when you cash out on that apartment, you'll be rich as Croesus and you won't have to marry that asshole."

"What apartment?"

"The one your mother gave you."

It was as if Norah was throwing random sentences together. "The apartment Mom gave me...?"

Norah held out a document. I hadn't noticed she was holding one. "Bert had one of his friends in the *gardai* deliver this." Norah presented a black-and-white photocopy, and I recognized my own signature. "It's the assignment of the lease. To you, with your John Hancock. And notarized." She pointed to the image of a circular imprint at the bottom of the last page.

My ears started to ring. The day of Judith's funeral when Mom brought in the black dress, she presented me with a document to sign. I hadn't even read it.

Mom actually *did* it. She gave up her lease for me.

"Oh my God," I stammered.

"Won't it be a pretty sight? You negotiating with your bridegroom for money. What'll it take for you to give up the lease? When will you tell him?"

"Rob doesn't know I'm Mom's daughter," I said absently. If Rob considered my mother at all, he knew her as Margot Conover. Angela was so desperate for my mother's approval, Mom was the one person whose secrets she wouldn't betray. Besides, in Angela's calculation, Mom was never going to block the deal.

Looking at the pages of the lease, *my* lease, I reeled from the implications. My mother had transferred her apartment to me. Why on earth would she do that?

The second I posed the question, I knew why. She thought I was getting married for money. This wasn't really true, at least not the way Mom thought. My engagement was a kind of surrender to fate. Obviously, Mom didn't see it that way.

I never wanted you to have to make choices like the ones I made.

Here was Mom's *more.*

"He knows." Norah flicked her pink Zippo.

I had lost track of what we were talking about. "Who knows what?"

"Goodman. He knows you're Peggy's daughter."

"What?" I whirled to Norah. "How?"

"I mightta let it slip."

"Norah! Why would you do that?" I felt blood drain from my face.

"I hated you," Norah said simply. "I didn't tell him when you first moved. I promised Peggy I wouldn't. It was after you stole Viviane's jar, when you started to get serious with him. That's when I told him."

My head hummed as if possessed by bees. If Rob knew... Peter Priest's words echoed. *He has an ulterior motive.* He asked me to marry him just as the Deal of the Century was revived. Was it possible the two events were connected? The timing was ominous. Did Rob simply want to protect his position at Number N? Marry me to get his hands on the apartment?

Norah was still talking. "...so when the day comes that Kathleen's flesh and blood falls in love with the shagging prince of darkness himself, son of her very killer, why should I give a fuck about promises?"

I felt a jolt. "What do you mean the son of her killer? What do you know about Howard Goodman?"

"I know he was in the building early that morning, the day Kathleen died, which he wasn't usually. Brought his son with him too. Fifteen. Nearly his size now. And here was Kathleen, standing in the way of everything." Norah's ash sizzled. "They both came hurtling down to my office. Goodman looked panicked. His son was in a sweat, too, all rumpled and red in the face. Goodman used my phone to call the police. He said to me, 'This was a suicide, Norah. You understand. A suicide.' Repeated it to his son, too. Strange comment to make, don't you think?"

"Why didn't you tell the police?" My voice was a thread.

"If you don't understand that, you're fucking simple," Norah spat. "Can you just picture it? Me, a woman super, sticking up for a queer? Who were they going to believe? I knew what the police would say, because it's exactly what they *did* say. She was *that* kind of woman."

"You could still have told them what you knew even if they

didn't believe you."

"Fuck what I knew! I did *better*! You want punishment? You want retribution? I'll tell you where it comes from—yours fucking truly! Year after year, keeping rents low. I told Howard I'd keep my mouth shut on one condition—if I got to run the building how I wanted. Every time a lease was signed—four hundred dollars for a two-bedroom!—the knife went in a little bit more."

"Howard Goodman just went along with it?"

"That's how I was sure it *was* him. He would have told me to fuck off if he had nothing to hide." I braced myself against the upright of the awning.

"And you thought sticking it to him over rents paid for her murder?"

She savored a long drag on her cigarette. "Let me tell you something about someone who loves money. He loves it like his own right hand, like his one true woman. He'll die for it. He'll kill for it. He'll rot his soul for it. What Kathleen tried to do—preserve a little bit of space in this city for herself and you—I did it for her when she was gone. Now, it's all for shit."

"Jesus, Norah." All this time, I'd been living with Norah at Number N. She'd seen Howard and Rob Goodman that day and had kept it a secret. Listening to her now, a horrible thought sparked in my mind. "Oh, my God," I heard myself say.

Norah went on. "I changed my opinion about Howard that morning, tell you that much. I never thought he had it in him—to kill someone. Howard was a bit of a lily. Son's the opposite. Always with a temper. Must be from the mother's side."

The idea-spark kindled more brightly, raising the hairs on

my arm. "After his father died, why did Rob Goodman let you keep running things, low rents and all? Losing money on the apartments. Why would he do that when it didn't matter anymore with his father gone?"

Norah shrugged. "He started that hedge fund. I guess he was too rich to give a fuck."

This was exactly what Rob told me, more than once. It was what I always assumed. Yet it went against everything I knew of him. He was a money man.

"Would you tell what you know? Now, I mean, if you had to?" I put my hand on Norah's arm. My ring glinted diabolically.

"Now, why would I do that?" Norah shook me off her arm.

Kathleen planned to leave it to you one day, Rosemary had said. Now Mom had fulfilled that wish.

What I would do next was as clear as anything had ever been in my life.

"I'm going to keep the apartment, Norah. I'm going to stay."

Chapter Forty-Six

Τα μάτια σου δεκατέσσερα.

May you have fourteen eyes. (Eyes in the back of your head.)

—Greek exhortation

NORAH STUTTERED AND choked. "I'll be shagging fucked," she finally said. She went for another cigarette, shook the package to raise one, lost her grip and dropped it in a puddle by the curb. With no fag for her mouth, and finding herself at a loss for words, she threw her hands in the air, turned, and stomped down to the basement on the hunt for another pack.

Alone on the sidewalk, I used the awning pole to steady myself and caught my breath. My spark of a theory strengthened and grew.

Rob's words echoed.

It would have changed our lives.

When someone has no price, I'm like a different person.

And Norah's.

He was fifteen and nearly his size now.

Always with a temper.

My theory was strong. Was it anything more than a theory?

I drummed my fingers on the awning pole. I had come to my own conclusion about Aunt Kathleen—that she didn't kill herself. Rosemary, the person she'd loved and for whom she'd made a great sacrifice, ratified that conclusion. It was enough. I'd thought it was all I would ever have.

Until now.

Was it possible, at long last, to know the truth? Could I prove she was killed and, at the same time, discover who murdered her?

I lined up what I knew. I thought back and viewed the incident with Viviane through a different lens. Was it *all* Angela's idea, or had Rob recruited her? Rob said it himself. When someone defied him, he became a different person.

Here I stood, ironically, in the same position as Aunt Kathleen twenty-three years ago. A lone woman capable of blocking the Deal of the Century.

What if I could prompt Rob to repeat the past as well?

My plan quickly took shape. I would call Rob and tell him I was Mrs. Condon's daughter. He wouldn't actually be surprised, because he already knew from Norah, but he would act as if he were. We would laugh. Then, I would relate the amazing news, that Mom had signed her apartment over to me. We might chuckle some more at the irony. If I knew him, which I did, I would begin to hear an edge in his voice.

Then I would suggest I was thinking about keeping the place. I would remind him that with all his new financiers and backers and opportunities in distressed real estate, surely there would be other deals and money enough.

What would happen next? I imagined he'd offer money first. Then, when I didn't agree? What Viviane-like plots would ensue? Unlike Aunt Kathleen, I would not be caught by surprise. I would be prepared for what Rob would do. It would tell me everything I ever wanted to know.

It was risky. When he didn't get his way immediately, Rob could grow threatening. He might go after me, or even Mom. But by then, I planned to alert Bert and Seamus Rivera. I had friends in the NYPD. I could convince Norah to recount her story, that both Rob Goodman and his father were there that day. That Goodman Sr. instructed her to call it suicide. That they agreed to her blackmail—first the father, then the son. Maybe things would end differently than they had twenty-three years ago. Maybe on the side of justice. Aunt Kathleen had sacrificed her life trying to preserve a space for me. I might be able to prove who was responsible for her death. If there was even a possibility, I had to try.

I heard Norah coming back up from the basement. After a brief conference and after extracting a promise, I had to get moving.

First things first. My phone was dead. I needed retrieve it from upstairs and find somewhere to charge it. I would call Mom and Bert. It was probably a good idea to get myself out to Centerville.

But how?

All the way up in the elevator, I thought of ways to get to Long Island. Could I walk across a bridge and somehow find a ride in Queens? Maybe one of my cop friends would lend me a horse. I was imagining riding over the 59th Street Bridge on Whitey when I opened my apartment door.

Inside, Rob sat on my couch, long legs stretched out in front of him and crossed at the ankles, smiling his chip-toothed grin. "Hello, Delia."

I commanded myself to steady. "Rob! Hi!" I forced delight and bemusement into my voice. "I didn't expect you here—with the storm and everything." I couldn't recall ever giving

Rob my key. Then I remembered—he was my landlord.

"I'm checking on my interests," he said levelly. "You know, with the storm."

"Things seem fine," I said, walking past him and trying to be casual, setting my bag down alongside the bookcase. "Really quiet. Norah has things under control, as usual."

"Good." Rob got up and went to my kitchen. I heard the refrigerator door open. He emerged in the threshold, a beer in his hand.

"You know how I was trying to reach Mrs. Condon?" His beer top popped. I gave a small start. He took a long draw. I adjusted the positions of the Saint Francises on the yellow bookcase. "Though I suppose if she's my future mother-in-law, I should start using a different name."

I forced myself to laugh. "Sorry I never told you about that." Branches struck my window and a touch of bird-yellow streaked my peripheral vision. "Mom's really private. She didn't want anyone to know. How did you find out?" I knew it was Norah, but I needed to keep the conversation going so I could have time to think. At least Rob didn't yet know Mom had assigned the lease to me.

Rob took another sip of beer and frowned at it because it was warm. "It's strange the way people assume Peter Priest is the only one with a research department."

A dig meant for me. I took a long breath. I went over to the window, nonchalantly evaluating the state of the birds. "It doesn't matter." I shrugged. "It's not really relevant to anything." The birds flapped and preened.

"Your mother seems to think it is. I just got off the phone with her."

"With Mom?" I felt dread in my stomach, heavy like lead.

"It took a while, but she finally returned my calls. She said she had news." The lump expanded and the tips of my fingers grew numb.

News.

Was it possible Mom called Rob to say she gave her lease to me?

Then I realized—of course she had.

I saw it all clearly. I knew my mother. She would be satisfied about what she'd done. Perhaps even a little proud. I could picture her picking up the phone to Goodman, telling him that, for his information, Delia Mulcahy was *her* daughter and the new leaseholder of apartment 13B. Mom would say all of it in her most dignified tone meant to convey, *No daughter of mine needs to marry for money.*

"Don't worry, Delia." Rob set his empty bottle on the faux colonial coffee table and ambled toward me. "I'm not mad. It's just business. You have a position now, and that position is worth something. I'm here to negotiate. I was going to offer your mother money for her lease. But now I'll offer it to you."

My heart thumped palpably. I made an effort to think as I might do on a horse. I needed to focus and make decisions. I tried, but suddenly I realized how angry I was. I was standing here with the man who, it seemed clearer and clearer, killed Aunt Kathleen. Not just standing with, but actually engaged to that man. "I suppose you hoped a situation like this would hold off until we were married?" I hissed. "And it was all in the family, so to speak?"

Rob laughed and shook his head. "C'mon, Delia. You have to admit, we're a good match." I felt shock. He wasn't denying it. He *had* planned it this way. I wondered what kind of tricky lease-negating language he was preparing to insert in the prenup. Rob came closer and put his arm around my waist.

"We've just stumbled on a small complication." His tone changed to seductive. "I actually think it's kind of fun, writing my soon-to-be wife a huge check." He touched my nose with the tip of his finger.

Rob's manner suggested all he needed to do was sweet-talk a petulant bride, one very much under his control. My anger blazed, and I blurted, "What if I don't *want* your money?"

Keeping hold of my waist, Rob regarded me steadily. "Be serious, Delia. It's fine if you want to drive a hard bargain. To be honest, it turns me on." He pulled me to him, and I could tell that it did. I realized, with ice in my stomach, I had played my hand badly, letting my anger get the better of me. We were alone. I had no phone. The city was on lockdown. Defying Rob here was definitely not a strategic charge into no-man's-land.

I searched his face. All those years ago, the Hungarian taught me to discern the light and dark souls of horses, which, of course, was about more than white stockings, forehead blazes, and rims of eyes. And it was also about more than just horses. In that moment, and exactly as I'd learned, I looked for Rob's true nature. His blue eyes were both laughing and aroused—and beneath that, something much darker. It was all I needed to know. The moment's pause helped me to ground myself and summon my Hungarian training.

I unwound myself from Rob's arm. "That's not what I meant." I could do *petulant bride*. "I don't want to take the money now. I don't really want to talk about it at all now. It's too stressful with the storm. Let's sort it out next week."

"No, Delia." Rob's voice had an edge. "I want this sorted out today. In fact, you'll never guess who's here."

A man appeared in the kitchen threshold behind Rob.

"You remember your old pal, Mitch?"

Chapter Forty-Seven

You cannot choose your battlefield,
The gods do that for you;
But you can plant a standard
Where a standard never flew.
—Nathalia Crane, "The Colors"

"HI THERE," MITCHELL said.

If I had confirmation from looking into Rob's eyes, I now had confirmation in the flesh. Rob had seen the Deal of the Century disappear once, and he was not going to let it happen again. "You two worked together every day. I'm sure you heard the rumors about him."

"What did you used to call them, Delia?" Mitchell asked. "There was a phrase you used."

"Urban legends," I supplied, my mouth going dry.

"That's it," said Mitchell.

"I have the contract here." Rob extracted an envelope from his pocket. "It's revised with your name instead of your mother's. It's a lot of money. You're going to sign it."

I clutched the windowsill. I could yell, but there was no one around to hear me. Thoughts whirled in my head, like the winds still rattling the branches outside. I wanted to run.

Then I heard the long-dead Hungarian in my head. Retreat was not the answer. *Leg! Leg! Go! Go! On through no-man's-land!* Suddenly, an idea flew into my brain, like a traveler blown off course. Could it work? There was no choice but to try. Two women tried to give a legacy to me. One had died for it. I felt a familiar mixture of fear, recklessness, and steely resolve—exactly the kind of courage it took to ride a white-eyed horse.

"The thing is, Rob, you are not the only one to negotiate with."

"I'm not?"

"What about Peter Priest? You're both in this deal together, aren't you? I was there when he called you a few days ago."

"I don't know what you're trying to do, Delia. You're just wasting time."

"Let me ask you something. Why does the money have to come out of your pocket alone?"

Rob paused, struck by what I'd just said. He hadn't expected this. He thumbed his papers. Rob was, as previously noted, a money man. "What difference does it make to you whose pocket it comes out of?"

"Well." I let a mischievous smile turn up the corner of my mouth. "I think I might get more if Priest is involved."

He narrowed his eyes. "Why's that?"

"You said it yourself a long time ago. Sometimes someone is interested in something other than money. They have a soft spot in the deal." I cocked my brow coyly.

Rob smiled and shook his head. "You were right, Mitch. I always did underestimate her."

"I'm just saying." I turned to the bookcase and addressed a St. Francis. "I know what you're willing to pay. But not what *he's* willing to pay. And I won't sign anything until I talk to the two of you together." A bird on Saint Francis's shoulder seemed to nod in encouragement. "It's to your benefit."

Rob looked at Mitchell. He shrugged. "Peter and I don't have a meeting until later in the week."

"He's at the embassy right now. You're so hot to settle this, then let's go." I picked up my purse. My heart throbbed. I hoped Peter really was there. I headed to the kitchen, passing so close to Mitchell I could smell his sweat.

"What are you doing?" Mitchell asked, turning as if to block me.

"While you guys debate about this, I'm going to feed the birds. That okay with you?"

Mitchell stepped aside, giving me a few seconds to slice an apple. Hiding my movements behind apple coring, I scribbled on a business card. I went to the window and spread the apple pieces to conceal my other motions. I heard the men's voices rumbling low, conferring.

I shut the window. When I turned around, Rob was beside me, close and intense. Had he seen what I had done? No. It wasn't that. The look in his eyes was something else.

"You want a meeting with Priest? Fine." Behind him, Mitchell melted back into the kitchen. "But you're going to have to negotiate with me for it first." Rob pulled me into him, his arms tight to my back, purpose in his eyes, his erection a rock.

I didn't want to have sex with Rob. He knew it and that turned him on more. I'd called him a ravisher long ago for his forceful style of lovemaking. But now I realized I had been literally right. Facing the full implications of what that meant, I felt revulsion. Involuntarily, I stiffened. Rob closed his fingers, which now gripped hard on my rib cage. He chuckled. "*You* know how deals affect me, Delia. What you don't know yet is the tougher the deal, the more it turns me on."

Maybe the Hungarian, my first lover and—I now realized—my first true love, had succeeded in creating a soldier of me after all. I fully understood, when charging into no-man's-land, sometimes a soldier had to sacrifice herself. Today, that warrior was me. Because as much as my revulsion rose at the thought of what was about to happen, Rob was handing me exactly what I needed—time.

"And what if I don't like your terms?" I knew this would egg him on.

"You don't have a choice of the terms."

Rob pulled me into the bedroom and shut the door. He pushed me down and he held me down with force. He ripped off my jeans and jerked apart my thighs. He was more aroused than I had ever seen him. As he unzipped his fly, unable to control my need to resist, I struggled briefly. I felt a crack across my face. My cheek stung. He found the violence so pleasurable he could no longer hold back. He instantly wrenched me open and shoved his length inside. His deep thrusts were painful, like blows, both punishment and threat. He came quickly, and then went back for another more extended round.

Deals really did turn him on.

Afterward, I heard Mitchell's footsteps through the wall. I was shaking as I showered, Rob hovering in the bathroom doorway. He seemed to fear I would do something. He didn't realize I already had. He watched me going to my closet and sliding hangers aside. I felt Rob's eyes on my naked back as I found what I was looking for: a dress that had been my mother's, vintage Diane von Furstenberg. It was a wrap-around, and I sensed its former owner's presence as I tied the clingy fabric.

Mom and I were both doing Hungarian things today.

As we left, in my peripheral vision I saw the yellow-green bird and his new mate examining the card, propped in full view of the webcam.

WE ENTERED THE bird-whittled study that once belonged to my great-grandfather, now temporarily inhabited by Peter Priest. Rob was on one side of me, Mitch on the other.

"Well." Priest rose behind the computer monitor on the great carved oak desk, his face a mask of businesslike focus. "This is an interesting group."

Rob put his hand on my back to guide me into the room. My skin revolted at his touch. I braided my fingers in front of me to control my reaction. A question mark passed across Peter's face. I smiled steadily. Pushing away thoughts of the last hour with Rob, I wondered how long it might take for a message by bird to arrive.

"Sorry to barge in," Rob said. "We were next door."

"Be my guest." Peter positioned a chair for me. As he did, I smelled his scent. I inhaled to gain strength from it.

"There's a development in our deal I need to discuss with you," Rob said.

"Now?" Peter asked. Rob nodded. "Is *he* necessary?" Peter gestured to Mitchell.

"My right hand," Rob said. "You know that."

Peter looked at Mitchell, the one who stole Odyssey's code all those years ago. "I, of all people, am familiar with what Mitch does for you."

"When we spoke last week," Rob continued. "I told you I

was tying up some loose ends."

Peter nodded, taking a seat and looking at me out of the corner of his eye. "A buyout agreement, I recall, with your rent-regulated tenant."

"Mrs. Condon." Rob leaned his elbows on his knees to deliver his next statement. "Delia's *mother.*" Rob searched for surprise on Peter's face. When he didn't see it, his expression grew darker. "But it appears you somehow knew that," Rob said after a pause. Peter, however, had his head down, looking in a drawer for something. He took out a pack of cigarettes and toyed with them. Rob went on. "It seems she's just assigned her lease to Delia."

"I see." Peter remained impassive, seeming almost bored.

"Since you and I are both in this transaction together—" Rob paused for an acknowledgment from Peter; Peter gave one nod "—Delia wants to talk price with both of us."

"Price?"

"Yes, price. I already spent some time this afternoon, *negotiating* with her." Rob smiled, putting a possessive hand on my leg. I managed to remain still, but Peter watched closely. His shoulders grew rigid. Taking a long moment, Rob let his hand slide up my thigh, pushing up the edge of my skirt. Higher. Then higher still. "Seeing you know so many personal details about her, I'm suspecting you may have had your own negotiating opportunity."

Peter was around his desk, pulling Rob out of his chair and landing a blow on his jaw.

Mitchell lurched between them.

Rob caught himself on the desk and put out a hand to wave Mitchell away. He pulled himself straight, squared his shoulders, and readjusted his jacket. For a long moment he and Peter held their positions. Finally, Rob let out a little chuckle and said, "Feel better? Maybe you should have done that years ago. Then we could have just gone on doing business together."

Peter looked at me. I raised my fingers in a barely perceptible gesture to say I was fine. Peter saw it and regained control of himself. He exhaled, still looking at me. "Doubtful," he said finally and walked over to the long casement windows. "But you're right. I do feel better." He gazed up and down Fifth Avenue. A slight hope fluttered in my chest.

"My enthusiasm's spoiled, though," Rob said. "I'm not so eager to write a check to a woman who's got another guy taking a swing at me while she's wearing *my* ring."

"You'll get over it." Peter reached into his jacket for the cigarettes.

"You're forgetting what old friends we are," Rob said. "The only time you smoke is to cover your tell in poker."

"I haven't forgotten." Peter shook the pack to raise the shaft of a cigarette. He opened the window—seemingly a gesture to let out the smoke. Did he hear something? He flicked a silver lighter and inhaled. I saw him glance once again down the street. Was that a four-beat sound I heard? I thought maybe it was. Peter looked back at me. "So, Delia. Tell us. What *is* your price to leave the apartment? I think I can guess."

That was my cue.

"No price," I said. "I'm staying at Number N."

Rob pushed away his chair. "That's why you wanted to come over here? Because you thought *he* would protect you? It's not going to work. You just dragged him into it." Rob's voice was low and threatening.

"I'm not leaving," I repeated. "The lease is mine and I'm not taking any money for it."

Rob pointed to Mitchell. A matte black gun appeared in his hand, small and hard, like an indisputable fact. "It's amazing the number of people who are missing after the storm," Mitchell said. "You could be a story in the *Daily News* again. Fiancée of Rob Goodman went to check on some of his tenants. Concerned for their safety. You were caught by the storm and didn't make it out."

The smoke from Peter's cigarette formed a perfect plume starting from his fingertips and spooling out the window, where I was now sure I heard a familiar sound. "You've made your position clear," Peter pursued calmly. "I'm confident Delia understands it. Surely you don't want to complicate things any further. What do you propose?"

"I don't know what's gone on between you and Delia, but I infer, at minimum, you care what happens to her. You need to convince her of what she needs to do. She can walk out of here. I'm a generous guy so, despite everything, I'll still pay her to release her rights. It's her only option."

"You underestimate Delia," Peter said, walking back to his desk. "It is definitely not her only option, since I was prepared before you came."

Rob's eyes narrowed. "Prepared? How?"

"As I believe you say in English, 'A little bird told me.'" Peter took out his cell phone. "I was working when my phone suddenly went crazy—with dozens of text messages from strangers."

In a swift gesture, Peter turned his computer monitor around. There, the brace of parakeets preened each other on the Gotham Bird homepage. In the center of the field sat Priest's business card, the one he handed to Bert with his cell phone and my quick additions.

URGENT send this text to 917-555-1212:
Delia coming to embassy. Need help.

The counter below the video said 132,560.

Through the open window, the unmistakable sound finally rang clear. It multiplied and swelled. Metal met pavement in a clanging beat, echoing down the canyon avenue. It was a primal rhythm forged by the first man and beast to go to war together. I went to the window.

Horses' flanks glistened, and tails streamed. Buckles and bits jingled and chimed. Riders sat astride in their midnight uniforms, vibrant yellow trouser stripes ending in gleaming black boots. They formed a phalanx as if stepping out of the pages of an epic tale.

Only, unlike in a legend, I recognized all the faces. I'd taught each of them to ride.

Chapter Forty-Eight

The isles of Greece! The isles of Greece
Where burning Sappho loved and sung,
Where grew the arts of war and peace,
Where Delos rose, and Phoebus sprung!
—Lord Byron, "The Isles of Greece"

WHILE GOODMAN AND Mitchell went to the window to gape at the phalanx gathered there, I slipped out the door. Sergeant Seamus Rivera and his partner alighted and approached the embassy, spurs chinking. I recognized his partner as Officer Kate McCarthy, a fine rider who could mount a horse at a canter from the ground.

I met them on the sidewalk. "Bert called." Rivera put his hand on my shoulder. "Said you had some emergency."

I quickly related the situation to Rivera. I told him about Mom and the apartment and that I was ambushed by Goodman and Mitchell. I recounted Rob's threats and Mitchell's gun.

We looked up to see Rob jogging down the steps like a political candidate, cool and purposeful, Mitch Mitchell behind him. Both Rivera and McCarthy rested their hands on their service weapons.

Mitchell put up his palms up in defense, and Rob asked casually, "Is there a problem, officers?" Peter appeared behind them in the threshold.

I backed away. "Don't go far, Delia," Rivera said, and turned his attention to the three men.

I made my way along the line of horses to Whitey. I took his reins from the officer holding him, who nodded at me in recognition. Whitey exhaled a long warm breath with a soft nicker of greeting. I stroked his shoulder, taking strength from his rippling muscles. As Rivera interviewed the three men on the embassy steps, the still-churning wind brought me partial sentences. I heard Peter say, "threatened" and "gun."

Rivera addressed Mitchell. I heard "carry permit." Mitchell handed over his gun and a plastic square that looked like a driver's license. Rivera reviewed it seriously. A concealed weapons permit. Rivera nodded at the card.

Mitchell pointed to Rob's jawline. A visible abrasion was turning red. "Fiancée," Rob said pointing to me. Then to Peter, "attacked me." McCarthy had her head down, writing on a thick pad. Rivera shot me a concerned look. I leaned against Whitey's neck. This was not turning out the way I wanted. It looked like two guys fighting over a girl in a bar.

Rob knew it. He gave me a victorious smile that made my stomach turn.

Had I really expected knights in armor? Triumphant battles and vanquished enemies? Magical cloaks? If such things ever existed, they sure didn't now. It seemed as if the world was entangled in a baffling web of evil. A diabolical Penelope kept on weaving the stuff, forgetting to unweave, spinning a shroud to encircle the universe. The fabric couldn't be penetrated by bright battalions, nor brave soldiers, nor any other Hungarian thing.

"Can you hurry the fuck up?" a voice shrilled. "You eat too many fucking donuts!"

Norah hustled down the street, a beefy cop trotting with her. When they caught up to us, the cop was panting.

"I'm Tom Cicalese from the 19th," he huffed to Sergeant Rivera. Graying and thick, Cicalese looked as if he might be the desk sergeant left at the precinct while everyone else was responding to hurricane-related emergencies and preventing looting. Cicalese regarded the line of horses, astonished. "What the hell is going on?"

"It's a fucking parade!" Norah interposed. "I'm here to report a murder!"

She was keeping her promise.

BEFORE I'D LEFT her, I'd told Norah my theory: it was Rob, not his father, who killed Aunt Kathleen. I pointed out that Norah herself said Howard wasn't the type, and Rob was the one with the temper. At nearly his size today, he could surely have done it. Howard Goodman said it was a suicide to protect his son. After his father was dead, Rob had no reason to abide Norah's blackmail. Yet he had.

"That makes more fucking sense," Norah admitted. She gave me her word that she would tell what she knew when the time came. I hadn't expected her to decide the time was right now.

"She walked right into the precinct," Officer Cicalese said to Rivera. "Going on about a murder at Number Ten. She says some lady got thrown off the roof and landed in the embassy garden."

"Better fucking believe it!" said Norah.

"She described the incident in great detail." Officer Cicalese continued talking only to Sergeant Rivera. "Finally, I ask, when *was* this murder? And she says twenty-three years ago."

"She's out of her mind," said Rob, but I thought I saw a hint of concern on his face.

Rivera held up a hand. Officer Cicalese lowered his voice. "I says to myself, maybe she's a little confused. But then I hear the call come over the radio about a disturbance at the embassy. Exactly the place she's talking about. You know what they say about coincidences? I think, maybe I better check it out."

"This doesn't involve us," said Mitchell.

"Let's go," added Rob.

"Don't let him leave!" shouted Norah. "*He's* the murderer!"

Rivera turned his entire attention to Norah. "*What* did you say?"

"I said he's the fucking murderer. He killed my friend twenty-three years ago."

"And how do you know this?"

"I saw both him and his father right after it happened. They told me to say it was suicide, so I did." McCarthy was now scribbling madly again on her pad. "I made a deal to keep quiet. First with his father, then with him."

"We had no deal," Rob said.

"You're admitting to giving a false statement to police at the time *and* to extortion?" Rivera asked Norah.

"And anything else you like. He killed my friend, and he won't do it again to her flesh and blood. Not if I have to go to jail along with him!" She held out her hands dramatically for cuffs.

"You can't be taking this seriously," Rob said. "I'm a businessman. I'm involved in Manhattan's biggest real estate deals. I'm friends with the wealthiest and most powerful people in the city. Where do you think any of this is going to lead?"

Rob, of course, was right. Perhaps he and Mitchell would be detained for questioning. But it was a case of they said, she said. As for Norah's belated testimony? It was hard to say what it would amount to, if anything.

Evidently, Rivera did not consider these future questions to be his problem. He was concerned only with what stood in front of him in the here and now. Which was a threat involving a gun against a might-as-well-be-cop's daughter along with a woman who said she witnessed a murder and confessed to extortion. Also, I think Rob's attitude pissed Rivera off. "Delia has friends too," he said. "I've got witnesses and suspects." Rivera turned his head to the radio pinned to his shoulder. It crackled to life. "Transport requested."

McCarthy rested her hand on Rob's shoulder, and a flush of anger spread across his face. "You think anyone is going to believe any of this? What we've got here is a cheating fiancée and rumors from twenty years ago!" Rob turned to Peter, his voice a growl. "I'm going to call my very expensive lawyer and I'll be out in an hour. Be the smart man I know you are. If you want things to work out for Delia, both now and *later*, consider what you're doing."

My spine straightened, and I felt fear throb acutely, right in the tender spots on my body Rob had left. I thought of Viviane and of all Rob's possible ways to get to me.

"I have considered," Peter said. "So while I was waiting for you to arrive today, I decided to call one of your investors."

Confusion crossed Rob's face. Then shock. Then I thought

I saw a hint of panic.

Two police cruisers arrived on the empty street, lights flashing silently. Blue uniforms loaded Rob and Mitchell into one, and Norah into another. Norah looked grim but determined. She met my eye and winked just before she disappeared. Mitchell's face was expressionless as he ducked his head. Rob, his jaw locked in rage, stared at me out the window.

With a single pop of a siren, the cruisers disappeared.

Sergeant Rivera swung up onto Whitey. The regiment turned as one. Tails swished at their heels. Riders waved gloved hands in salute, hooves clattering like castanets.

"Fine sight," said Officer Cicalese as broken syllables jumbled from his radio.

The city bridges were finally open.

THE SCORPION TAIL of the storm curled above the skyline, whipping up the most extraordinary sky. Patches of cerulean broke through the churning murk. Alongside anvil-gray thunderheads, white puffs glowed pink and purple. Peter and I watched the phenomenon from a bench in the embassy garden.

Peter shook his head. "He killed your aunt. If I had known that when I got your message—" His comment trailed off.

"I never thought I would know who did it," I said. "They always said she committed suicide. But I didn't believe it."

"There are times you just sense the truth about someone." Peter smiled down at me.

"This afternoon, I decided to find out for myself, if I could." I explained to Peter what I'd planned—how I wanted to elicit a reaction from Rob by refusing to leave, just as Aunt

Kathleen had done two decades before.

"That was brave," Peter said. "And foolish."

"Things didn't go quite as intended," I said, remembering all the specific ways it hadn't.

"Your original scheme didn't include an SOS using a couple of birds?"

"No." I shook my head. "That part was somewhat improvised."

With the wind, a curl of my hair strayed into Peter's face. He carefully repositioned it on my shoulder. His touch was apprehensive, as if he were trespassing, and his brows drew together. He looked at me, face serious. "It was an hour between when I got the text messages until you arrived. You were alone with Goodman. What did he...?" Peter didn't finish the question. I closed my eyes, took a deep breath, and didn't answer. But Peter already knew. In his vulgar comment, Rob all but revealed the truth.

I was battered in my heart, and also in the flesh, feeling the collection of bruises Rob had left. I had taken enough tumbles off horses to know what my body would look like when I undressed. Still, I knew I would recover—because I made a conscious choice, marching willingly into no-man's-land and putting my own body on the line.

Opening my eyes, I read concern and anger on Peter's face. But my hurt was too fresh, and not something I wanted to talk about right now. So I changed the subject. "How did you put everything together when you got my message?"

Peter held my gaze for a moment before silently assenting to the switch of topic. "When I got all those messages, I knew to call Bert. At first, he didn't understand why I thought you'd be in trouble. Then he said your mother signed her apartment over to you and called Goodman. When he told me that, I knew. I explained the danger you were in."

"Thank you." I rested my hand on Peter's arm. He looked down at it. There was still a ring on my finger. Peter considered it for a moment, then turned his eyes back to me.

"Bert acts like he's your father."

"I suppose he does." I remembered something. "Before, when you said you'd called an investor, was it…?"

"Conti," he supplied. I chuckled and shook my head. Peter put his hand on top of mine. My ring felt hard and cold between us. "Conti's another loyal friend of yours. I thought it was important for him to understand the situation."

"He'll pull out of the deal, I guess."

"More than that." Peter took a deep breath, expanding his broad chest, and looking into the distance. "Angelo Conti sees things in black and white. A trait I admire. I told him about Goodman, and he said that you and your aunt were good to his daughter. I think his exact words were that he would be 'happy to provide backup to the justice system if necessary.' Goodman won't be coercing you over the apartment, or anything else for that matter."

"Wow," I said. It seemed strangely appropriate to be relying on a gangster as my backstop and protection.

"Conti is the only guarantee Rob won't touch you. You know that?" Peter asked.

Of course, I did. Today, a legion of horses arrived like a shining anachronism to rescue me for a moment. Mitchell—he might face a gun charge. After that he would melt away and find another Goodman to work for. As for Goodman himself— would there be an investigation into a decades-old murder? And if there was one, where would it lead? When it came to justice, it was, at best, an uncertain future.

"Mr. Conti doesn't even know about Rob killing Aunt Kathleen. I wonder what he'll do when he finds out," I added.

Peter's arm muscles hardened through his sleeve. "That's Goodman's problem." Peter glanced back at the hand resting on his arm as if he had made a decision. He removed the pink diamond and presented it to me. I shook my head. He put it in his jacket pocket. I didn't know what he would do with it, and I didn't care. He, great returner of spoon jars, could dispose of that as well.

We sat for a moment. Priest dipped his head to scan my face, his eyes trying to fix on mine, questioning. If I decided to look into his eyes, I wondered what I would see. Concern? Pity? More?

The fact was, I had gone to Peter in desperation. I thought he would help me, and he had—cleverly, even protectively. Sitting here now, though, sore through my neck, shoulders, and into my very core, I felt as if Rob had hollowed me out. I made it through that ghastly no-man's-land, but it exhausted me body and soul. I didn't have the strength to look into Peter's face and see something short of cloaks and birds. A weary old part of me still didn't believe anything more was possible.

Iron hinges creaked, and Peter and I looked up. Mom glided through the gate, poised and beautiful, as if stepping off a runway. She came up to me and took my face in her hands. All mothers, probably even mothers like mine, sense the wounds of their children.

"I coulda chewed nails not being able to get here," Bert said as Peter rose to greet him. He shook Peter's hand hard. "I got through to the local PD in Centerville. They radioed to Rivera."

"Your man was here in time," Peter said.

"You should have seen all the horses," I added to Mom, smiling weakly. She looked at me seriously.

"Drove like a bat outta hell. Stopped in Astoria and waited for the bridge to open." Bert put a hand on Peter's shoulder. "Thank you for helping our girl."

"My honor," Peter said. Mom looked at him quizzically, then back at me.

"Hey," Bert said. "As we were driving in, I heard an alert over the scanner. Something about a murder suspect at the embassy."

I took a deep breath. Then I told them the story—from Aunt Kathleen, to Rosemary, to Norah, to my theory about Rob, to his threats when I wouldn't sign over the apartment.

"I put you in danger," Mom said and looked as if her legs would fail. Bert put his hand under her elbow. She gently removed it, straightened, and blinked hard.

"It's okay, Mom." I took her arm from Bert.

"You always believed in her." Mom squeezed my hand. She looked up at the window of Number N. "Oh, Kathleen." She turned to me. "She would be proud of you."

"She'd be proud of you, too, Mom."

I heard the small metal clasp on Mom's purse pop, as she reached inside for a handkerchief. She pulled out the one with my grandmother's initials in robin's egg blue. She dabbed her eyes. "You should really read things before you sign them, dear."

I laughed. "Next time, I will. I promise."

"If you hadn't gotten out of there…" said Bert, rubbing his head in disbelief.

"But I did," I reminded him. Then a thought occurred to

me. "What do you think will happen to Norah?"

"I'll go downtown and talk to the captain," Bert said. "Make sure she's treated right. She came forward in the end."

I drew Mom aside a bit, so as not to embarrass her in front of Peter. "I thought you really needed the money from the apartment."

Mom straightened. "A policeman's pension and one house will be more than enough for us," she said, loud enough for everyone to hear.

"Mom!" I exclaimed.

"I'd rather it was on Valentine's Day," Bert interposed. "But after fifty years, Peggy finally said yes."

Bert put his arm around my mother's shoulders in a way she had never allowed in all her life.

"Congratulations," said Peter, while I stood mute.

"From what I can see, you both make a pretty good team, too." Bert winked at me.

I smiled, a little sadly. Mom and Bert were finally together. As for me? I knew one heroic moment wouldn't change the entire world or even an entire person. I had been given my legacy, the apartment at Number N. It cost a lot, maybe all I had to give. It was enough.

"One billionaire is plenty," I said. "I don't think I'll go for two." I meant to make light of things, but in a way Peter would understand. I looked at him and got an unexpected reaction. He smiled broadly, as if concealing a really good secret.

"I agree," Mom said. "It may not be what other mothers might say under the circumstances, but a rich man is *not* my preference for Delia."

Bert guffawed. "Now, Peggy."

"You don't have to worry about that," Peter said. "I'm

broke."

"Broke?" Undisguised shock rang in my voice. "How can you be broke? You're worth billions."

"*Delia*," Mom said. "Don't be coarse."

"Well, as broke as men like me ever get. Let me assure you it wasn't easy. You might be surprised how hard it is to get rid of a fortune." Peter stepped beside me, brushed my hair back, and touched the back of his hand to the side of my face. "Your house set me back two hundred and fifty million. But I think I fell short in the presentation." Peter's mouth twitched with a smile. "So, I decided to buy you an island."

"An *island?*" It was Mom's turn to be shocked.

"Islands, plural, actually. In your honor, you could say." Peter was playing with one of my curls now, looking at it, then at me, eyes twinkling. "I had to outbid both the Russians and the Chinese."

"I thought you were just advising Greece," I said. "Not…"

"Buying things myself? How else is a man to dispose of such a large quantity of money? This specific group of islands, in fact, is highly desirable for its strategic port and its rumored cache of undiscovered artifacts."

"Peter!" I gasped.

"It's taken a long time for me to get a look like that from you. Worth all three billion it cost me." He ran a finger along my chin. "There's one thing I will regret. I always dreamed of having another picture painted of you, and now, it seems, I won't have the money. You were beautiful as a girl, and you grew into such an extraordinary woman." He traced up the side of my face. "Your eyes, though. They're the same."

Just then, I finally had the courage to really search his eyes—in the old Hungarian way. They were dark and expressive and black, as always, but now I saw they somehow held all the rainbow colors I could ever hope to see.

"What does a fella do with a chain of islands?" Bert asked. Mom touched him on the arm to remind him not to interrupt.

Peter turned to Bert. He gently slid a hand around my waist, unknowingly touching a tender spot on my hip. "For one thing, I'll build a museum, at the site of the island's ancient acropolis. Artifacts from the famous shipwreck will be moved there, where they were intended to arrive thousands of years ago. And I'll create a foundation. Greece is in trouble and headed for worse. There are refugees pouring onto our shores. I am hoping I can help those whose lives have been destroyed by what people like me have done to the world."

Mom looked at Peter, then at me. I could tell she was satisfied. "A museum. Quite clever," she said. "What gave you that idea?"

"I think you called it a spoon jar," Peter said, pulling me closer. A sensation traversed my body like warm sand running through an hourglass. I could feel it flowing from me into him.

"That's amazing," I said.

"What's a spoon jar?" asked Bert.

"This is all quite…" Mom carefully folded her handkerchief and returned it to her purse. "Extravagant."

"There is one inconvenience." Peter pressed my hand. I looked up quizzically. "I need help looking for an apartment. This mansion will house the foundation, and it isn't really appropriate for my lifestyle anymore."

"What a coincidence," said Mom. "I believe I know someone with an apartment."

Even Bert looked shocked at that.

IN TRUTH, I wasn't sure I wanted to go back to Number N, as dear as it was. If Peter weren't with me, I might have had trouble returning. But I knew it was somehow necessary. I could not permit Rob to transform the place into anything but what it truly was, a deeply treasured legacy.

As we stepped through the door, I realized I had never been so unsure of myself with a man. But Peter simply sat next to me on the couch and held me. As I leaned my head on his shoulder, the muscles of his long arm were strong down the side of my body, and it seemed maybe he could perceive what I'd endured.

After a while, in gentle low tones, he asked me to tell him what happened, and I did.

Many hours later, we watched the moon rise. Peter looked at me as if asking permission. When I nodded, he kissed me tentatively for the first time. I sensed my body welcoming him, as if he was offering the perfect start to healing. I was right, long ago, about how it would be—that I really hadn't ever felt like this with a man before. When Peter took his shirt off, I ran my fingers along his expansive chest and thought I recognized the *palikari*—the brave young hero—from our long-ago swim together.

Peter untied my dress, and it fell away. Seeing the scattering of purplish marks full on, he inhaled sharply. I could feel suppressed fury like an electrical current through his palms. I put my hand to his face to remind him what I'd told him earlier. That it had been my choice. I went alone and willingly into no-man's-land. Peter put his finger to a bruise on my shoulder, bent to kiss it, and didn't stop.

Epilogue

A harbor, even if it is a little harbor, is a good thing, since adventurers come into it as well as go out, and the life in it grows strong, because it takes something from the world, and has something to give in return.

—Sarah Orne Jewett, "River Driftwood"

GREEN YELLOW, BLUE gray, turquoise with a touch of white, the bird flock inhabiting the cloister at the back of Number N had grown to six members. Peter and I watched them a year later in the spring as we sipped our coffee on a new velvet couch that replaced the red tartan.

Our flock was now famous, eclipsing the Pale Male raptor clan. The city overflowed with enthusiasm for the birds. Postcards with their pictures sold on sidewalk stands outside the park. There was a documentary in the works. They were new media darlings.

In addition to the birds, the press also turned its attention to me, raising an inky eyebrow with the banner, "Rent-Controlled Princess Engaged to Second Hedge Fund Magnate." Peter, in contrast, received uniformly positive coverage: "Peter Priest Ends His Odyssey, Starts Foundation." As did Mom: "Society Queen Emerges from Decades of Seclusion, Marries NYPD Cop." Mom and Bert had a small ceremony by the fountain in the garden.

Peter's final extravagance, for which he kept funds in reserve, was to buy Number N itself. He paid more than it was worth. "I had to give Goodman a number he couldn't refuse," he said. Rob needed money.

One day, Rob Goodman might indeed have to grapple with Angelo Conti, but, at the moment, the justice system was doing a proper job. Rob's headline was, "Hermes2 Owner Suspect in Cold Case."

The DA was serious in pursuing Aunt Kathleen's death. There actually *was* an old box of evidence in a warehouse in Queens. One item it contained, Bert said proudly, was my notebook with the sketch I made of the scene as a stunned girl. With a birdwatcher's instinct, I captured many fine points not documented in the scant photos of the scene, including details of the body's posture and certain abrasions on Aunt Kathleen's hands that the medical examiner said were not consistent with a suicide. Rob had to hire his expensive lawyer and his bail was in the millions. The news said his trial would begin in the fall.

Angelo Conti visited us at Number N. He came the minute he heard Rob was accused of killing Aunt Kathleen.

"I plan on monitoring the trial," he said ominously.

"Sounds like Goodman's problems are just beginning," Peter said.

"I have another question for you," Conti continued to me. "I need you to tell me if Angie had anything to do with that woman's death. Her neighbor, the old art dealer."

I had been dreading the question. Angelo Conti had his own system of honor, and it did not include killing an elderly neighbor over an apartment. "I don't know for sure." It was, at least, truthful.

"I'm not a fool, Delia. I can see what you think."

So, Conti pulled in the reins on his daughter. Her Vermeer

trio of apartments went up for sale. I asked if he'd use Sarah as the broker. He agreed. Conti bought Angela a house in New Jersey, right next to his.

Angela's long-term prospects remained uncertain. Hearing about events in the neighborhood, Judith's children started asking questions. They wanted an investigation. Papa Conti might not be able to shield his daughter in the end.

In the short term, what hurt Angela most was a letter from Mom, who now knew all about Angela's treachery. Mom showed a copy of the epistle to me. Her handwriting perfect, her pen dripping with disdain, Mom required the return of the needlepoint pillow at Angela's earliest convenience.

The rest of Number N, including Viviane, got to stay. I wasn't sure if Viviane would ever forgive me for what I'd done. Some hurts just don't heal. But it felt good to have helped to preserve Number N for her and everyone who needed it. It was something.

After a brief hiatus, Norah returned as super at Number N, Peter having paid all her legal bills. She took a plea deal, admitting to blackmail and consenting to probation in return for her testimony against Rob Goodman. The DA wanted her to wear a plain gray suit for the trial. "Like I'm going to my own fucking wake," she said, but agreed.

Peter and Norah debated the running of Number N, sometimes congenially, sometimes just loudly. What was to be done as apartments became available? Was Number N to be an artist's colony? A haven for struggling families? Single working mothers? Students? Immigrants? Those in homeless shelters? Lighters were flicked, and streams of smoke unfurled from beneath Norah's door. In the meanwhile, lease applications came in and were decided on, a mixture of all the plans together.

It took a little while for me, but slowly, my conviction grew that there could be magical birds in the world. The proof was out my window. Our flock was like a colorful cloak of love encompassing Number N, finally healing the place, which had been the scene of too many crimes.

⌐◦⌐

"*OI THYSAVROI MOU.*" Peter laid food out the window, and a rainbow flurry of feathers flapped to him, parakeets perching on long fingers. I remembered Greek village women calling to their children this way: "My treasures."

"They sure are," I agreed.

Peter looked up, as if surprised I understood. He closed the window, put an arm around my waist, and drew me to him with a see-if-you-can-get-this-one grin. "*Kai esy.*"

That was easy. *And you.*

Great lover of irony that I was, I liked that *thisavros* aptly gave us "thesaurus," a treasury of words. And the original term for dictionary. In such a book, under *my* heading for *treasure* would be listed the half dozen parakeets. Also a spoon jar, a stone statuette, a reformed police horse, a cache of onionskin letters, some *Daily News* microfiche, the key to Apartment 13B, a new stepfather, a surprisingly Hungarian mother, a few no-quotes friends, a soon-to-be husband, the truth of Aunt Kathleen, and the voice of my own heart.

Peter had been right—I was a treasure hunter, and a very lucky one at that. I'd set off seeking wealth beyond belief, and, instead, discovered love past measure.

The End

If you enjoyed this book, please leave a review at your favorite online retailer! Even if it's just a sentence or two it makes all the difference.

Thanks for reading *Greedy Heart* by A.P. Murray!

Discover your next great novel at TulePublishing.com.

TULE
PUBLISHING

If you enjoyed *Greedy Heart*, you'll love these other Tule books!

All of Me
by Jeannie Moon

Once More With Feeling
by Megan Crane

The Other Side of the Bridge
by Katharine Swartz

Available now at your favorite online retailer!

Book Club Reader Guide
Greedy Heart: A Novel

1. Lightning round
Get the group moving with this lightning round! Pick one of the following, and comment in no more than 30 seconds:

- Did you love Delia or hate her?
- What tickled your funny bone?
- Who was your favorite character?
- Best moment in the book?
- Worst moment?

2. Sex
How is sex used in the novel? When is it used for recreation? For power? For love? Where do you see abstinence and why? How does sex change throughout the novel?

3. Mother-Daughter
The relationship between Delia and her mother is fraught. What do you think is at the heart of that? Does it remind you of any relationship in your life?

4. Greed
How is greed explored in the novel? What are the different depictions of greed and possession?

5. Honest Horses
Delia's first sexual experience is with the Hungarian riding master. What important life lessons does she learn from him? What impractical lessons does he leave her with?

6. God & Religion
How does Greedy Heart deal with God, religion and spirituality?

7. Animals
How do the animals in the novel (parakeets, migratory birds, hawks, pigeons, horses, rats), contribute to the story? What messages and meanings do they reveal?

8. Art & Artifacts
What is the importance of art and artifacts in the novel? What different objects does the author use? What is their connection to value?

9. Friendship
Discuss the different kinds of friendship that exist in the novel.

10. Climate
How does global warming make a kind of appearance in the novel?

11. Chapter Headings
What did you think of the chapter heading quotes? Was there one you particularly liked? Why?

12. Delia
What did you admire most about Delia? What did you like the least? Was she redeemed for you? By which action was she redeemed? Any hanging threads or lingering doubts?

About the Author

A.P. Murray's sprawling Irish Catholic family has roots in New York City going back four generations. Her industrialist great grandfather, Thomas E. Murray, Sr., co-founded Consolidated Edison, was second only to Edison the number of patents attributed to him, and is credited with establishing the mass distribution of electricity in New York City. Murray descends from this lace-curtain heritage and also from a working-class mother who rose to international fame as a fashion model.

A technology consultant by day, Murray began her career as a teacher and journalist before founding an early stage web company, which built many national brands' first websites. The firm, tmg-emedia, later expanded into broad-ranging technology consulting. Murray has won multiple awards for her technology leadership and as a woman tech entrepreneur. She lives in New York with her husband and business partner, Christos Moschovitis, and her whippet, Orpheus. Her horse, Hershey, resides separately in Connecticut.

Greedy Heart is her debut novel.

Thank you for reading

Greedy Heart

If you enjoyed this book, you can find more from all our great authors at TulePublishing.com, or from your favorite online retailer.

TULE
PUBLISHING